PRAISE FOR *SYCAMORE*

"Riveting. . . . A movingly written, multivoiced novel. . . .
A transporting vision of community, connection, and forgiveness."
—*Publishers Weekly* (starred review, Pick of the Week)

"Beautifully structured, compellingly plotted. . . .
Chancellor's story has well-developed characters, a complex
plot, and all the tension you expect from a mystery."
—*Star-Ledger* (New Jersey)

"Powerful and moving." —*Richmond Times-Dispatch*

"Absorbing. . . . Begins quietly, quickly gains momentum,
and ends explosively. . . . Gripping. . . . A must for readers
of literary fiction." —*Library Journal* (starred review)

"A meaty, suspenseful debut." —*Booklist*

"A powerful debut novel, one without flaw,
and it will slay you." —Kevin Wilson, author of
The Family Fang and *Perfect Little World*

"Haunting and elegiac." —Claire Vaye Watkins,
author of *Gold Fame Citrus*

"Keeps you up at night and haunts you through the day."
—Caroline Leavitt

PRAISE FOR *Sycamore*

"Chancellor's absorbing first novel begins quietly, quickly gains momentum, and ends explosively. . . . This gripping debut is a must for readers of literary fiction."

—*Library Journal* (starred review)

"A meaty, suspenseful debut."   —*Booklist*

"In this masterful performance, Bryn Chancellor explores the loss around which an entire community has calcified with humanity and wisdom. Chancellor digs deep in these pages, unearthing broken hearts, secrets, betrayals, passion, and—most impressively—grace. What a joy to find a book that is both propulsive and perfectly composed."

—Cynthia D'Aprix Sweeney, author of *The Nest*

"What's more wonderful than a novel that keeps you up at night and haunts you through the day? That describes Bryn Chancellor's *Sycamore*, about the discovery of a body that might belong to a vanished teenaged girl, a community pulling together and apart, and secrets."   —Caroline Leavitt

"*Sycamore* is an amazing showcase for Bryn Chancellor's great talent, the way she allows each of the various characters to shine on their own, but connects them with such subtlety that their light forms a constellation that maps out the grief, the regrets, and the strength of an entire community. This is a powerful debut novel, one without flaw, and it will slay you."

—Kevin Wilson, author of *Tunneling to the Center of the Earth* and *The Family Fang*

"[An] emotional and addicting debut. . . . [an] unforgettable page-turner. Four and a half stars." —*RT Book Reviews*

"Compelling. . . . Chancellor expertly takes us through Jess's days as she makes her way in the vicious social circles of high school, makes and loses a first friend, and then makes a longer-lived connection with a girl named Dani. . . . Chancellor takes readers beyond a standard whodunit and provides a more compelling take on what the experience does to the town."
—*St. Louis Post-Dispatch*

"Haunting and elegiac, Bryn Chancellor's *Sycamore* masterfully traces the fault lines of trauma and loss that resurface in the wake of a tragedy's second coming. Chancellor's multivocal narrative brims with intelligence and insight, and her subtle writing poignantly illuminates the ways in which we are sometimes bound, for better and for worse, by a collective sorrow."
—Claire Vaye Watkins, author of *Gold Fame Citrus*

"Bryn Chancellor explores the complexities of a small-town girlhood with insight and compassion. A page-turner and a heartbreaker, *Sycamore* marks the arrival of a shining new voice."
—Tayari Jones, author of *Silver Sparrow*

"Bryn Chancellor's *Sycamore* instantly reminded me of Tana French's thrillers: a small, intertwined community, a long-ago crime, the tension and intrigue that won't stop rippling. . . . Chancellor writes gorgeously, and her story is riveting and real. I love it." —Joy Castro, author of *Hell or High Water* and *Island of Bones*

"Bryn Chancellor's compelling debut novel, *Sycamore*, weaves a suspenseful web around a small town in the years following a disappearance. With astute emotional and psychological observations, Chancellor successfully shows the power of the unknown as various individuals explore the many what ifs and imaginings of what really happened."

—Jill McCorkle, author of *Life After Life*

"I love taking that first journey with a new author, filled with hope that the book I've just picked up will be a standout. Bryn Chancellor's *Sycamore* rises to that level, and then some. It is beautifully structured, compellingly plotted, and its multi-character cast captures the yin and yang of human behavior. . . . Chancellor's story has well-developed characters, a complex plot, and all the tension you expect from a mystery."

—*New Jersey Star-Ledger*

"Sycamore, Ariz., is a small town with loss and mystery at its heart. A visitor stumbles upon clues that dredge up the old memories and hurts." —*Philadelphia Inquirer*, "Need a Beach Read? 16 Great Choices"

"Intimate. . . . Half the book tells [Jess's] story of how she ended up in that town, the other half tells the story of the town as bones are recently discovered. Do they belong to the girl who went missing? Who finds them? It moves very well to piece the mystery together at the end."

—Nevada Public Radio, "From the Experts: Best Summer Reads"

Sycamore

A NOVEL

Bryn Chancellor

HARPER PERENNIAL

NEW YORK • LONDON • TORONTO • SYDNEY • NEW DELHI • AUCKLAND

HARPER PERENNIAL

A hardcover edition of this book was published in 2017 by HarperCollins Publishers.

FIRST HARPER PERENNIAL EDITION PUBLISHED 2018.

Designed by Bonni Leon-Berman

The Library of Congress has catalogued the hardcover edition as follows:

Names: Chancellor, Bryn, author.
Title: Sycamore : a novel / Bryn Chancellor.
Description: First edition. | New York : Harper, [2017]
Identifiers: LCCN 2016042150| ISBN 9780062661098 (hardback) | ISBN 9780062661111 (ebook)
Subjects: | BISAC: FICTION / Literary. | FICTION / Psychological. | FICTION / Coming of Age.
Classification: LCC PS3603.H35595 S93 2017 | DDC 813/.6—dc23 LC record available at https://lccn.loc.gov/2016042150

ISBN 978-0-06-266110-4 (pbk.)

18 19 20 21 22   LSC   10 9 8 7 6 5 4 3 2 1

For TW

We are tangled

We are stolen

We are living where things are hidden.

—JOHN DOE, "THE GOLDEN STATE"

CONTENTS

YOU ARE HERE
January 1991

HER FIRST NIGHT IN SYCAMORE, the girl snuck out of the house. Wearing frayed purple canvas shoes and a new puffy vinyl winter coat the red-orange of an ocotillo bloom, the girl paused on her tiptoes on the threshold when the front door hinges creaked. Her mother, deaf in her left ear, didn't stir, and the girl shut the door with a click. This wasn't the girl's first time to slip out the door late at night, and it wouldn't be her last. (There would be a last time, but not tonight.) For now she had this night, her first in a small northern Arizona town where her mother had dragged her. She shoved her notebook inside her coat and hurried down the driveway. Her breath smoked in the desert winter air.

At the end of the driveway, beyond the porch light's bowled halo, she stopped. No Phoenix streetlights. No swish of tires from nearby Seventh Avenue, no shouts echoing from the bus stops and bars, no jet engines from red-eyes at Sky Harbor. She stared into a cold, silent darkness so vast she grew dizzy. An eerie quiet. *Un*quiet. Sweat pricked her armpits, and she widened her eyes, thinking about the owls that roosted in their neighbor's ash tree back home, that prizefighter bob-and-weave as they gauged what lay before them.

She looked up, and the silence stopped. The carbonized sky howled as the Milky Way cracked its sternum, exposing its galactic heart. She clenched her eyes shut as if she'd stared into a klieg light. Back in central Phoenix, in a neighborhood blanketed by the grapefruit haze of streetlights, the night sky never sank into black. Even out in the desert, beyond the city's glow, stars and planets hung back like shy children. Her nostrils flared at the sudden smell of mint, and she shivered with the sensation she had tumbled down a hole. She thought, Oh my god, I'm Baby Jessica! I'm in a well! Help! It's dark in here! She laughed with a hard exhale, and the sound surprised her. She opened her eyes. That was her father's laugh, a caw that veered into honk.

Her eyes began to adjust. The shapes of trees and shrubs and rooftops sharpened, and neighbors' lights emerged as pushpin dots along the edges. Her new street stretched before her, a single stripe down its center. Roadrunner Lane. *Beep beep*, she thought, picturing childhood cartoons, and as if on cue, coyotes began to yip in the distance. The silhouette of the Black Hills loomed—to the west, she knew, because the sun set over the hills—salted with the lights of Jerome. Her nose, ears, and feet growing numb, she hopped up and down for warmth, trying to decide if she should go inside for a hat and thicker socks. Instead, she began to jog the mile east toward town.

Though she was tall and long-legged—she'd hit five-ten that year—she was not a graceful runner. Arms flailing and feet dragging, she felt more like a branch caught in a rushing river, lurching over rocks and roots, tumbled forward by the force of mass and gravity. Sixteen had been the Year of Hips, and she had to cinch the waistbands of her wider pants with belts and safety pins. And look at those feet. Ridiculous. It was a wonder she didn't trip over them every second of the day. She'd quit ballet last year, self-conscious now of her body in a leotard, of her lumbering leaps and thuds on the studio floor. How had humans evolved into these stupid, unaerodynamic bodies? Still, she was outdoors. She was moving forward, gulping down clean, cold air. In the low end of the foothills, the road swelled and dipped, crossed washes in the depressions. Downhill, she picked up speed. Her puffy red jacket made a pleasing slushy sound as her arms swished against it, her notebook tucked against her heart. Impetuously she leaped, a quick jeté, jeté, jeté, defying gravity for three brief spans.

The impulse to be *out*—she'd had it since she was young, when she would burst through the door and leap off the steps en route to the playground, the yard, the swimming pool, back when she was young enough to perform along the way, all extended arms and chassés and pas de bourrées. On her recent late-night excursions in Phoenix, she usually went only as far as the backyard; she stretched out on a blanket in the grass with a flashlight and a book, or on irrigation nights splashed through the flooded lot, feeling the earth sink and squish between her toes. Once she had her license, she would sometimes take her father's pickup, rolling it silently to the end of the drive with the engine off, and after he packed up and left, she did the same with her mother's brown sedan. She didn't always go far, mostly up and down the grid streets of her neighborhood, listening to mixtapes on the stereo. She'd park under a streetlight and write in her notebook, scratching out her lousy poems, trying to calm her itchy nerves. Like now, she wasn't seeking trouble or mischief or clandestine meetups—well, she once had been, when she was with the Boy, but not since they broke up almost six months ago. Instead, she was easing the tightness that grew in her all day as she bumped her way through the school halls with her newly belled hips, as she evaded the Boy and his smirking friends, as she navigated her parents' arguments, the tense conversations that stopped short when she entered the room. Here in her new town, she didn't know what she was seeking. Out. Go—that was the impulse.

Breathless, the girl stopped atop a slope from which she could see the center of town. In Phoenix, when she viewed the city from some height, the sprawling city hissed and spit, defiant in its radiant heat. The little town of Sycamore struck her as something out of a fairy tale in its smallness, in its cluster of businesses along Main Street, its small college on one side, her new high school on the other. Though it seemed to emit a gentle sigh, a sleepy breath, she thought not of sweetness but of *Frankenstein*: "By the glimmer of the half-extinguished light, I saw the dull yellow eye of the creature open." As soon as she thought it, she grinned and rolled her eyes. Such *drama*. As her mother always said, Lighten up, J-bird. You're sixteen years old.

Almost seventeen now. She didn't know why, but that was important. One step closer to people taking her seriously. One more step away from this sucky year.

Earlier that afternoon, her mother had driven them to the high school. As her mother filled out paperwork to sign her up for classes, the girl leaned against a pillar and watched the other students walk the halls, slouch against the rows of yellow lockers, scatter like dice when the bell rang. About the same as in Phoenix: plenty of shit-kickers, jocks, and cheerleaders overly fond of hair spray. She did see one kid who clearly worshipped Morrissey and another with a safety pin in his ear, wearing a Misfits T-shirt, so maybe all was not lost. *Mis*fit. Ill-fitting, like a too-tight coat or shrunken gloves, like her stupid pants belted tight at the waist. Why was it she recognized herself in the prefixes, in altered meanings: *Un*settled. *Un*easy. *Mis*shapen. Atypical. *Ex*-girlfriend. *Ex*-daughter.

Two boys, wearing flannel shirts and jeans and wrestling a large cardboard box, shuffled by. They both looked at her and smiled; once they'd passed, they whispered over the box and glanced back, laughing. Those laughs: at once flirtatious and threatening. She tugged her sweater over her hips and fought the urge to crouch.

She thought of the Boy, whom she had forbidden herself to think of, and how she'd once gotten a buzz from his flattery, a rush of heat from his touch. She crossed her legs and twisted into herself.

Afterward, her mother drove them around town for half an hour. Up and down Main Street, through the bordering neighborhoods, around Sycamore High and Sycamore College, to the post office where her mother would start work in two days, up the hairpin switchbacks to the tiny abandoned mining town of Jerome and its tight streets, where houses teetered on steep slopes. The girl tracked road signs, freshly memorized for her driver's license test: Do Not Enter When Flooded. Road Slippery When Wet. No Passing. Yield. Stop Sign Ahead.

At a gas station in town, the girl kept her face to the passenger window. A woman at the next pump wore mismatched striped socks and a giant yellow ribbon safety-pinned to her sweater. Across the street was a motel, the Woodchute Motor Lodge, which was built to look like cabins, all connected by a covered wraparound porch. Behind it loomed a strange black outcrop, a small mountain in the middle of town.

Her mother sighed. "The silent treatment is getting old, J-bird."

"What is there to say?" The girl shrugged. "We're here. It's done."

"There's plenty to say. Tell me what you're thinking."

She was thinking of everything as usual, her head spinning with a mess of the mundane and the profound: the president announcing war, how the rows of lockers looked like stained teeth, whether the letters on the Woodchute's sign were hatched to resemble logs, the question of reality, of knowledge, of love. Her breath fogged the window, and she traced an X through the moisture. X marks the spot. You Are Here. Or was she? Were any of them?

Her mother went on, "I know we've been over it, but it's worth repeating. It's a big change, and it all happened fast. Too fast. I know, and I'm sorry. We have a lot to figure out. It's just you and me now. I need you on board, okay? I need you—" Her mother tugged on the girl's arm. "Look at me, would you?"

The girl pulled her arm away.

Her mother shook her head. "The aggrieved teenager thing doesn't suit you."

"I guess you would know," the girl said. "Mother knows best."

"Right." Her mother laughed.

"It's not funny," the girl said. "It's not a *joke*."

Her mother rubbed hard at her forehead, pinching between her brows. Her voice rose as it did when she forgot to modulate, as if she were speaking over the din of a crowd. "Look. I didn't want to get into all this before, because finances are my problem, not yours, but the fact is, even if I'd wanted to stay, we couldn't. I had to sell the house. I couldn't buy your father out, pay the lawyer, all the bullshit I didn't want in the first place. That's the part of divorce no one talks about. It's expensive. It breaks you. Financially and otherwise." She sighed again, tugging on the lobe of her bad ear. She lowered her voice. "But even if that weren't the case, I needed a change. A fresh start. We both do."

The girl slumped lower in her seat, thinking of her father. In California with his new blond wife, his new baby girl. Beautiful girl, something he'd once called *her*. The sister she'd wanted when she was younger, whom she'd begged her parents for (not understanding what her mother meant when she said, "We can't have any more kids, honey"). She could not reconcile this new image with the mental family picture she had always known. It was as if she and her mother had been cut out and replaced with two strangers' faces. Not a sister but a replacement. His new beautiful girl. It seemed like a bad dream creeping in during the day, and she'd think, No, that's not real. Except it was. And her father was the one holding the scissors and paste. She had decided she would not speak to him again. He didn't want them? Well, fuck him. Fuck. Him.

Her mother said, "We're here. You have a year and a half left of school, college to think about. Give it a chance."

The girl turned and looked at her mother, who sat facing the windshield, her jaw flexing as she tried not to cry. In her mother's profile, the girl could see herself, the longish chin and straight nose, the messy curls her mother pinned with combs, the laugh lines fanned at the corners of her eyes. Like a snapshot of her future self.

She reached out and touched a freckle on her mother's wrist.

Her mother wiped under her eyes and smiled at the girl. "I had a wild thought. What if we *like* it here?" She gasped and clutched at her heart.

The girl rolled her eyes. "Heaven forbid."

Her mother grinned. She turned the key ignition and tapped the steering wheel. "You want to drive? Come on."

The girl hid a smile in her sleeve. They switched sides, and she settled herself behind the wheel, latching the seat belt.

"Check your mirrors," her mother said. "God, I can't believe you're taller than me now. Taller than your dad even."

Your dad, instead of Dad. Another among all the changes.

The girl said, "Can't wait for the witty repartee at school. 'Hey, how's the weather up there?'" She stuck her finger in her mouth and made a gagging sound. She thought of those laughing boys in the hall, of how she'd slumped against the pillar, trying to hide. After the Boy and his dumb lies, that's what she'd been doing at her old school: hiding in plain sight, ducking from the sense of shame that dogged her like a shadow. Her shame wasn't about the sex so much as being duped, as being stupid: she'd *believed* him. Her, the girl who questioned everything. Love—ha.

Her mother reached over and squeezed the girl's arm. "Try. Okay? For me? Come on, it'll be an adventure."

Her mother fell silent, and she did too, knowing that had been one of her father's favorite phrases; he'd say "adventure" with a goofy French accent. She revved the engine and checked her mirrors before pulling the car to the parking lot exit. She started to flip the turn signal but realized she had no idea which way was home. Home. A house on a street she didn't yet recognize. She put her forehead on the steering wheel and blinked hard.

"Left, J-bird," her mother said, reaching over and cupping the back of the girl's neck.

Her mother's palm, warm as a sun-heated window. She had the strange sense she was hearing a secret, the universe whispering hot into her ear: *Don't blink.*

The girl sat up. She pulled her shoulders back and pressed her spine against the seat. Okay. No more hiding. From here on out, head on.

Standing in the dark, her breath slowing, the girl marked an X in the air, over the town in the short distance. You Are Here. She leaned against a stop sign and pulled her notebook from her jacket. She rolled off the rubber band that kept the pen wedged inside and then put the band in her mouth and bit down. She liked the pressure of the rubber between her teeth, the slight squeak and resistance. She liked the oddity of writing when she could barely see her hands, the words sprawling crooked and unruly across the page. When she finished her thought, she snapped the band around the book and zipped it inside her coat. Then she walked to the center of the road and lay down on the pavement.

The rocky asphalt dug into her scalp, scuffed her jacket and jeans.
She drew an X across the sky. You Are Here. And where in the
world was *here* in relation to all *that*? What were the soldiers in
Iraq, the Iraqis themselves, seeing right now? How easy it would
be for her, for everyone, to disappear. If they even existed at all.
She thought, It's thoughts like these that make you so fuckin'
popular. Where's your school spirit? Rah rah *rah*. She laughed,
breaching the quiet. Her father's laugh. But her mother's looks
and humor. And all her own, too.

Seventeen. Who would she be then? Who would she be here?

She opened her eyes as wide as she could. Don't blink, she told
herself.

Something rustled in the bushes next to her, and she jumped
up fast. Too cold for snakes and lizards. A jackrabbit? Javelina?
Or a mountain lion—weren't they nocturnal? Or, she thought
as she scuttled backward, a human? She turned and ran home in
her gangly lope. Elemental, rushing, a force to be reckoned with.

The girl let herself in the house, the soles of her canvas shoes
squeaking on the tile. Home. Same worn plaid twill couch with
grandma's quilt across the back. Same shelf of faded green A–Z
encyclopedias, the dictionary, Big Red, open on top. Same rocking chair with her old one-eyed teddy bear in its seat. Yet nothing
was the same.

In the bedroom, her mother hadn't budged, sleeping on her
right side with her hands tucked under her cheek, her brown
curls obscuring her bad ear. She'd been sleeping a lot these days,
climbing into bed soon after dinner, staying under the covers on
her days off. She slept hard, seemingly immune to slammed cupboards or clanking dishes or thudding doors. The girl stood close
and watched her. Her mother began to whimper, and the girl

saw a glint of wetness. Crying in her sleep again—the only time she really ever saw her mother cry. She sat on the bed and put her hand on her mother's shoulder. Her long hair brushed her mother's arm.

Her mother stirred. "Jess? Is that you?"

"It's me," the girl said. "I'm here."

IN A CREVICE OF THE EARTH

THOUGH IT WAS LATE JUNE, with temperatures climbing into the 100s, Laura Drennan walked her new town during the afternoon, the heat pressing right through the soles of her tennis shoes. She slathered on sunblock and wore the only hat she could find in the moving boxes: a stupendous lime-green foam visor emblazoned with a cartoon frog slamming a tequila shot, which emerged from under a pile of shoes, a faint tread mark on the brim (her best guess: it had belonged to the Girlfriend, she of the jean skirts and pencil hips, acquired on a little clandestine trip down to Tijuana with Charlie). And so Laura wore it—why not!—as she walked in a high-stepping stomp to ward off the diamondbacks she *knew* were coiled in the foxtails (though so far she'd seen only skittish lizards and grasshoppers, plumes of gnats, quail darting under the brush). Despite the sunblock, her arms and legs darkened to the color of a terra-cotta bowl—even the tender band of skin on her now-ringless ring finger had faded. Dust nested in the cuff of her sock, leaving a geologic circle above her anklebone.

In her new neighborhood, a subdivision of 1970s and '80s homes on large lots behind the high school and town ball field, she set one foot on the gravel berm, one on the pavement, memorizing street names: Rojo, Blanco, Yucca, Dry Run, Bottlebrush, Alameda. Her street was Arrowhead; her white clapboard two-bedroom rental with puce-colored trim had belonged to an old woman who lost her mind and dug holes in her yard at night—this according to Laura's mail carrier, Maud, a woman Laura's mother's age who stopped on the porch to chat and shouted questions as if boxing Laura's ears. Laura skirted strangers' yards, cataloging oddities: a mannequin head with a flowered swim cap; soda cans wedged into chain link in a Z shape; a three-legged dog cooling itself in a play pool; a man on a Segway pausing to peer into neighbors' garbage bins; a child's fire engine toppled on a wheelchair ramp.

She walked, and her mind whiplashed from present to past, trying to process the changes: small-town Sycamore, Arizona, instead of San Diego; 4,000 feet instead of sea level; gravel berms instead of sidewalks; lobed cactus instead of ice plants; bushy pines and junipers instead of eucalyptus and symmetrical rows of skinny palms; year 2009, almost twenty years out from her high school graduation. She walked, smelling dust and hot pine needles instead of the briny fog of the Pacific. She bent to collect rocks the way she used to collect seashells, and her pockets grew gritty with sediment in the seams. She walked in a land of strangers instead of in the land of her parents, her older brother and nephews, her colleagues and friends, her husband of eleven years. She walked in her alien landscape, in her ridiculous visor, and she told herself: Buck up, Drennan, you chicken shit. This ain't summer camp.

When she *stopped* walking, she sat on the couch, ignoring her huge to-do list (unpack, tweak syllabuses for fall semester, reply to new department chair's week-old e-mail about her IT setup, research and work on article, talk to neighbors? GET SHIT TOGETHER). Instead she watched baseball and tracked the pitches—sliders, split fingers, cutters—as she cupped her fingers around an imaginary ball. Nights cooled down enough to open the window, and she could hear cheers and the muffled voice of an announcer on the PA, remembering how she and her brother had narrated their backyard practice sessions (*Drennan throws a nasty slider in the dirt, oh and he chases!*). Through a slit in the blinds, she could see the glow of the ball field over the tops of the sycamores and cottonwoods, and she thought about walking over but didn't. Instead she obsessively checked her e-mail, or read forums about venomous snakes, poison ivy, and black widow spiders, or investigated reasons for the new ache in her knee—arthritis? Baker's cyst?—or she browsed social media for the friends with whom she'd lost touch during her marriage. She'd tried to block news of Charlie and the Girl-friend but twice stumbled on photos, and she zoomed in on the girl's smooth face, looking for acne but finding only adorable freckles. The girl looked straight at the camera, her chin tilted upward, and Laura thought, Look at her. Standing there in her little jean skirt as if she had all the time in the world.

When she didn't walk, she left voicemails on her parents' home phone, sometimes twice a day, as she always had, but now they didn't always return her calls as promptly; they were newly re-tired, busy traveling and sprucing up her childhood home to sell it. She called her brother but chatted with her sister-in-law be-cause he was working overtime on a delayed bridge project as well as hauling his sons to music camp and swim lessons and Little League games. She heard her mother's voice in her ear, a sliver from the litany of the past months: *At least you're young enough to start over.* As Laura watched the Padres lose to the Giants *again* and picked at the dirt under her fingernails, it dawned on her that she and her parents were on a parallel path. All starting over. Except, of course, her parents' do-over was part of a long-held plan—their fortieth anniversary was in two months. Hers was an attempt at an entire split from the past. Burn the whole fucking thing down and see if she could rise from the ashes. As she and Charlie had divided up and sold their sweet little ranch near Rose Canyon, as she took the only tenure-track job she was offered, her mantra was *Tabula rasa, motherfuckers*! But it turned out she had no idea where such a blank slate ended and where she began. She grew exhausted with dissecting herself, with seeing the shrunken, formaldehyde parts of her laid bare. So she walked. She walked because she knew how to do it *without* thinking: one foot and then another. There she found only immediate stimuli: heat, rocks, insects, trash bag nestled in weeds, maybe-a-snake. She walked, she walked, she walked.

By July, she began to vary her routes and walked in the mornings to beat the afternoon storms, which Maud and others called the monsoon—a debatable term, according to the Internet, for the storms that rolled up from the Gulf of Mexico. Whatever they were called, they flayed the sky with lightning and carved channels into the dry earth with ferocious bursts of rain. Some days, though not often, she rose early enough to see a man on a bicycle deliver copies of the local newspaper, tossing them from his basket like wrapped fish. She walked down Main Street, where she memorized the stores in what Maud called the District, a stretch of shops and eateries bordering the college, where her new office and new students awaited. She walked on the brick sidewalk past the Snip and Clip, Pie in the Sky Pizza, and Wolf's Den Books, close enough to run her fingers along windowpanes. She walked past the Patty Melt Diner with its red vinyl booths and whiffs of onion rings, past Casa Verde Restaurante and its apple-green door, past the tinted windows of the Pickaxe Bar and Grill. She stopped at the Woodchute Motor Lodge to admire a parked car decorated from hood to tail with bottle caps and colored glass; she waved to an elderly couple lounging in a vintage red-and-white metal glider outside Room 8. At Alligator Juniper, the one coffee shop in town, she dug change out of the rocks in her pockets for an iced coffee, heavy on the cream. She splurged on a bear claw at the bakery next door. She walked to the grocery store, using her credit card for soup and generic granola bars and veggie burgers and peanut butter; she wouldn't get her first paycheck until the first of October, and the divorce and move had drained her dry. As she walked, locals glanced up, smiled; she imagined they whispered once she passed—*New history and Latin American studies professor, lives alone in Ms. Byrd's old house behind the high school*—details delivered, no doubt, by Maud. Soon she would see students everywhere: no doubt they would wave and call out, Hey, Professor Drennan! Hey! Is our paper still due tomorrow? She walked, and she pulled her lime-green visor low over her eyes.

One day she didn't walk and instead hopped a train, the scenic railway that ran on tracks once used to haul supplies and passengers up to the mines of Jerome. She made her way through the vintage cars, back and forth, engine to caboose, past elbowy tourists wielding camera phones; she paused to lean on the open trolley railing, taking in the slopes tufted with shrub oak and junipers, the giant mining slag heap pushing through its rusted containment fence like a hernia. The craggy red canyon walls were so close on one winding pass, she could almost reach out and touch the rock. Other days, she hopped in the car, covered now with rain-spattered dust and cat prints, and drove to nearby destinations to walk—Sedona, Jerome, even once to Flagstaff. On her thirty-seventh birthday, she walked up the red, sandpapery sides of Bell Rock, where, according to Maud, thousands of nitwits once gathered to wait for the mothership—"Harmonic convergence my ass!" Maud had shouted, her eyes glinting. Laura sat at the top of the rock and tried to call her parents, who hadn't called yet. They'd never forgotten her birthday before. She didn't leave a message; instead, she found a sharp gray stone and scratched the sandstone into a fine red powder. As if she were playing dress-up, she smoothed the powder on her cheeks like blusher, rubbed it into her temples and jawline and the backs of her hands. In Jerome, on a mountain made of Precambrian rock, the abandoned open pit mine in the side like an open wound, she walked up long narrow stairs and rattled the bars of an old jail cell and ate a grilled cheese in a converted brothel. When she caught a glimpse of herself in a window—stringy and tanned, collarbones like a scythe—she stopped and thought, And who the hell are *you*? Standing there in your stupid hat, as if you have all the time in the world.

Back in Sycamore, she walked a dirt path the town had cut along the river, where fluffy cottonwood seeds floated across her vision and stuck to her sweaty forearms. Shrubs and low trees crowded the banks and obscured her view of the river, but on Sycamore Bridge, she could lean on the railing and take in the stretch of brownish-green water. She thought of the strong and lovely Crystal Pier, whose railings she'd leaned on throughout her life, watching the surfers and sky, salt and wind in her nose and eyes. Here all was still: the heat seemed to shimmer off the ground. The water meandered, sluggish, nothing like the relentless push and pull of the ocean, that enigmatic expanse with lurking fault lines and reefs, the tectonic scarred ridges of continental drift, the answers to the Earth's beginnings. If the river's surface rippled, she jumped—a harmless water snake? Or a water moccasin, a member of the pit viper family known *to climb into people's canoes?*—but it was usually the fat twitching tail of a fish.

Usually she turned around at the bridge, but one morning she walked farther than normal, though she had drunk most of the melted ice she'd brought. The path curved beyond the bridge, and she wasn't sure what waited around the bend. In the short distance, she could see rows of trees, which must belong to the pecan orchard she'd read about. Farther still were the curls of smoke from the cement factory on the far outskirts of town.

When she rounded the river's bend, she was surprised to find a concave stretch of land on the path's left side. She shielded her eyes. The surface, parched and scratched with fissures, had also been covered with stones in spiral patterns. On the far side was a pile of stones about the size of a small car and what appeared to be a wooden dock. She remembered then from her Internet research: this must have been the small lake that disappeared when a sinkhole opened up overnight. Arroyo Lake.

She walked around the lip of the old lake toward the dock. The cracked mud looked like map markings, a crisscross of boundary lines and highways, streams and county roads. She remembered reading that the Verde Valley had been an ancient freshwater lake, layers of limestone and mudstone and volcanic deposits. She climbed onto the wood dock and walked to the end. At the lowest point was a five-foot gash about the width of a tree trunk. Large, smooth stones curled around the hole, as if protecting it, and then spiraled upward along the sides.

From behind her, a voice called out, "Hello."

Laura stifled a scream and turned around so fast she lost her balance, throwing her arms out to catch herself. A woman wearing a large yellow sun hat stood a few feet away, pushing a green wheelbarrow filled with stones.

"You scared me," Laura said.

The woman shrugged but said nothing. At the pile of stones, she tipped the wheelbarrow until the rocks tumbled out and then leaned for a moment on the handles. She was short, her tanned arms and legs ropy with muscles. When the woman took off her hat and wiped her brow, Laura glimpsed a streak of purple dye in her fair hair, as well as a reddish-brown port-wine stain birthmark on the right side of her face, spreading along her cheek and jawline and down her neck. The woman was closer to her own age than she'd first thought.

Laura pointed at the stones in the old lake. "Is this yours? I mean, did you do all this?"

"No one comes here anymore," the woman said. She turned around and pushed the wheelbarrow toward what Laura saw was a sloping ravine. Laura had read about these dry washes being carved by rains throughout the desert. They could be as wide as bedrooms or as narrow as hallways, the sides as short as porch railings or as tall as rooftops. During flash floods, walls of water gushed through, pushing tons of mud and sand, ripping out trees, and tumbling boulders. She'd clicked through to multiple stories about unsuspecting hikers, campers, and migrants killed in flash floods in and around washes like this one. Swept miles away, buried in mud or never found at all.

Laura followed the woman, who had climbed up the other side of the wash and was pushing the wheelbarrow along a well-worn path. A car whizzed past, and with a blink, Laura realized that the District was only a hundred feet or so from where she stood. She could see the sign for the Woodchute Motor Lodge, a flash at the intersection. She shook her head, disoriented.

"Hey!" Laura called out to the woman, although she wasn't sure why.

The woman turned and looked at her.

Laura swept her arm at the space behind her. "It's beautiful. What you're making."

The woman nodded and seemed to smile. "Nice hat," she said.

Laura bent the brim of the visor and watched the woman disappear through the scrub. Then she stomped her way home past the snakes in the weeds, brushing at cobwebs that draped like bunting across the path. The rocks in her pockets clacked like marbles, and the sound gave her the shivers even as the sun blasted down.

One evening in July, she opened the window after the summer storm-monsoon-rain event-thing had blown through. Through the buzz of cicadas she heard a distinctive metallic *ping*: an aluminum bat connecting with a ball. She turned off the computer and walked toward the sounds of the game. She crossed a wooden footbridge that connected the ball field to the neighborhood, and as she walked closer, she could see men and women leaning on the fence, the toes of their tennis shoes in the chain link, cheering for kids up to bat. She could smell the stale popcorn and hear the clang of hard soles on the metal bleachers. Memories rushed in like high tide, foaming at the edges.

She didn't think of the ball games with Charlie, although those were legion, those old date nights full of hot dogs and peanuts and beer and sex, or of the nights when their relationship began to fray and she'd sit in the bedroom and watch the game alone. Her mind went farther back—to long days at the beach when it really did seem she had all the time in the world. When she, tomboy girl child dreaming of becoming a ballplayer, would shag pop flies and throw pitches with her dad and brother in the low surf. Her dad squeezed and shaped her hand around the baseball, bent her pliable arm. His reedy voice in her ear: *Throw hard, the more speed the better. Find your balance, there's a girl. Plant your feet, get grounded. Focus. Work from instinct, from the heart, don't think too much.* For the first time, as she watched those parents lean on the fence, she recognized the larger life subtext of his advice. And she had done none of those things.

Laura wanted to join the crowd, get some stale nachos and a soda and climb to the top of the bleachers, but instead she turned around, full of a sudden unnamed fear, a gripping force that made her keep her eyes on her feet. She walked toward the house of a woman who had lost her mind, and she thought of one of the final moments with Charlie: he'd grabbed her by the shoulders, his eyes narrow, and said, "You're such a goddamn little girl, Laura. You're such a fucking child. An infant." Then he began to sob, and watching his puckered face, she'd thought, Well, there's irony for you.

Midstride, she hauled off and kicked a rock, sending it skittering across the pavement. As her knee twinged again—bone cancer? bursitis?—she wondered if he wasn't right. She certainly felt childish in her homesickness, in her creeping fear of darkness and creaks in the house and the eerie yowl—coyotes? cats in heat? starving mountain lion stalking humans?—she heard each night over the clanking evaporative cooler. She called her parents and brother too much because it seemed as though they were the only part of her she recognized anymore.

She tracked the rock she'd kicked and scooped it into her pocket. She rubbed the rock's pitted surface with her thumb and gazed at the darkening sky, still luminous at the edges. An image of the ocean rose beneath it like a palimpsest. She missed it as if it had died. Or as if she had. And part of her had, hadn't it? Where was that fearless young girl on the beach, baseball in hand? Who was this woman in the near dark whose walk turned to a run? Who was this woman who flew up the sidewalk to her front door, keys in hand, belonging nowhere and to no one?

When she finally slept, she dreamed a spider had eaten a hole in her knee.

On the last day of July, Laura timed the walk from home to her new office at Sycamore College: twelve minutes, door to door. She walked in blue cross-training shoes with books stuffed in her pack. She walked through the iron arches of the renovated entrance where just beyond, the Black Hills flexed with sun and shadow. She walked the no-frills cement paths of the young campus, built in the early 1960s to serve the fast-growing Verde Valley. She walked through the buildings' breezeways, admiring the sandstone walls and benches. She walked inside the linoleum halls of the stuccoed Humanities building, stopping to read the comics and notes and news clippings on office doors. She paced at the front of the lecture hall, still nervous at the prospect of all those eyes on her, though she could lecture on the Treaty of Guadalupe Hidalgo in her sleep.

Back home, she called her mother, who told her about her father up on the goddamn roof despite his limp—his retirement is going to kill me, she said. Her mother talked about the Padres losing to the goddamn Dodgers, about their upcoming trip to Taipei, and when the Realtor called on the other line, she hung up before Laura could ask, "When are you going to come visit?" She tried not to cry, like the fucking child she was.

She decided to tackle a few moving boxes. Much of what she'd packed in haste was crap, anyway, cheap tin pots from college

days, tattered gift baskets, expired medicine she should have
tossed, but today she slung clothes into drawers and shelved a
few books. On that last day of July, she slit open a cardboard
flap to discover she'd accidentally packed the box Charlie had put
next to the dryer as a trash can for lint. Inside was a soft bluish
pile: fibers from their clothes, scales from their skin. She reached
in and grabbed the wad, squeezing the sloughed-off parts of a
past life, and she was struck by an oceanic wave of grief. She
dropped the lint back, folded the flaps down, and went to bed.
She did not walk that day, nor the day after, nor the day after
that. She did not get out of bed, and she left the TV on all night,
the brittle laugh tracks reverberating on the tile. When she finally
checked the mail, Maud had left a note in the box: "Everything
okay in there? Holler if you need anything."

In early August, Laura finally rose early and walked again. Out
on the path she saw a runner, a bald man with a big smile and
bigger ears who gave a wave and wide berth—cues he wasn't a
threat—as he loped past her with a long-legged grace she envied
in her slow plodding. His face was nice enough, but those legs:
heroic, dense as quarry stones. She couldn't help but think of
how they would feel locked together with hers, muscle and heat
and bones, and she created an elaborate, very sweaty sexual fan-
tasy right there on the dirt path. The next day, when she saw
him again, she was embarrassed and could barely meet his eyes,
pulling her stupid visor even lower.

    The next day, she rose late after a night of tossing and turn-
ing but decided to walk anyway, in the early afternoon when the
heat seared her skin, when the storm clouds had gathered in the
east. She set out with two frozen water bottles strapped to her

waist like pistols, in a new blue floppy canvas hat she had bought on sale in the District. She wanted to see the old lake again, to see what the woman had added to her art. When she reached it, the wheelbarrow sat empty next to the dock, but there was no sign of the woman. She again climbed up on the dock and peered down at the spiraling stones. She stared at the gash in the bottom, thinking of the red stain along the woman's jaw.

She pulled a rock from her pocket, took a deep breath, and swung her arm underhand, aiming for the hole. It'd been a long time since she'd taken aim. She let go, and the stone disappeared into the dark space. She listened for a splash but heard nothing. In the stillness, she could hear only her own breathing. She took off her shoes and socks and looked down at her feet, frighteningly pale against her tan.

In the woman's pile, Laura spied a round one of the perfect size and picked it up, tossing it between her hands until it cooled enough to clench in her fist. Stepping onto the dock, she planted her right foot behind her, lowered her shoulders, and cocked her elbow. She narrowed her gaze and pinpointed a target: a small tuft on the rim of the lake that wasn't a lake. With her breath barely a whisper, she went into her windup, thinking, Don't think. Speed. Go.

The rock flew. She watched it sail across the chasm, clear the lip, and bounce into the brush inches from where she'd aimed. She pumped her fist and did a twisting shimmy, the wood hot and scratchy on the balls of her feet. That strong-armed part of her: it was still there, even if she'd forgotten.

She breathed hard, hands on her hips, looking at the land around her. A lake made of stones, trees that didn't look like trees. The whole landscape was so absurd and otherworldly she started laughing. She *lived* here. Holy shit. She looked down at her feet. They looked smaller, elfin. Nothing was recognizable, not even her own two feet. And yet: there she stood.

Laura slid her bare feet into the tennis shoes, grabbed the wheelbarrow, and scooted down into the dry wash. At the bottom, she checked the sky: storms still a ways off. Lining the wash above her were mesquites, shrub oaks, junipers, yuccas, and other pointy stalks she made a mental note to look up later. She stepped with care on the uneven surface, liking the crunch of rock, the buzz of insects, the softened whiz of car tires overhead. She hummed a little under her breath, warmth in her cheeks. The walls of the wash were high enough that no one could see her down there. What a strange sort of secret, to walk in a crevice of the earth.

She walked with her eyes on the ground, scanning, kicking the smooth pebbles and shale under her shoes. No sign of snakes. No signs of people either, except for the plastic bags, cellophane, and wrappers plastered in the weeds. She would return later to pick up trash, but for now she picked up stones, beautiful smooth ones that fit the heart of her palm, large round ones that lined the floor like fresh citrus. She plucked and weighed her choices, liking their loud clunk in the wheelbarrow.

She pushed the wheelbarrow farther from the lake, her eyes on the bed, scouting, following the wash's twists and turns. Its walls grew taller as she progressed, too steep to climb out easily. At a crack of thunder, she looked up. Fat black storm clouds crept overhead. She needed to head back before she got soaked. She needed to get out of the wash, but the walls were too steep here, more like a small canyon.

She swung the wheelbarrow toward the lake. At the base of the west wall, she spotted a gray stone so smooth it shone. As she reached for it, she noticed a stick protruding through a crevice in the wall. A snake. She let out a short scream and scrambled backward. But the stick didn't move. She squinted and then eased closer to it. She drew a sharp breath. Not a snake. Not a stick.

She kneeled against the wall and studied the shape, the notched end. A tibia. She hissed through her teeth. Her heart kicked, and she glanced around. No one there. She climbed the sloped wall, digging the tips of her shoes into the dirt to get closer, pushing her hat aside. The sky rumbled, the thunder louder and closer now.

The bone appeared to be weathered, porous and cracked. Buried shallow in the crevice, or perhaps the dirt had been eroded by gushing water and rain, or perhaps an animal had been there digging. She brushed at the dirt above the protruding bone, and there: what seemed to be the curve of a rib.

She slid down to the bottom of the wash and dusted the dirt from her knees. She straightened her hat, trying to stay calm. She might be wrong—it might not be human. She walked through the wash to the dry lake and climbed out. She walked around the lake to the river path—to home, to the phone—as the rain began to fall. After a few steps, she began to trot, and then to run. She was a hundred yards away, almost to the bridge, when she realized she'd left the stone-filled wheelbarrow in the wash and her socks and water bottles on the dock, but she did not turn back.

Laura ran, her breath coming as hard and blotchy as the rain, which pelted her skin, stinging, and knocked her new hat off. She didn't pick it up. She ran. The stones in her pocket rattled, and though there was no way she could know by sight, she thought: A girl. Somehow she knew. A girl who, not so long ago, stood somewhere, her gaze long and steady, as if she had all the time in the world.

SOUNDS FROM INSIDE

THE NOISE AGAIN. CHATTER AND laughter, the clang of hand trucks, the drone of air-conditioning, a hiccupping thrum that ping-ponged off the metal cases and concrete floors. To Maud Winters, who stood at her case with her back to the mailroom, it sounded as if a fidgety child were twisting a radio dial, skipping across static and stations. As she pulled letters and flats from the crook of her arm and slid them into the correct slots, she clenched her teeth until her jaw bulged. Mornings like this, she wished the right ear would go all the way, too; in her darker moments, she fantasized about jamming a pick in the canal. Strike it fast, like a snake, and all would fall silent. She'd stopped wearing her hearing aid years ago because it amplified the din instead of tuning it in, and because it didn't help with the one voice she could not stop hearing.

She paused with her hand on a white envelope, the address scrawled in blue ink. Every time, her heart made a little twitch, as if tugged by a piece of twine. She closed her fingers on the envelope, and a wave of warmth washed through her. It had been several days since she'd found one—fewer and fewer letters these days. The address was 125 Arrowhead, the last street on her route, Ms. Byrd's old house where the new professor had moved in. Maud cased it in the correct slot, bottom right corner, the lone piece of mail in the box for the day. She repeated the address under her breath to remind herself, as if she would forget.

Maud drained her coffee and began to pull down the now-organized mail from the slots to rubber-band it and put it in her delivery trays. A voice cut through the din, seeming to come from behind her. Maud jumped and spun around. No one stood there. Luz Navarro was on the other side of the case, peering around the corner. Maud cupped her good ear. "Say again?"

Luz pointed. "Packing tape. Can I borrow? Mine disappeared."

Maud nodded and handed it to her. Luz's side of the case was plastered with photos of her teenage girls, the gaps between their front teeth matching hers. One was an older high school portrait of her with her brother Roberto—Beto, everyone called him— both with long feathered hair and oversize collars; another was of a young man in a soldier's uniform—her brother who'd died in the run-up to the Gulf War. Maud's side of the case was blank. She reached up and scratched at a sliver of old tape and sticky residue where the Missing poster had once been; she'd taken it down in the tenth year, when Jess would have turned twenty-seven, far removed from the kohl-eyed teenager in the picture and long since local headlines had faded from view. That also was when Maud had stopped holding anniversary memorials or trying to get the paper to do a follow-up. People had begun to look away from the posters and from her, unsure of what to do with their pity. Sometimes people asked what she planned *to do*—a euphemism for the question they couldn't ask: Will you declare your daughter dead? Her answer, always, still: I don't know. Rachel Fischer had met Hugh Leitner and gotten remarried then, and her and Rachel's strange, unexpected friendship, those lifeline meetings over coffee and wine in Maud's living room or on Rachel's deck, had dwindled to occasional phone calls. Of course, Esther still brought bagels or Danish on Fridays, and Iris called frequently and brought over bags of pecans every winter. Detective Alvarez still called or stopped by on occasion, and not only when bodies were found, either; he chatted with her about the weather or the Lobos' winning season, his salt-and-pepper hair growing saltier over the years, as had hers. They never stopped checking in. They never asked what she planned *to do*, even after almost two decades.

Luz leaned around the case and handed back the tape with a smile of thanks, the gap between her teeth as thick as a penny. Luz had known Jess—she was a couple of years older, her brother Beto in Jess's class. They knew the story. Even if they hadn't known Jess, they would know. Stories like that never died in that town. Transmitted through water or something, like cholera. Or through mail carriers. Her customers told her everything, good and bad, unburdened themselves on their front steps: sore backs and bunions, busted appliances, nephews getting married, lecherous bosses, secret affairs.

For god's sake, don't disappear.

Maud shook her head at the inner voice, those old words.

Luz asked, "Any big weekend plans?"

Maud said, "Paris, London, Rome. Hot date with a trapeze artist. The usual."

Luz's eyes widened a moment before she laughed, and Maud reminded herself: Watch the volume, Maudly. When she was younger, Maud had trouble regulating, and kids would mock and tease her, cupping their ears and yelling, What? Pardon? Say what? Say again? Then Maud learned to let fly, jokey, outrageous. To hell with them. Jess had tried not to get embarrassed, tried to make a joke of it. *You're at freight train levels again, Mom.*

Luz said, "We're all going to the Pickaxe for happy hour after shift. Beto's working—sorry, *Roberto*, he hates when I call him that. He'll give us free drinks. You should come."

Maud glanced at the bottom corner cell in her case, 125 Arrowhead, again feeling the tiny twitch in her heart. She said, "Thanks, but I can't. Gotta wash my hair." She pretended to toss back long locks and patted her fuzzy gray curls, which she used to color a glossy dark brown but had let go in the past few years.

Luz smiled. "One of these days I'm going to drag you out, mamí."

Luz. A good egg. A good kid. Trying so hard to make it okay. Maud wrapped a rubber band around a stack and snapped it, remembering, every time, how Jess used to chew rubber bands like gum. She said, "One day, maybe I'll let you."

Maud finished packing her trays. She loaded her parcels into the large canvas roller bin, stacked the trays on top, and hauled the bin out to her truck. Before she headed out, she ran through her supplies: water, sun hat, lunchbox, pepper spray, pens, strap cutter, pink slips, phone, scanner, lip balm.

Her route for all her eighteen years in Sycamore had been a combined walking and driving one, in the older Riverbend subdivision behind the high school. She had enough seniority to switch to one of the few all-curbline routes, like those in her own neighborhood in Roadrunner Heights or over at Juniper Meadows near the highway to Sedona. Luz, in fact, had jumped at the driving route in Roadrunner Heights, but Maud liked to walk, even in the heat, even with torrential bursts of monsoon rains, even with a forty-pound satchel hanging off her shoulder—even now, at fifty-seven, when she had to wear a brace on her creaky left knee, when her shoulders and hips ached and she knocked back ibuprofen with her morning coffee and again in the evening before bed. She pictured her father's stooped shoulders, his swollen knees. He hadn't loved it like she did. He had taken early retirement and spent his afternoons puttering around with house repairs (and

driving her mother up the wall) until he got a part-time job at the
neighborhood hardware store. She remembered her father saying
he knew his mail route better than his own neighborhood, and
this was true for her, too. No matter what else happened in her
life, each day she could at least walk her streets.

Each day advanced the same: starting in the truck over at
Overton Orchards. That morning, Iris was out on the tractor and Paul, home for a visit, was carrying a ladder across
the field. Maud stopped and watched him a moment, noting
the pronounced hunch of his shoulders, the shine of his now-
bald head. She whistled, sharp and quick, and Iris turned with
a wave. Then Maud drove the truck over to Riverbend and
parked. Her satchel grew lighter at the end of each relay, the
steps counter at her waist clicking from the hundreds to the
thousands, and she marked her progress by yard features:
the oak stump with kids' carved initials on the corner of Dry
Run; the tilting streetlamp on Bottlebrush; the hairpin cul-de-
sac on Alameda. She knew the dogs, the pitch and lengths of
their barks and growls. She knew which box hinges squeaked,
which swayed on loose posts, which were dented and scratched
and rusted. She knew what it was to pull down the little metal
door, anticipating what lay inside, so she took care stuffing the
boxes. Some part of her felt as if she were watching over it all,
keeping everyone safe. And in some ways, she was: she had
called ambulances, police, and family members. They watched
out for her, too, old women and men waiting at the door with
smiles, with envelopes of cash and boxes of fudge at Christmas.
The path of her day was clear-cut, waiting for her every morning like a faithful pet, and she did not veer. Some would find
this mind-numbingly monotonous, but not Maud. She needed
the sureness of pavement, of brick steps, of concrete driveways

under her rubber-soled shoes. She needed to feel the strike of her feet on surfaces that would not disappear beneath her.

After the mornings when she found letters, Maud tended to be distracted and jittery all day, walking at a faster pace, her satchel thumping her hip. Long-ago images and sounds snuck in when she was like this, tunneling under the wall of her defenses. All the tricks she'd learned in counseling with those other families of the missing, learning how to take care of herself, to stop the spiral of obsession—pushing air into her belly, a countdown from ten to one in an elevator that opened onto her safe place, tying the thought to a balloon and watching it disappear into the sky— none of it worked. There was Jess's voice, or what had become an approximation of it, like words and phrases from her note- books, or the outgoing message on their old answering machine. The words buzzed like swarms of cicadas at dusk. Maud pressed her finger to her good ear, closing it off, as if she could block the sound of memory.

In the early years, Maud heard and saw Jess everywhere. In her dreams at first: Jess turned up without explanation, the same age, suspended in time, waiting on the doorstep or inside the house. *Oh, Mom, I know you love to worry. I'm right here.* So Maud took a lot of sleep aids to stay in that world as long as she could. When she wasn't at work, she was in bed, trying to get closer to the dreams. But then Maud began to see Jess in broad daylight. She'd see Dani Newell, or Angie Juarez, or other kids around town, all those young smooth faces, and behind them she'd see Jess ducking around pillars and street corners, ghost girl, her voice and long curls trailing.

And then there were the imaginings, the speculation about what had happened: body snatched, body bloated, body burned, body naked, body floating, body bleeding, body buried alive. Maud's counselor taught her how to replace her terrible images with a more positive one: Mexico, their family vacation spot before the divorce, the last place they'd traveled together the summer before Jess disappeared. The last place Maud remembered Jess being happy. Maud had trained herself to see one image: Jess standing at the blue-gray Sea of Cortez at sunset. The water lapped over Jess's ankles, and she smiled, bathed in the final light of day.

As she walked her route, Maud tried to get to that image. She managed to get in her mental elevator and count down; the door dinged and opened to her safe beach: Mexico. But there was young Jess on the beach in a stretched-out tee and floppy hat, drinking a bottle of 7UP, chewing Chiclets, saying, "Mama, mama, watch!" as she hurled herself at the spawning grunions at sunset. "Mama, look!" There was Jess riding on her father's broad back, the three of them standing together in the low surf at sunset. There was Jess and Dani Newell, her first best friend, sipping their sodas, toes in the sand. There was Jess, infant—body tiny, body spongy, body rocked and nursed, squalling and red-faced and perfect—and teenage, rolling her eyes at Maud from the passenger seat. Jess, staring down the Thanksgiving table at Adam Newell. Jess, huddled on her bed, crying as if her heart had turned inside out. There was Maud's counselor, a kind woman, asking, "What is it you see for yourself, Maud?" which Maud never could answer. Lately, when she had tried to think about this question, she had been conjuring the fireflies on her grandparents' farm in Tennessee, the summer when she'd lost the hearing in her left ear and most of it in her right. When the counselor gently pushed, asking, "But what else? What about the future?" Maud couldn't say. She could see backward but never forward. Only the endless now.

The days moved faster, too, when Maud found a letter. Before she knew it, it was lunchtime. She took her half hour in the shady parking lot of Juarez Autos. She waved to Angie Juarez working in the bays with Luz's brother Beto, at Rose Prentiss and her daughter Hazel in the front office, but stayed in her truck to eat her PB&J, even though sweat soaked her shirt and shorts. She watched all of them—grown, healthy, their bodies heavier but still taut with youth. She tried to place Jess among them, to re-see her, transform her into an adult. But she couldn't get the image to crystallize: Would her hair be prematurely white now, like Angie's? Cut short into a bob like Dani Newell's?

"I like your hair like that," Maud had said to Dani last week, when she'd gone to have blood drawn for her annual checkup. Dani had worked at the medical center for a couple years now, though she'd been in town since she'd failed out of Stanford so quickly. For years, Maud would see her at whatever job she happened to have—the deli counter at Bashas', stock clerk at the HealthCo—or she'd spot her out shopping or walking or driving. Dani kept her head down, eyes averted, even when Maud waved hello. Maud knew Dani was renting Esther's guest house now. Everyone in town knew Dani's story, too.

"Thanks," Dani had said, not looking up from her hands as she tied the rubber tube around Maud's upper arm. She flicked for a vein at Maud's inner elbow, scrubbing at her skin with an alcohol swab. They sat so close, Maud could see a brown mark on the sleeve of Dani's scrubs, a mottled red flush on her cheek, a vein thrusting at her throat. Her hands, though, remained steady.

Dani said, "A quick sting. There. Okay, we're in."

Maud looked away from the tube filling with her blood, her palms sweating.

"Relax your fist now," Dani said. When she pulled the needle

out, Maud heard her make a sound, a soft moan. She looked up
to see Dani with eyes brimming, her jaw locked tight, nose red
at the tip.

"Sorry," Dani said. "Just thinking."

Maud said, "It's okay."

Dani turned away to wipe the tears. Maud couldn't remember
the last time Dani had met her eyes. Dani unwrapped a bandage
and stuck it on Maud's arm, her eyes still downturned. "You're
all set," she said.

"Say hello to your mother for me," Maud said.

Dani nodded, pulling off her latex gloves, her short hair
swinging.

In the parking lot, Maud wolfed her sandwich, downed some
water, stopped in the Juarezes' bathroom, and then headed to
Riverbend, working her way north in an east-to-west zigzag. She
reapplied lip balm and sunblock. Cumulus clouds of the monsoon broiled to the east, cranking up the humidity. She tied a
handkerchief around her neck to catch the sweat.

Finally, Maud parked at the end of Arrowhead, her last street.
She opened the truck's hatch. If a supervisor lurked anywhere, all
he would see was her loading her satchel with her final stacks. He
wouldn't see her finger the mail for 125 and slide out the letter,
leaving it in the tray.

At number 125, Maud didn't turn up the driveway, but Laura
opened the door and stepped onto the front porch, perhaps because she saw Maud coming. Maud hadn't seen Laura in several days; in fact, she'd even left a note in the mailbox. Two days
ago, the mail and the note were gone, so Maud hadn't called the
police to have them check on her.

Laura had thankfully replaced her lime-green foam visor with
a wide-brimmed canvas hat, but she looked too thin, her shorts

bagging to her knees. Divorce, Maud had guessed, or a death in the family, from the way she dragged herself around town in the heat. She had to be Jess's age or thereabouts, thirty-five, thirty-six. They resembled each other a little, too, although Laura was fair-haired. After a moment, Maud realized she was standing still, staring at Laura.

"Nothing today!" Maud called, louder than usual, a flush at her neck.

Laura waved, smiling. She adjusted the water bottles strapped to her waist and pulled on the brim of her hat. If she said anything, Maud couldn't hear it.

"Think it's going to rain," Maud called and waved back. She heard a voice she both knew and didn't: *You are here*. She turned and looked behind her before she could stop herself.

It was after five by the time Maud swung her sedan into the driveway, a bag from the Patty Melt and her lunchbox with the letter tucked inside on the passenger seat. Her wet shoes squeaked on the brake. The sky had waited to unhinge until after she finished her route, a swift, furious deluge that flooded the station's parking lot while she wrapped up her tasks for the day. The storm had let up, and the streets were nearly dry again as the water soaked into the parched earth, seeping into the aquifers below.

She turned off the engine and sat listening to the rain spatter on the hood, watching the steam curl up. The square stucco house looked the same as when she'd bought it in 1991. For years, her parents had wanted her to move home to Phoenix—*Come home, Maudly. Honey, come home*—but Maud stayed in Sycamore. In the same house. Same address, 825 Roadrunner Lane. Same phone number. Same good old car, now pushing 200,000 miles, thanks to Angie's miracle working. She'd repainted the house, but in the same Navajo White. When the jacaranda near the breezeway died, she had planted another one. For better or worse, this was home. She could stay here and wait. She could do that much.

She climbed out, her shoes squishing on the driveway. At the mailbox, she held her breath as she pulled down the little metal door: bills, an ad mailer, nothing else.

Inside, Maud kicked off her soaked shoes and socks and changed into jeans, a T-shirt, and flip-flops, and then put the kettle on to boil. She ate her hamburger standing over the sink and then scarfed three of Esther's cinnamon swirl bites. Sipping her soda, she unpacked her lunchbox and held the letter over the kettle's steam until the flap lifted. Then she took the letter to Jess's room.

Maud had left the room the same for a while. Around year six, she had taken down the music posters, filled the holes with spackle, and asked Rachel Fischer to help her paint the walls with a fresh coat of Garden Mint. She had bagged the clothes and books and photos and put them in the storage shed. After all, if—when—Jess came home, she would not be a teenager. She would be an adult, ready to move on to her own space. Maud had replaced the double bed with a burgundy twill sofa sleeper, adding throw pillows, an ottoman, and a small television and DVD player.

The one thing she had left the same was Jess's desk, which had belonged to Maud when she was a girl and which sat as it always had under the window facing the street. A simple white cottage desk with three drawers and a hutch, where Jess had done her homework and written in her diaries—her notebooks, she'd called them. Plain black-and-white composition books, their sturdy covers held shut with rubber bands. After Gil Alvarez returned the notebooks, which he and the police had scoured for clues, Maud hadn't packed them away, storing them instead in the lower desk drawer, along with the old answering machine. She pulled them out sometimes, reading them again even though she knew every word. Couldn't stop knowing them. Two years' worth, except the notebook from her last weeks, which she must have had with her.

She pulled one out now, pressing the spine open with the heel of her hand. She ran her finger over the pen and pencil marks, feeling the indentations. She skimmed the first entry, written the day they'd arrived.

> *January 1991*
> —*So here we are. Sycamore, Arizona. God's little slice of heaven. The whole place is about the size of five blocks of our old neighborhood. What in the name of all things holy was Mom THINKING? Tells me, We need a change, J-bird. Yeah, so schlep your only daughter to the flat-fuck middle of nowhere? GREAT idea.*

Maud scanned to the end of the entry, to the poem whose stanzas slanted down the page.

> Tonight you watched the universe
> from the pavement
> the sky so black
> it howled
> Or was that you?
>
> You lifted your finger to find
> your place in space
> X marks the spot

You Are Here.

You: flat-backed
in the flat-fuck middle of nowhere
staring at a galactic heart
nestled in a nest of stars

Are: the verb to be
(or not to be)
Conjugate it:
I am
You are
She is
When will you finish the sentence,
fill in the blank?

Here: A new home
small and minty
with salted black hills
tiny speck on the pale blue dot

You are here
Dog-ear the page of yourself
don't lose your place
For god's sake
don't disappear

Maud could hear Jess's voice, or what she thought of now as her voice, husky, as if she'd just woken up. She pulled the answering machine out, too, plugged it in, and played it.

There it was, tinny on the cassette: *You've reached Jess—*

and here, Maud's voice, chiming in—*and Maud Winters. You know what to do and when to do it, so do it.* Then Jess's honking laugh, before the beep. Maud rewound the tape and played it again. And again.

Maud could see Jess sitting there, hunched over the desk, filling the pages with her looping scrawl. Back then, Maud had thought this was normal, a good sign. A teenage girl writing in her diary— thank god. She had believed Jess was working out her anger and hurt about the divorce, getting it down, getting it out. And then came Thanksgiving. Maud could still taste the mouthful of dry turkey she'd been chewing, could still see Rachel's dark eyebrows pulled tight together, Dani putting her forehead down on the table and retching onto the carpet. Adam, pale as the mashed potatoes. And Jess: hiding her face behind her brown curls, eyes gleaming, cheeks flushed, flapping her hands as if she could shake it away.

She flipped to the last page, where she'd taped Jess's final note:

Mom,

I'm going out for a walk (it's about 4:45). I need to clear my head. I'll be back in a couple hours. Don't worry.

Love, J-bird

Maud closed the notebook. None of it mattered now. None of it helped. No answers, no hidden clues. All suspects with airtight alibis. The prevailing theory: Just another teenage runaway who didn't want to be found.

Except Jess wouldn't have run. Maud knew it. She knew that much.

The letter was like all the others in the past few years: hand-written address, thin, maybe a sheet or two. Maud never took birthday cards. Never bills or credit card statements or envelopes marked Urgent. Never postcards. She never kept a letter for long, a day or two at most. When she finished, she always resealed it with a glue stick and shuffled it in with the outgoing mail. She always delivered it. It wasn't stealing in the strictest sense, but it was definitely tampering and a gross violation of privacy; if caught, she would be fired. She didn't do it for the thrill, or to snoop, or to meddle. She didn't have bad intentions.

She did it because after eighteen years, every time she opened her own mailbox, she still held her breath. Every time, she shuffled through the envelopes, looking for the scrawl she knew by heart. Every time, nothing. She couldn't count how many letters she had carried and delivered throughout her life. She could see the scads of them in her mailbag, feel the rough fibers, their sharp corners as she slid them into boxes. Thousands upon thousands. She wanted only one.

The letter she had today was addressed to Laura Drennan and was from Mr. and Mrs. Robert and Ellen Drennan. Her parents, Maud guessed; the penmanship was neat, tight cursive—the mother. Maud held it up to the lamp. Looked like one folded sheet.

As she eased her opener under the loosened flap, she pictured Laura Drennan standing on her porch, wearing those saggy clothes. Her face, in all those times Maud had shouted at her: a bird that had flown into a window, stunned into stillness.

And Maud remembered Rachel Fischer saying that—"I feel as though I've smacked into a window. Flying along fine, and *bam*." She'd shown up one afternoon at Maud's house some months after Jess hadn't come home, months after Maud had delivered the letters Rachel blasted across town, only later learning their contents: "Dear Sycamore Friends: I write to tell you some news." In the return address field, she'd used their stamp—"Adam Newell and Rachel Fischer-Newell"—and scratched out his name and her hyphenate with blue ballpoint pen. She hadn't named Jess, had written only "an underage girl." Maud had stared through the screen at Rachel, who stood on the step, cradling a bottle of wine and crying so hard she couldn't speak. Finally, Rachel had said, "I wished bad things for him. For her. But I never wished for this. Never." Maud had opened the door.

Now she set the unopened letter on the ottoman.

She looked out the window. The rain had stopped, the low-hanging sun breaking through unsettled clouds. Friday. Happy hour. She ran her hand over her frizzy curls.

Rachel didn't answer the front door. Maud peered through the sidelight window. No movement, no flicker of the TV. No Hugh in the kitchen, with his loud, tuneful whistle even Maud could hear. No one home. Maud got in her car and started to drive home, but at the intersection of College Drive, she took a right instead of a left, toward the District.

In the Pickaxe's lot, Maud parked next to Luz's zippy red convertible and stepped out into the humid evening, her flip-flops crunching on the gravel. She looked at the little red car and some part of her reached back, saw herself at twenty-one, just starting out. Back then, she'd been waiting tables at a sandwich shop near the Phoenix community college where she met Stuart in her Intro to Art History class, tumbling in and out of his bed and marrying him within six months. At the sandwich shop, she'd set down plastic baskets and big red tumblers on the checkered tablecloths, and she'd pause to look at the shining band on her left finger, thinking how lucky she was to find her true love, thinking of her future: they would finish college, get good jobs, buy a little house with a yard, travel the world. Simple, happy. On her and Stuart's weekend honeymoon in Mexico, in the months before she'd gotten pregnant and taken the civil service exam and started her career as a letter carrier—in her father's footsteps, as it were, though he'd wished her a different path—she'd stood on a balcony naked and watched the sunrise while her new husband slept. Watching the shimmering expanse of the Gulf, she'd thought, There's the whole wide world, and she stretched to her tiptoes, reaching for it.

Now Maud reached for the bar's door handle, holding her breath.

Inside the front door, Maud let her eyes adjust to the dimness. Luz stood with some coworkers near the pool table. Luz looked toward the door. "Hey, it's Maud! Mamí! You came!" She waved her arms as if hailing a ship.

As Maud walked toward those waving arms, she could not remember the last time she had been inside this bar. She knew it was early on, when they'd first moved to town, and she'd gone on a few dates with that charming Hector Juarez, who up and got cancer the same year. She remembered Hector's stark white hair—like Angie's now—but she didn't remember anything about the dark paneling, the neon signs, the clacking pool balls and murmurs, the muted televisions perched in the corners. She couldn't remember the last time she'd walked into a place she did not know. She couldn't remember the last time she'd faced noises and voices and walked *toward* them. She couldn't remember the last time she had walked toward someone without an armful of mail, carrying only herself as an offering.

As she weaved through the tables, Maud thought of a different past, one before marriage and parenthood and divorce, before these years of loss and yearning: those fireflies on her grandparents' farm. After her terrible fever broke, Maud, six years old, had folded herself onto Granddaddy's wood-splitting rock near the barn at twilight. She couldn't hear out of either ear then, and she was weak, disoriented, wrapped in a blanket despite the warmth of the evening. And there they came, flickering up from the grass with a yellow-green flash, hovering around the corners of her vision, like a magic trick she had seen at a fair, a man flicking silver coins between his fingers, like the colors and shapes she'd seen in her fever dreams. The strangeness of it made her clasp her knees, holding tight, as if she might disappear if she let go of herself. As she sat there, the world was both too big and too small, and she wanted all of it at once. She reached out and caught one, and the creature bumped against her palms, tickling. She peeked at its glow through the cracks of her fingers. It was like nothing she'd ever known, as if from another world, one with all her heart she wanted to find. She whispered, "Go," and opened her hands. And it did.

Maud left the Pickaxe and drove up Roadrunner Lane to find a police cruiser in her driveway. Her first thought: stolen letter on the ottoman. The second: driving after two glasses of Chablis. It hit her as she pulled next to the cruiser and saw Gil Alvarez standing next to it.

Maud stepped out, unsteady both from the wine and the fact of Gil. Under the streetlight, his hair looked silver. She blinked and realized it *was* silver. She hadn't seen him in person for more than a year, not since his wife's funeral.

"Did you find her?" Her voice surprised her: steady and clear, despite the Chablis, despite the lurch of her heart into her throat.

"We don't know yet, Maud."

"But you found something."

"We did. I didn't want to call. But it's late now, and you can come on down tomorrow."

"I'll come now."

"It's dark. We're not going out now."

"Where is she?"

"We don't know it's her—"

"Where?"

"In the wash. Past the bridge, past the old lake. It's dark—"

"So get a goddamn flashlight." Maud grabbed her keys and purse from her passenger seat and climbed into the front seat of his cruiser.

At the old lake, Maud followed him into the darkness. The flashlight beam jerked across the path. The sky had cleared, but the waxing moon was a mere thumbnail sliver. She kept her eyes on the ground, stepping only where Gil stepped. The thud of his footfalls seemed to come from a distance.

They reached the dry wash. Gil scanned with the beam, and he pointed at the trail down the slope. "Watch your step."

Maud started down. Her shoes skidded on the loose dirt, and she threw her arms out, stumbling the last few feet but staying upright. As they walked through the wash, she stayed close to Gil's back, and she almost bumped into him when he stopped. He lifted his arm.

The beam lit the wall of the wash, cordoned by yellow-and-black police tape. Maud stepped forward and lifted the tape.

"Maud, please don't touch anything. The forensics team is coming up tomorrow from Phoenix. We need to keep it clean. I don't need to tell you how much trouble I could get in for bringing you here like this."

She leaned against the sloped wall, her knees pressing into the dirt. "Shine the light."

He did. A pack of coyotes began to yip. The high-pitched calls bounced across the air, sounding to Maud as if they were feet away.

"We don't know it's her." Gil's voice, low, behind her. No, he leaned next to her.

"But it's someone," she said. Even through the dirt and brush, she could see the notched bone.

He clicked the flashlight off. The negative image floated in her vision, unearthly black, bone white.

"The rain," she said. "The whole town was flooded that night." She remembered the sky as vengeful, mythic with rage and thunder, as if it wanted to punish the earth, pummel it into submission. Body drowned, body bloated, body buried alive.

"We just don't know yet. Those folks coming tomorrow, they're good. They can tell a lot with bones. We'll know more soon." He patted her arm, his hand warm and assuring. He stood up. "Come on. It's late."

The coyotes howled. The sounds moved in from all sides. She pressed her finger against her ear, closing it off.

But she could not mute the sound of her own breath, as shallow as the crude grave just a few feet away in the dark. She could not stop the voice that lived on: *Mama, look! Mama, Mama, watch me! X marks the spot. You Are Here. For god's sake, don't disappear.*

THE NEW GIRL

WORKDAYS, ANGIE JUAREZ LEFT THE house before sunrise, long before Rose or Hazel woke. That early, Angie could take her time setting up the shop, drink coffee, read the paper, hum low in the silence. Early mornings had been her papa's habit, too, and she used to think it was an awful chore to get up before dawn, but now she understood. There was nothing quite like waking with the sun, in her own special quiet place, watching the world yawn and stretch around her.

Half asleep, in the glow cast by the nightlight, Angie pulled on her flannel shirt, jeans, and boots. Rose lay sprawled across the bed, the sheets twisted and tangled like a clump of seaweed. Angie sat on the corner of the bed and patted her bare leg, but her girlfriend didn't budge. She'd been up late again. She'd been up late a lot, prowling the living room and eating handfuls of dry cereal and watching reruns, which meant something was bugging her. When Angie had asked, "What's wrong, hon?" Rose teared up and said, "I don't *know*." Angie tried to let her be. Rose would talk when she was good and ready, not a second before. Could be anything: her mother selling her home and moving into the guest house, the two-year anniversary of her father's death, something to do with the motel and her sister Stevie, more bullshit from her boss at the bank, her upcoming birthday. Angie worried if she pushed too hard, Rose would run. After all, there was a time when Rose *had* run. Even now, so many years into their life together, those dormant memories erupted: waiting up until the sun seeped through the blinds when Rose didn't come home, waking up to find her gone. A night, a couple days, sometimes longer, young Hazel oblivious in the crib. The last episode had been four years ago, when Hazel was away for a week at the YMCA camp in Prescott. Three days, no note, and then Rose was home without a word. Then Angie had told her if she did it again, that was it, *she* was gone, and Rose had fallen to her knees in sobbing apology, begging, promising. That morning, though, as Angie squeezed Rose's warm foot, recognizing those signs, she wondered if she would ever stop waiting for the moment she'd wake up to find Rose gone. Her throat tightened, a familiar lava heat and fear tinged with anger. She pressed at the hollow of her neck where unspoken words lodged, poised and sharp as a scorpion's tail.

After Angie let out the dogs, and fed them, the cat, and their new turtle, she stopped in Hazel's room. She kissed her on the forehead and stroked her smooth brown hair. Hazel was the one good thing to come out of Rose's disappearing acts, the product of a brief affair with a feckless young man when Rose had moved to Phoenix for a couple years. Hazel, now fifteen, whom Angie had helped raise since she was two—though Hazel called her Ang, not Mom. Hazel, her almost-daughter, whom Angie's father had missed meeting—he'd died the month before Rose came back to town with Hazel on her hip. Papa and Hazel were bound in her memory by the proximity of his death and her arrival, his terrible absence offset by Hazel's wondrous presence, by the enormity of both what she'd lost and what she'd found. Hazel half woke and said, "Can we practice driving later?" and Angie said, "Sure thing, hon. Sure thing." She smoothed her hair harder, tucked her blanket tighter. "Don't forget to feed the zoo this afternoon."

As Angie backed the Impala out of the driveway, a lamp in Rose's mother's garage apartment clicked on. The rest of the town, though, slumbered as she drove through its streets, the houses and stores dark except for Yum Bakery, where she caught a glimpse through a glowing window of Esther Genoways leaning over her stainless steel prep table. The other place alight was the office at the Woodchute; Angie knew Stevie was inside, brewing coffee and setting out Esther's bite-size muffins and rugelach for guests. Stevie may have been an odd duck, but no one could argue with how she'd turned the motel around. Listed in the Best-Of tourist guides, booked solid through Christmas with visitors en route to Tuzigoot Monument or Jerome, college parents in for visits, tourists headed to Sedona who couldn't afford to stay there.

At the shop, Angie set the coffee to brew and flipped through the day's invoices. Iris Overton's jeep was up first. Yesterday, Iris's son Paul had dropped it off. She had told him how sorry she was about his wife. They'd known each other since kindergarten, though they hadn't been friends in high school. Such youthful divisions faded as time slipped away and nostalgia crept in, as they settled deeper into their adult lives, her growing white-haired and him bald—and now losing his wife to cancer. He was in town with his young son, not sure how long they'd be there. They chatted about the heat, about who from high school was still in town or had come back, a little gossip about who was dating whom. About the jeep she'd said, "It's on its last legs, but your mom won't listen." He'd smiled and said, "Yeah, she's stubborn." Angie had laughed and said she'd do what she could. "Take care of yourself," she told him when he turned down a ride back to the orchard and jogged off down the sidewalk.

The newspaper landed with a fat thump outside the door as the coffee finished brewing, and Angie waved at Beto—Roberto—as he pedaled off on his ten-speed. Roberto now. She smiled. He'd been trying to get that to stick. It was true he looked nothing like the scrawny, shy kid he once was—he was tall and lean now, ruggedly handsome in his low-slung jeans and snap-button cotton shirts—but in her heart he'd always be Beto. He'd be at work here in a couple hours, and then after the shop closed, he'd pick up a shift at the Pickaxe. Angie didn't know how he did it all. "Keeps me young," he said, rubbing at his ever-thinning hair, at his broad forehead that seemed to be growing broader, but Angie knew, too, he was helping with his mother's doctor bills, not to mention hooking up with college students, those clueless, sweet young women who didn't give him any trouble. Exasperating as it was, part of her couldn't blame him—envied him, even. Roaming, free of commitment, no worries about being left behind.

Angie slid the rubber band off the paper and smelled the fresh ink. Her fingers would be black by the time she'd finished reading, but then again, they'd be black all day long until she got out the orange pumice, and even then, hints of grease would linger in her cuticles and stain her knuckles. She sat in her father's old reclining rocker and unfolded the front page.

She blinked and pulled the paper taut. She turned on the desk lamp and put on her reading glasses. The article was brief: Bones found in dry wash by a Sycamore College professor out for a walk. Would be tested by forensics team. Police investigating whether the bones belong to Jess Winters, a seventeen-year-old girl who went missing in December of 1991. Had lived with mother at time of disappearance. Mother, Maud Winters, unreachable for comment. No arrests or charges ever made in connection.

She touched her finger to the page. There it was, the news most everyone in town worried they would see some day, the news they'd been waiting for even when they forgot they were waiting. That girl. Angie rubbed the paper until ink smudged her finger.

She'd waltzed into fourth-hour Humanities midway through class, wearing red-framed sunglasses, a red puffy jacket over an orange baby-doll dress with zebra-striped leggings, and worn purple Chucks. Silver star- and moon-shaped studs lined her lobes, up into the cartilage, and she twisted them as if tuning the pegs of a guitar. Her long, curly hair was the honey brown of fresh motor oil. She was as tall as, or taller than, most boys, slim up top but broad at the hips, like a chemistry beaker.

The girl slid into the desk next to Angie. She smiled and said, "Hey," as if they'd been friends forever. Surprised, Angie's face heated up, and she smoothed down her bangs, where she had already sprouted a slim silver streak. Like her father, she went white by thirty-five, but at sixteen she had only that streak like a stick of spearmint gum. A clump of girls whom Angie thought of as the Ra-Ras turned and gawped, their eyes sparkling with glitter shadow and malevolent intent.

"She doesn't talk," one of the Ra-Ras said, indicating Angie.

The new girl didn't answer. She pushed her sunglasses to the top of her head and cracked a piece of neon-green gum until the Ra-Ra turned around and slid down in her seat. Angie kept her eyes on her graffiti-carved desk but snuck a sideways peek at the girl. Despite the earrings and the gum, with her riotous hair, oval face, large brown eyes, and tiny mouth, she reminded Angie of a figure in a Renaissance painting, like the ones Ms. G had shown them. Sort of glowing but sad. For some reason, Angie thought of xylophones. Perhaps because of all the bright colors, or perhaps because of the sudden range of notes in her percussive heart.

After school, Angie worked in the bay at her father's auto shop. With the garage door open, she could see the white steam of her breath, but she didn't care. She layered up with a down coat, wool hat, and gloves with the fingertips cut off. Under the hood of a car she was no longer the quiet girl in the back row. Here, with the thrum of an idling engine, she was animated, singing low to the pop songs on the radio blaring from the shelf behind her. She was going to run her own shop someday, somewhere far from this place where kids spit in her hair or bumped her with brick-weight backpacks or elbowed her in the throat in auto shop, even though she knew more about cars than any of them. "Shitheads, all of 'em, mi'ja," Papa said. "Don't know nothing from nothing, verdad?"

She worked on the belts and filters on her '69 Impala, checking the tension on each part as her father had taught her. Cuidado, he'd say, easy now. He'd been protective even before her mother ran off to California in search of a bigger life with a man who sold real estate. That according to her letter, anyway. Angie didn't see her mother or her bigger life at all. It'd been her father and her alone so long she hardly remembered it any other way. At the shop, he let her work on her own. If he did help, he leaned next to her at an alert distance, gave her quick pats on the back. Pat, pat. Used to be she could sit on his lap and hug him close, breathing in his smell of orange pumice and sweat. Still, he was always around. Lately he had been making noise about how he wasn't sure what he'd do without her there, and she didn't know what to say, so she didn't say anything, as usual.

Papa came out of the office into the bay. He had circles under his eyes, and his shirtsleeves bagged around his skinny arms. He stumbled on an errant pipe wrench. Though no one saw but Angie, she had the urge to defend him, to announce how much he could carry, everything from tires to bedsprings to even her, like the time she had her wisdom teeth yanked and had to be hauled, drugged and dead-weight, from the dentist's chair to the truck.

He held up an invoice. "Can you run over to Eddie's for me? His guy's out sick, and I need this belt."

"Sure." She set down her crescent wrench.

He handed her the invoice and gave her a quick pat on the shoulder.

Slow and careful, she backed the Impala out of the garage. Outside the bay, the day shone bright despite the cold, and the sun heated her face and hands through the windows. As she pulled away, Angie glanced in the side mirror. Papa stood in the bay, smiling and waving, his white hair tinged gold by the sun. *Cuidado*, she could hear him saying, and she resisted the sudden urge to gun it.

Eddie's Auto Parts was on the south side of town, the newer side, off the intersection of the highway that led to Sedona, Flagstaff, and the Grand Canyon. The town had had a growth spurt, with cheap motels and gas stations and a few chain eateries cropping up like crab grass along with a SuperMart and the HealthCo and a new medical complex. Most of the town, though, still seemed the same: the college and the District, with historic brick stores and houses and tree-lined neighborhoods; her father's shop on Main south of the District; the slag heap hunkered low and black behind the fairgrounds; one supermarket, one movie theater, one high school, one pecan orchard, one cement plant, one nice restaurant—Shane's on the Bluff, with a nautical-Western theme—and one river, a lazy, curling thing that smelled of fish and moss, where the sycamores and cottonwoods grew dense, setting loose their fluffy white seeds in the spring and summer.

All tucked tight against the rolling Black Hills range with its rough ridges, the Woodchute and Mingus Mountains, the town of Jerome nesting on its side.

On her way back from Eddie's, caught up in the roar of the engine and the sun warming her through the windows, Angie decided to make a quick detour out to Arroyo Lake and took the dirt turnoff next to Sycamore Bridge. Few other kids went there—they all headed to the river or to Peck's Lake outside town to fish and swim and slug cans of cheap beer and then drive home fast on graveled roads. She preferred Arroyo, which was smaller, right in town but secluded behind trees and shrubs.

Coming around a bend, she swerved to avoid a person walking on the side of the road. Her tires skidded on the gravel, fishtailing, and she yanked the wheel too hard. The back end swung until she turned into the spin and braked hard, screeching to a dusty halt. Her body unleashed a flood of adrenaline, and she sat panting at the wheel.

She jumped when someone knocked on the passenger-side window. With a dumb blink, she realized the person was the new girl. Angie leaned across the seat and rolled down the window.

The girl leaned in the car, frowning and looking at Angie over the tops of her sunglasses. She said, "Whoa. That was quite a spinout. Are you all right?"

Angie nodded, trying to catch her breath. The girl's eyes were almond-shaped, more hazel than brown, Angie saw now. Despite the cold, the girl's brow was sweaty, her cheeks flushed. Angie squeezed her arms tight against her sides, feeling the same warmth as when she stood in the school bathroom and smelled the other girls' perfume, their hair spray, their glistening strawberry breath. She'd never once had a boyfriend, nor had she wanted one, but she wanted to believe Papa when he told her:

"Ah, Angie, just you wait, mi'ja. You'll find love. You'll find the right boy." Pat, pat. He was her father. She wanted to believe him.

The girl stared at her with raised eyebrows.

Angie said, "I didn't see you at first." Her voice came out tiny, warbly as a cricket.

The girl grinned, and Angie saw that her two front teeth protruded. Not bucked exactly. Tilted, Angie thought, feeling heat in her neck.

"So you do talk," the girl said.

Angie shrugged. She wanted to talk. She always could feel the words. She thought of them as glass beads, a constant marbled roundness in her throat.

The girl gave her another toothy grin. "I'm Jess." She threw one arm out. "Jessica Violet Winters, all the way from Phoenix, Arizona." She said it loud and twangy, a beauty pageant contestant. "Jesus, it's cold today." She blew into her gloveless hands. She wore only a jean jacket and thin striped scarf. She snapped a red rubber band at her wrist and then took it off and popped it in her mouth.

Jess thumped the door. "This is a great car." She chewed on the rubber band and drew out the words with a long sigh. She paused, ruffling her hair. "Definitely makes you look like you're from somewhere way cooler than this place. Light-years beyond."

Light-years beyond. No one had ever told Angie such a thing before. She only knew she didn't belong, and that it was somehow her fault. She held the wheel tight, her breath still unsteady.

"Do you need a ride?" Angie asked. She picked up the box from Eddie's off the front seat and threw it in the back.

"Sure," Jess said. "I was just out walking. I'm not really going anywhere." She slid in next to Angie on the bench seat and clicked on her seat belt. "Where you headed?"

Angie shrugged. She didn't want to talk about her father or

the shop. She didn't want to be that careful girl right now. She recalled the urge she'd had to gun it down Main as Papa watched.

She wanted to go fast for once.

She stepped hard on the accelerator, and Jess laughed, letting out a whoop as the wind through the open window whipped her long curls. Dust plumed behind the bumper. Angie's palms sweated, and once she almost swerved off the road, but she laughed, too. At the lake pullout, she bumped into the makeshift parking area and slammed the brakes. They both jerked forward as the engine stalled.

Jess laughed. "Congratulations. I think you might be the world's worst driver," she said, and Angie smelled a hint of rubber and sweet shampoo mixed with gas fumes.

They sat in silence, staring out the windshield. Besides the shop, Arroyo Lake was one of the other places Angie felt okay, bigger than her public self. Behind the tufts of creosote and shrub oaks, Angie could see the water flash. It was so quiet she could hear the nasal *ka-kah* call of a quail, a rustling in the thin brush under the mesquites and junipers. On the horizon, the cement-plant smokestacks smoldered at the tips.

Her papa had taught Angie to swim at this lake when she was a girl, long before these days of bras and embarrassing toiletries, when she could float in his arms without him gently pushing her away. Good, *bien, mira, mira* like this, he'd say as she kicked and sputtered. He bobbed and frog-kicked below the dock, as-suring her, and she jumped out into his waiting arms again and again. He taught her to dive from the dock, too, kneeling first with her arms tight like an arrow over her head, until she grew stronger and braver. Then she would run to the end of the dock and spring out, flying, flying, until she torpedoed into the brown water, larger than she'd ever been.

Jess ran her finger on the side window, made an X mark. "The middle of nowhere. I live in nowhere." She propped her feet on the dash. Her tennis shoes were the purple of plums, the canvas thin at the toes. The laces were too long, knotted three times, and it looked as if she'd shoved her feet in without untying them, breaking down the heel. She had drawn black diagonal lines along the white rubber trim. Like tick marks. Or jail bars.

Angie made a noise in her throat, something between a sigh and a whimper.

Jess said, "You don't have to talk. I don't mind." She scratched at her neck. "In my opinion, not talking isn't the worst thing in the world. A lot of people I know ought to shut up more often." She chewed hard on the rubber band. "My dad, he's got this whole other family now. Like ours wasn't good enough, so he went out and got himself a new one. Like we were old shoes. Like my stupid Chucks." She tugged at the shoelaces. "Last thing he ever bought me." She spit her rubber band into her palm, put it on her wrist.

Jess's chin quivered, and her eyes blurred with tears. "I'm sorry," she said. "I don't know what's wrong with me."

It's okay, Angie wanted to say, but it came out as a soft sigh.

Jess fell over onto Angie's shoulder, limp as a drop cloth. Her plastic sunglasses dug into Angie's bicep.

"I haven't been sleeping. I get up and wander around in the dark." Jess sniffled and sighed. "I feel like I want to go somewhere, but I don't know where. Somewhere far away." She took two hard breaths and fell asleep.

As the sun liquefied and seeped into the horizon, Angie rubbed a slow circle on Jess's forearm. She knew her father would be waiting for her, starting to worry, but she didn't want to move. The round glass rose in her throat, and she pressed her thumb on the butterfly indent of her neck. She could feel something there, tender as a swollen gland.

For a few weeks, they were inseparable. After school, Angie drove them around town in the Impala. Though it was cold, they rode with the windows down, drinking gas-station sodas from cups the size of oil cans. Jess would pop in cassette tapes of music Angie had never heard on the radio—R.E.M., the Velvet Underground, X, a Patti Smith mix she called Plush Patti. She talked about Phoenix, the desert city down the hill, a place that in Angie's imagination was as large and dangerous as a samurai sword, lawless and glinting with cars and malls and desert parties, radio stations and rock concerts and movie theaters with first-run films, worldly-wise girls and boys who had the inside scoop on the world. But Jess made it seem much more normal. She talked more about her childhood than anything: riding the roller coaster at Legend City or the carousel and paddleboats at Encanto Park, pedaling bicycles up and down the graveled paths along the canals. She talked about watching British sitcoms and *Saturday Night Live* late into the night on weekends with her parents, all three of them together. Now the two of them.

"You're a good listener," Jess told Angie. "A good friend," and Angie nodded in agreement that Jess was too, a friend, a good, good friend.

Weekends, Jess often spent the night at Angie's. Angie stayed at Jess's only once, tucked in a sleeping bag next to Jess's twin bed. Jess's mother, Maud, ordered them pizza for dinner and then disappeared into the bedroom before the sun had set. Jess explained that her mother had to get up at four thirty to get to the post office, so she went to bed early. Angie had nodded. Her father had to get up early, too, so she understood. But at Angie's house, Papa cooked dinner for them after he cleaned his hands, washing them over and over with orange-pumice soap though he still wound up with grease in the cracks. He fixed them quesadillas or breakfast for dinner, their favorite, stacks of pancakes and huevos, all served on yellow melamine plates. Papa stayed up late with the girls on weekend nights when he didn't have to open the shop in the morning. They played gin rummy, pinochle, or Texas hold 'em, or watched TV until the sun peeped through the curtains.

They slept in Angie's double bed, which sagged in the center. When Jess's knee grazed Angie's, Angie almost fell off the side. Sometimes, when Angie knew Jess was deep asleep, snoring a little, she would dare to touch her. Trail her fingers down her cheek, along her bare thigh. She'd slide her pinkie under the rubber band at Jess's wrist, feel the pulse against her knuckles. The glass inside her swelled. She imagined them hopping in the Impala and driving off down the hill to Phoenix, or to California, or to some town in Colorado. Angie would open an auto shop, and Jess would go to college and work in a record store. They could make do. Angie worried sometimes that her father knew her secret, what she was imagining for herself and her friend. A few times he caught her staring at Jess. He tilted his head, a frown between his brows, and she blushed and looked away.

Late one night, something woke Angie. She jumped out of bed, disoriented. Jess wasn't in the bed, or in the room. Angie stumbled into the hallway. A light was on in the living room.

Jess was curled up asleep on the couch, a magazine dangling from her fingers, the lamp on low on the side table. Angie plucked the magazine from Jess and started to cover her with an afghan. As she did, she kicked over a tumbler of water Jess must have put on the floor next to the sofa.

Angie got a towel from the kitchen and knelt to sponge up the water. Her arm bumped Jess's bare knee. She sat on her heels as her stomach twinged, as heat spread everywhere. She reached out and touched that knee deliberately, cupped it in the heart of her palm, holding her breath and watching Jess's face. She moved her hand up Jess's thigh and under the blanket, her fingers as directed as a trail of ants. She kneeled closer, lifted her other hand toward the curve of Jess's shoulder. She wanted all of her under her hands. She thought her body would crack open from the pleasure of this sensation, from the bright discovery of this feeling in herself.

Jess opened her eyes. Beneath the lamp, they seemed dilated, space-black. She blinked at Angie. "What are you doing?"

"Angela," Papa said.

Angie yanked her hands away and scrambled to her feet. Her father stood in the darkness of the hallway. He leaned on the wall, his face unreadable in the shadows.

Even if she had the words, she couldn't have spoken them.

Jess sat up, yawning. "I couldn't fall asleep, but I guess I did. What's going on?"

Papa stepped into the room, and Angie saw his face then, except it looked nothing like his own. It looked locked up tight. Lights out, no one home. A stranger who wouldn't meet her eyes.

"Go back to bed," he said. "Vas. Ahora."

Angie started to shake. The glass moved onto her tongue. She coughed and then spit onto the brown carpet, next to the damp spot under the towel.

Angie ran to her room, locked the door, grabbed her coat, and climbed out the window. She ran to the Impala, and when she turned on the headlights, she saw her father in the doorway, Jess standing next to him. She gunned it down the drive and into town. She drove up and down Main and through the District in a trance, not glancing at the closed-up shop windows, her eyes on the yellow and white lines of the road. She didn't know where to go. She wanted to leave, but she didn't know where, and she had no money anyway. She wondered how far those pavement lines stretched, where they would take her if she followed them past the outskirts of town—south to Phoenix, north to Flagstaff and to the reservations. And then to where?

Finally she drove across the bridge to Arroyo Lake, parking in the dark pullout with the engine running, huddling for warmth in her coat. She didn't sleep, the images of her father's face, of Jess's knee, fluttering behind her eyes. At dawn, stiff with cold, she got out of the car and climbed to the solace of the lake.

The lake was gone.

Angie stood on the dock in the hazy dawn, blinking down at a fissure in the bottom, a jagged gash the length and width of a body. The muddy surface glistened with bloated sucker fish and soggy weeds, pockmarked with once-buried things—what looked like a broken fishing pole, a beer can, a tarp or maybe a deflated raft, the heaving back of a boulder. Around the lip, the mud was cracking, the water already soaked into the thirsty earth.

She squatted on her heels, her toes over the end of the dock, and wrapped her arms around her knees, fighting a shiver. She knew about sinkholes; in Earth Science, they'd learned about deep-down aquifers and the porous, fragile rock of the Verde Valley, but she also had grown up hearing stories about kids falling into them during hikes and bike rides, the legends of childhood. Devil's Kitchen in Sedona was hundreds of feet down, and everyone *knew* there was more than one banana-seat bike down there. Bones rotted, metal rusted. The earth could eat you. Now it had eaten the lake.

The sun crept higher, the sky no longer gray but not yet blue. A non-color, something like the inside of a tin can. Crouched close, she could see more things in the lake mud. Cigarette butts, gum tinfoil, a condom wrapper—condoms, something she hadn't ever needed. She swatted the gnats around her face, and her nostrils flared at the rotting smells. The images of Papa and Jess flicked and fluttered. She wanted to scream into all that ragged space. She couldn't remember the last time she had screamed, had let fly until her throat burned. She opened her mouth, but nothing came out.

Her thighs cramped, so she stood up, grimacing, shaking out her muscles. Her right foot was numb, and she stamped it, hopping on it. As she did, perhaps because of the dimness and the lack of sleep, she lost her balance. She whirled her arms, trying to throw her weight backward, but it was too late.

The scream trapped inside came out now as Angie fell into the empty lake.

She landed on her side with a hard thump, the mud certainly not as yielding as the old lake water. She tumbled and skidded down the slope toward the gaping hole until the mud slowed her. She stopped a few feet from the sinkhole, in a seated position, as her rear end and legs sank down into the mud.

She swam her arms in the air, trying to wade forward, but the sucking mud held her legs fast. "Fuck," she said, "Fuck," her voice piercing the hushed morning. She began to cry a little, hiccupping, grit in her nostrils and mouth. A little girl stuck in the mud. A stupid skinny little girl. No wonder Jess didn't—no wonder.

The mud was rough with sand and rocks. She pawed at it, scooping up a lump, and chucked it with all her strength at the sinkhole. It landed several feet shy of it, which made her so furious she punched the mud with both fists, the rocks scraping her knuckles. She got another good handful, but instead of throwing it, she rubbed it into her mouth. She shoved in another mouthful, lungs burning, before retching it up.

A siren wailed somewhere in the distance. Then someone called her name.

She craned her neck. Her father stood at the top of the lake, his white hair wild. At the sight of him, despite everything, the first thing she felt was a spurt of relief.

"Angela Juarez," Papa called. "Jesuchristo. Get the hell up out of there."

She shook her head.

"What do you mean, no? Ahora. Venga."

"Stuck," she whispered.

"Mi'ja. Please. Come up out of there. Let's talk about this."

She shook her head again.

"Maybe I misunderstood—"

"You saw," she said, louder now. "You saw."

"Talk to me. You can tell me, verdad? You can tell me anything."

She thought about how he had seemed like a stranger in the hallway, and she started to say, "I *can't*," when the lake let out a ripping groan. A mammoth wedge of mud alongside her fell away, exposing a slash of blackness. She stared at the menacing hole in the earth, and the reality of where she was struck her hard. She screamed again. Hot adrenaline rushed into her limbs, and she tried to lunge upward. Her arms were sucked into the unforgiving mud until she was stuck up to her chest.

Papa yelled, "Don't move. Dios. Mierda. Don't move. Hold real still."

She held as still as she could, breathing in shallow spurts. Sweat poured down her face, dripped on her lips. She thought she heard a splash.

Papa was sliding down the lake on his backside and hands, crablike, inch by inch. He said, "No, no. Angela. Ya voy. Ya voy."

She was up to her neck. Her feet dangled beneath her, pulled by the dark gravity below. Mud pushed up around her ears and chin, and her mouth, until she was only eyes, eyes taking in her father. Papa, white-haired and wide-eyed, nostrils flared, plastered with mud. Papa, digging down and grabbing her shirt. Papa, his mouth moving fast—Por favor, he seemed to be saying, por favor—and pulling and pulling, all muscles and veins and tendons, making her think, again, about how much weight he could carry.

He got a hand, then two hands, under her arms, and he pulled her to him. Breathing hard, she pressed her face against his chest, let the thud of his heart echo into her. The glass rose higher. This time it shook loose. She let it roll on her tongue and then spit it into the air. "Love," she said, but it was unintelligible, more like a grunt, against his body. Her voice was froggy, the deep croak of a stranger. It burned, that new voice, and she touched her throat.

"Ay. More than you know," Papa said. He locked his arms around her.

Though it wasn't possible, Angie swore she saw the glass take shape before them, a tiny fragile orb, bright as water. She would see this image again at moments throughout her life, from what felt like a million years from that day, when she lay in bed with Rose, the cats curled on the comforter, Hazel asleep in the room next door, the dust motes floating in the sunlight in the window. She would see it the first time with Rose, in Rose's parents' motel, the rain flooding the parking lot as Beto Navarro stood guard in the Impala—the first time a girl had returned her touch. She would see it when Rose ran off the first time, spooked by the dawning awareness that what they were doing in secret was *real*, it wasn't going away. She would see it when Rose turned up on her doorstep, bouncing Hazel on her hip. She would see it when they visited her father's grave tucked in the little cemetery in town, when she rearranged rocks into a heart shape over where she thought his heart might be. She would see it every morning as she woke in his house, as she opened his shop in the town she never left, the lines of the road taking her right here, a place both new and old.

She saw it again now as she stared down at the newspaper and looked at that girl's face again, still seventeen years old, a bright xylophone chime of a memory. Her first secret love. The girl who'd opened Angie's heart and pushed her in the direction of her true self, even if she'd never known it. The girl whose friendship Angie then severed, unable to see past her own shame and confusion, retreating again into silence. The girl who didn't come home one rainy winter night, and about whom Angie never stopped wondering: What if I'd been a better friend? What if I'd told her? What if she'd said yes? What if I'd seen her that night? What if she showed up on my doorstep? The girl whose disappearance seemed to soak into the porous rocks of the town, a mystery lurking beneath the surface, becoming as much a legend as those of bones and bikes in sinkholes.

Angie pressed the newspaper to her chest, breathing hard. No, these were real bones, the real bones of a real person—not a myth, not a story. And she remembered that day in the mud, how she'd held tight to her father as he pulled her to safety. How she watched as the glass drifted silent between them and then floated out of the muck, rising above their heads, up and up, beyond them.

UNEARTHED
February–May 1991

IN THE FIRST WEEKS THEY called her the new girl, and then
Phoenix Girl. Not everyone, mainly those who roamed the halls
in packs, boys with their hair gelled into spikes wearing polo
shirts and smirks, girls with cocked eyebrows and wads of pink
gum. At first they said it to each other, nudges and whispers she
overheard (that's her, the new girl), but then they said it to her:
"Hey, it's the Phoenix Girl. What's up, Phoenix Girl?"

Jess found this baffling. She could sense an undertone, but she
couldn't gauge it; she decided it probably was a dumb inside joke
or a test of some kind, not recognizing how much of their tone
was rooted in pride, insecurity, and self-preservation, a wariness
that she, girl from the city, would dare to look down on them, the
rural kids. After all, they'd seen this their whole young lives—
from the news, from movies, from the very books in their backpacks, from other new kids before her: *Rednecks. Dumb hicks.*
She should have recognized the tone; she'd heard it enough from
her mother, about anyone with a better house, a better car, a
better-paying job: *They're not better than us, J-bird. They just
have more money.*

Whatever was going on, Jess knew enough to keep her mouth
shut, clutching her books to her chest, eyes straight ahead.
"Ignore them," her mom told her. "Take the high road." She
could do that. She imagined a literal high road, a berm or a
bridge a few feet off the ground, and she fixed her gaze on the
square alarm bell at the end of the hall. It was like in ballet
class: keep your eye on one spot as you turn so you don't get

dizzy. They weren't allowed to wear headphones at school, but she acted as though she had them on, as if she could hear only lyrics and guitar.

One day a girl wearing a yellow scrunchie in her hair called after Jess. She said, "God. Stuck-up much?"

Jess should have ignored it. At most, she should have shaken her head or said a simple *No, I'm not.* But that week, after Angie had had that strange fight with her father, roaring off in her car and leaving Jess to sleep alone in her friend's bed, Angie had stopped returning her calls, had stopped waiting for her after school or offering rides. Had mumbled, "I can't do anything after school anymore. I have to help my dad." Her one lifeline in this town had been razored in half, leaving her reeling, untethered. No more eating pancakes or playing poker or watching TV with Angie and her nice dad, no more rides around town with music blasting from the speakers, thumping into her chest. Nights, she watched TV, but lately the news blared footage from the Gulf—wind-whipped sand and bombs exploding over the capital, burning oil fields, Iraqi soldiers on their knees— which tied her up in knots. She lay in bed and stared at the ceiling or watched her mother sleep and cry until she couldn't stand it and ran outside. Last night, the moon had dodged in and out of the clouds, lighting up the edges, so the sky looked like a map of the earth. She wouldn't have been surprised if the land and air *had* changed places. If the little lake could disappear like that—boom, drained into a sinkhole overnight—then why not the land and air? Nothing made sense. Friendship: How could it be even more elusive than love? What had she done wrong? What was wrong with her?

In the hall, with the scrunchie girl in her peripheral vision, part of her warned, *Don't. Keep walking. Ignore. High road, high road*. The other part of her, though—the one worn thin by too much thinking, too much worry, not enough sleep, the weeks of navigating these halls and their whispers—had something else in mind: *Head-on. Don't blink*.

Jess turned and looked at the girl. She pulled her book bag from her shoulder and held it by the strap, testing its weight. She carried everything in that bag so she wouldn't have to stop at her locker. Books for US history, trig, Humanities, and chemistry, her notebook, pens, her hideous polyester gym clothes, copies of *Bloom County* and *Life in Hell* she hadn't returned to the Phoenix library. A good fifteen pounds, if not more. She gripped the strap tight.

The girl lifted her hands, mocking. "What? You got something to say, Phoenix Girl? Oooh, Phoenix Girl has something to say." She flipped her head to look at her friends, and her stupid ponytail whirled like a helicopter blade. They all laughed as if it were hilarious, as if any of them had the first clue about funny.

Jess said, "Yeah, I got something to say." As the words came out, she took three long steps and swung the book bag underhand as if fast-pitching a softball. Fast, but not fast enough. The girl jumped back so the bag grazed her arm but missed nailing her upside the head, where Jess had been aiming. She stumbled into another girl to her left, and the whole clot of them stared at Jess, blinking, at first too surprised to react.

The weight and momentum of the bag had wrenched her shoulder, but Jess ignored the twinge. She slipped the straps over both shoulders and continued down the hall as if nothing had happened, as if she had nothing at all to do with the swarm of girls who had begun to buzz and screech behind her. But her heart beat fast, and she swallowed hard. That, she knew, was a mistake. A big one. She smiled and lifted her chin, spotting the alarm bell at the end of the hall and almost pirouetting toward it.

Sure enough, the next day—her seventeenth birthday—the little charmers started tagging her locker. "Bitch." "Slut." "Cunt from hell." "Jess Winters *spreads*." Jess walked past the locker as if it wasn't hers. She didn't try to cover it, let the words scream into the hall. She didn't tell on them. She wouldn't tell her mother. By midmorning the custodians had scrubbed it clean, leaving faded marks on the paint. When Principal López called her in to ask if everything was all right, squinting at her over his bifocals and tugging at his bushy mustache, she said she was fine. No, sir, she had no idea who was writing on her locker. No, sir, she didn't need a new one. She was fine, thank you. No, sir, she didn't need to talk with a counselor. Yes, she was going to apply to colleges. Yes, she had signed up for the PSAT.

Because of that meeting, she was late to Humanities. Ms. Genoways was already hot in the middle of reading out an Edna St. Vincent Millay poem. She wore silver rings on every finger, even her thumbs, and her hair looked as though someone had snuck in and given her a perm while she was sleeping. Before Jess could hand her the late pass, Ms. G held up her arm to Jess's face and said, "See? The shivers—now that's literature." She went on to tell the class that Millay and other authors such as Oscar Wilde were banned all the time for their risqué content. She went on to say that love and all its permutations—she paused and wrote it on the board, "LOVE = permutations"—was the great question at the root of all literature. Was it Capital L Love? Or lowercase? Or lust, or longing, or loneliness, or loss? What was the difference? How did we know? A great big beating heart of a puzzle, she said. The great unknown.

Jess slid into her seat, ignoring the glares from the girl she'd knocked back, ignoring Angie's averted eyes. She found a spot on the wall: a poster of James Baldwin, who was shown sitting in front of a bookcase with his chin in his palm, looking away from the camera. She focused her gaze on the twin grooved lines between his brow. Deep, like a river gorge.

After class, Ms. G told her to wait a minute, so Jess hung back near her own desk. She caught Angie's eye and gave a quick wave, and Angie smiled before ducking her chin. After the last student left, Ms. G turned to Jess.

She tilted her head. "I let a couple of students have lunch in my classroom. Not everyone. Those who might need—" She paused, considering. She twisted the ring on her thumb. "Some space. You're welcome, okay? If you like."

Jess started to say, "Thanks," but her throat seized up. She nodded and hurried out the door to her next class. The St. Vincent Millay lines Ms. G had recited ran through her mind: *but the rain / Is full of ghosts tonight, that tap and sigh / Upon the glass and listen for reply.* The words were wet and warm under her tongue, and sure enough, the hair rose on her arms.

That night Jess's mother brought home pizza and a birthday cake from Bashas'. White frosting with blue trim, a blue bird in the lower left corner with a large speech bubble: "Happy 17th birthday, J-bird," it read, as if the bird were talking.

At the kitchen table, her mom lit the single candle. "February 17. Your golden birthday."

Jess looked at the flame. The inside of the cake, she knew, was marble, her and her father's favorite. Her father had sent a birthday card—in Caroline's handwriting. "To My Beautiful Girl, With Love from Dad, Caroline, and baby sister Noelle." Capital

L Love. Jess had torn it in half and tossed it in the wastebasket under her desk.

She tried to smile. "A regular pot of gold at the end of the rainbow. Little leprechauns are just shitting gold."

"Jess."

"I know. Sorry."

Her mom sat down across from her and started to sing "Happy Birthday."

Jess looked at the cute talking bird on the cake, at the candle beginning to melt. She started crying. It was just so sad, Capital S Sad, the two of them sitting there, with the little candle dripping blue wax on the frosting.

"I'm sorry," Jess said.

Her mom got up and hugged her. "It's too much. It's too much for anyone. But we'll get through it. I promise." She squeezed herself on the chair next to her, holding her tight, and Jess breathed in her familiar scent, a salve of mint gum and clean sheets.

She rubbed Jess's back. "You have your whole life in front of you. This is a blip on the radar. I know you don't see it, but you have this glow about you."

Jess sniffed and wiped her nose with her sleeve. "Radioactive."

Her mother laughed. She tugged on a strand of Jess's hair, pulling the curl straight and then letting it spring back. "No. You're my Starshine, my strong blue-winged girl."

Before bed, Jess wrote herself a big note in her notebook, in bright purple marker: "Capital P Perspective. Get some! Also: Get a job. And a CAR." She wrote a sloppy draft of a poem based on the prompt Ms. G had given them: "Write a poem or scene that includes the sky."

When we weren't looking
the sky talked the land into switching places.
(The sky's sly that way.)
So now we walk on patches of blue,
knock stars from our shoes,
skate around the corona of the sun.

Look up.
Boulders move fast across the dirt,
and the trees are setting.
Their veiny leaves burn on the horizon,
and the grass is in our eyes.

She wrote: "WRITE MORE. DO BETTER."

Classes, if not school altogether, helped with the perspective. In history, Mr. Manning began a unit on the Holocaust, and he assigned the comic book *Maus*. Jess read half of the first volume in one sitting, holding the book tight to her knees in bed. When she put it down, she let out a long exhale—as if she'd been holding her breath the whole time. She'd had to read Anne Frank before, but these scratchy black-and-white comics made it more real and true than the mythic nightmare she'd imagined. Somehow, the writer had even made her laugh at times. Her head spun with the size of the story, with how to hold all its truth inside. How did the world not rupture because of that event? Like, literally rip in half. She got up and pulled the torn birthday card from her wastebasket. She taped it together and stuck it instead in the back of her desk drawer. She fell asleep clutching the book to her chest, her finger marking a page.

The next day in Humanities, Ms. G began an art unit on the pre-Impressionist period. Artists were shifting to realistic paintings, which irritated the Salon, which Jess understood to be a bunch of dudes in charge of the art then. Ms. G showed slides of the work, pausing on a French painting called *The Floor Planers*, which showed three shirtless men on their knees scraping a wooden floor. This was scandalous, Ms. G said, not because they were shirtless but because they were workers. The Salon did not value depictions of ordinary life, working life. In their view, that was not the subject of art. "But look at that light," Ms. G said, and she touched the screen, tracing the shine on the floors and on the men's muscled backs. "Shivers!" she said, holding up her arm, and Jess got them, too. "The beautiful in the ordinary," Ms. G said, and Jess wrote it down. Of course, the lights were off and half the rest of the class was sleeping, so Ms. G took off her shoe and chucked it against the wall, yelling, "Wake up! Wake up!" Under her breath she added, "Christ on a crutch." Jess laughed her father's loud honk, forgetting to try to hide it.

At lunchtime, Jess knocked on Ms. G's classroom door. Her teacher opened the door with a smile, welcoming her with sweeping wave. The radio was on low, streaming classical music.

Jess went to her normal seat at the back of the room. She dropped her hefty book bag, pulled her brown lunch bag out of it, and slid into the desk before she realized another girl was there. She was sitting across the room under the James Baldwin poster, her face tipped toward a book on the desk.

Jess knew her name was Danielle Newell. They were in trig together. Dani, the teacher called her. In math, she always knew the right answer although she never raised her hand. When Ms. Simmons asked a question and it was clear no one would answer, she would turn to Dani, who would answer without prompt. "That's right," Ms. Simmons would say, and the class seemed to groan and sigh and hiss in one shared breath. Jess admired how Dani never flinched, never looked behind her. Straight ahead or down at her book, her shoulders straight.

Ms. G said, "Dani, this is Jess. Have you two met?"

Dani raised her hand in greeting without looking up from the book. As always, she wore her dark hair in a low ponytail. An enormous pair of eyeglasses, the lenses as round as navel oranges, dwarfed her small face. She looked tiny in the desk, childlike.

Ms. G stared at Dani's head and then looked at Jess. "I'll be over here, grading, if you need anything. Stay as long as you like." She turned the volume up on the radio.

"Thanks," Jess said. She pulled out a bruised banana and a PB&J, squished on one side from the weight of her books. She opened *Maus* and began to read. The room filled with the strains of piano and violin, the wheeze of the heater, the shuffle of papers, a few loud sighs from Ms. G, an emphatic scratch of her pen. Out the window, fat white clouds moved fast across the blue sky, and when she leaned forward, she caught a glimpse of the snow-tipped Black Hills, of the lump of black mountain she knew now was a slag heap from the old mines. She tried to chew her sandwich without noise, pressing at her clicking jaw, which her mother blamed on the rubber bands.

After a few minutes, though, she settled into the peace. Mouth full, hunched over the desk and immersed in the comic, she glanced up to brush a strand of hair out of her eye. As she did, she caught Dani Newell staring at her, her eyes wide behind the huge frames. Jess smiled, because of those ridiculous glasses. Dani looked away, but Jess thought she saw her mouth twitch.

In March, Jess interviewed for a part-time job working weekends at Overton Orchards, the pecan orchard about a half mile from her house—an easy walk, an easier bike ride. Her mom delivered mail at the orchard and had got to talking with Iris Overton, the owner, who said she was looking for some help with answering phones and with the gift shop.

Iris was tiny, maybe five feet tall, with little tan bird arms and legs, and she kept her head shaved. Like Sinead O'Connor, but silver. Jess thought she looked a bit like a pinball, and in fact she had the energy of one. She bounced into the room wearing large rubber boots, with a rake slung over her shoulder.

After introducing herself, Iris said, "Have you met my son Paul? He's a junior, too. Tall? Needs a haircut?" She raised her arm over her head and stood on her tiptoes.

Jess shook her head. "Not yet."

"You might see him here sometimes, but it's track season, so he's out running all the live long day. Or off with his girlfriend." Iris smiled. "Takes after his dad. Took after." Her smile faded. "Beau died last year. Unexpectedly. His heart," she said, placing her palm on her chest.

Jess's throat tightened. She kept saying she didn't care if her father lived or died, but such a picture, one with her father cut out, didn't fit, either. She hadn't spoken with him in three months now, though he'd called and left messages on the machine she shared with her mother. *Call me, honey, I love you and miss you, beautiful girl*. Blah blah blah. What did he expect her to do? Get over it? She was the daughter he didn't choose.

Her voice hoarse, Jess said, "I'm sorry."

Iris said, "Honey, don't I know it. Listen, don't worry about that. The job's yours if you want it. Now I can't pay much, four bucks an hour, but it's not nothing, right? Let me guess: you're saving for a car?"

Jess nodded.

Iris laughed. "I was the same way. Let me show you around."

She gave Jess a tour. The main building, a cabin with heavy wood beams and a green tin roof, housed the gift shop and office. It was built in the early 1900s by her husband's family when the mines still flourished and the town was flush. In the 1950s, when the mines went bust, the family turned to farming, which in that climate was best for crops, cattle, poultry, or dairy—or, her husband later learned, pecans, planting the first row in the 1970s when he inherited the land. Their house was off the back, connected by a covered breezeway. Beyond was a large barn, the cleaning shed, where they processed the pecans during fall harvest. Iris explained the three primary seasons: In winter, the dormant season, they planted new trees and replaced dying ones, pruned limbs, repaired the tools and cleaning sheds. In spring and summer, the growing season, they tested irrigation lines, watered, fertilized, mowed, and checked for insects and root rot. In late summer, the shells ripened, turning green and round as the pecan nut formed. Come October, the shucks would toughen and break open as the nut reached maturity. Time for harvest.

"Fall, all hell breaks loose," Iris said. "Our busiest time. The shaking season."

"What's the shaking season?" Jess said.

"That's how we get the nuts out. Shake the trees. Used to be we whacked them with big sticks. Now we have a tractor with a long mechanical arm, although last season it kept seizing up and we went back to sticks." She shrugged. "Something's always needing to be fixed around here. It's a long season. The buds will break soon, in April, and we'll be busy making sure they stay healthy and grow right. In the fall and winter, we'll start staying open late on the weekends, selling bags of nuts and pies for the holidays. Sundown at the Orchard, we call it. I'll definitely need your help then."

Jess walked behind Iris through the trees, almost skipping to keep pace with the bald pinball woman. She tried to determine the smell: a lemony tang, combined with wet dirt and sun-heated grass. *The buds will break soon. The shaking season.* The words flitted through her mind, and goose bumps rose on her arms.

On Jess's second weekend working at the orchards, as she addressed envelopes for the monthly sales flyer, a young man in a tank top and nylon shorts jogged past the office window. Paul Overton, she guessed. He was tall, several inches taller than her, as Iris had said, and whip-thin. He had dark curly hair, unruly as a fern and hanging to the middle of his neck, now plastered to his sweaty forehead and cheeks. As he passed the window, he lifted the hem of his damp shirt to wipe his face, and Jess glimpsed his lean, muscled stomach. The sight made her mouth soften, a nervous flick in her belly. She remembered the Boy, his warm flesh against hers, the flare of his hipbones under her fingers, before she tamped down the memory.

About a half hour later, Paul came into the office. He'd showered, his mass of wet hair dripping onto a dry T-shirt and shorts. He lifted a hand in greeting.

"You must be Jess," he said. "I'm Paul. My mom said you started working here."

"That's me," she said.

"How's it going so far? Do you like it here?"

"The orchard? Or Syc-to-my-Stomach?"

He laughed. "We call it Suck-a-more."

She grinned back. "Noted."

The bell on the office door dinged, and Jess turned to greet the customer. Dani Newell stood in the doorway. Jess blinked, confused. What was Dani Newell doing at the orchard? She had started to call out a greeting when Paul grinned. He stepped forward and pulled Dani toward him, lifted her right off the ground and almost to the ceiling, her tiny feet dangling, her giant glasses knocked askew.

Jess looked away from their embrace, trying to hide her surprise. Dani Newell was his girlfriend? In ten million years, she never would have guessed they were a couple. Caught up in his hug, Dani laughed, red-cheeked, so different from the wound-tight girl who sat across from her, avoiding eye contact. Even her hair had loosened, the sides falling around her face.

Paul dropped her to the ground, and they whispered to each other. Jess pressed a stamp on an envelope and smoothed its ridged edges.

Dani said, "How are you?"

Jess looked up, and Dani was staring straight at her. *Me?* she almost said. She sat up straighter. "Fine."

Dani said, "I hear you scared the hell out of Marci Tennant."

Jess rubbed the stamp, wondering if this was a trick of some kind. She gave a tentative smile. "I don't know. I guess. She definitely hates my guts."

"She's an idiot," Dani said. She shook her head, pushing her glasses up her nose.

Jess smiled for real then. "Blithering," she said. "She and her wicked scrunchie minions."

Dani nodded, the corner of her mouth quirked. As Paul took her hand and led her toward his house, she turned and waved at Jess. "See you at lunch then."

Jess waved back. "See you." A lump rose in her throat, and she swallowed hard on it. Seeing. To be seen. She pressed her thumb hard on the stamp.

The next day at lunch in Ms. G's classroom, Dani sat at her desk again, wrapped up in her reading, and for a moment Jess thought nothing had changed. She moved toward her usual seat.

Dani spoke without lifting her eyes from the book. "There's a chair here." She pointed at the desk next to her. Jess saw then she'd angled the desks. So they could talk.

Jess said, "Sure." She slid into the desk and dropped her bag.

Ms. G watched them and nodded. "About time. Thought I was going to have to issue a written invitation." She smiled and returned to her grading.

Dani kept reading, and Jess peered over at her book.

"*Maus*? For Mr. Manning?" she asked.

"Yep."

"Me, too." Jess pulled the books from her bag.

"I figured. What do you think?"

"About the book? It's great," Jess said.

Dani looked up, her eyes large and serious behind her glasses. "No, don't be facile. What do you *think*?"

Jess tilted her head and leaned back in the desk, stretched her long legs. She shrugged. "I think it exposes the largeness of the evil through the smallness of the detail, through its attention to moments. I think it doesn't flinch. I think Art Spiegelman is a genius. Does that meet your approval?"

Dani smiled her hooked smile. "Fucking A." She launched into her own analysis, gesturing with her hands, her owl eyes bright. As she spoke, she held out a baggie full of chocolate chip cookies. Jess reached out and took one. Biting down on the cookie, she wished she had something to offer in return besides a handful of browned apple slices and some crumbled pretzels. She chewed, content not to speak, to listen, to hear the happy thump of her heart.

On the Saturday of the first week of May, a few weeks before school was out, Jess finished up her shift at the orchard in the afternoon. Before leaving, she rode her bike through the trees, her sweatshirt tied around her waist, her puffy coat already stuffed into the closet. Grass grew tall and dense in the rows between the trees, and the bike wheels left a narrow wet cleft. The once bare branches now teemed with green leaves and long, hairy strands—pollination time, Iris said. The nut clusters would be forming soon, and then they'd begin mowing and irrigating. Iris said Jess could have more hours once school was out, that she'd show her the ropes outside. Jess let her feet dangle off the pedals. The grass tickled her bare shins, and the spring sun warmed her face. Quiet, except for wind in the shells of her ears. The air smelled to her like grated citrus rinds and iron. Earth, she thought. Crust, mantle, core. How far down was the core again? She pictured the diagrammed images from her science textbook, the world peeled and cored, splayed open to the molten orange layers and hot white center. *Un*earthed. And what did *that* smell like?

Instead of taking the right turn to Roadrunner Lane, she turned left on Quail Run and kept riding toward town, taking College Drive toward the neighborhood across from the college. She was going to Dani's house, to work on their final Humanities paper and to study for a trig test. They'd met twice at the school library with Paul, but Paul was away at a track meet that weekend, so it would be just the two of them—and the first time she'd been invited to someone's house since Angie's. She hit a slope and picked up speed. The wind plucked at her hair, and she stood up on the pedals, lifting her face skyward.

She rode past the iron gates of the college and turned into the neighborhood—built for the miners and their families in the early twentieth century, but taken over by faculty and staff in recent decades. During their drives, Angie had called the area Yuppieville. Dani's narrow street, Piñon Drive, was shaded by large pines, ash, and sycamores, though they weren't as dense as the clusters along the river. Unlike in her own neighborhood in Roadrunner Heights, the yards had no rusty patio furniture, no bicycles ditched and upended on the dry grass. Instead there were neat squares of grass behind low pickets, shrubs edged with military precision. Pulling into Dani's driveway, Jess dragged her feet on the cement to stop the bike. The house was old and red brick, with an arched entryway to a shaded porch. Jess propped her bike against the porch railing and climbed the steps, taking a deep breath before knocking. Through an etched sidelight window, she could see movement.

A man swung the door open with a smile. He wore a white T-shirt smudged with what looked like black grease and jeans, but no shoes.

"Hi there. You must be Jess. I'm Dani's father. Adam." He started to hold out his hand, but then wiped his palms on his jeans. "Sorry, just washed up. I was in the garage. Lost track of time, and now I'm running behind."

"Hello." She reached out and shook his hand. It was warm and still damp, but she could feel calluses on his palms. She would have known he and Dani were related from looking at him. Same round face, same gray-blue eyes blinking behind glasses, though his frames were smaller, square, and black. His nose was big, with large nostrils and a knuckle-like knot at the center. He looked more like an older brother than a dad. Nothing like her father, whose thinning gray hair tended to stick up in flyaway wisps, whose belly had grown round and soft, a warm pillow on TV nights.

"Come in, come in. Dani!" he called out behind him. "Your friend is here."

Jess stepped inside, hefted her backpack higher. She was almost as tall as him, and she slouched down a little.

He said, "She's in her room. Can I get you anything? Something to drink?"

"No, sir, I'm fine, thank you."

"No need for sir. You can call me Adam. We're not very formal around here."

She nodded but doubted she would. She tried to imagine one of her Phoenix friends calling her father Stuart. Not a chance. She watched his back as he walked away, his bare feet noiseless on the wood floor.

Jess stood still in the entryway. The foyer—was it foy-*er* or fo-*yay*?—with its mahogany walls and grandfather clock, its polished wood floors, its welcoming breath of cinnamon potpourri. No chipped ceramic bowl crammed with keys and pencils and receipts, no hooks cluttered with jackets and purses and tote bags. None of her mother's guilty-pleasure celebrity gossip magazines—her Trashy Mags, she called them—piled on the end table, or dust bunnies that Jess had been supposed to vacuum and forgot. She fought the urge to check the bottom of her shoes.

"Jess?" Adam stood smiling at the end of the hall, his head tilted in question. "You can come in."

"Thanks," she said. She took her pack off and hugged it to her chest. "Your house is really nice."

"Thanks. We like it. Of course, it's old, so it's been a work in progress. Always a project. And we've had a bit of family upheaval of late." He pointed to a stack of boxes at the end of the hall. "Dani's room is this way." He led her through the living room and dining room. Jess glimpsed large bookcases full of books and knickknacks, a brown tweed sofa and rocking chair, a long dining table with a vase of wildflowers in the center.

They went through the kitchen, which was stark white, from cupboards to sink to tile. Jess was admiring the cherry-red towels when a woman rushed in, wearing a loose robe, her hair wrapped in a towel, a toothbrush sticking out of the side of her mouth. She saw Jess and started, her eyebrows jumping. Her dark eyebrows were arched like wings.

"Oh!" she said around the toothbrush. She went to the kitchen sink and spit. "I'm so sorry. I'm a mess and running behind as usual. You must be Jess. I'm Rachel, Dani's mom."

Dani walked into the kitchen, her brow furrowed. "What, Dad? Oh, Jess. Hey! It's already three?" She saw her mother, and the corner of her mouth hooked into a grin. "Nice outfit."

"I'm so late," her mother said.

"Shocking," Dani said.

"I'm going to get us out of rehearsals by dinner, though." Dani's mother returned to brushing her teeth, spit again, and then cupped her hand under the faucet to rinse. She wiped her mouth with the robe's sleeve. "Scout's honor."

Dani's father said to Jess, "My wife teaches at the college, in theater. She's in rehearsals for *Hamlet*. Lots of late nights and weekends."

Dani sighed. "First stop, Sycamore, next stop, Broadway."

Her dad said, "All right, smart-ass." He ruffled her hair, and she wrinkled her nose at him. "Pizza for dinner?"

"Sounds good," her mother said. "I'll be home by seven. At the latest."

Dani and her father groaned in unison and rolled their eyes, smiling identical hooked grins.

"Seven! Bet me, clowns," she said. "Jess, you're welcome to stay."

"Thanks," she said.

"Definitely stay," Dani said.

"I'll have to call my mom to let her know."

"Good news. We have a phone." Dani quirked her left eyebrow, her grin still hooked.

"How modern." Jess smiled, too.

Dani's mother glanced at the clock. "Crap." She yanked the towel off her head, and her long dark hair spilled down her back. She rushed toward the hall, trying to drop a kiss on her daughter's cheek, but Dani ducked out of range. "Later, gators."

Dani's father frowned and checked his watch. "Me, too. I'm supposed to show a house in fifteen minutes. Oops." He pressed at his grease-streaked shirt, and his big nostrils flared. "See you in a few hours, clever girls."

Dani pulled Jess by the sleeve toward her room. "Don't mind them. Another ordinary day at the mental asylum."

Jess was surprised to find that Dani's bedroom was messy. Clothes were piled on the two twin beds taking up one side of the room, and her desk was strewn with loose paper and drinking glasses. A yogurt cup with a metal spoon lay toppled on its side. One wall was a bookcase, crammed with books and magazines shelved both upright and stacked on their sides. Above the desk was a giant world map, the globe of Earth cut and spread flat. Multicolored pushpins dotted multiple countries.

Jess pointed. "Are those the places you've been?"

"Not yet. Where I'm going to go."

Jess peered closer. Colors in all continents, in countries Jess couldn't even name. She wasn't sure what her own map would look like. She had the vague word *overseas* in mind, images of trains, of bicycles with a loaf of bread in the basket, of tile-roofed casitas perched on a steep hill. Sometimes she pictured a loft—massive windows, burnished wood floors—in an unnamed city, skyscrapers strung like a child's paper cuttings; sometimes she saw Phoenix and its clean, straight lines, its dusty flatlands and jagged peaks.

"Check it out," Dani said, pulling her by the wrist closer to the desk, where a microscope sat. "I found a dead horned toad in the yard today."

"You have a microscope?"

"My mom got it for me. A hand-me-down from a biologist at her school. Look."

The reptile lay on a piece of cloth next to the microscope. The creature looked intact, not squished or injured. She'd always thought of the sharp spikes on their heads as Mohawks. Punk-rock lizards. "I used to call them horny toads when I was a kid," Jess said.

Dani put her eye to the microscope and twisted a dial. "*Phryno-soma platyrhinos*. When they feel threatened, they shoot blood from their eyes. Here," Dani said, pointing at the lens. Jess leaned over and peered in. Cells whooshed into focus, a cluster that looked as if it had been scribbled and scratched in pencil, the lines fuzzy and blurred.

"That's part of its *eye*," Dani said.

Jess pulled her face away and looked at Dani, whose face was lit with energy.

"You're a weirdo," Jess told her.

She grinned. "Well, how often do you get to see a lizard's eye like that?"

"Not often," Jess said. "Practically never."

Dani changed her voice, affecting the accent of a hokey 1940s movie director. "Hang with me, kid. I'll make you a star." She waggled an imaginary cigar.

Jess laughed. "What?"

"I don't know," Dani said. "Just in a goofy mood." She

shrugged. She took off her glasses and wiped them with the hem of her shirt, then sighed and put them back on. "I guess we have to study."

"I guess so," Jess said.

They sat across from each other on the beds and pulled out their books and notebooks, spreading them across the matching blue bedspreads. No, *duvets*. The cloth was soft as talc.

Jess had finished most of her Humanities essay on *Antony and Cleopatra*, so she thumbed through the play, double-checking her quotations, and then they exchanged papers. Dani wrote notes in the margins with a purple pen. Sometimes her lips moved as she read, and when she focused intently, she put the tip of her tongue against her teeth.

Dani said, "God, I'm going cross-eyed." She pushed her glasses up and rubbed her eyes and then shut her book with a snap. "Let's do something else. Something we don't usually do. What do you usually do?"

Jess thought about it. Write bad poems. Read. Listen to music. Watch sitcoms with her mother over dinner. Flip through the dictionary and encyclopedia, close her eyes, and pick entries at random. Sneak out and roam around in the dark streets of a town she still didn't know. Try not to think of the Boy, of her father with his new family, of her mom crying in her sleep, but then think about all those things anyway, the images flipping fast behind her eyes like an animation.

"Not much," she said.

Dani said, "Do you think being only children makes us smarter? Or weirder?"

Jess shrugged. "Both, probably." Except she wasn't an only child anymore. She said, "I have a sister now. My dad had a kid."

"Really? Where are they?"

"California."

"Do you visit him?"

"No," she said. She wished this was because she'd refused, but the truth was, he hadn't asked. He had started including his phone number in the cards, though, with a note: "Call if you need *anything*."

"Do you miss him?" Dani said.

Jess looked at the microscope, at the lump of the toad next to it. She had told herself she didn't, but in that moment she could feel his shoulder where she so often rested her head, the scratchy hair on his knuckles. She smelled the scent of basil from his "world-famous" spaghetti. She heard the sound of his honking laugh. She didn't know how to express this kind of missing. It was as if he was both there and not there, like the horned toad, and she squinted at the microscopic moments, looking for answers. She didn't know how to say any of that. She nodded instead, offering a small shrug.

Dani said, "I hope you get to see him soon."

"Thanks," Jess said.

Dani hugged her knees. "Have you had sex?"

Startled by Dani's bluntness, Jess stuttered a moment but then admitted it. "With one guy, back home." That was the first time she'd said it to anyone. Not even to her mother.

Dani flopped backward and kicked her feet in the air. "I can't believe how much I love it. I mean, *love* it."

Jess watched as Dani pointed her toes and pedaled her feet, trying to reconcile this giddy version of her with the stand-offish girl in the classroom and wondering what else she had misjudged. For her, sex hadn't been terrible, but it sure as hell didn't make her want to kick up her feet. The sharp pain would start to ease, but as she would begin to feel a tingling warmth and lift her hips higher, the Boy would groan and stop moving. And that was it.

Unsure of how to respond, Jess walked over to the horned toad and peered down at it. Still dead. She touched the long spines on its head, the shorter ones on its tail.

Dani sat up and folded her feet under her. Her neck splotched with red, she pushed her glasses up her nose and looked away toward the window. Jess realized Dani was embarrassed, and she squeezed her hands into fists, trying to think of what to say to make it okay.

"Sorry," Jess said. "I don't know how to do girl talk. If that's what this is."

"Me either," Dani said.

"I spend most of my time talking to my mom. Or to myself."

Dani smiled. "Me too." She gazed out the window as if searching for something, and then turned to Jess. "I know. We could do faces." At Jess's blank look, she said, "You know, like makeup. My mom has a ton of theater stuff upstairs. She used to practice on me, making me up into characters. I haven't done it for a long time."

"Like who?"

"Whoever you want. Come on."

Jess followed her to a narrow set of stairs at the end of the hall, dodging the stacked boxes. They thumped up to the top floor, entering a small room with a pitched ceiling. On one side was a double bed with a cedar chest at the foot; the other half of the room held a tilted table spread with drawings, an easel with a half-finished painting, and a table with jars of paints and brushes. Several canvases were stacked along one wall. A large rectangular window overlooked the backyard, and the ceiling on both sides of the pitch had skylights.

Dani swept her arm. "The guest room slash Dad's studio slash storage room slash my old play room." She opened a closet next to the bed and began to pull out boxes.

Jess stood in front of the easel. "This is your dad's?"

The painting was soft and smudgy—watercolor, she guessed—depicting a grove of bare aspens in a field of bluish snow, a burnt brown forest in the background.

Dani said, "Yeah. He was an art major in college, and when they were in New York, he did a lot, but he basically stopped when we moved here. He started up again a couple weeks ago. After his mom died."

"Your grandma died? I'm sorry."

"Thanks. It's okay. I didn't know her. My dad never talked to her or saw her, so I didn't really think of her as my grandmother. She was a famous painter." She pointed at the canvases along the wall. "Those are hers. My dad went to pick them up in Colorado. She lived up there in a cabin. Frances Barnes. She's totally in the encyclopedia. An American realist in the tradition of Andrew Wyeth and Edward Hopper."

"Wow," Jess said. She looked at the half-finished painting again. It made her think of day trips to Flagstaff, avoiding the expensive downhill slopes on the Peaks and instead renting cheap cross-country skis and taking the offbeat trails near Mormon Lake. Swishing through the trees, following her father's tracks, her eye on his gray sweater ahead of her, checking behind her for her mother in her red wool cap. Stopping on the rustic benches to eat their home-packed picnics, fat ham sandwiches thick with mayo, apples cut in quarters and tart with lemon juice. How hungry she'd be, wolfing the sandwich, gasping between bites, as the bright sun warmed them at the picnic bench.

"Your dad's a Realtor now?" Jess asked.

"Lately. He thought he'd teach a couple classes at the Syc when they first moved, but he didn't have the right degree, so that didn't work out, and then he thought about getting certified to teach high school, and then changed his mind, and then, I don't know. He works on the house, does a lot of errands to help my mom. He sold a house last month, though."

Jess said, "My dad is an insurance adjuster. The world's most boring job." Unless, of course, you fall in love with a coworker and you leave your family for a whole new life. She bit her lip and gazed at the painting, tilting her head. She wasn't sure what she was trying to see. She didn't think it was very good—nothing like the paintings in Ms. G's class. It struck her as hazy, like a milky eye. "I like it," she said.

Dani shrugged. "I guess. I don't think he ever finishes anything. I don't know if he runs out of time or gets bored or what. He always says art is about failure, but then my mom says art is work, persistence. That's the only time I see them argue. Whatever. I'm going into science."

Dani hauled out a large hardside suitcase and what looked like a fishing tackle box, plunking them both on the bed. Inside the tackle box were squished tubes, pencils, vials, brushes, and compacts. In the suitcase were scarves and hair adornments, a peacock's spread of silks and sequined pins and sparkly barrettes.

"Voilà," Dani said. She rifled through the box. "I'll do you first. Who do you want to be?"

"I don't know."

Dani pursed her lips, squinting. "How about Cleopatra? Timely." She opened a round compact that held a puff and white powder. "Close your eyes." She leaned in and patted Jess's forehead and cheeks and chin. "Okay, open." She picked up a mascara wand. "Don't blink," she said. She widened her own eyes behind the glasses, her mouth pulled into an O.

"I won't," Jess said. She glanced at the dark painting on the easel. A line from the play looped in her head. Act 5, when Cleopatra is memorializing Antony. She said it aloud, inflecting as she remembered Ms. G had: "His legs bestrid the ocean: his rear'd arm / Crested the world." She loved that word, *crested*. She never wanted to stop saying it.

Dani smiled. She said, "But, if there be, or ever were, one such / It's past the size of dreaming." She rested the side of her palm on Jess's cheek and daubed at her lashes. "This is why we're friends," she said.

Jess smiled back. She held her eyes open as wide as she could.

She called home and asked if she could stay for dinner, and her mother shouted her approval through the line. She and Dani ate pizza and ice cream in their makeup and headgear, she as Cleopatra, Dani as a glittery-eyed Titania—Dani's parents both got it on the first guess. Dani's parents drank red wine and regaled them with stories about their years working in New York, Dani's mother as a playwright and actor and Dani's father as a painter before they moved to Sycamore for Dani's mother's job at the college. Dani rolled her eyes and said, "Here we go again, the great New York saga." Jess smiled at her but leaned closer to the table. Really, Dani's mother told her, we were waiters and cooks. Sycamore was hardly thrilling, but it was stable, she said, especially with a two-year-old in tow. Definitely not thrilling, Dani's father said, laughing. Turned out he was a better Realtor than painter. Unlike my mother, he said. Cheers to my mother, he said, raising his glass, still laughing, but it sounded to Jess as if he laughed a little too hard, or maybe that was the wine, and Dani's mother looked down at her lap.

Before Jess left to go home, she and Dani stood side by side in the guest bathroom with its plush pink towels and wiped their makeup off, laughing at their smeared eyes and cheeks, making faces in the mirror, filling the wastebasket with blackened tissues. Jess washed her face with soap in the shape of a starfish, scrubbing with a pink washcloth. Because it was late, Dani's father loaded her bike in the trunk of the Squareback he was fixing up for Dani and drove her the quick few blocks home. The engine, a low thunder, vibrated in her chest.

"Thanks again, Mr. Newell," she said as he pulled into the driveway.

"Adam," he said. "Not a problem, Jess. Hang on, that door sticks." He leaned across her, tugged on the handle, and gave the door a firm push. Then he got out and unloaded her bike from the trunk.

She took it from him, gripping its handlebars. "Thank you," she said again, but she couldn't bring herself to call him by his first name.

Under the porch light, he smiled and pointed at her face. "Missed a spot," he said.

She scrubbed at her cheek.

"Here." He reached out and wiped the place where her eyebrow met her temple, showing her the smudge of black on his thumb. She thanked him and pushed her bike to the front door as he got in the car. She turned and waved as he backed down the driveway, watching the headlight beams cut through the dark. She watched until the taillights disappeared at the end of the street.

Inside, though it was only nine, her mother was dozing on the couch. She sat up fast, blinking, when Jess nudged her shoulder.

"You're home," she said. "How'd it go? Did you finish your paper?"

"Done."

"Good. Was it fun? How was dinner? How was everything there?"

Jess opened her mouth to tell her, to let loose the effervescence building in her as the idea reverberated—*I have a friend*—when she saw a stiffness in her mother's smile. Jess knew that stiffness: *They're not better than us, J-bird. They just have more money.* A queasy sense of guilt turned her stomach, still full of three slices of pepperoni pizza and a scoop of mint chip.

So she didn't tell her mother about the makeup that had caked her cheeks and swooped across her eyes. She didn't tell her that when she saw herself in the mirror, dark-eyed and glamorous, she'd thought, I look pretty. Exactly like my mother. She didn't tell her how hard she'd laughed when Dani messed up her eye makeup, deliberately blinking until the black smeared her cheeks and eyebrows. She didn't tell about the starfish soap or plush pink towels. She didn't tell about the microscope, or the dead toad, or the bright-white kitchen with its cherry towels, or the big dining table she'd had the urge to slide across. She didn't tell about New York. She didn't tell about the painting studio, she didn't tell about missing Dad. She didn't tell her Dani's father had driven her home. She didn't tell her how he had wiped at a smudge on her temple. She certainly didn't tell her that the moment he had, she'd felt a low fire somewhere in her, like the namesake of her hometown rising from the ashes, a shiver on her arms as if he were a poem, the word *crested* on her tongue. Something strange and uneasy, something she couldn't tell herself yet.

All this she did not tell, holding it in her throat until it hummed, its own kind of burn.

SKATES

ANGIE SAYS IT WON'T BE much longer on your car. About ten minutes. Can I get you anything? Water? I don't work here, but I'm filling in till Beto gets back from lunch. Hope he hurries. I took a day off to take my mom to the doctor and deal with errands, and I still have to get to the grocery store. They never have enough lanes open during the week, do they? I always think it will be better with students gone for the summer. With work, I can't ever get there more than once a week, so I end up with a total mess. Half of it's not even food. Our daughter's in this phase where she won't eat anything but cheese slices and cereal without milk. My mom likes those stupid Hungry Jacks. When my dad died, she swore she would never cook again. Stood by it, too. Lets me do it now, ha. Within a year she retired, sold the house, and moved into the garage apartment we'd renovated. The three of us and now my mom, my sister sometimes, two dogs, a cat, and a turtle named Slow Poke. A regular zoo over at our house.

I'm sorry, but haven't I seen you out walking? You're the one who found the body, right? Not to get in your business, but people talk, you know. Oh my gosh, I couldn't believe it when I saw the paper. You must've been freaked out, huh? I guess you don't know the whole history. Everybody around here knows the story, has a theory about what happened. The cops never did figure it out. There were all these rumors about something going on with her best friend's father and maybe he had her killed, stuff like that. I don't know. Most people think she ran away. A lot of kids want to run away from here. But with the body being so close by, I don't know now. Maybe they'll be able to tell how she died. If it's her. She was a year older than me. She came into the Patty Melt a few times when I was working. The last night anyone saw her, in fact. I served her fries and a Coke. Lots of ketchup. Kids tell ghost stories about her. Jess Winters is coming to get you. Isn't that terrible?

You teach at the Syc, right? Thought so. It's a good school. I went for a semester, but long story short, I had Hazel. Couldn't keep up. I might go back, though. California—really? If I were from California, I'd never leave. I lived in Phoenix for a couple years, but that was a total disaster, so I ended up back here. I went to California senior year of high school for the class trip to Disneyland, though. Took a bus over at the crack of dawn, rode the rides till midnight, and then hopped on the bus home. We're always talking about taking a beach vacation, but you know how those things go. I've always wanted to go to New York, too. Lots of places. Angie feels pretty bad about it, wants us to be able to go. With running the shop and helping at the motel, and now with my mom at home, seems like we can't ever get ahead, you know? I guess that's the way it goes sometimes. And we're going to get married now, and so we have to save up for it. Boston or Connecticut, probably, or Vermont if it passes. Thanks. It is.

Listen to me! Going on. You have kids? Lucky you. Just kidding. I love my daughter. When she's not working my last nerve. Cheese slices and cereal. Hazel, yes. She's fifteen, almost sixteen. When did that happen? She wants to practice driving every second, says she'll get her license the second she turns sixteen. Seems like it was yesterday she was wearing shoes with skates in them. God help us.

You know, I just remembered, my mom went to New York

once, when my dad was in the army, before my sister and I came along. I forgot that. There's a picture of them by the skating rink, the famous one? Rockefeller Center, right. They look cold in that picture, but happy too. So young. It's hard to see them as your parents when they look like that.

Speaking of which, if you ever have visitors come to town, we own the Woodchute Motor Lodge down in the District. My sister Stevie runs the place, and I help out when I can. We've made a lot of improvements in the past few years. Well, Stevie has. You might have seen her around, pushing a wheelbarrow with her rocks? She drives a car covered in bottle caps and glass? She's harmless, just not all there sometimes, if you know what I mean. Keeps making her art, as it were. Anyway, we're booked up a lot these days, but she'll work with you. She'll give you a discount, since you teach at the Syc.

Hey, did you know there's a recall on peanut butter? Salmonella. Thought that was chicken. Anyway, I don't know if it's all brands or what, but watch out. Oh, and now Hazel has decided she wants to be vegetarian. Veggie burgers! That's on my list. Have you tried them? My mom says they look like cow shit and probably taste that way. Well, I'm going to get them for her anyway because at least it's not cereal. I don't know if I'd be able to do without meat. When I was pregnant with Hazel, I could not get enough. I'd eat it raw. You're not supposed to, but she turned out fine. Wasn't like I was smoking or drinking or anything. Although if I was, that's my business. That was one thing I hated about being pregnant, how everybody felt like they could come up and tell you what they thought was best. They'd put their hands on you. Reach out and lay a hand on your belly. Like you're public property. I mean, excuse me? That's mine. 'Course, it's not like I'm not used to people saying things. I wasn't married or even with the father, and to put a cherry on it, I went ahead and shacked up with Angie a couple years later, so you can imagine.

You know, a couple weeks ago, I took Hazel out to practice driving and we went down to Phoenix without telling anyone. We kept on going, headed out to I-17, just us girls. Told my boss at the bank I was feeling sick and couldn't come in, faked a cough. Told Ang I had to run some errands. I don't know what got into me. I haven't done that in a long time. For a while there, I thought, What if we keep going? I don't know where. Somewhere. Ended up in Phoenix, though. I took the wheel, and we got lost even though I used to live there. I have a terrible sense of direction. I went down a one-way street the wrong way. Hazel was trying to read the map on her phone, and everyone was honking. Finally, finally, we got ourselves downtown and parked. We were so hungry, I spent twenty-five dollars on two sodas and two pieces of chocolate cake at this snooty place, at that one hotel with the restaurant at the top overlooking the city. The waiter got into such a huff about us making fun of that cake, stomping around, his nose in the air. We cracked up. We laughed and laughed the way you do. Hazel. She's a good girl when she wants to be. I worry about her. This place can be hard. People are, I don't know. Mostly live and let live, but it wasn't always that way. I used to be scared shitless of who I was, and so was Ang. But we made it, and I can't imagine my life without her. Hazel will have to figure it out, too. But damn, you don't want your kid to suffer, you know? Almost sixteen. Not much younger than Jess Winters. Who knows if another place would be any better, though. Trouble can find you anywhere.

Anyways! Can you believe it's 2009? Remember when the 2000s seemed like a million years away? Stevie used to think we'd have flying cars, and we'd go roller-skating on the moon. 'Course she's like that. When I pointed out the teeny-tiny detail about gravity, she'd said, It'll work. You'll see. Anyway, here we are. Time's the one skating right on by. I'm going to be thirty-three years old next month. Thirty-three. The age of Christ, ha. When did that happen? I used to think I'd be somewhere else. Or maybe not somewhere, but something. Sometimes I wish—well. If wishes were nickels.

Thanks. She is. Listen to me! You came in to get your car fixed, and here I throw my entire life in your lap. Let me go check on your car. You have things to do. I'm Rose Prentiss, by the way. Nice to meet you, Laura. Hey, I hope you like it here. Don't listen to me. It's not so bad, really, once you get used to it.

AZALEAS

A WOMAN WALKED INTO A bar. She said to the bartender, "A man walks into a bar." The bartender said, "Ouch." The bartender knew his jokes. He knew his customers. He knew *this* customer once as his high school Humanities teacher, and he still called her Ms. G even when she said, "It's just Esther now, honey." He knew her as the woman who owned the bakery that made his stomach growl in the mornings when he rode by on his bike, the teacher he'd always loved just a little. She seemed a bit drunk already, and the bartender frowned as she pulled herself onto a barstool. She lived around the corner, though, and had most certainly walked instead of driving, so he poured her a short whiskey and Coke, no ice. She drummed her fingers, and her silver rings caught the light.

Esther took her drink and thanked the bartender, a boy she could bookmark in her mental file of former students, from hairspray helmets to pixie bangs, at Sycamore High (Go Lobos!). Beto Navarro, younger brother of Luz Navarro, who by all accounts raised him. This corner bar, the Pickaxe, could be straight out of that time too. For years students—herself included, back in the day—had snuck in here with fake IDs after school dances, reeking of knockoff perfume sprays and strawberry wine. Either that, or they drove out to the Drag, a patch of desert on the outskirts of town, and built bonfires out of wood pallets stolen from behind Bashas'. She had taught this boy and half the rest of them in this bar, too. All these teenage-now-adults roaming around town and showing up in her bakery, their faces and bodies broader and creased, their own teenage children in tow. She still pictured them with their soft cheeks and springy curls, so she was startled to see this boy's retreating hairline, the deep lines around his eyes and mouth. Of course he was long out of short pants—she chuckled into her highball at this phrasing. Speaking of which, she should get herself some. Shorts. Or pants. She was wearing a full-length black polyester slip as a dress under a flannel shirt Sam had left behind, and she slithered half off the vinyl barstool, revealing a good breadth of pale plump thigh, before catching herself. "Whoa Nelly!" she said. At forty-eight, a few years into her second career as a bakery owner, she favored loose drawstring pants and flowery A-line skirts; as everyone in town knew, she was a smart, creative woman with her ducks in a row. At the very least, she usually *wore clothes*. This slippery slip business would get out. Oh well. Couldn't be helped. Tonight, after getting a little stewed in the living room, staring at the newspaper and its awful news and at the square lighted windows of the guest house where Dani Newell was surely thinking about the same news, Esther was not thinking about clothes. She was thinking of flash floods, the speed at which the water gushed, whipping through the channels of the high desert like a comet, rolling mud and boulders with monstrous force. She was thinking about what it felt like to gasp for air. To be choked and held under.

Jess Winters. Bones in a wash, for Christ's sake. Drowned, then. At best. Esther knew it was she. Had to be. The truth clicked into place like a well-oiled lock. That girl was no runaway, though Esther had once thought otherwise. The day Jess had showed up in her class, all wild brown hair and silver earrings and narrowed eyes, Esther had taken one look at her and sighed in both exasperation and pity. Capital T Trouble and Troubled. She'd thought she could see it a mile off. She was thirty then and more than a wee bit smug about how much she knew about the world. Thirty, ha! She'd been wrong, of course. Trouble had found Jess, but she was not the source of it. She was a smart, gorgeous kid with a bonfire of an imagination.

Righting herself on the stool, Esther ignored the bartender's glance of concern. Since Sam moved out a month ago and ran off to San Francisco and married Kevin, a man not yet thirty (thirty!) he'd met online, her friends had adopted the same look. Iris circled her as if she were a wounded animal, poking her with offers of hot tea and walks. Iris didn't ask questions. Iris knew she would talk when she was ready. Iris was maddeningly sane that way. Esther loved having an older friend. When she'd been a teacher, she'd always been the one shelling out advice. It was nice to be advised sometimes, to *ask*. Iris did say, "So what, Esther? So what if he's making a mistake? So *what*? He's in love."

She twisted her rings, starting with the ones on her left pinkie and working her way across to the right pinkie, a nervous habit she channeled into jokes and mixing bowls. She glanced at the bartender. Beto Navarro. A boy, all grown up. Two young women at the end of the bar, probably Syc students—she didn't know them or their parents—threw glances and smiles at him, tossed their glossy hair, and Esther watched him with new eyes. Yes. Handsome now, his gawkiness stretched into angularity, a lean ranginess. She watched the flexing muscle of his forearms as he squeezed a rag, and a little heat snuck in her belly. He was what, thirty-four, thirty-five now? Oh, his brother, that lovely Tomás. He'd died in the Gulf War—no, in the run-up to the war, in train-ing. Humvee crash. What a terrible thing. Of course, people said that about her, too, having lost both parents when she was five and been raised by her grandmother. She remembered being happy when Beto started palling around with Angie Juarez and Rose Prentiss. Kid needed a friend. All of them had. She had always remembered him for his large forehead, how the skin seemed almost translucent, and she remembered, too, that he'd been a wonderful writer, his otherworldly stories underpinned by an almost painful beauty. No, he didn't write much anymore, he told her. No, no kids of his own. Never married, nope, not him, he said with a laugh. She didn't have to say, Me neither—everyone knew this about her. Everyone here knew her, or *thought* they did. He said he still worked at the auto shop with Angie. Still had the paper route twice a week, but picked up some weekend bar shifts to save up for vacation. "Keeps me young," he said. He showed her a picture of his nieces, Luz's girls. Luz still worked at the P.O.—with Maud, she thought. Esther had been at Maud's house earlier; she and Iris had brought food and stayed with her. Maud had played with the burger and potato salad on her plate and then before the sun set, said, "I think I'll hit the hay early tonight." Esther took a large wallop of her drink, let it burn.

Staring at the bartender's broad forehead and strong arms, as the twitch of heat intensified, Esther thought of herself at Jess Winters's age, the only age Jess would ever be: seventeen, the age at which Esther had lost her virginity, an awkward, embarrassing event that catapulted her into life as a sexual creature. After that, she had warded off pregnancy with a potent cocktail of birth control, condoms, and long stretches of celibacy. She ticked off on her fingers the number of men she had slept with in her forty-eight years. Twelve. Like the months. Like the steps of AA. Like the apostles. The last one set loose a hacking laugh. So *that* was what she'd been doing in erratic bursts these past years: dating the apostles. The absurdity comforted her, and the tightness in her lungs eased. She decided she'd make the apostles her shtick, the way some people had six toes or had climbed Everest or could tie cherry stems in knots with their tongue. Sam would love it. She'd call and tell him when he and Kevin got home from their honeymoon.

"Beto, can I borrow your pen?" When he handed it to her, she grabbed a napkin from the fanned pile in front of her and scrawled down the rest of the apostles' names, somehow still lodged in her brain from years of Sunday school indoctrination at the church not four blocks from this bar, in this town she'd never left. She held up the napkin with the twelve names and laughed. She laughed and laughed, falling forward until her forehead bounced off the padded bar rim.

"Ms. G," said the bartender/mechanic/former student with the sexy forearms. "Hey. Hey. Ms. G."

"I'm good, Beto," she said. "It's just Esther now. Maybe some water."

She righted herself on the stool and ran her fingers over the list, transposing the apostles' names over the real ones from her memories, trying to figure out how to construct such a joke.

Andrew, the first. Seventeen years old, she straddled him in the vinyl backseat of his VW bug in the parking lot next to Juarez Autos, which now housed Starz Nails but then was only gravel overrun with bristly foxtails and tumbleweeds. Poor Andrew fumbled with her triple-hook bra while she joked to shroud her smarts and long chin and frizzy hair and the roll of fat at her waist. She wasn't thinking of the boy beneath her. She had been saving for college, and she was almost there, ready to beat cheeks out of Sycamore to the university in Tempe, only an hour-and-a-half drive but a world away from Grandmother's House of Repression. She was thinking about urban skylines, coffee, poetry, letters to the editor about global injustices, foreign accents, moody singer-songwriters, everything that existed elsewhere. Despite the dubious yearbook honor of "class clown," she was a dreamy girl. She believed in things like signs, and ESP, and kismet, snarfed them down as if they were a side of hot, salty fries. But later for dreams. First, the virginity. Andrew pumped once, grunted, shuddered. He looked at her but ducked his head, his chin tucked in shame and vulnerability. He looked close to tears. She smiled hard and chucked him on the shoulder. "Wow, that was great!" she said, her voice as high and pitched as a circus tent. He dropped her at her house—the same house she would inherit when Grandmother died and in which she would live for forty-three of her forty-eight years. If someone had told her that then, she would have laughed and laughed. *Hilarious.* Then, she could only see that the lights were off and she could sneak in the window without Grandmother knowing she'd been gone. She slid between the two azaleas, whose magenta flowers had burned in a late freeze. The now-brown blooms crumbled and stuck to her pant legs. They flaked across the carpet like fish food.

Thomas was her first semester at Sycamore College, which had given her a tuition scholarship plus room and board—away from her grandmother, even if down the street; she'd save money and leave town before the ink dried on the diploma. A philosophy major, Thomas drank a twelve-pack every day and had the sweetest Carolina drawl. He slept with her even though he doubted *everything*, including his sexuality, poor kid. It did not go well. She could not remember that boy without thinking of Sam, who'd arrived in town a few years later to teach at the high school. Twenty-two years old, with the sleek, buoyant beauty of a seal. Once, early on, they drank too much wine and fumbled around in her living room before he pulled away, tears in his eyes.

"Goddamn," he said. "I don't want to pretend with you, okay? I don't want to pretend anymore. Do you know what I'm saying?" She did. "Would you like a cinnamon roll?" she asked, because she had learned she liked to feed people, and herself, when she was nervous, or sad. Happy, too. "I made them this morning," she said. He laughed and cried at the same time. "Yes, please," he said. And so they ate them straight from the pan, wiping their faces and hands on paper towels. She didn't know yet how their lives would become entwined, feed off each other, a twenty-year-plus friendship that would fill them full to bursting.

But that was later. Next up was Matthew, whom she met in one of those themed secret-pal dorm games—he was Sid and she was Nancy. *So* punk rock. He wanted to start a band, said she could write the songs. Save the world with their angst and rock and roll. But soon he dumped her for a sorority girl, and she cried in her dorm bunk for two days. She wrote haikus about minor chords and tuning pegs.

James the Lesser gave her impetigo around her mouth about the time she moved Grandmother into the senior care home. She wrote a limerick about a young woman who wore a rubber Richard Nixon mask to conceal her scabby face rash and brought it to her poetry class. It did not go well. "Always with the jokes," her professor said, her voice tired, waving her white sheet of paper in surrender instead of asking, again, "Why should I *care*? What is at *stake* here?"

James the Greater was tall and spindly-legged, a runner she met at the track. She had moved back into Grandmother's house and started teaching at Sycamore High—a short-term assignment, she'd move on in a year or so—and was in one of her zealous exercise periods, when she still stuffed her chunky waist into brand-name jeans and hadn't learned the wonders of drawstrings and A-lines.

He did a dead-on impression of Ronald Reagan—*It's morning in America again*—and he praised her fledgling poems and made her feel like a million bucks. She mistook this for intimacy because she was twenty-three, and he had eyes as blue as a gas flame. But when it counted—when she was late, and he said, "How?" and she said, "This ain't the Immaculate Conception, for Christ's sake"—he ran as fast and far as his long legs could carry him. She wasn't pregnant after all, but she held onto his two hundred dollars anyway.

Thaddeus—not Thad, but Thad-*deus*—was from back east, taught at Sycamore High for a grand total of two years. Wire-rims, soft hands, read Kant and Hegel on their camping trips while she set up the tent and ate bags of wicked marshmallows and drank his wicked Rolling Rocks and wrote a villanelle about his goatee. Thad-*deus* had a mean streak. One night, after they'd been out drinking, he called her a stupid, fat bitch. Sam said, "We can break his kneecaps. I know a guy," and she laughed too loud and made a giant batch of peach-walnut muffins she snuck out and ate over the sink in the middle of the night. When she visited her grandmother in the home, Grandmother said, "You don't watch it, you're going to end up washed up, a fat spinster with no one but that queer friend of yours for company. You're going to die alone." And she fired back, "Like you?" It was one of the last exchanges they'd have. She stormed out, but she stayed with Thad-*deus* for two more months.

Philip was a divorced parent of one of her seniors. He'd split from the mother and moved two hundred miles away to the foot-hills of Tucson, so in between visits, they had phone sex, during which she often did the dishes or spackled her walls or worked on a sestina about a UN ambassador who was having sex from pay phones around the globe. When the boy graduated and Philip took his vacation in Sycamore, it was over by the end of the week. Sam gave her what she called the Eyebrow: the damn thing cranked up so high it disappeared into his hairline.

John was married, two kids, lived in Sedona. At the Sycamore Arts Festival, having told his wife he was at a conference, he bought her a silver ring and slid it on her left finger. Esther was old enough to know better, she was about to turn thirty (thirty, ha!), but she let him. In return, she bought him a leather brace-let. Sam unleashed the Eyebrow again but said nothing. On the night of her birthday, the married man didn't show up for their clandestine date, and she sat alone in her bedroom, too embar-rassed to tell Sam. The next day, she had what would turn out to be her last conversation with Jess Winters. Jess's words ran through her mind as she drove fast down the back roads toward her house: *Oh my god,* fuck *poetry. Why can't you answer a question straight for once? If you can't tell me what to do, tell me what you would do.* What would she do? Without hesitating, she chucked the goddamn ring out of her sunroof.

She met Bartholomew in an online Scrabble group, and they took to chatting on IM though not in person. The sex was sur-prisingly good despite the typos and Times New Roman font. A comma splice here, a dangling participle there, but it did the job.

Simon the Zealot was a Scottish slam poet—awful teeth, a butterfly tattoo on his skinny rump—who wandered into town one summer during his travels. Six months in, he needed a green card and married a waitress in Phoenix. Late one night, she drove down there and contemplated setting fire to his garbage can but settled instead for tipping it over. The bastard didn't recycle, which gave her a split second of comfort as she strewed beer bottles and soup cans and something resembling a human liver out onto his dusty lawn. Later, she told Sam, "I'm *that* woman now. I'm the woman out on the fucking lawn." Sam rolled a joint and they knocked back a bottle of wine, and it was a good old-fashioned rip-roaring pity party, because, Jesus Christ on a Crutch. How hard was it to find someone, anyway? Sam said, "Hey. Why *does* Jesus have a crutch? I mean, he can heal lepers but not sprained ankles?" And with that, they lay on the kitchen floor in hysterics, contemplating holy injuries and knowing they were going straight to hell.

Simon Peter called Peter was short. Troll-short. Think jockey. One day he stopped calling. He disappeared so fast that for a few days she thought she had imagined the whole thing until she found his plaid flannel shirt in her laundry. When she held it to her face, it smelled of aftershave and cigarettes, a hint of something bitter, like marigolds. The truth of him emerged, again, when she was late, again, when her breasts swelled and the smell of coffee made bile rise in her throat. At thirty-six, she was the oldest woman in the Flagstaff clinic by a good decade. As she waited, she picked off her chipped lavender nail polish and fixed her gaze on the gardening magazine in her lap. She traced one of the titles, *We Love Azaleas!*, over and over, up and down the yellow letters. Months later, she wrote a poem of the same title, exclamation mark and all, though it wasn't funny, that one. Not a joke in sight. She didn't tell Sam. She told no one.

Judas. The last one, two years ago now, a customer new to town who showed up at Yum when she was up to her elbows in flour and debt and worry—what kind of maniac left a stable teaching job with a pension and weeks off in summers to open a bakery?—when her ovaries were in their last gasp and spewing hormones everywhere and she was swollen again, a sensation that harkened azaleas, and she thought her breasts might explode right there over the stainless steel prep table and new industrial mixer (she'd named the mixer Spinster. No one got the joke but her, but she thought it was *hilarious*. Spinster: Christ, what a word). Judas had gapped front teeth, an immunization scar on his left upper arm shaped like a clover. She often traced it as he slept. His hands were preposterously large; even now, she could feel the ghost of his colossal palm pressed flat against the small of her back, a sausage-sized thumb smoothing her eyebrows.

But he wasn't a Judas, a name synonymous with betrayal, a man who took his life outside Jerusalem. It just ended. He moved home to Oregon, and she stayed put.

Story of her dating life. And Sam's, too, till Kevin. All these years down the line.

A priest walked into a bar, carrying a ceramic duck under his arm. It was late, near closing. He sat next to a woman who doodled on a bar napkin, who didn't seem to notice him or his duck, which he clunked down on the bar when he ordered a pint from the bartender with the large forehead. He took a long drink. The carbonation made his nose tingle.

The woman, clenching the napkin, turned to the priest. Her eyes gleamed like an icy road at dawn. She said, "Father Tom, did you hear the one about the woman who dated all the apostles?"

The priest sighed. He was tired. His clerical collar was chafing, his socks slipping. The duck, a gift from a parishioner he'd been visiting with for the last four hours, was heavy and cumbersome. "Hi Esther," he said.

"Hey yourself."

He heard it then. A hairline crack in her voice. He had spent his life listening, and he knew that universal sound. Injured hearts, broken souls, lost faith. He shook his head. He said, "I haven't heard that one."

She peered at him through the dim haze of the Pickaxe. She

leaned down and pulled up a sagging white sock, and the priest glanced away from her ample cleavage, the dimpled thigh exposed by a deep slit in her dress. She said, "It isn't much of a joke, to tell you the truth. No punch line." She stuffed the ink-covered napkin inside her highball.

The priest nodded, waiting. He had learned that over time: just wait.

She reached out absently and petted the duck, rested her thumb on its beak. She started to talk then, but not about the apostles.

"I used to write poetry," she said. "It was terrible, but you know, I used to have that impulse. To notice things." Her head bobbed, and she pulled her shoulders back. "I used to think, No apologies, no regrets. Leave a trail of wreckage, and so what? That was living. But then I never did, you know."

"Leave a trail of wreckage?"

"Live."

She pointed at the wadded-up napkin. "I was going to save the world. Who wasn't? Like it needed my help." She laughed, but her eyes welled. "That girl, Tom. That kid. In a wash. And Maud." She stopped.

He folded his hands. "I know it, Esther. It's awful news."

"Sam's gone." She twisted all her rings, one by one. "And she's found."

He looked at the two glasses in front of her, one stuffed with a napkin, the other brimming with brown liquid. "We don't know it's her yet. And Sam is still your friend. You'll still see him. I know you're sad, Esther, but think how happy he is."

"He is, isn't he? I never saw him look quite like he did at the wedding, and I thought I knew him best." She lifted the glass and sniffed it. She shook her head. "I don't understand what I'm feeling. I *am* happy for him. Mostly. But I also feel like I'm going to die of grief. I don't understand it. I have a wonderful life. It's astonishing, really, how much I have. Most days, I look around, and I think, This is exactly right. This is my path, and it's a god-damn good one. At the very least, I'm sitting here. Still here."

He said, "It's a big change. How long did he live at the house with you?"

She tilted her head. "Twenty-three years. I was twenty-five when he rolled into town and he was twenty-two. Babies."

"Long time." He sighed. Tics of exhaustion pulsed at the back of his eyes, and something else, too, a bright, tight ache of memory, his young past self fumbling with conviction, fumbling with a girl in the dark hallway of a dance hall, her braid in his hand like a rope to safety. Conflicted, he'd fled from his plans for priesthood to the secular life, to pharmacy school, to this town. But he'd re-turned to his faith. He'd found his way back on his own.

He turned to reflex and said what he always said. "Have faith. Lean on God."

"Oh, come on, Tom. Give me something I can use."

He took another swig of beer, and he thought again of that girl. Peppermint breath, pink-tipped fingers clutching his tweed lapels, tracing the crooked scar on his cheek he'd gotten from a childhood dog bite. She came to him on nights like these, when his guard was down, his faith a little frayed at the seams.

He set his glass down hard. "For shit's sake," he said. "Why does everyone think I have the answers?"

She smiled. "Isn't that the deal? Straight line to God?"

He leaned close to her. "Go *home*, Esther," he said. "The an-swers aren't here."

She pushed the glass away and raised her hand to the bar-tender. "A house is not a home, honey." She nodded at his glass. "At least let me get you one."

He clenched his hands in his lap. He tried a smile. "All right. Sure. One more."

The bartender brought the priest a beer and slid the woman a glass of water. She smiled at the bartender, that boy turned man. "Beto Navarro," she said. "You look great. You look like a million bucks."

He smiled back. "Thanks. You too. It's Roberto now."

The woman said, "Roberto. Yes. Lovely." She stared at him a moment longer. "You wrote so beautifully. About something in space, yes? I remember a ship sailing across the sky."

"Yes," he said. "Once."

"Yes," she said. "I remember it was beautiful."

She turned to the priest and started to talk again. She said something about how she liked to watch sunlight, the way it filtered through dust in a window. She told him about her grandmother, how she wasn't always so rotten but she'd had a hard life. Lost her daughter, inherited a five-year-old kid out of the blue. She said, "She was a good baker." She asked, "Do you think she'd be proud of me now?" She told him about Judas's hands. "Like kielbasas, seriously," she said. She smiled, and then looked at the far wall, long into the middle distance. Those azalea bushes in her front yard—still there, still blooming like mad every spring. How was that possible? Such fragile blooms—one freeze, and it was sayonara, sweetheart.

The priest let her go on. He checked his watch once, feeling the lead of his limbs, the exhaustion rimming his eyes. He nodded and said "Um-hmm" and "Sure" and "I see," his smile pinched. He thought of Stevie Prentiss, who'd come into the pharmacy all those years ago with her fake injuries. He'd tried to fix her anyway. He humored her as he humored the woman now because no matter the time of day or place, it was always someone's dark hour.

She wiped under her eyes and said, "A priest, a rabbi, and a duck walk into a bar. Bartender says, 'Hey, what is this, a joke?'" She laughed and slapped the bar.

The priest said, "Good one."

She said, "And then he quacked up. No, no, he cried fowl!" She howled with laughter, loud enough that other patrons glanced their way. Then she placed her head down on the bar. Her back heaved, buckling with the force of her sob.

The priest put his hand on her shoulder. "Come on, Esther. Let's get you home. Time to go home."

She nodded, slipping off the stool, hiding her face in her hands.

A woman walked out of a bar, crying, holding the elbow of a priest, who left his duck behind. The handsome bartender with the broad forehead watched her go, a tightness in his chest. He remembered the story she'd mentioned, one he'd written in a frenzy at the kitchen table. He remembered how in high school, she would pace at the front of the classroom as if caged. He remembered how she said one of the great questions of literature was about knowledge, about how humans know one another. "Think about it," she'd said. "Do we really know anyone? How?" She'd leaned over his desk, her face close enough he could see the faint blond fuzz over her lip. "You can't see my thoughts. You can't see my heart. My heart is an *inferno*," she'd said, thumping her chest, "but how would you know?" The other students had laughed and rolled their eyes, at her over-the-top, vein-in-the-throat passion, at her *weirdness*—and of course they'd snickered at him frozen in his seat, because people snickered at him then. But he hadn't laughed. He hadn't then, and he didn't now as she slurred and stumbled out with the priest. As she opened the door into the warm night, he squeezed his hands into tight fists and lifted them to his face. Each the size of a heart. Beating. Ablaze.

TRACES

June–August 1991

BY JUNE THE SCRATCHED-GLASS SKIES in Sycamore seemed larger than oceans. Time, too, stretched wide. Unlike most kids from school, who went to Peck's Lake with twelve-packs smuggled from the Circle K, Jess, Dani, and Paul spent their days off at a mellow river spot on the Overton property, a clearing under a giant sycamore with a rope swing hanging from one of its large limbs. They started calling themselves the Onlys—a club of only children, but *only* for the three of them, fuck you very much. They carried an assortment of sandwiches and chips, sodas they cooled in a shallow part of the river. They hauled along a crappy tape deck that sometimes ate their cassettes, making them cuss as they pulled out the shiny entrails and rewound them with pens and pinkies. When they got hot, they grabbed the rope swing, climbed to the top of a small hill, and hurled themselves over the bottle-green water, angling their bodies away from the submerged shin-breaking boulder.

The first time Jess did this, when she let go of the rope, she seemed to fly upward and hang suspended, a moment wholly wild and without name. She learned to leap midair, to slow time by kicking her feet up and arching her back. When she fell and hit the water, smacking the soft skin of her inner arms, the cold stole her breath. She swam with jerky strokes to the muddy shallows, the stones slick under her bare feet. She smelled of fish and moss, minerals and silt, her hair tipped the color of butter.

Dani and Paul would take their towels and sneak into the far end of the trees, and Jess would put on her headphones—it was bad enough to be a third wheel; she for sure didn't want to *hear* any of it—and lie down with her eyes closed. The music pulsing in her ears, she would fall into a drowsy state, somewhere on the cusp of sleep, and in those moments, she understood what people meant about the golden haze of youth. Out here, drying off on a towel atop the warm dirt, she didn't think about the divorce or her dad's new life or her mom sleeping like the dead or the fast-fading Boy. She stopped worrying about what it meant to exist, about what awaited in the wide, wide world. Wrapped in that languid heat, she stopped thinking altogether. Here, she simply *was*.

At the orchard, Jess spent her days outside now too. The pecans were no longer the strange pods of earlier spring, with their furry sea-anemone tufts. Now the pods were round and green and soft, protecting the inner shell where the nut formed. Jess had learned from Iris that the outer shell, the husk, was called the pericarp, and the hard inner shell was the endocarp. Prefixes, again: *peri*, around, *endo*, internal. She loved learning that. She loved knowing how fierce and tough the pods were, how many layers grew to protect the tiny nut. Her new knowledge brought a rush of pleasure that reminded her of how it felt to skip a stone: a perfect flat rock bouncing across water, defying gravity.

Dani had gotten a job at the HealthCo as a cashier three days a week, and Paul worked with Jess at the orchard, though they were often on their own. Iris put Paul on larger maintenance tasks, such as painting the shed and repairing equipment, and he handled the riding mower and weekly supply runs to Flagstaff. Jess would catch glimpses of him up on a ladder, or in the rows of the orchard, an arm, a leg, a shaggy hank of hair. They'd wave at each other through the trees. Over lunch, they talked about the orchard or college—he wanted to go to Arizona State if he could get a track scholarship, or to California, where Dani wanted to go, though he wasn't sure about his grades for Stanford. He wasn't sure what he wanted to study. Journalism, maybe. He liked working on the school paper. Jess told him she hadn't decided, either—if she even went, which her mother insisted she would. *You're not making my mistake, J-bird.*

When Dani didn't have to work, she'd come and hang out at the orchard with a book, lounging on the deck in a broad straw sun hat. When she could get it to start, she drove her Squareback, its paint the deep blue-green of an aloe vera stalk, its polished chrome bumpers and tire rims reflecting the sky. She gripped the wheel tight, a pillow tucked behind her hips. Driving made her nervous—all those morons out there, racing around, heads up their butts. Fixing up an old car had been her dad's idea. He thought they'd work on it together, hoping she'd get more comfortable if she knew the car's mechanics, but it ended up being just him, late at night or when he had time, and really, Mr. Juarez did most of the work at his shop. Her father tinkered, Dani said with a wry shrug. He was a mad genius with Turtle Wax. A car for Dani was matter-of-fact: As long as it worked. As long as it got her from point A to point B.

When Jess rode her bike home alone, the bleeding citrus sky at her back, she couldn't decide what she envied Dani the most for: her nonchalance about having a car; a father, working on a project for her; a boyfriend who climbed inside with her, heading off together; or the car itself, its goofy, sweet shape, its rattle and hum, its stink of oil and gas. But her envy was brief, a quick sting, like lemon juice on chapped lips.

In mid-June Jess installed a line of irrigation at the orchard. She loved digging the trench, chipping away at the hard-packed dirt with the shovel, the impact sending a jolt into her arms. The only digging she'd done before was in garden pots with her mom or tunneling in the sand at the beach in Mexico. By the end of the day, she had sweated until her shirt and the brim of her canvas hat were soaked through, and she'd drunk a gallon of water straight from a jug. As she wound a garden hose to return to the shed, she could smell the must of dried sweat on her skin. Her stomach growled, and she remembered she'd be on her own for dinner. Her mother was going on a date—with Angie's dad, Mr. Juarez, with his mop of white hair. When her mom had told her, Jess had hugged her hard, feeling protective, happy, and bereft all at once. But happy, mostly. What if this meant she and Angie could be friends again? (Or, oh my god, sisters!) At the very least, her mom deserved a night out. Jess's stomach grumbled again. She would make herself a giant pile of egg noodles and butter, eat it straight from the pot.

Jess glanced up to see the Squareback coming up the driveway. She smiled, hefting the coiled hose to her shoulder. Dani must have gotten off work early.

But it was Mr. Newell who climbed out of the driver's side.

"Hello!" he called to Jess. He wore a long-sleeved oxford shirt and tie and shiny black shoes. A yellow pencil stuck out from behind his right ear. "I've brought Dani her car. I'm a little early."

Jess shook her head. "Dani's not here. She's at work today."

He slapped his forehead. "That's right. I'm supposed to meet her at the HealthCo. We're meeting here *tomorrow*, for dinner with Paul and his mom. It's been one of those weeks." He shook his head, knocking loose the pencil, which bounced on the ground. He bent to pick it up and put it in his breast pocket. He smiled at her. "You're working hard," he said, nodding at her dirt-streaked clothes, at the hose on her shoulder.

She dusted at her shorts and shirt with her free hand. "I installed a line of irrigation today. All by myself." The skipping stone feeling again, though this time it was *her* skidding on the water, sending ripples outward. She remembered her mother teasing her on the day they'd arrived: *I had a thought. What if we like it here?* She grinned and shrugged.

"That's great," Mr. Newell said. "A budding botanist, perhaps. Or horticulturist."

Jess knew nothing about botany or horticulture; it was as if he'd suggested she become an astronaut. She stuck her thumb inside the metal end of the hose. "Maybe. I'll have to look into it. Definitely." She'd hit the encyclopedias when she got home.

"The Syc has a good reputation for agricultural science, actually. Because we're so rural. But you probably don't want to stay here."

"No," she said. She thought of Dani's map and pushpins, still unsure where she wanted to sink her own. "I don't know yet where."

"Don't rush it. That's the beauty of being young. You have time." He laughed but looked away, staring at the trees in the orchard. "We tell Dani all the time she should look farther afield, even though she'd get a tuition break here. We want her to see the world. I don't want her stuck." He shook his head. "Not that people here see themselves as stuck. They're not. They have all kinds of reasons for staying. A lot of people love it here."

"Don't you?"

"No." He smiled. "Sometimes I do. I've made peace with it, I guess. It's not easy, to be the spouse of an academic. I showed up here with no role to play. I had to let go of ideas of what my life would be. It's stable here. Safe. Good for Dani. We've made it work. Of course, now she'll be leaving." He blinked behind his square glasses and then checked his watch. "Sorry. That was more than you needed to know. Are you done now? Do you need a ride home?"

"I'm good," she said. "I have my bike."

"It's no trouble," Mr. Newell said. "We can put it in the trunk again and drop you off before I scoot over to pick up Dani. We have time."

"Oh. Okay, sure." She put the hose away in the shed, said good-bye to Iris, and wheeled her bike to the car.

Once he loaded it in the hatchback, he held out the keys to her. "Want to drive?"

She grinned. "Really?"

"Sure. Do you know how to drive a stick?"

She nodded. "My mom taught me on hers."

She slid in behind the wheel, and from the passenger seat he pointed out the gear lever and told her to be careful with the brakes—he had tweaked them for Dani but hadn't gotten them quite right. He leaned close and turned the key in the ignition, and the engine rumbled to life under her hands and feet. Up close, she could see dark circles under his eyes, a patch of gray hair behind his left ear. The pencil slid out of his shirt pocket and rolled onto the seat.

"It's a good little car. I just drove it up to Colorado this past week to get more of my mother's things."

"I'm sorry. About your mother, I mean," Jess said.

"Thank you." He stared down and rubbed the vinyl seat with his thumb. "It was a beautiful drive. That part of the country." He shook his head and looked up. He said, "Dani's funny. She doesn't like to drive. I thought if she had a different car, kind of unusual, she might like it better."

"I know," Jess said. "I'd kill for a car like this."

He laughed. "It's been a lot of work. Do you know what you want?"

"Not really. I'm saving right now. Whatever costs a thousand dollars and won't die on me. My dad was going to help, but." She shrugged. "My mom said she'd cover insurance."

Frowning, he buckled his seat belt. "That's hard. I'm sure it's been hard for you. I'd be happy to help you look for one when the time comes. If you want help."

"Thanks," she said. She pressed her foot hard on the brake.

He nodded at the windscreen. "All right, ready when you are." He loosened his tie and rested his arm on the open window.

She shifted into first and let out the clutch. The car lurched once, but she adjusted, coasting down the orchard's gravel driveway. "Good, you got it!" he said. When she hit the main road and picked up speed, the wind knocked her hat off and swept tangled strands of hair across her face. She held the wheel tight, and he picked up her hat from where it landed at his feet. Dirt crusted her knuckles and streaked her forearms, and her muscles, strained from digging, gave off a faint feverish ache. The bright summer sky had softened to a whisper of itself, burnished and dusky, and the air smelled of smoke, perhaps from a nearby brush fire. Her beehive mind started buzzing with questions—Smoke: Was something burning down out there? Was it someone's house? What *was* botany? Would Mom have a good date tonight? Would Dad find out she was dating?—but her physical exhaustion and a sense of gratification beat the thoughts back. She sank against the seat and relaxed her arms. She felt the tremble of the engine in her thighs, a flush in her cheek. She felt—happy. She started laughing.

"What's funny?" Mr. Newell said.

She shook her head. She raised her voice over the engine and the wind. "Nothing."

His smile faded as he turned away and stared out the open window, holding her hat in his lap.

In late June, when the monsoon began to lumber in, Jess's mom took her and Dani on a camping trip to San Felipe, Mexico—their old vacation spot, the first time without her father. The trip was a first for Dani, too—her first time tent-camping and her first time in Mexico, a new pushpin for her travel map. Jess's mom bought a second tent for the girls and hunted up coolers and snorkels and rafts from the storage shed, wedging it all in the trunk for the eight-hour drive. They drove through Phoenix and Gila Bend and Yuma, past the thrumming cars at the Calexico-Mexicali border and into Baja, speeding across a desert dotted with creosote and salt bush and ocotillo until there: the glimmering Sea of Cortez. On a secluded beach at the cheap campground, the girls slathered themselves in coconut-scented suntan lotion and body-surfed and snorkeled and watched the grunions spawn at sunset. They wore cutoffs over their suits, plastic flip-flops on their feet. In the afternoons and evenings, Jess's mom, her hair knotted atop her head, sat on the beach under an umbrella with a fat paperback and a cold beer. "All I want to do is read and watch the tides," she said. They walked into town, bought carne asada tacos from a roadside stand and groceries and supplies at a small *mercado*, pleased when their Spanish was good enough to be understood. They stopped at a beach bar and ordered piña coladas with nutmeg on top, growing tipsy and giggly a few sips in. They didn't shower for four days, their hair stiff with salt, sand in their seams and waistbands and in between their toes.

In the tent, its screened vent open to a patch of starry night, they learned to talk to each other. They talked about Paul and other boys and stupid things like their tan lines, yes, but then shifted to what they didn't know yet: where would they go to college—*of course* they would apply to the same places, or at least schools near each other—about their futures, their careers. And they talked about what they didn't know *how* to know: divorce, and family, and God, and love, and fear, and what it meant to be alive.

Their last night, Dani rolled over on her stomach. "Trace me," she said.

Jess could see the tan lines from her bathing suit, white ghost straps, and she started to write letters between her shoulder blades with her finger.

"F," Dani said, her voice muffled in the sleeping bag. "I. S. H. Fish. Come on. Make it worth my while. And why fish, you weirdo." She laughed. "Do another one."

Jess wrote *grunion*, and *botany*, and *lozenge*, and *pristine*. Dani guessed half of them, her voice sleepy.

"Now me," Jess said. She turned over with her face in her pillow. Dani's finger on her back felt like an eraser. "Not so hard," she said. Dani eased up. She wrote *fusion*, and *esoteric*, and *sunstroke*, and Jess guessed all but the second. On the last, Jess, drowsy, couldn't tell what the word was.

"Song?" she asked.

"Nope." Dani moved her finger in the same place, over and over, until Jess got the chills.

Jess struggled to keep her eyes open. "Doll? I can't tell."

" 'Love,' you simpleton," Dani said. She sighed and lay down.

Jess laughed into the pillow. She rolled on her side and opened her eyes. Dani curled like a shrimp inside her bag, her glasses off, eyes closed. The sky yawned above them, too, and Jess closed her eyes against the shimmering, star-scarred blackness. She fell asleep hard and fast, the kind of sleep she could rarely find at night—heavy, dreamless—not waking until late the next morning, sweltering in the damp tent.

Then she and Dani climbed in the back seat for the drive home, propped up on sandy pillows, sunburned and sticky, the taste of salt on their lips. Jess took one last look out the window at the place where the desert met the sea. Next summer would be their last trip together before she went off to college. This, the penultimate. And never again with her father and mother together. This last thought snuck up on her. She blinked back the sting of tears.

Dani said, "Thank you, Maud. This trip completely made my summer. My life, really."

"You're very welcome." Jess's mom looked in the rearview, frowning when she noticed the tears.

Jess smiled, waving her off. "Completely. Best Mom prize for sure." She plumped her pillow and leaned against the window, pressed her palm against the warm glass. Lulled by the sound of the engine, safe in her mother's care and with her friend beside her, she slept again. She woke disoriented, staring at a strange stretch of road. She lifted her head and looked to the front of the car.

Her mom smiled at her in the rearview, reached back and patted her knee.

"Not too much farther," she said. "Almost home."

On the Fourth of July, Jess went with Dani and Paul to the fireworks at the ball field. A friend of Paul's from the track team, Warren Smith, whom everyone called Smitty, joined them on the blanket they'd spread in right field. He sat next to Jess. As the evening progressed, he reached out and hooked two fingers around her right pinkie. Jess kept her eyes on the fireworks that streaked and flowered against the onyx sky. When she jumped at the booms of the duds, Smitty squeezed her pinkie. When they said good night, he kissed her on the mouth, a quick peck with firm, dry lips. She smiled, her heart warm. He was sweet. She couldn't help but think of his first name: Warren. A rabbit's den. A sweet rabbity kiss.

After, Jess stayed the night at Dani's. They climbed into the twin beds and debriefed about Warren and his pinkie squeeze, and when her parents went to bed, Dani snuck out her bedroom window to meet Paul. Left alone, Jess tossed in the bed, unable to sleep. She went to the living room and sat on the sofa, peering at the familiar objects—books, picture frames, figurines—rendered strange by darkness. The stiff tweed cushions scratched her bare thighs. She couldn't curl up here as she would on her sofa at home, cocooned in worn plaid twill, the shelf of green encyclopedias and Big Red in her line of sight.

She opened the sliding glass door that led onto the Newells' redwood deck, where more than once she had sat in the wooden Adirondack chairs and eaten a sandwich or sipped a soda, her feet propped on the railing, her friend's house fast becoming her second home. She plopped down now in one of the chairs before she realized someone else was there. Mr. Newell. He leaned against the railing, smoking a cigarette.

Startled, she pulled her nightshirt down her thighs and scrambled to get out of the low chair. "Sorry. I didn't know anyone was out here."

He said, "Stay. It's fine. Don't tell Dani I'm smoking, though. I quit. Is she asleep?"

"Yes," Jess said, looking at her hands.

"But you couldn't, huh?" He crushed out the cigarette. "Me either. Thinking too much."

He dragged a chair to sit next to her. Because it was dark, he misjudged and scooted the chair too close, and when he sat down, their knees brushed. Jess flinched and pulled her knee away, and he did the same. They sat there, unmoving, knees so close she could feel the heat from his skin. She breathed as if through a fireplace bellow: air sucked from her lungs and then blasted back in. But he didn't move the chair.

She tried to think of something to say. She glanced at his profile. That beaky nose with its knuckle in the center. A yellow pencil behind his ear again. She thought of his aspen painting upstairs, soft and milky, and she smelled snow and lemon-soaked apples, and time seemed to slow for her. Dream time, supple and lethargic. Her breath shallow, she pressed her knee closer, skin to skin, almost as an experiment to see what he'd do.

He didn't move. He kept looking straight ahead, but he put his hand on his knee so the edge of his palm brushed her kneecap. A wisp of contact. He still didn't look at her. In her dream state, she reached out and took the pencil from behind his ear. When she did, she heard him give a little sigh. The pencil was warm from his skin, and she held it tight.

He said, "You should go inside. It's late."

His voice startled her. She jumped up from the chair, tugging her shirt down, her legs shaking. All of her, shaking. She stumbled inside, tripping over a rug in the doorway. She climbed into the bed in her best friend's room, listening to her best friend's father move down the hall and climb the stairs to his painting studio. She listened to the creak of footsteps above her. She clutched the pencil, running her thumb down its ridges. She put it lengthwise across her lips and bit it, feeling the soft wood give between her teeth.

When Dani snuck through the window an hour later and whispered, "Hey, are you awake?" Jess feigned sleep. But she did not sleep. She dressed and slipped out the door before Dani was

awake, leaving a note: "Had to get home. Call you later, gator."
Walking home in the cool morning, she shivered, but she wasn't
cold. The opposite. As if someone had struck a match and lit her.
Or more like she was the match, scraping across the red striker
pad, and whoosh. Phosphorescence.

For weeks, she did not see him again. When she came by Dani's
after work or slept over, she would hear footsteps but see no sign
of him. She began to believe she'd dreamed it. Even when she
held the pencil dented with her bite marks, she couldn't be sure.
Because how could she believe it? He was Dani's father. Even if
it had happened, it was an accident. He did not feel what she
did. That heat, that match-struck feeling—that was her problem, not his. She told herself it was no big deal, but when she
saw Mrs. Newell—who seemed always to be dashing from
house to college to theater to home, her dark, winged eyebrows
pulled low—Jess couldn't quite meet her eye, her face aflame.
Her mother went on more dates with Mr. Juarez, and Jess went
on a few dates alone with Warren the Rabbit. When they said
good-bye, she kissed and rubbed up against him. Once she got so
carried away, she bit his lip and drew blood. He pulled away in
surprise. "Ow," he said, as if she'd hurt his feelings.

She worked at the orchard, the days hot and sluggish, making
sure the trees had enough water. Iris called July and August the
water stage, a time crucial to the growth of the nut. A hundred
and fifty gallons a day. Though the monsoon helped, the storms
were not enough. Jess checked and fixed irrigation lines, carried hoses, pushed a wheelbarrow piled high with branches. She
cleared weeds and drove the mower for the first time, cutting
the grass low to keep it from competing for water with the trees.

So much work to protect and nurture those tiny little nuts, and she remembered *botany*, which she'd circled in Big Red's pages. The scientific study of plants. From the root *botane*, "plant." Throughout the day, Jess, too, needed water, gulping it straight from the hose.

On breaks inside, the A/C cooling her sweaty face, she helped Iris map out plans for Sundown at the Orchard, those fall and winter nights when they'd stay open late and sell nuts to the holiday crowds. Jess suggested lining the driveway with luminarias, winding the posts with twinkle lights. "I can help bake," she told Iris, and Iris said, "You'll have school." But Jess wasn't thinking about school. She was thinking about the brush of a palm. She was thinking about hands she had no right to think about. She was looking up the meaning of *spontaneous combustion*.

On her nighttime excursions, she walked into town, up and down through the dips of her unlit road. Once she reached the bottom of the hill, she turned onto Quail Run, passed the swath of the orchard, and then turned onto College Drive, the street that bordered Sycamore College and led to the District. Occasionally she saw people or headlights coming toward her, and she would dive into the shallow drainage ditch and hold her breath, waiting until the footsteps or tires passed. She never went onto campus, even though it was right there, two blocks away from Dani's, less than a mile from her own house. Something about the iron gates created a sense of a barrier, even though they were open, unlocked, and she could see college students along the lit paths, hear shouts and calls and laughter. She was sure the second she set foot inside, they would know she didn't belong.

When she reached Main Street and the District, she sat across from the Woodchute Motor Lodge in the shadowed alcove of a vacant building. From there, unseen, she watched the windows of the motel rooms, the cracks of light through the closed curtains, wondering who was inside, what they were doing on the beds. She caught sight of Stevie Prentiss, the girl with the birthmark, through the window of the office. She wondered at the birthmark's splotchy shape, its visibility even from a distance, and she touched her own face. Birthmark. Marked from birth. What did that mean? Marked for *what*? She watched her drunken classmates gather across the street at Casa Verde and the Patty Melt and next door at the Circle K gas station, hollering to each other out open car windows. Marked to be assholes, fools, fuck-ups. One night she saw Angie Juarez's Impala swing into the motel lot and park in front of Room 7. Angie, Stevie's younger sister Rose, and Beto Navarro hopped out of the car, and Rose ran to the front office. Angie and Beto waited, leaning against the car, until Rose skipped out and unlocked Room 7, and all three headed inside. Jess felt that old twinge of sadness about Angie, their friendship severed for no reason Jess could fathom. She didn't resent her finding new friends, but the moment reasserted a lingering sense of shame, as if she had done something wrong—as if something was wrong with her. And something *was* wrong with her, wasn't it? With Dani, she had finally found friendship, a second family, a welcoming space she wanted to crawl inside and burrow. And now here she was obsessing about a surreal moment with Dani's father, consumed by a ridiculous heat. She didn't know how to fix herself, only that she better figure it out before Dani disappeared too.

She walked through the darkened college neighborhood, past the pretty houses with their tidy shrubs and recessed porches, their soft lights and watered grass. She turned onto Piñon Drive. She passed the Newells, standing in the street to watch the glowing attic window.

In her notebook, with a tooth-gouged yellow No. 2 pencil, she
wrote:

> The nuts grow in clusters,
> oblong and taut,
> tender as limes to the touch.
> They cling to the branches
> afraid of falling
> though fall they must
> come fall
>
> Summer is too soon
> for the shaking season.
> So what is this tremble they feel?
> What is this hot change
> that pushes their skin outward
> their seams like scars?
> Shaking now, shaking
>
> Come, fall.
> Hurry.
> They're losing their grip
> They can't hold on much longer.

Then she erased it, scratched and shaded the page in a fine
sheen of carbon.

In August, weeks before her senior year began, in the last-gasp
days of summer freedom, Jess stayed over at Dani's again. They
stayed up late watching movies and eating Dusty Roads, bowls
of vanilla ice cream sprinkled with malt powder and chocolate

syrup. When Dani fell asleep, Jess lay in bed, straining to hear footsteps, but the house was silent aside from the occasional muffled creak or clang. She went to the kitchen for a glass of water. A door off the kitchen led to the garage, and a strip of light shone beneath it.

She opened the door. Mr. Newell was inside, leaning into the hood of the Squareback. The door swung shut behind her, hitting her heels, and he turned.

"Hello," she said. She lifted her hand but then dropped it. The cement was cool under her bare feet.

"Hello, Jess." He picked up a rag from the workbench and wiped his hands. He wiped and wiped until there couldn't have been a speck of anything left. He sat on the front bumper, his hands braced on his thighs. Then he looked straight at her. Hawk nose, hawklike intensity.

She understood then she hadn't imagined the night on the deck. She knew why she hadn't seen him since. He didn't have to say it. It was there in the solemnness of his face, the furrowed brow, the pulled-down corners of his mouth. She locked her legs together and held the doorframe.

"Sorry," she said. "I'll go."

He said, "It's not your fault."

"What isn't?"

"You know what I mean," he said. He sighed, long and hard, and he pressed down on the bumper, half lifting himself. "You're the age of my child."

"I'm not a child," she said.

"You think you're not." He laughed a little.

At that laugh, the confusion of the past weeks—really of the past year—bloomed into anger. "Don't laugh at me," she said. "Don't assume you know me. You don't know me. I'm not your daughter. Just because you've been this age doesn't mean you know me."

He nodded and wiped his forehead, leaving a black streak. "Sorry. You're right."

Though her skin burned, her teeth began to chatter. She took a step closer to him.

"Stay over there," he said.

"I wasn't—"

"I'm Dani's father. I'm a married man. I love my family. Do you understand?"

"Yes," she said. She shook her head. She understood what he was saying but not what she was feeling. Her bones ached, as if they were growing right that minute, straining against the muscle. She pointed at him. "Is this even real? You're sitting right there?"

"I'm here."

"So what *is* this?"

"I don't know."

"You don't know."

"I don't *know*, Jess." He slapped the rag against his leg.

"But I didn't imagine it, right? You feel it, too?"

He twisted the rag. "We need to forget about this."

The car rocked as he emphasized his words with the weight of his body. He clenched his jaw. He clenched the bumper, the veins in his hands popping. In his body, she saw the truth: it was real. Her first reaction was relief: she was not alone in this feeling. She hadn't made it up. Someone else felt it, too.

He said, "We have to forget it. We have to go back to normal."

Meaning this, what she was feeling, was *ab*normal. That she was abnormal. Wrong. Nothing new there.

Her initial relief turned to excruciating sadness, and tears stung her eyes—which made her furious. Fury that she didn't understand her own emotions, or his, fury at her abnormality, fury at herself for that lustful shaking heat inside, for wanting something she knew to be wrong. All these conflicting emotions surged, combusted, strangely alchemic. She pulled herself to her full height, rising to her tiptoes. *Her rear'd arm / crested the world.*

"Go ahead, Adam," she said, his name in her mouth for the first time. "Forget me."

MAYBE YOU ALREADY KNOW

HI LOVE, IT'S ME. I'M back. I guess I don't need to announce myself, although who knows. I thought I'd kicked this habit years ago, but here I am. I still have days when I want to *talk* to you, like we used to. Sit out on the deck after putting Paul to bed, mix up a gin and tonic, shoot the shit. The worst part is I'm having trouble hearing your voice. I can hear the crickets and cicadas and the fizz of the tonic, I can smell the lime, but I can't remember your damn voice.

I'm out on the deck now. It's late. I just got in. A long day. Lots to tell. The moon's hanging low on the horizon, and the stars are out by the millions. The monsoon blew through earlier, and I can smell the damp grass. You better believe it's pretty, buster. I hope you can see it. I think of you up there as particles, floating above me in some part of the universe. I figure you had to go somewhere. It's like you always quoted Carl Sagan: We are all made of star stuff. I loved how you said that, imitating him. *Starrrr* stuff. *That* I can still hear.

Well, first off, Paul's come home, with Sean. First time since Caryn died. Got here a couple of days ago. Maybe you already know. I don't know how he's doing because he won't tell me anything. You should see him. He looks like my father, with those bushy caterpillar eyebrows. Maybe his will turn gray too. And he looks like you, of course. Those big old ears. Some days he'll turn and I'll see his profile and catch my breath. Smart as ever, but also lost. And angry. That tension still radiates from him. I guess you never saw that part of him, although maybe you know. Heaven forbid I ask him anything. Hates it when I fuss and worry. I hate it myself. I've turned into a big fat worrier, like my mother. I'll bet you can guess how much I like admitting that.

After you died, I used to sneak into Paul's room and stand over his bed and watch his chest rise and fall. I'd stand there in the dark and conjure elaborate scenarios of someone trying to hurt him, and I'd grow murderous in my imagination, punching and kicking at the air, at the fictional intruders, while he lay there sleeping, having exhausted himself from running god knows how many miles. Some nights he wouldn't be there, and I knew he was sneaking out to meet Dani but I never busted him or let on I knew. I worried about him out there, but I worried more if I held too tight, he'd never come home. Well, he's home now.

I know it's not easy for him to be here, but the truth is, it's not easy for me, either. Because it makes me think about you. About how much we lost, about what I'd thought my life was supposed to be. All those emotions I thought I'd buried come rushing back. Because I want to be done—I'm done grieving you, damn it. But that's not how it works. Not for him. Not for me. Coming up on the nineteenth anniversary of me finding you out in the orchard, lying next to the trimmers like you were sleeping. Just taking a nap.

God, we were so young, weren't we? A couple of idiot college dropouts, backpacking around the West, hitchhiking, sleeping under that great big moon, thinking we'd live forever and a day. When your granddad died, us thinking, yes, yes, let's work the land. Another adventure. I remember those early days, here with Paul on my hip, shaking scorpions out of my shoes, whacking at the trees with a broomstick to get the pecans to fall, and thinking, Dear god, what have we done? And there I was not even that much later, a widow at forty-one. Now here I am, almost sixty, an old woman talking to herself out on the porch. Christ on a crutch, as Esther would say.

But you know all this. I'm repeating myself, as always. While we're young, Iris, right? Funny, I know you said that all the time, but I can't hear *how* you said it. Well, we're not young anymore, that's for sure. But I made it. Still here, keeping it together. Mostly. I made it this far without you.

The other big news. A new woman in town, she's a new professor at the Syc, was out walking in the dry wash out by the old lake where you used to fish—shoot, I don't know if I ever told you that story. Not long after you died, a sinkhole opened up under it, and whoosh—it was gone overnight. Maybe I already told you. Anyway, the woman was walking in the wash, said she was looking for rocks to add to Stevie Prentiss's pile. Oh, Stevie. You should see her now. Still as odd as she was as a kid, and for years she's been gathering up stones and placing them inside and around the old lake. She moves them, changes the patterns, adds new circles and lines. It's lovely, actually. Our own strange *Spiral Jetty*. Anyway, the professor! While we're young, Iris! I'm not good with straight lines, buster, never have been.

The point of this is, the professor found bones. Wedged in a deep crack in the wash. They think it might be Jess Winters. I know you never knew her, but maybe you know anyway. That was a tough one when she never came home. I hired her out here, oh, about six months or so after you'd died. She and her mother Maud moved here alone, and Maud delivers our mail here, and I told her I was looking to hire someone part-time, so she sent Jess on over. Great kid. Great worker. Sharp, funny. Quirky, really. Struck me as a kind of old soul. Then all hell broke loose with Adam Newell, and Paul right in the middle of it, like he needed *that* to worry about on top of everything. I didn't know Jess well, certainly not like Maud knew her. She was a lovely girl, but that wasn't it. She loved the orchard, and the fact is, she reminded me of you. She was fascinated by the trees. She soaked up everything I told her—all those things you and I figured out as we spliced together our life out here. And then she was gone, too.

It's hard to believe how long it's been. Maud—every day, she still brings the mail. Neither rain nor sleet nor snow nor missing child. Jesus. Some days I can hardly stand to see her coming. She's changed so much. So gray now, her back humped. We've all been waiting for this news. For any news. Something. I was over there tonight after Esther called me. Esther and I brought food. Sat with her. What else can we do? Rachel would have come, but she's out of town. At this point, there's nothing much to do but wait. The police are running tests. I haven't had a chance to tell Paul yet. He was in bed by the time I got home.

After all this time, still no one knows what happened. I mean, we know what happened before, of course. I was at Thanksgiving dinner, and Rachel blasted the town with that letter. But the night she disappeared, he was in Flagstaff. He still lives up there, I guess. Haven't seen him since. Rachel still doesn't talk to him. I don't know if Dani does. Rachel remarried, gosh, what, ten years ago now? Hugh's a good guy. Town attorney. Ten years younger, good for her. But Dani, poor kid. I know I wasn't sorry when she broke up with Paul. They were too serious, too young. But I didn't think she'd fall apart quite the way she did. Got into Stanford and you better believe Rachel scraped together that tuition. Then she failed out, came home, worked odd jobs. She finished her degree a year ago, finally. Hallelujah, as Rachel said. She works out at the medical clinic now. A phlebotomist. She's living in Esther's guest house. Aside from Maud, I think it hit her the hardest.

So much for plans, eh, Beau? So much for dreams.

Do I need to speak? Maybe you can read my thoughts. Maybe I've breathed you in.

The truth is, Beau, I'm tired. I'm tired of running this place. Our place. There. I said it. Thinking about retiring. About what's next. That's the age I am now.

If Paul comes home for good, then great. He can take it over. If he decides not to, well, then we have a decision to make.

We. After all this time, I still do it. We have a son, we have a grandson, we own an orchard.

I have a decision to make.

I still have the acreage up in Payson. I still think about our plans: selling the orchard, the land, the house. Taking our profits and building our retirement home in the mountains. A house with pine beams and a big fat deck overlooking the lake and not a pecan tree in sight. Hiking, cooking, traveling, reading books, taking care of the grandkids. A perfect life. I'm sure it would have been, or pretty near to it. I don't know. It's easy to sentimentalize, to idealize you. You sure as heck weren't perfect, buster, and neither am I. But somehow we were perfect together. Don't you think?

Anyway, now I have to think about *my* life. I've outlived my husband and a seventeen-year-old girl and friends and too many young soldiers to count and god knows who else. You would think by now I would have a goddamn clue what I want. You'd think I'd have figured it out by now.

Do you know what's in my heart, Beau? What I don't tell you? Can you see inside of me?

Because I've been thinking. Thinking and thinking and thinking. And you know what I want to do? I want to go to college. Almost sixty, and I think it's time for this old girl to learn a thing or two. About art, and philosophy, and literature, and the whole blooming universe, all that *starrrr* stuff. To get out of my body and into my mind for a while.

I wish you were here to tell me if I'm right. I wish I could hear your voice.

THE SHAKING SEASON
September–November 1991

THE ENVELOPE, WITH HER TYPED name and address in the center but the left corner blank, arrived on a Saturday in her mailbox in early September after school had started. Jess collected the mail after work as usual and almost missed it. There was never anything for her, except for those cards from California with her father's phone number, which she stuck in her desk drawer.

Inside was a torn slip of paper folded in half. At the top were two words: "I can't." Beneath was an address and a date—Sept. 7, 1991—followed by the words "after midnight." Adhered to the sheet with two strips of masking tape was a silver key.

Jess sat on her bed and stared at the paper, crushing it in her grip. Of course she knew it was from him, but she didn't understand. She ran her finger over those two cryptic words: *I can't*. If he couldn't, then why was he giving her an address? Was he asking her to meet him, or wasn't he? Can't *what*? See her anymore? Figure out what to do? She recalled her last words, her bold admonition on the last night she'd seen him: *Forget me*. She gasped as she understood.

Her mother pulled into the driveway then, and Jess jumped up from the bed in a panic. She ripped the key from the paper, balled up the note, and threw it in the wastebasket under a tissue and string of floss, then pulled it out and shoved it in the drawer with her father's cards. Her mom called out, "I'm home, J-bird. I picked up dinner. Come eat—I'm starving!" Jess stuffed the key in her pocket, pulled the crumpled paper from the drawer, wrote the address down in her notebook, and tore the paper to bits. Later, she would sneak the town map from the car's glove box, but now she hurried out to meet her mother. That skipping sensation again: a stone across the lake, her ripples bending outward.

At midnight, Jess again opened the front door and slipped outside. Again, she ran on long legs, loping down Roadrunner Lane toward town, a silver key loose in her jeans pocket. A cracked eggshell moon, three-quarters round, lit her way. The desert around her rustled. Nocturnal, like her. In the distance she saw what she thought was another person, but she didn't try to hide, just turned the corner and kept running. Catching speed, she leaped across the low dips and then lunged upward, her thighs burning.

The address was a house on a secluded dead-end street not far from her own. A car sat parked at the end of the street, but not one she recognized. She squinted at a sign in the yard: For Sale. No porch light, no car in the driveway, no movement in the drape-drawn windows. She stood on the curb and scanned the house, unsure what to do next. The only light was at a neighbor's house several yards up the street.

She walked up to the front door. Still uncertain, she slid the key in the lock and turned it just as the door opened.

"Quickly," he said. He moved to let her in, and she stepped over the threshold.

Inside, her nostrils flared at the warm air, stagnant with lemon cleaner and cigarette smoke. The back window's curtains, partly drawn, let in a shaft of moonlight, and she could see that the entryway opened into a large carpeted living room. Not a stick of furniture. No trace of who once lived here. He knelt in the center of the living room, where he'd spread a blan-

ket, and turned on a small propane camping lantern. Its fabric
bulbs glowed white.

"Come in," he said, gesturing toward the blanket.

She hovered near the blanket and then sat cross-legged in the
corner of the room, her back against the wall. She hadn't yet
looked him in the face. "Whose house is this?"

"A client's," he said. He wore loose Bermuda shorts and tennis
shoes without socks, a windbreaker left unzipped. "It's been on
the market a while. Listed too high, though they won't listen
to me." He spoke faster than usual and fiddled with his jacket
zipper. Instead of sitting, he began to pace along the edge of the
blanket.

She pulled her knees up and rested her chin on them, watching
his feet move back and forth on the carpet.

"It's—safe," he said. "They moved out of town. No one will
come."

"I see," she said. The words sounded dramatic, suggesting she
understood the subtext, which was the farthest thing from the
truth. She saw nothing. She couldn't see beyond her own hands.
She couldn't see his face. And she did not feel in any way safe as
the musty air pressed down on her, as the silence stretched.

He said, "I wasn't sure you would show up."

"I wasn't sure I should."

"I know. This is strange." He rubbed his hand over his hair.
He began to walk the whole square of the blanket, stepping along
its sides as if it were a maze. "I wanted to talk to you," he said.
"In private."

"What about?"

"Jess," he said. He stopped pacing and knelt on the blanket,
facing her. He gazed at her across the lantern, his face in shadow.

"We're supposed to forget it. Go back to *normal*," she said.

That was the word she'd repeated to herself in the last three weeks, as she trudged through the orchard in the heat, the ground slick and muddy from monsoon rain, as she huddled on the couch next to her mother watching *Masterpiece Mystery*, as she curled in her bed with a book open, unread, as she started her senior year, walking the halls with her best friend but unable to meet her eyes.

He crawled toward her in the corner. She could see his face now, the shadow of stubble, the knuckle in his nose, a divot in his left eyebrow she hadn't noticed before.

He said, "I can't sleep. I can't stop thinking about it. I feel like I'm losing my mind. Trying to figure it out. To explain it away. I keep going round and round. All the reasons it's wrong, all the reasons I'm a terrible person for even *thinking* about it."

She nodded. If she understood anything, it was spinning thoughts and feeling terrible. She couldn't remember the last time she'd slept through the night. She wanted to punch a hole in her skull to release the pressure.

"Nothing's changed," he said. "It's still wrong." He moved closer. He kneeled in front of her, his face lit from below, mottled with shadow. The knot in his throat moved up and down. "I don't understand what's happening. Is this a midlife crisis? Is this what everyone talks about?"

"I don't know," Jess said.

"No." He laughed a little. "Neither do I. I guess I wanted to see you face to face. To try to make some sense out of it."

She stared at him through the lantern's glow. "Here I am."

"There you are. God. I look at you, and—" He took an unsteady breath and tapped his chest. "This is what I'm worried about. This thing here." He thumped his sternum. "This is what I'm afraid to name."

She thought of Dani tracing her back in the tent in Mexico, the last word on their last night, the word she could not name either. Her toes curled inside her sneakers, and her jaw locked with the force of sensation in her.

He held up a shaking hand. "Actually I'm terrified." He dropped his hand. "What do you think about this? What are you thinking?"

That was the thing: for the first time in weeks, she wasn't. Her mind was an exquisite blank. All she had was her flushed body, a toe-curling heat. She wanted to touch him, to have him touch her too. She unfolded herself and rose to her knees, thinking, yes, yes, *unfold, un*fold.

She leaned in, reaching for his face—the face that had been at the fringe of her consciousness all day and night, the face that materialized behind her eyes at the orchard, in the grocery store, in the shower, in her school desk, on her pillow, his knuckled-nosed, dark-eyed face above her, beneath her, between her hands.

The doorbell rang.

Jess fell backward and scrambled to her feet. Adam jumped up too. He put a finger to his lips, miming quiet.

"Who is it?" he called out.

"Detective Alvarez," the booming voice said. "Sycamore Police. We had a call."

Adam kept his finger at his lips and pointed to the hallway. Jess rushed to the hall and ducked into the bathroom, hiding behind the door.

She heard Adam open the door, the murmur of voices. She closed her eyes, crossing her legs tight at the ankle. The bathroom smelled of pine cleaner. Her foot hit the spring bumper on the bottom of the wall and set off a loud twang. She held her breath, but the voices didn't pause. Tears stung her eyes, and she clenched the key in her pocket. What was she doing here? What the hell was she thinking? She thought of Dani, curled up asleep in her twin bed, sure her father was asleep down the hall, not in a stranger's house in the middle of the night with her best friend.

The door shut, and after a moment Adam called, "Jess? It's okay to come out."

She returned to the main room. Adam stood next to the blanket.

He said, "A neighbor called. Saw movement. Thought it was a break-in. I told the officer I was alone, doing some paperwork."

"So, not safe after all." She gave a twisted smile.

He shoved his hands in the pockets of the windbreaker, his head bowed. Seeing him like that, in an ugly jacket with his baggy shorts and sneakers, it was as if someone had snapped the lights on. A father. Dani's dad. This was not what she had been imagining. This was not what she dreamed.

He held up a hand. "Nothing happened. It's okay. But we can't tell anyone. This is—"

"Wrong." As in abnormal.

"Yes," he said.

"I won't tell," she said. Not her mother, not Dani, obviously. The only way she could tell would be to write it in her notebook, but she already knew she wouldn't write a word about it. Because she didn't have the words.

"No harm done," he said.

Except that wasn't true, was it? If they could tell no one, especially not her best friend? If she had the sick sense of carrying a secret inside?

"I have to go," she said.

And go she did. She ran to the front door and bolted through it. With her long legs, she leaped off the low step, her tennis shoes crunching on the gravel walkway and then thudding on the pavement. She ran all the way home, the key bouncing in her pocket, chased by the rustling darkness, by what she had wanted, by what she had *almost* done, by what she could not tell.

Normal. Okay. She could do this.

Days, she walked the halls. She went to physics and learned about chaos theory and Schrodinger's cat and mass and gravitational force. She went to AP English and learned about comedies and tragedies, about the nine circles of hell, and wrote about the meaning of the color yellow in *The Great Gatsby*. She recited French phrases to her French teacher, she ran the spongy track in PE. She slumped in desks, taking tests, taking notes, taking in her teachers' wisdom, ignoring the desire that surged through her body like a virus. Days, she ate lunch with Dani, Paul, and Warren. She rode in the Squareback with them to pick up burgers and fries from the Patty Melt and tacos from Casa Verde, snuggling with Warren in the back seat, whispering to him about meeting over the weekend. Normal. A girlfriend moving to the next level with her nice boyfriend. Days, she did her homework. She studied with Dani at the library but stayed away from her house, claiming her mom wanted to spend more time with her this last year, her final year of high school. Nothing out of the ordinary. A regular teenager.

Nights, she met up with Warren, both with her mother's knowledge and without. Young rabbity Warren with his sweet dry pecks, his earnest rubbing through his jeans. She grabbed him and tumbled down with him into the rabbit hole of sex. They fumbled and twisted in the back seat of his car, wishing they had more space, and she whispered, I know a place. They parked at the end of the street of the For Sale house and, bent low, snuck through the unfenced yard to the back door, where she pulled the silver key from her pocket. Warren, caught up in the moment, didn't even ask how she got it. Into the house they went, naked house, bereft of furniture and light. She, too, stripped naked, clothing wadded on the carpet, as she tamped down the memory of the man she first came here with, of the face that still showed up in her dreams. She moved out of her head into her body, happy to find that this boy had more finesse than the first one, with his hurried thrusts and clumsy hands. Lit by the moon through the window, she moved atop him and beneath him—voracious bodies, celestial bodies, entwined. She replaced her secret desire with this one, her jawline rashed from that enthusiastic boy's stubble.

In October, nights grew crisp. Pumpkins appeared on porches, and clusters of crimson and yellow dotted the Black Hills. Jess pulled her red puffy coat out of the closet again for those nights that dipped into the forties and her breath turned white. Those nights, her coat became a pillow on the flat floor, soft against her neck and spine as her heels and knees dug hard, as she braced herself against walls and doorjambs. Teenage sex, condom wrappers, trying out new positions in a stranger's house they snuck into. Normal. This was normal.

"I love you, Jess," Warren said. "God, God."

And Jess, her night self, said it back, on her back: love, Warren, God, her own kind of trinity, not sure which one she was calling for. She rolled over and straddled him, rocking faster, making herself believe.

Days, she turned in papers late and zoned out in class. Her grades fell as the SATs and college application deadlines loomed.

Days, she woke sore, her hips and thighs aching. The raw, dry air stung her chafed skin, and she rubbed lotion on the carpet burn on her knees and backside. She looked to the side of the

mirror, unable to meet her own gaze, this day person, this peripheral girl with the shadowy eyes.

Days, her mind broke through the surface, gasping. Love,
Warren had said. Love, she'd said, too, but she knew it wasn't
true, at least not how she felt for him, the boy to whom she'd
transferred her desire. As to what she felt in her secret heart, she
didn't know. Capital L something, all right. She checked the the-
saurus. Lustful. Lewd, Libidinous, Licentious, Lascivious. Liar.
She filled in the blanks of herself: I am, you are, she is.

Days, she touched the marks on her locker where those hateful
words had been scrubbed off: slut, cunt, Jess Winters *spreads.*
Not true before, but now they were—at least the last part, and
even then she shivered with the force of her night desire, the
image of someone pushing her knees outward. She rubbed the
marks with her thumb, shut the locker door with a soft click,
holding her bag tight to her chest. She looked at her feet instead
of finding a spot on the wall. She shuffled. She did not leap.

Days, Dani said, "Are you okay? You seem, I don't know, distant." And Jess said, "No, just tired," but she couldn't meet her
eyes—eyes like her father's.

Days, Jess thought of her own father in California, well into
his new life, his cards with their scrawled bleats—*Miss you, my
beautiful girl. Give me a call sometime*—stuffed in her desk
drawer. Her father, the great betrayer. She thought of her low
moans in the night house as she pictured a forbidden face, her
secret thoughts on nights she lay in bed alone, and she wondered
if her father had felt that way too: the shame and pleasure fused,
hating himself but doing it anyway. Perhaps she was his daughter
after all.

Days, she didn't open her notebook. She didn't write a word.
She chewed rubber bands until her jaw ached.

Days, over dinner, her mother leaned across the table. *What's going on? Tell me, J-bird. Do you need a tutor? What's the problem? I thought you were doing better. This isn't you.*

No, it wasn't her. At least, it wasn't all of her. It was the normal part trying to kill the other part. Two halves, split in two, day and night, night and day. She didn't know which side she was anymore, or how to fuse herself together.

The end of October brought the start of the shaking season. On weekend days at the orchard, Jess watched Iris and Paul and two hired men haul out the sticks and the three-legged machine with its extended mechanical arm and clamp. The machine's arm clutched the tree's trunk and *shook*. As the ground vibrated and the shells rained down, Jess planted her feet as if she might be knocked off balance and flung to the ground herself.

She helped rake the branches, dried leaves, and nuts into windrows, which they shoveled into small trailers and hauled to the cleaning shed. Jess raked until she had blisters inside her cloth gloves, until she had no strength to grip the handle. She pushed herself to exhaustion—into her body again, again to forget, or maybe to punish, she wasn't sure. All she knew was she could fall asleep those nights, her fingernails and nostrils crusted with dirt.

In the shed, they separated the nuts with screens and blowers, and then sanitized and dried them. They shelled some, cracking open the burnished brown outer layer and harvesting the nut, and left others intact, before bringing them to the office for packaging. Packaging became Jess's job. Her hands in plastic gloves, she scooped and tied the sacks, labeled them, and boxed them for shipping. She kept her mind on the monotony of the routine— scoop, scoop, tie, label. But sometimes she stopped and held up a shelled pecan. Here it was, that tiny nut formed, emerging into the world with its strange bumps and ridges. Without its shell, it seemed vulnerable, exposed.

She bit its soft flesh, trying to savor its rich taste, but instead she thought of pencils. She spit it into her palm.

The end of the month was both Dani's eighteenth birthday and, of course, Halloween. Jess, Dani, Paul, and Warren were going to dress in costumes and go to the town festival. A few days before, Dani stopped Jess at her locker. She grabbed Jess by the elbow, squeezing hard. Jess froze. But then Dani loosened her grip.

"Can you come by the HealthCo after school? It's important," she said. Her eyes grew red and watery behind her round frames.

Jess nodded yes, and after school, she waited for Dani at the pharmacy counter behind another customer—Stevie Prentiss, the girl from the Woodchute Motor Lodge. Looking at Stevie's birthmark, Jess touched her own cheek. Stevie turned and caught Jess doing it.

"It's not contagious," Stevie said.

Jess dropped her hand, and her face flamed. "I'm not—" She wanted to say she wasn't mocking, only curious, but she realized how awful that sounded. Stevie wasn't a sideshow.

"Sorry," she said.

Stevie shrugged and turned to the counter.

Dani came out of the back room and called to the pharmacist, "I'm going on break." She grabbed Jess's hand without a word and pulled her down the aisle to the HealthCo bathroom.

Inside, the small bathroom held a toilet, a pedestal sink, a metal trash can with rust stains down the side, a mop inside a bucket, and a wire shelf cluttered with boxes and cleaning bottles. The sickly sweet air freshener made Jess think of choking down purple cough syrup.

Dani locked the door, lifted her shirt, and pulled out a box from her waistband. "I'm late," she said.

Jess stared at the box and then at Dani's face. "Shit," she said.

"No kidding. I didn't want to do this alone." She pulled out a wrapped stick. "I already read the instructions. Pee on the end and then wait two minutes."

Jess looked away as Dani stepped to the toilet and unzipped. Dani peed and flushed, holding the stick out with two fingers. She set the stick on the toilet tank and checked her watch before pumping chalky pink soap into her hands. "Two minutes," she said.

Jess checked hers too. "Got it."

"Okay," Dani said. "Okay. Talk to me. Tell me things. Distract me." She shook her hands dry and paced the room in two steps.

"What do you want to know?"

"Anything," she said. "Everything."

Jess couldn't do either. She couldn't even come close.

She said, "It's going to be fine."

Dani gave a jittery laugh. "But what if it isn't?"

"Then we deal with it," she said.

"I can't have a *baby*." She looked at herself in the mirror and slapped her cheeks, hard, twice, three times, until they bloomed red.

"Don't," Jess said. "Dani, stop."

"Time," Dani said.

"One minute."

"I feel like I'm going to pass out. It's stifling in here. God," she said, pulling at the neck of her T-shirt, stretching it limp. She took off her glasses and wiped the lenses with the hem. "What if it's positive? My parents are going to freak."

Jess looked at her tennis shoes, tapped the toes. One of the laces dragged on the linoleum. "It won't be."

"I missed a pill a few weeks ago. I'm an idiot."

"You're not," Jess said.

"Wouldn't everyone love that. Valedictorian gets knocked up, ruins her life."

"Okay, time," Jess said.

Dani rubbed her hands on her jeans. "I can't look. Will you? Please. I can't."

"Of course." Jess leaned over the toilet and looked at the lines. She smiled and gave a thumbs up. "Negative."

Dani whooped. She launched herself at Jess, hugging her around the waist, her glasses digging into Jess's collarbone.

"Thank you," she said. "I don't know what I'd do without you."

Jess patted Dani's back, her nostrils flaring as she caught the scent of her hair. The same shampoo as her father.

Dani pulled away, wiping under her eyes. "I better get going. We'll celebrate this weekend. With a cornball hay maze and the world's stupidest haunted house. Spaghetti brains and grape eyeballs. Seriously." She tossed the box and stick into the metal trash can. "Can you stay over this weekend? Please? We haven't had any time."

"I'll ask," Jess said.

Dani gave her one more quick squeeze. Over Dani's head, Jess watched the metal trash can lid swing like a broken jaw.

Warren called the next day, and she told him she couldn't go out. She wasn't feeling well. He called again, and she didn't answer. The machine clicked on and off, on and off.

Finally she picked up.

"Jess?" a voice said. A man's voice, but not Warren's. "It's Adam."

"Oh." Her heart thudded hard, and her stomach dropped. "Hey."

"I just want to talk a minute. To check in."

"Okay."

"How are you?"

"Fine."

"You don't sound fine."

She bit her lip, covered the receiver with her palm.

"Jess? Are you there?"

"I'm here," she said. "I don't know. I guess I don't have anything to say."

He paused for a long moment. She almost said hello, wondering if he'd hung up.

"Done with the old man, are we? You had your fun?"

She blinked at his low voice, the anger in it. She frowned. "It never got started," she said. "Remember? And it wasn't fun. None of this has been fun."

"Like with your little boyfriend?" He laughed. "I saw you at the house."

Jess frowned. "Are you following me?"

"Stay out of there."

"I'm not doing anything wrong," she said. "I'm doing what I'm supposed to be doing."

"What's that? Breaking into houses and fucking boys on the carpet?"

"Yes. *Fucking*." She spat the word, one she never used for sex, but it felt good to say it, angry herself now. Angry *at* herself, at him, at all of it.

He breathed into the receiver, and she plucked a loose thread on her shirt, breaking it off. "It wasn't real," she said. "Between us."

"It's real to me," he said.

"They're real," she said. "Your daughter and wife."

"Jess," he said. "I—"

"Don't say it," she said. She hung up, staring at the receiver as if it might speak.

After the Halloween festival, around midnight, Jess, Dani, and the boys piled out of the car in Dani's driveway, two rumpled flappers with wilting feathers in their headbands and two gangsters with crooked mustaches. Giddy from sipping the beer Warren brought, Jess kissed him, happy to be young again, to find herself a teenager out on a Halloween night. A festival, a six-pack tucked in the wheel well, jokes and music hovering in the air with their pluming white breaths. A boy her age with beery kisses and a gentle smile, pressing his hips against her on the front fender outside her best friend's house. She had handfuls of mini candy bars in her bag to share with her mom tomorrow after dinner— chili and cornbread, their favorite fall meal. She had Dani, waiting on the porch, and they'd go inside and talk late into the night.

Normal.

She kissed Warren hard on the mouth and looked up at the dark attic window. She was sure she saw the blind twitch.

In November, the week before Thanksgiving, in the heart of the harvest, Sundown at the Orchard began. Jess helped Iris blast the town and region with flyers and coupons to get the word out. She and Iris wrapped the shop and outlying posts with hundreds of twinkle lights, lined the gravel driveway with brown paper luminarias, decorated and organized the bags of pecans and pies and pecan sandies Iris baked with the help of Ms. G and other women in town. Tourists flocked in from Sedona and on their way down from Jerome, bundled in their coats and hats except the ones from back east in their shirtsleeves, who scoffed, "Cold, ha! It's three degrees at home right now!" They loaded up on gifts and mingled with the locals, who made jokes about their accents and cowboy boots after they left, who gossiped in the corners and drank cider and coffee from little Styrofoam cups.

After nine on the Wednesday before Thanksgiving, when they'd almost sold out of pecans, Jess helped Paul and Iris clean up and around ten bundled herself in her puffy coat and a wool cap and gloves. Since she'd had to work late, she had her mom's car. The engine churned twice and then kicked, and she goosed the gas, tucking her knit skirt around her calves for warmth. She turned on the headlights, and that's when she noticed a piece of paper tucked under the driver's-side wiper.

A note: *Meet me? Last time, I promise. I'll leave you alone. I'll be in the orchard.*

She looked around for him, but Iris had turned off the shop lights. She and Paul were in their house, headed to bed.

She turned off the car and got out. She peered down the dark rows of trees and walked into them. The moon was almost full, bright enough she could see her shadow. The shells they'd missed in the sweep crunched under her shoes. She thrust her hands into her coat pockets, moving farther into the trees, checking behind her when she heard a muffled crack. Just the wind in the branches.

He leaned against a tree at the end of the row. He stood up straight when she reached him.

"Thanks for coming," he said.

"I'm not staying," she said. "What do you want?"

"To talk a minute. To say a few things."

"Okay," she said. "Talk."

"I know I handled this terribly." His voice rose, and she understood he was angry. Angry with her. "I understand why you have to shut me out. I get it. But don't act like you didn't feel it. You felt everything."

She folded her arms. "What is your problem? Nothing happened. It's over. I'm not going to tell, if that's what you're worried about. Dani's my best friend. I wouldn't hurt her."

He raised his voice. "I have to watch you kissing that boy in my driveway. You're bringing sweet potatoes to my goddamn house for Thanksgiving tomorrow. Jesus Christ." His voice broke. He bent at the waist and covered his face. His eyes gleamed. That got to her. That, and the desperate choke in his voice.

"I'm sorry," she said. She slumped against the tree, the bark scratching her jacket.

"No, I'm sorry." He grabbed handfuls of his hair and pulled. "I don't know what's wrong with me. I don't know what I'm doing. I've never done anything like this before. Everything's a mess. I'm trying to deal with my mother's house, and I swear, I don't even know what day it is."

"Thanksgiving," she said.

He laughed a little and stepped closer to her. She didn't move away.

He reached out and cupped her cheek. "God, Jess. Look at you. I can't stop looking at you. It's like I'm seeing for the first time."

She didn't push his hand away. She lifted her head and stared up through the bare branches, unblinking. For a brief moment, she pressed her face into his palm, and then something moved in the periphery of her vision.

"Did you see that?" She scanned the trees but could see nothing, could hear only a faint rustle, the low hoot of an owl in the distance.

"No. What?" He glanced behind him. "Nothing's there. Jess, listen."

"But what if someone comes?"

"I love you," he said. He traced her eyebrow with his thumb. "That's what I wanted to say."

"No," she said. "I love Warren."

He laughed. "No. You don't."

"Shut up," she said, sighing as he touched her cheek. "Don't tell me who I love."

He slid his hand to her neck, leaned down, and kissed her forehead. "Me," he said.

"No. I can't love you."

"Can't, or don't?"

She pulled her face away from his hand. She looked over his shoulder, through the trees toward the orchard office, catching a glimpse of the twinkle lights. "I have to go," she said.

"Please stay." His breath was warm on her forehead, and that traitorous heat snuck in, coiled in her belly. She wanted to wrap her legs around him, let him push her up against the tree, let the bark chafe her jacket and scalp. She wanted to do with him what she did with that sweet boy in the night house. Rutting, she thought, and her whole body flushed.

She pushed his chest and stepped around him. "Go home to your daughter, Adam. To your wife. To your fucking family. You love them."

"Jess—"

"Shut up!" She pulled her hat lower and covered her ears. She ran through the trees to the car, hands to ears, blocking out his voice behind her. In the driver's seat, she fumbled with the keys, her fingers numb. All of her, numb, frozen with fear.

WHO, WHAT, WHERE, WHEN

SIXTEEN FEET UP A LADDER, Paul Overton scraped dried paint off the fascia boards of the orchard's cleaning shed. The dry flakes fluttered down, dusting the tops of his boots and the ladder rungs and the gallon of Old Forest Green at the bottom. The extension ladder, propped at a steep vertical pitch, snapped against the roof like a sail in sharp wind with each jerk of his arm. He knew better. His father had taught him how to set a ladder, but these days he was having trouble remembering what day it was. Who, What, Where, When, Why, How: the journalist's credo. Get it in the lede, tight, no frills, and now fuck all if he couldn't do it for himself. *Who?* Who knew anymore. *What?* Good question. He couldn't remember *what* was on the grocery list or *what* he was about to say in the middle of a sentence or *what* bills were due *when.* He couldn't remember *what* to eat, *when* to sleep, *when* to go to work, *where* he was when he woke up or *how* he got there or *why* he couldn't stop the ball of rage expanding in his stomach.

Instead, his head was cluttered with images. He kept seeing Caryn: how she rose earlier and earlier in the weeks before she couldn't get out of bed at all; he'd find her in the kitchen, lit by the streetlight, sheet creases in her cheek. "I don't want to sleep," she'd say, staring out the window, at the sun on the cusp of rising. "I don't want to miss any more of it." (*Why*: Because she was dying, at motherfucking thirty-four years of age.) He kept seeing Sean on that bike. (*When*: Two days ago, four months after they buried his mother.) The boy swerved toward the curb at the same moment Paul realized he'd fallen too far behind to grab him (*Why*: Because he'd been lost in thinking about his late wife), and then Sean was off the curb and into the street, and Paul was shouting and running faster than he'd ever run. He heard the squeal of brakes as he flung himself toward the bike and knocked Sean to the pavement. Both of them lay on the hot street, the bumper of a car above Paul's shoulder, Paul's left wrist ballooning and Sean with a scraped elbow and knee.

And so Paul had brought his boy—and himself—home, to figure out what to do next. Stay in Phoenix? Sell the house? Donate her clothes? And fuck all if now he hadn't added a film reel of his childhood to the images clogging his mind: his father carrying this aluminum ladder around the orchard, leaning it on a pecan trunk and then climbing high into the branches. His mother, her cloud of hair shaved into the sink the week after his father's funeral. Dani Newell beneath him, her skirt up around her waist. Jess Winters, her hands flailing. And now, now, the news about the bones. He didn't think he could take one more picture in his head. He scraped until he was out of breath and had to grab the roof with his injured hand to keep from flying backward.

Paul rested his forearms on the roof and took a sip of coffee from the mug he'd set on the attached paint tray. He tried to catch his breath. The morning air was still cool, a bit humid, rich with the smell of dirt and citrusy tang of the pecan trees. At home in Phoenix, it'd be well over 90 degrees. He'd grown to love the wild, never-ending summer heat, when it was 100 degrees at midnight when he stepped out of the newspaper office after filing a breaking story. He'd go running at that late hour—the best way to get rid of any simmering anger, which had over the years led him to throw and break tools, to kick and punch through dry-wall, until Caryn got him to see a counselor. After his run, he'd stop to stretch, the sidewalk still hot under his fingers, and then he'd go home to his wife and baby son. He'd step inside, and except for the glow of a nightlight in the hall bath, all was dark, the windows blocked with blackout curtains to help with the heat and with Caryn's bouts of insomnia. A silence like the orchard, solemn and protected among the trees. He found his way to them with his eyes closed. "Where are you?" Caryn would say, flinging out her arm from the sheets, and he'd say, "I'm right here." And he would think of another sense of *right*: restored, safe, healthy. Yes, he'd think, touching his wife's cheek. He was right, here.

He craned his neck and looked at the symmetrical rows of trees, shaggy now with their tooth-edged leaflets and bent with the weight of the ripening pecans. Paul used to run inside those trees, up and down, for miles. He'd been assured by the linearity, the routine in a world upended by his father's sudden death. In these days he'd been home, he'd been running them in the early mornings, taking the eastern rows to the river path on the far end. He'd then loop the town, waving to Stevie Prentiss at the old lake and to the woman who walked in the bright green visor and to Angie Juarez on her way to the shop, but otherwise keeping his head down.

Though he had yet to admit it, he knew why he had come. This visit was more than a visit. He was trying this on for him and Sean, seeing if he could be here again, if he could move from journalist to pecan orchard owner, from city to town, from his future to his past. His mother told him he was welcome to stay as long as he needed. She told him she could help with Sean. She said, "This is your home, son." But was it? He couldn't explain the relief he felt (and guilt for that relief) away from here. He couldn't tell her he'd only felt able to make a family once he'd left this place where everything had fallen apart. Nothing was right, here. Of course, now the family he made had fallen apart too. Caryn was gone, and Paul had no choice but to change. *Who*: a widower, a father of a four-year-old boy.

"Dad!" Sean called.

Startled, Paul turned, and with the sway of his body, the ladder popped off the roof. He pitched his weight forward until it snapped tight again. His son stood near the base of the ladder with Iris, who held Sean's hand and waved a newspaper. She wore her slippers and cotton nightdress. She said something he couldn't make out.

"Can't hear you!" he called. He could hardly hear her in the house, either. In her socks or foam slippers, she whispered around the wood floors. She was sixty now, an age he could no longer ignore, her silver hair still cropped short.

"Come down," Iris said. "Esther's here. You'll want to see this." She shook the paper, and even from that height he could see the loose skin drooping on the underside of her arm like a wet sock. He looked at the fascia board. She had lived long enough to turn sixty. *Who*: his mother, a widow for almost twenty years. He knew what she wanted to show him, the news he'd seen in the paper at the coffee shop early that morning. *Who, what, where, when*: Jess Winters, a girl gone missing at age seventeen from Sycamore almost two decades ago. *Why, how*: No one knew.

He said, "I saw it."

"Are you okay up there? Be careful. That ladder looks off."

"Mom, I'm fine." He tried not to bristle at her tone, her constant clucking and worrying. "I'll be down in a minute, okay? Let me finish this stretch."

Iris didn't answer. When he glanced down, she gazed at the orchard rows, shielding her eyes.

"Miss Esther brought *doughnuts*, Dad," Sean said. "Doughnuts, doughnuts, doughnuts." He dropped Iris's hand and started to run in circles, his pajama top ballooning with air. The white bandage on his knee flapped loose.

Iris squinted up at Paul and swatted the paper against her open palm. "Come down, honey. And be careful." She walked toward the house, seeming to float across the grass.

He sighed and started down, keeping his weight forward. He needed to reset the ladder anyway.

"Hey, Esther," Paul said, leaning into her hug. She still smelled like the vanilla lotion she'd kept on her school desk—he always thought of her when Caryn used a store tester. Esther had been the first one there when his father died, bringing box after box of pastries and answering the door and phone and running errands. She didn't look much different than she had then, a little heavier around the hips maybe, a little grayer in her frizzy curls. Her face, with those sharp blue eyes and round chin, reminded him of a cat. Or an elf. It always had shamed him when he would get aroused when she'd pace in front of the class in all her loud strangeness, her skirts swirling like a dust devil. Of course, he could get aroused by a stiff wind then. Hell, just the word *stiff* would do the trick. But she was the one who taught him how to write. "Stop bullshitting," she'd write in the margins. "Say what you mean. Shut up and get on with it, darling. SNORE. Get to the point. Careful with commas; they can change everything."

"Hey yourself, honey," Esther said. "Goddamn it. I hate it for you. Hate it."

He pulled away gently. "Thanks."

"Fucking cancer."

Iris said, "Esther," and nodded at Sean, who sat at the counter with a doughnut on a plate in front of him. His eyes were round.

Esther said, "There's a time and place for swearing, darling, and this is one of them. I'm sure your father knows."

Paul said, "We left the cuss jar at home, didn't we, buddy?"

Sean nodded and stuck his finger in the hole of his doughnut. "The f-word's a quarter."

Esther laughed. "Smart kid." She pointed at the white pastry box on the counter, printed with YUM in bright yellow block letters. "Have one. Save me from myself."

Iris pointed at Sean's doughnut. "Eat. Don't play with it."

"I am," Sean said. He broke off a piece but didn't put it in his mouth.

Esther touched Paul's arm. "Tell me about the news racket. I keep track of your bylines. You keeping those crooks in the legislature on their toes?"

"Trying," Paul said. "I'm on leave right now."

"Of course you are." She smacked her forehead and then tapped the paper folded at her elbow. "You saw the paper today?"

He nodded. "This morning when I went for coffee."

Iris said, "I still can't believe it. I can't believe it's her."

"Who?" Sean said.

"Oh, a friend of your father's from high school," Iris said.

Paul shook his head, irritated by the description. "Not exactly a friend. Someone I knew."

Iris frowned at him. "She was a friend. A good kid," she said. "I don't care about the rest of it." She picked up a cloth from the sink and wiped the counter.

His hands curled into fists. "You don't care about what they did to Dani? Or Rachel?"

"They didn't do it *to* Dani and Rachel. It happened."

"It didn't just happen. It wasn't an act of God, like a hurricane or something."

"So what?" Iris said. "That's not what we're talking about. What is wrong with you? Think about her mother. Think about the bigger picture here."

"Bones in a dry wash," Esther said. "A goddamn ditch."

Sean looked at Paul. "What bones, Daddy?"

Paul patted Sean's back. "Nothing. It's okay, buddy." He knocked his sprained wrist against the counter and winced. He rubbed at the elastic bandage. "I forgave them a long time ago."

Esther narrowed her eyes. "Forgave them? How noble of you." She snorted. "What did you have to forgive? What business was it of yours? I love Dani and Rachel, too, but, honey, this isn't the time for petty teenage grievances."

He started at the vehemence in her tone. "They were like family to me. In a way."

"They weren't your family," Iris said.

"I said 'like' family. But they might have been if—"

"You weren't going to marry her," Iris said. "You were too young."

"Marry who?" Sean picked at the bandage at his elbow. "Mama?"

"No, buddy. It's okay. Leave that alone."

Iris scrubbed at a spot on the tile. "I did my best, you know. I did my best without him. I made the best family I could."

Paul blinked. He saw her standing over the sink with the clippers, buzzing her head, the clouds of hair falling to the basin. She'd said, "Who needs it?" She'd never grown it out again, kept it cropped short.

"Mom, I know that. That's not what I'm saying."

Esther folded her arms on the counter and rested her chin on her forearms. "Adam was like your father."

"No," Paul said. He pictured Adam Newell, the man with his face contorted at the dinner table, the man in the moonlit orchard. That old angry heat expanded in his stomach, a sensation that had died down once he'd moved away but with which he always wrestled. *Deep breaths, love,* he could hear Caryn say. *I don't want your heart to blow.*

"He wasn't like my father. He was in no way like my father."

"No, I mean he was like family, like a father figure," Esther said. "That's why you took it to heart."

He clenched his jaw. "He was not like my father in any way."

"Okay." Esther sighed. "Whatever you say."

"But he was *Dani's* father."

"Dani's father," Esther said. "But not Jess's."

The heat pushed its way up into his limbs. He leaned over the counter, folded the top of the doughnut box down, and then squashed the box with the heels of his hands, flattening whatever remained inside. They all stared at him. Sean peeled off his elbow bandage and stuffed it inside the hole of the doughnut. His elbow scab had turned a reddish purple.

"Well, I guess that's that." Esther stood up and dusted her hands.

"Paul," Iris said.

Paul pointed at the crushed box, angry at himself now for losing control. "Can we talk about something else?"

Esther said, "I have to be going anyway. I have to get to the bakery. Stop by if you like. Dani's renting my guest house now. She works at the medical clinic. Alive and well." She picked up her purse and walked to the door. She opened it and looked at him. "Adam's still up in Kachina Village, as far as I know. Alone." She smiled and shut the door with a gentle click.

Paul stared at the flattened box. Out of the corner of his eye, he could see Iris watching him as she wrung the cloth in her hands. Sean swiveled his stool from side to side. His fingers were brown with maple glaze.

"Don't ask me if I'm okay," he said to Iris.

"I'm not. I won't."

To Sean, Paul said, "Okay, let's get you cleaned up, buddy. Grandma's taking you to the library for story time."

"I am," Iris said. "You bet."

"We're family, right, Grandma?" Sean said.

"That's right, honey," she said to Sean, but looking at Paul. "We sure are."

Paul lifted Sean from the stool and carried him to the sink, biting his lip at the pain in his wrist. He turned on the faucet and lifted the boy up by the waist. "Rinse."

Sean rubbed his hands under the stream of water. "What happened to your friend, Daddy? Did she die too?"

"I don't know, buddy." Paul glanced at his mother, who cupped her hand over her mouth. He held the boy tight and let the water run.

Paul reset the ladder at the right pitch and climbed up. He kept scraping. The old paint had blistered and cracked, and he had to scrape down to bare wood. He'd have to prime before he put on another coat. His father had taught him that, too. Not Adam Newell. If he had a father figure beyond his own, it was Caryn's father, Ken, a retired police detective who cried at old songs and weddings and baby pictures.

If Paul was honest, though, it wasn't as simple as his denial to Esther and his mother. The Newells indeed had been a family to him, and Adam a kind of parent. Of course they had. Given the timing—he'd started dating Dani six months after his father died—it would have been strange had he not attached himself as he had, if he hadn't lunged to the safety of their vessel, clinging like a drowning victim. The first time Paul had walked into the Newells' house, in fact, he'd had the sensation of floating. No sense of waking in the dark and wondering where he was, if anything would be right again. No blanket of grief smothering him until he ran into the orchard and *ran*. No dreams and imaginings of his father's last moment before he fell over dead with a rake in hand. No Iris hovering, worrying, checking on him every five minutes, wanting him to quit track because he could get hurt. With the Newells, he found a family intact, dazzling in their wit and stories, comforting in both their togetherness and their autonomy. Adam, Rachel, and Dani Newell. Father, mother, daughter. All three of them, nuclear, unexploded. Their steadiness steadied him. He felt all right, there.

And of course he'd found Dani there, too. Pretty, brainy, privately wild Dani Newell, whom he thought he'd love until the end of days. Until the night when everything began to unravel, when the anger first forced its way through.

The night before Thanksgiving, Paul helped his mother and Jess close down after Sundown at the Orchard. He waited until Iris climbed in bed, and then he crept outside, running through the orchard toward the river, to the path that would take him the back way into town, to Dani's. The bright moon guided him through the trees. Nestled in his backpack was a new box of condoms. It wasn't very late, after ten, so he wasn't sure if he'd be able to climb in her window, if Adam would still be up painting or if Rachel would be up reading or getting ready for tomorrow's dinner. Maybe they could sneak out into the backyard. The thought was sexy: to be out there in the cold dark with the glowing window above them, the moon lighting up their bodies. He felt himself grow hard. God, he loved Dani, and god, he loved sex. Fucking, she called it sometimes, in his ear, and he thought he'd lose his mind. Fuck me, she'd say, and Jesus, he'd almost go right then before he was inside her.

He was deep in the trees, almost to the river trail, when he heard a noise. A scuffling, a low swish of leaves, a crack of twigs. His first thought was javelina, and he stopped, looking around. It would be bad to startle a pack. Then he saw the source: two people standing against a tree. He'd started to walk toward them, puzzled, thinking at first they were tourists. A man and a girl. He'd been about to call out, *Hello, what's going on? Can I help you?* when the man stepped forward and touched the girl's face.

The man said, "God, Jess. Look at you."

The voice startled Paul so much he fell to his knees. He knew that voice. He crawled toward a tree trunk and pressed himself against it. He held his breath. An owl hooted. He peered around the tree, trying to calm his gasping breaths. He stared at Adam's face, at the sharp curve of his nose in profile. He recognized Jess's puffy coat then, her curly hair sticking out from her wool cap. He couldn't look away.

"I love you," Adam said, his hand on her face.

Paul kneeled in the damp grass and watched as Adam kissed her forehead, and then he began to crawl along the path toward his house. He crawled and crawled and then leaped to his feet and tried to run. But he was aroused. He was shocked and aroused and ashamed at his arousal all at once. He stumbled at an awkward gait, his pack slamming his spine, chased by the image of Adam's face and his declaration in the moonlight, by the burning rage building in his belly. Not a father. A man, his jaw clenched with desire.

Paul scraped paint all afternoon and into the early evening. His wrists, shoulders, and back would be sore tomorrow—his sprained wrist throbbed—but he didn't want to stop. He kept thinking, One more patch. Iris and Sean came home in the afternoon with a sack full of library books, and Paul took a break to eat a sandwich and read to his son. When Sean went down for his nap, Paul went outside. He stepped up and down the ladder to refill his water bottle and reapply sunblock, making sure to reset the ladder each time. He took a break when the monsoon swept through, a brief furious rain that washed away the green flecks of paint and cooled the air. He breathed. He breathed his way to calm, the way his counselor taught him when he'd finally agreed to go at Caryn's insistence.

Iris called to him to come in for supper, and he waved her off, told her he'd be in in a minute, to get started without him. He wanted to finish the last stretch so he could start priming tomorrow. He was still working when the sun set. His mother called to him again.

"Paul!" she said. "Come on. Sean's going to need a bath before bed."

He sighed. "One minute!"

He thought he heard her say, "Jesus Christ." She turned on the outdoor lights. The house lit up with twinkle lights. Those lights. She left them up all year.

They had been Jess Winters's idea. He could still see Jess out here with his mother, twisting the cords around the posts, his mother locking them in place with a staple gun. The night she'd disappeared had been a Sundown night a few days before Christmas. Usually one of their busiest times but slow that weekend because it had been pouring rain for two days. Almost a foot of snow had dumped on Flagstaff, closing I-40. He remembered the details because he'd had to tell the police several times. He hadn't seen Jess that night, not at all, but that wasn't a surprise; she hadn't been coming to the orchard since Thanksgiving—the last day he'd seen her.

The details of Thanksgiving were less clear. He'd barely slept after he returned from the orchard, trying to make sense of what he'd seen, trying to figure out how to tell Dani. The rage had simmered all night. Rage, plus a sick sense of shame for being turned on by seeing them, plus a strange feeling of betrayal. Adam wasn't the father he'd believed him to be. And his father: still gone. Nothing was all right after all. He'd not planned to make a scene, but at dinner, as he watched them smile and pass heaping bowls and share pleasantries, the boiled-over rage blindsided him, pushing him out of his chair. He could still feel the cold weight of the butter knife in his hand, the satisfying thud it made against the wall. He could smell the cinnamon and nutmeg of the crushed apple pie. He could see the terror on Jess's face, hear the whimper in her throat. Her hands, thrashing like a hummingbird trapped against a window. When the memories crept in like this, the two moments sometimes conflated: Jess against a tree in the orchard, Jess frozen at a dining table. Trapped, he realized now, first by Adam, and then by him.

It was almost dark when Paul finished scraping. Twilight. Dusk, Caryn called it. Her favorite time of day. The time when things slip through, she said. He heard her voice in his ear, something she'd murmured in her last days. *Meet me in the dusk, love. I'll be there.*

Paul stood on his father's ladder and he called out, "I'm right here." Right here. Right, here. A comma could change everything. And everything could change in the smallest space, the smallest breath of time.

He looked at the lights twined around his mother's house, at the lights of Jerome up on the hill. Ethereal, Dani had called them, when they sat in her car and watched them together. Before she'd stopped seeing him, stopped talking to him altogether. Here he was, at his family's house, in the ethereal dusk. Home.

He took a step down, and his foot slipped. He missed the step. In a panic, he flung his right arm out away from the roof, and the ladder lifted. He lunged forward, trying to correct, and for a moment the ladder hovered and seemed to stop straight in the air. But then gravity won, and Paul was falling. He let go of the ladder and jumped, some twelve feet off the ground. He tried to turn his body to land on his feet so he could take the tumble in a forward roll. He almost made it. Almost. He landed on two feet and rolled forward, but his shoulder wrenched beneath him.

Stunned, he lay in the grass—thank god it wasn't cement— and assessed the pain. Ankle, a little twisted, but he could move it. Shoulder, throbbing, on fire. But he was breathing. He lay on his back, not yet touching his shoulder. He groaned as the pain rose to the surface, and he choked back tears. *What*: A father, an idiot man not paying attention, crying like a boy on the lawn. *Where*: Right here. Home. If he could ever make it right. *Why*: Because too many people he loved were gone, buried in the earth, leaving him—boy turned man, man turned father, but still a son, always—lying faceup in the grass, weeping, alive.

AT THE FRONT DOOR

AT SUNSET, RACHEL FISCHER HURRIED home from the theater, half skipping, half running down the sidewalk. She was late for dinner. Hugh was cooking them an anniversary meal—eleven years!—and she forgot. Forgot! Though it was summer and she was technically "off"—ha!—she was helping stage-manage the town's production of *Cat on a Hot Tin Roof* because many of her students had roles. Dress rehearsal was tomorrow, the opening in two days, and Jesus, Mary, and *Joseph* were they behind. She'd been marking the stage, rolls of neon spike tape shoved up her arms like bracelets, her knees and spine screaming from crouching and kneeling on the wood, when the clock tower struck. She'd run out of the black box and into the fading sunshine, wincing at the brightness, the tape rolls clacking around her wrists.

She darted up the driveway and checked her watch. Ten—well, fifteen—minutes late, but that wasn't good. They had just spent three days—three days she couldn't afford to take off from rehearsals—with Dr. Steve in Prescott talking about their exasperating habits: her constant lateness and absence, her tendency to be distant, her obsession with work; his neediness stemming from lack of self-esteem, his hypersensitivity to perceived criticism. She shoved the tape rolls in her bag.

"Honey, I'm here!" she called, out of breath. "I'm home."

For a moment, she forgot and expected the Captain to stumble out with his sweet hoarse bark. Poor doggy. They'd boxed up his dishes and toys and put them on a shelf in the garage, as she couldn't bring herself to donate them yet. The house seemed so quiet now. Even though she wished Dani had handled things differently with the Captain, Rachel was relieved she hadn't had to make the call to put him down. Almost seventeen years she'd had him, bless his heart. Such a little guy, but he'd filled up the emptiness. Maud had been the one to name him. Well, hello, Captain Barks-a-Lot, she'd said, giving him a pat. He hopped right in her lap.

Maud. Rachel had called and left a message, and then got caught up in the production, forgetting to try again. Jesus, what was wrong with her? *When* was she going to get her head on straight?

"Hugh! I'm here." No answer. "Sweetheart, I forgot the olives," she said. "Hugh?"

He wasn't in the kitchen. He wasn't in the bedrooms, or the garage, though his car was there, or up in the attic, or on the deck. The house smelled of garlic and onions, and the oven was on. She peered in. Veggie lasagna. Her favorite. Her stomach growled— what had she eaten today? O hell-kite, she couldn't recall. She washed her hands and looked around for a note. Nothing.

She sat down at the dining table, which was set for two with unlit candles, a bottle of chilled white. "Hugh!" she yelled, irritated, half expecting him to pop out from a hiding place and surprise her. But he didn't. He wasn't there.

Well, didn't that beat the band. She poured herself a glass of wine. He must have forgotten something at the store. He wouldn't *leave*. She was only ten—well, fifteen—minutes late. She remembered his face at Dr. Steve's, plaintive, lip quivering, and what was wrong with her that she felt not sympathy but irritation? She was *busy*. Staging a play took time. Not to mention she had classes to prep, and don't get her started on committee work. She was in charge of new faculty orientation this year, and she was already behind. Thank god they had only two new faculty members, Laura Drennan in history and Wyatt What's-His-Face in English. God, Laura Drennan. What a thing to have happened. New in town, and you find a body. Anyway, that was how it worked at the Syc, too much to do, not enough time to do it. At Dr. Steve's, she had promised Hugh she would be more conscientious. Yes, she would make a plan to retire in the next few years—yes, it was time, yes, she wanted to spend time with him, yes, yes, yes. But now here she was, two days later, back to her old habits. What could she say? They were old habits for a reason.

She stared around the dining room, feeling disoriented. When she was in the theater, she tended to forget everything but the production—she was engrossed in making a story come to life onstage, guiding and correcting students, worrying about lighting and lines and timing. This demanded close observation, her full attention, and it was hard to return to this world from that one. When Dani was little, Rachel would come home and sit with a glass of wine at the kitchen table. Dani would say, "Mama, are you back yet?" And Adam would say, "Give her a minute, she's right around the corner." They turned it into a game, teasing her: *She's on the front lawn! No, no, she's on the front porch! Now she's at the front door!* And then she would shout "Boo!" and grab Dani, who would shriek with delight. And Adam—he would smile. How he smiled at her then. She took a long sip of wine.

She got up and pulled the recycle bin from under the sink, digging out yesterday's newspaper. Dani had left a message, telling her to read it, but she hadn't. And then Iris and Esther had called, so she hadn't needed to. She already knew the news. When Rachel got home, she'd picked up the paper and folded it, sticking it down beneath the milk jug and soup cans.

Now she opened it and looked at the article. At that girl's photograph. Maud's girl. Dani's erstwhile best friend. As she read, her breath caught and her cheeks burned. In the aftermath of that Thanksgiving dinner, Rachel had wanted hell to rain down on the two of them. She'd wanted to go Greek tragedy on his ass. She'd wanted to spit blood from her eyes like a horned toad. She'd wanted to watch the two of them implode, watch that young, fresh-faced girl reject him, hear the crack and squish of his betrayer's heart. She wanted to see his face *then*, for him to know what it was to be left behind.

But that changed when Maud's girl went missing. Rachel wouldn't speak with Adam, and Dani refused to talk about it, but oddly enough Rachel began to speak with Maud. Before Rachel met and married Hugh, she'd be sitting in her house, which once had been filled with her child and husband and now was a shell of itself, and she'd thought, if she was feeling this bad when Dani still lived down the street, what must Maud be feeling? And so out of the blue, she swung by to see her. They'd shared a number of comforting afternoon and evenings, drinking coffee and wine and swapping stories about their kids. About their ex-husbands. How she never would have believed it of him, never saw it coming, never in a million years. But over time, she saw more: how they buried themselves in work, away from each other, her at the theater, him in the attic. Her career fine, his stalled, a stew of resentment simmering on each side. The sudden death of his estranged mother, his increasing distance. It wasn't surprising he'd looked elsewhere. What she couldn't get past was who he'd turned to. A child. A girl their daughter's age.

As she stared down now at Jess's picture, her eyes so blurred she could hardly see the photo, Rachel pictured Maud sitting on her sofa, staring out her large front window with its view of the driveway and street, where she so often sat, waiting. She set down the article, choking off a sob. She never wanted *that*, even in her darkest hour.

She ran her hands along the dining table. Her mother's. A beautiful Mission style with two extra leaves she'd had restained after Adam moved out, when she repainted and rearranged and reupholstered what she could. She couldn't get rid of this table, but she could change it, make it unrecognizable. That was what she'd done with everything from that time, physical and intangible: removed it, scrubbed it clean, pushed it far away from herself so it was as if it had happened to another person.

This old table. The place of that last dinner—the Last Supper, ha. A night so ridiculously dramatic that if such a script had shown up in playwriting workshop, she'd have shredded it for its overwrought screeching, its utter over-the-topness. She'd have asked, Do we believe these people? Do we believe this situation? She'd have counseled restraint, razoring the dialogue, slicing away sentimentality to reach sentiment. Perhaps that's why the moment always returned to her as a play, something she could watch from a distance—something she could critique instead of relive. Something she could rewrite, retell, redo. But of course, she couldn't change a thing.

She rubbed the table. She rubbed and rubbed.

THE LAST THANKSGIVING
A Play in One Act

Setting
1991. Dining table that seats eight.

CHARACTERS

Adam Newell, 44
Rachel Fischer-Newell, 42
Dani Newell, 17
Iris Overton, 42
Paul Overton, 17
Jess Winters, 17
Maud Winters, 39

ACT 1, SCENE 1

Lights up on dining table. Behind it, sliding glass doors overlooking backyard. Carved turkey in center of table. Kitchen stage right, piled high with dishes. Pies cooling on sideboard stage left. Silverware clinks against china. ALL eating hungrily except PAUL, who toys with his food and watches JESS across from him. ADAM is at one end of table, RACHEL at the other.

MAUD: Delicious, Rachel.

ALL (*speaking over each other*): Yes, thank you, wonderful, delicious, I'm so full!

ADAM: Yes, lovely, honey.

(*PAUL drops fork on plate with loud sigh.*)

RACHEL: Thank you. There's plenty. Please.

DANI: God, I can't move. I'm going to die, I'm so stuffed.

JESS (*holding stomach*): Me, too. So full.

PAUL (*picking up fork and tilting it at JESS*): Full of it.

IRIS: Paul.

JESS: What's your problem?

PAUL: No problem.

JESS: You've been saying shit under your breath to me all day.

MAUD: Jess. Language.

DANI: Paul, what's going on?

JESS: I don't know what I did.

PAUL (*laughing*): You don't know what you did. (*Leans across table.*) How about you, Adam? Do you know what she did? Do you have any idea?

(*ADAM sets down fork and wipes mouth with napkin. Takes drink of water.*)

IRIS: Paul, for Pete's sake.

RACHEL: I'm lost. What's happening here?

DANI: Paul?

(*PAUL stands up, leans over table, and grabs a roll from a basket. He remains standing and tears roll in half, squeezing it and then dropping it on his plate. He looks at ceiling.*)

PAUL: Adam, how's it going up there in your studio? Did you get a lot of painting done last night after Rachel went to bed?

IRIS (*tugging on PAUL's shirt*): Sit down. What are you doing?

ADAM: Some, yes.

PAUL: Some. (*Laughs.*)

ADAM (*folding hands on table*): Please don't do this, son.

PAUL: I am not your son.

DANI: What is going on?

(*JESS pushes back chair and stands, flapping her hands. MAUD sees this and stands, too. Her chair tips over, and she scrambles to pick it up.*)

JESS: Paul, can I talk to you outside?

PAUL: Outside. Yes, you do like it outside, don't you?

RACHEL: Can someone please tell me what is going on here?

MAUD: I don't think she's well. (*Walks around table to JESS.*) We should get going. Let's get on home. Get your coat. Thank you for dinner, Rachel.

JESS: I need to talk to Paul first.

PAUL (*still standing*): Nope. I'm fine right here.

IRIS: Sit down, Paul. What in the world's the matter with you?

(*Adam stands, too, looking at JESS.*)

ADAM: It's okay.

RACHEL: Everyone should sit. Sit down, please. I'll make some coffee.

DANI: No one wants coffee, Mom. Jesus. (*To PAUL*) Just say it. Tell me.

JESS: No. It's over. It's over.

MAUD (*pulling on JESS's arm*): Get your coat. Now. We're leaving now.

(*PAUL picks up a butter knife and points it at ADAM.*)

PAUL: Are you going to tell them, or am I?

ADAM: Please. Not like this.

PAUL: Like what? You mean like this?

(*PAUL throws butter knife against wall. He turns around, grabs a pie, and turns it upside down, shaking it over tablecloth.*)

IRIS (*grabbing PAUL's arm*): What the hell are you doing?

MAUD: Now, Jess. Let's go.

PAUL: Him (*points at ADAM*) and her (*points at JESS*). See? Get it? Your husband (*points at RACHEL*) and your father (*points at DANI*) is sneaking around the orchard in the middle of the night confessing his undying love to your daughter (*points at MAUD*). To your best friend (*points at DANI*). Kissing her against trees. That is the matter. Are we all clear now? Is everybody clear now about what the matter is?

(*PAUL sits, slumping in chair. ADAM stands frozen. MAUD pulls on JESS, who is crying now.*)

JESS (*to DANI*): Nothing happened. I swear it.

(*DANI scoots chair away from table, puts forehead on tablecloth, and retches onto carpet. RACHEL stays seated, looking at ruined pie.*)

RACHEL: That was a beautiful pie. I was really proud of that pie. Lattice crust. (*To ADAM*) Is this true?

ADAM: Not exactly.

PAUL: You fucking liar. I saw you.

ADAM (*to JESS*): Go home now. It's okay. This is mine to do.

(*MAUD lets go of JESS and runs at ADAM. She pushes him, and he stumbles.*)

MAUD: You don't tell her where to go. Who do you think you are? She's *mine*. Don't talk to her. Don't even look at her.

RACHEL (*To MAUD*): Please get your daughter out of my house.

ADAM (*pulling himself upright, straightening his collar*): It's true. I fell in love with her.

JESS: Wait. No, please—

RACHEL (*laughing*): You fell in love. Isn't that sweet. Isn't that a fairy tale.

ADAM: I'm sorry. It's not what you think.

RACHEL: You sick, pathetic man. She could be your daughter.

JESS: I'm not his daughter.

DANI: I'm his daughter.

RACHEL (*slowly*): Get out of my house.

IRIS: Let's go, Paul.

PAUL: Dani? (*Touches her back.*) Come on. Let's go. Let's get out of here.

(*DANI stands up, wipes her eyes and mouth.*)

DANI (*to PAUL*): Don't touch me.

JESS: Dani, please, wait. It's not what you think.

DANI: What I think. (*Laughs.*) My father loves you? Are you, I mean, are you kidding me? What am I supposed to do with that?

ADAM: Dani, please. Listen.

JESS: I didn't do anything. You have to believe me.

DANI: Well, I don't. I don't believe you.

(*DANI exits.*)

IRIS: Dani, wait.

RACHEL: Oh, shut up, Iris. Let her go. All of you, get the hell out of my house. Dinner's over. It's all over.

(*MAUD grabs a red coat off rack and pulls JESS out door. IRIS and PAUL shuffle out behind them. ADAM sits next to RACHEL.*)

ADAM: I wasn't looking for this. I wasn't looking at all.

RACHEL: Is that supposed to make it okay? She's seventeen years old.

ADAM: Nothing happened.

RACHEL: What does that mean, nothing happened? Clearly something happened. Clearly.

ADAM: I didn't touch her. Not like that.

RACHEL: Like that. Like what? Like you didn't fuck her? You didn't stick your dick in a seventeen-year-old girl? You didn't lick her little teenage cunt?

ADAM: Jesus Christ.

RACHEL: What? Too much? Worse than finding out your husband is in love with a seventeen-year-old girl? Having his cake and eating it, his sweet little seventeen-year-old cake and his dried out forty-two-year-old cake. All the cake, all for him. Man, I hope you choke on it.

ADAM: I wish you would listen for a minute. Let me explain. Nothing happened. Yes, I feel something for her. Yes, I'm sorting it out. But it's not like you're making it out to be. We can talk about this.

RACHEL: What is there to talk about? You think you're in love with a seventeen-year-old girl. You should be talking to a prosecutor, not to me.

ADAM: I didn't touch her. And she's almost eighteen.

RACHEL: Oh, eighteen. (*Laughs.*) Well, okay, then.

ADAM: Rachel, please. Please. I'm sorry. I never meant for you to find out this way.

RACHEL: You never meant for me to find out, period.

ADAM: No. I never meant for it to happen. This is—I don't know what this is.

RACHEL: Is this about your mother?

ADAM: No. Jesus. No, of course not. Why would you ask that? Don't be ridiculous.

RACHEL: It's not ridiculous. You never—

ADAM: This has nothing to do with her. You don't know anything about her.

RACHEL: Well, that's true.

ADAM: This is not about her.

RACHEL: Can you hear yourself? Poor Adam—

ADAM: Shut up, Rachel. Leave it alone.

RACHEL: Don't you dare tell me to shut up.

ADAM: I'm sorry. Jesus. I'm not—I didn't plan this. I swear, I don't know what to do. Tell me what to do.

RACHEL: Like the birds.

ADAM: What birds?

RACHEL (*pointing at back window*): They used to smack into the glass before we put the glaze on. Flying along, everything clear as a bell, and then bam. Lights out.

ADAM: What are you talking about?

RACHEL: Nothing. None of your business. You're pathetic. Seventeen years old. Get out, Adam. Go. Leave your things. I don't want to see you here again.

(*ADAM exits. RACHEL stands up. She holds edge of table, looking out window.*)

(*Lights out. End scene.*)

Rachel blinked at the dining table, at the sweating bottle of wine. She was standing up, out of her chair. Her knuckles were white as she gripped the edge of the wood. She saw herself sitting at this table eighteen years ago, writing that poisoned letter in the heat of the moment. *Dear Sycamore Friends: I write to tell you some news. Adam and I are no longer living together as a married couple since he has decided he is in love with an under-age girl. I will be filing for divorce and returning to my maiden name. Sincerely, Rachel Fischer.* She saw herself flipping through her address book and the phone book, emptying a box of enve-lopes, fueled with vengeance instead of thinking of her daughter weeping in her room, of her daughter's best friend up the street, huddled in her own bed. She saw herself scratching and scratch-ing and scratching through his name on the mailing labels. She tasted the too-sweet paste of the stamps.

Mama, are you back yet?

I'm at the front door. I'm inside the front door. Boo.

The timer on the oven dinged, and she smelled smoke. She called, "Hugh!" She turned off the oven and pulled out the lasa-gna, which was bubbling and crisp around the edges. Where was he? She thought, Oh. I've pushed him away, too. She ran to their bedroom, pulling open the closet. She let out a pent-up breath. All his clothes and shoes were there. The suitcases, still there. Unlike that day when she'd ripped every last piece of Adam's clothing from the closet and thrown it on the lawn. When she'd shoved Frances Barnes's exquisite paintings out the attic window, watching them plummet onto the driveway like shot geese. She saw herself as she must have looked, screaming and wild-haired, an actress chewing the scenery in a B movie. She saw Adam on his knees, begging Dani, Please, please, please. She remembered thinking, Beg me to forgive you. Beg me, knowing somewhere in her deepest heart she might have. But he never had.

The kitchen smoke alarm started to blare. She climbed on a

chair and yanked at it. She couldn't get the battery out, so she pulled the entire disc off and threw it to the floor. The plastic shattered across the tile. She turned on the ceiling fan and slid open the glass door to the deck, fanning at the smoke.

"Rachel!" Hugh called.

Rachel stepped out onto the deck. Hugh stood in the almost dark yard near the back fence, holding a glass of wine and a flashlight. He flashed it at her.

"There you are," she said. "Have you been here the whole time?"

"Sure. I was waiting for you. I saw movement, and I thought something was digging out here by the fence." He shone the beam at a patch of dirt in the corner. "But come here and see. Oh, the lasagna!"

"I got it." She walked over to him. "I'm sorry I was late. I really am."

"It's okay." He smiled and waved her closer. "Come see."

He pointed the light near the base of the velvet mesquite, where dried grass and weeds grew dense beneath the low bushy limbs. "There."

She heard the alarm call—*pit pit pit pit*—as she saw the nest in the brush. Gambel's quail. A covey, a female and her young brood. The male was somewhere in the branches.

"I'm surprised they're on the ground," he said.

"They like the ground. They nest in low brush. They're good at hiding," she said, remembering it was Dani who'd taught her that.

"Isn't that dangerous for them?"

"They can fly if they need to." Low flyers, quail. Big birds. It always surprised her to see them take flight, their stout bodies lifting, surprisingly swift and graceful once they got going.

The female made a distress sound, and Rachel touched Hugh's hand. "Turn off the light. We're making them nervous."

He did, and they stood in the dying light of the day. She turned and faced the house. The kitchen and dining room were illuminated, and through the glass she could see everything: the table, the wine, the broken fire alarm scattered on the floor, the lasagna cooling on the stove. Dinner. She saw her old self that old night, staring down at the ruined pie, addressing envelopes, scratching, scratching. She saw her own girl, retching on the carpet as her life fell apart. Her daughter's beautiful, sad, and unforgiving face as her father kneeled before her, begging. She saw Maud staring out her window at home, waiting, waiting, waiting.

Rachel touched Hugh's arm. "I need to call Dani," she said. "And Maud."

"Sure." He put his hand on her back. "Let's go in."

She looked at his face. Her young, kind, neurotic husband. He knew that past, of course, but they hadn't spoken of it in a while.

She pointed at the house. "What do you see when you look at that window?"

He frowned down at her and then turned toward the glass. "At, or through?"

"Both," she said.

He tilted his head. "Is this a test?"

She laughed. "No test."

"I don't know. Glass, I guess. Home." He put his arm around her. "Like coming home."

She pressed her face into his shoulder, breathing in his damp heat.

I'm around the corner. I'm at the front door.

"Come on," she said. She took his hand and led him inside.

LIGHTS IN WINTER
November–December 1991

WHEN THEY RETURNED HOME FROM Thanksgiving dinner, Jess's mom stood facing the living room window, her arms crossed. "Go to your room, Jess. I need a minute."

It was almost funny. Being sent to her room, a child's punishment, for the fact of a grown man confessing his love for her. But Jess didn't laugh. She didn't argue. She went.

She sat on her bed, her body stiff, her feet planted on the floor, and stared out her window as the sun slunk behind the Black Hills. She didn't take off her coat, her leaden guilt pinning her in place. She could smell Dani's vomit, see the yellow chunks on the carpet. She wasn't sure if the smell was a memory or spattered on her shoelaces or pant legs. She couldn't bring herself to check.

After some time, her mom came into the bedroom. She pulled the desk chair next to the bed and sat down, crossing her legs at the ankle.

She said, "I want you to tell me everything. Don't lie to me, Jess. Enough lying. Tell me so we can figure out what to do."

Jess pulled her coat tight around her. She said, "Mom, nothing happened."

"Something happened. Come on. *How* did it happen? Did he coerce you?"

"No. It wasn't like that. He didn't—we didn't do anything."

"If he touched you, I need to know. Aside from being flat-out wrong, it's illegal, Jess. You're a minor."

"Nothing happened. Nothing physical. I swear it."

"You didn't have sex with him?"

"No."

"Oral sex? Other touching and kissing?"

"God, Mom. *No*."

Her mother sighed. "Well, that's something, I guess." She frowned. "So what's going on? Tell me. From the beginning."

How to even begin? "I don't know. We were out on the deck late at night—"

"What were you doing on the deck late at night with him?"

"I couldn't sleep."

"Let me guess. He told you his sad story, how sad his life was, how awful life with his wife was. How stuck he felt."

"It wasn't like that. Not at all. I know you think he manipulated me somehow—"

"I *know* he did, Jess. Of course he did. You can't see all the pieces. You haven't lived long enough to know, but this happens all the time. All the time. Exactly like this. He's trying to get his life back through you. It even has a name. Midlife crisis. We don't even have to look far for an example. Look at your father."

"He's *not* the same as my father. It's not like that. It's not a midlife crisis. There was no crisis. He didn't seek me out."

"I'll bet you a million dollars he did. You couldn't see the signs. Didn't know how to read them."

"He didn't," she said, but she hesitated, thinking about the night on the deck. The night in the garage. The letter with the silver key, the first night in the empty house, his phone call, his note under the windshield wiper.

"No." She shook her head. "He pushed me away."

"That's what he wants you to think. And now he's told you he's in love with you."

"Yes."

"How is that not manipulative? Telling a young, confused girl what she wants to hear?"

"It's not what I want," Jess said. "I don't know what I want anymore."

Her mother let out a disgusted sigh. "What did you think was going to happen, Jess? He would divorce his wife, leave his daughter, and marry you when you turned eighteen?" She laughed. "You'd start a sweet little life together? Happily ever after?"

"I didn't think any of that. I didn't think—"

"No, you didn't, did you." She raised her voice until she was yelling. "He is using you, Jess. Using your youth, your beauty. He is a *vampire*, sucking the life out of you. He will use you to death. He will drain you until you are nothing, and you'll wake up one day, and it will be too late."

Jess plugged her ears. "Stop yelling."

"I'm not yelling!" She lowered her voice, though. She exhaled hard through her nose. "Jesus. If this fucker thinks he can mess with my kid." She shook her head. "Nope. Not on my watch."

At first Jess felt relief. Her mother was on her side. But she was shaken by the yelling, which made her want to yell, too. "On your watch? Ha! When are you ever awake long enough to watch anything?"

Her mom narrowed her eyes. "This isn't about me."

"Why not? Why are you allowed to behave however you want, and I have to sit and take it? Because you're the so-called *adult*? You don't even know what you're doing. You spend half your days in bed. You can't even do the bare minimum: stay *awake*."

Her mother stood and tucked the chair against the desk. "Enough. We'll talk about this later. I need to go out and get some aspirin. My head is killing me. For some reason."

Jess said, "It's Thanksgiving. The store's closed."

Her mom whirled to face her. She yelled, "I know what day it is!" She pushed on her bad ear, holding her finger against it. "Goddamn, Jess. I can't believe you did this. How could you be so stupid?"

Jess's cheeks stung as if her mom had slapped her. She had never seen her mother look at her like that before, her face inflamed, the tendons in her throat distended. She'd never called her stupid before.

"I didn't do anything." Jess burst into tears, knowing it was technically true but that she was guilty, too, in her heart. She curled on her side and pulled her coat and covers around her, trying to fold up inside herself. She wept into her knees, choking on the force of her sobs. At the same time, she waited: for the bed to dip as her mother sat next to her. She waited for her mother's hand to smooth her hair, pat her back. She waited to hear her loud voice: *It's okay, J-bird. We'll figure this out together.*

Instead, she heard the front door open and click shut. She heard the sound of the engine in the drive. She heard her mother pull away.

If her mother didn't believe her, who would?

By Monday, Jess was sure everyone knew, and she knew everyone would say it was her fault. She seduced him, she was a home wrecker, a little slut who ruined a family. She could have stood that. What she couldn't stand was the thought of seeing Dani. Dani, who blamed her. Who wouldn't believe her, who would look straight through her. Who would never speak to her again.

So she stayed home from school, and her mother agreed to it for now, until they could figure out the best way forward. She might finish out the school year in Camp Verde or Prescott. Her mom swung by the house on her lunch break and picked up Jess's homework from the school. She made dinner for them, and they sat together at the table, and after, in front of the TV. Every day, her tone brusque, she asked, "Have you heard from him?" When Jess shook her head, she said, "Good." Her tone softened then, as did her face. After a week, when they sat on the sofa, her mother reached out and put her arm around her, but her body remained rigid. Jess knew she was disappointed, angry, and disapproving but trying not to show it. Jess cried so hard she burst a blood vessel in her right eye, a tiny squiggle from pupil to inner corner.

It was true she hadn't heard from him. She didn't know where he was, and she didn't want to know. She didn't want to think of him at all. When the phone rang in the afternoons, she didn't answer it. Whoever it was didn't leave a message. Warren didn't call, either, so she gathered that he knew. She gathered that that relationship was dead, too.

One afternoon after school, her teacher, Ms. Genoways, came by the house, bringing her homework.

"I heard you were sick," she said. "You don't look sick."

Jess pressed at her bloodshot eye. "Scarlet letter fever," she said.

Ms. G smiled. "Funny."

Jess said, "You know, though, right?"

She scratched her cheek. "Well, yes. It's quite the pickle you're in, honey. But that doesn't mean you should be locked up in the house. This isn't the nineteenth century."

"I'm not locked up," she said. "I don't want to see anyone, anyway."

"Okay. Fair enough," she said. "I brought a couple of books I thought you might like."

Jess looked at the books. *House of Light* by Mary Oliver and *Enormous Changes at the Last Minute* by Grace Paley.

"Thank you," she said. She took the books from her teacher. "Does everyone know?"

"Some," Ms. G said. "The adults, anyway. Don't worry—they're focused on him, not you."

"I haven't talked to anyone about it."

"You don't have to. That's not why I came." Ms. G sighed. "I was worried. I worry too much. I don't know. I thought at this age I'd be less worried, but nope. Worse."

"I didn't do anything," Jess said. She hesitated and then added, "But I wanted to." That was the first time she'd said it aloud, confessed the truth. "I almost did."

"But you didn't," Ms. G said. "And even if you had, you're not the one at fault, kiddo." She shook her head and muttered something that sounded like "that motherfucker."

"We always talked about love in your class," Jess said. "What makes it true. What makes it real. But we never found an answer."

"There is no answer. There is no one way. That's what makes it so complicated."

"In literature or real life?"

"Both," Ms. G said. "All."

"Do you believe in it?"

Ms. G hugged her purse to her chest. "I believe people believe in it. I believe it has enormous sway when we do believe it."

"He told me he loved me."

Ms. G laughed. "Oh, honey. Of course he did. He probably even believed it."

Jess shook her head. "I go back and forth. It was real, it wasn't real. I believe it, I don't believe it. It's like he was pretending, playing make-believe, because it could never happen. But I hurt everybody. That's real. What kind of love is that?" She pressed at her chest, at the terrible animal weight crouching there. "How do I fix it? What should I do?"

"I wish I knew. I wish I could tell you."

"Say I *am* you. Say you did this, and now you're older, and you're looking back, and you know what to do."

"Jess," Ms. G said.

"Please." Jess scratched hard at her scalp and then clawed at her neck until red welts appeared. "I just want someone to tell me what to do."

"You know I can't. Poems and stories"—Ms. G tapped the cover of one of the books—"they help me when I'm lost and confused. Which is often."

"Oh my god, *fuck* poetry," Jess said, her voice rising. "Why can't you answer a question straight for once? If you can't tell me what to do, tell me what *you* would do."

Ms. G slung her purse over her shoulder and stared at her a moment. "I'd finish high school, however I had to, and then get the hell out of here. Go to college. Put it behind me. Live my life."

"Run from it, you mean," Jess said.

"Run toward something else."

A week before Christmas, after her mother fell asleep around ten, Jess snuck out for a walk to see the holiday lights. That had been one of their traditions in Phoenix, walking and driving the neighborhoods to ooh and ahh, to laugh and wonder at the over-the-top displays, at the skinny paloverdes wrapped tight with bulbs, prickly pears dripping with icicles. They hadn't put up a tree or any decorations this year—their first Christmas in Sycamore, Jess realized—though they always had in Phoenix. There, the three of them would spend hours untangling cords and wires before tacking them along the roofline and wrapping the porch.

Tonight she walked down Quail Run past the orchard, where Iris had left on the twinkle lights, a ghostly glimmer against the black swath of trees. She wandered through the neighborhoods across from the Syc, admiring the colorful bulbs strung through bushes and wound around lampposts. She peered through windows to catch the flicker of trees and tinsel. On Piñon Drive, she passed Dani's, where there were no decorations. No lights at all, in fact, the porch and windows blank. When she reached the District, she huddled against the wind in her alcove, watching the sparkling strings at the Woodchute blur behind her tears.

Around midnight, when she returned home and approached her driveway, a man stepped out of the shadows and into the porch light. She barked a scream.

The man held up his hands. Adam. "It's me," he said. "It's okay."

"God, you scared me," she said. "What are you doing here?"

"You haven't answered the phone." He had a scruffy beard, and his eyes looked bloodshot. "I've been at a hotel in Flagstaff, but I got a room at the Woodchute tonight. I wanted to talk to you."

"I'm not going to a motel with you," she said.

"I didn't mean—never mind. My car is down the road," he said. "I don't want people to talk. I don't want to make it worse."

She laughed. "Worse?"

"Can you please—" He stopped, his voice choked up. He looked at his feet.

"All right," she said.

He carried a flashlight and lit the way to the end of the street, where the Squareback sat on the side of the road. She climbed in the passenger side and crouched over her knees against the cold. Two trash bags crowded the wheel well at her feet, and the back seat was piled to the roof with more of them. She pushed at the plastic, and something sharp dug into her palm.

"Sorry for the mess," he said.

Jess nudged the bags with her foot. "What is all this?"

"My things," he said. "What's left of them. Clothes. My mother's paintings. I found it all on the lawn. I haven't been in the house since."

"Why do you have Dani's car?"

"She didn't want it anymore," he said. "She said, and I quote, 'I don't want anything that reminds me of you.' " He turned on the engine and adjusted the heat vents.

"How is she?"

"I haven't seen her since that night. She won't take my calls, either." He shrugged. "The only thing she said was, 'Why? Why did you?' "

"What did you tell her?"

"I said I didn't know."

Jess pressed her calf against a bag, let something sharp dig into her skin. She hadn't imagined the possibility others could find out, or what would happen if they did. Now she could. Vomit on beige carpet. Flying knives and an upside-down pie. A car stuffed with black garbage bags. An unlit house. Everyone bloodshot and nauseous and hiding from the world. Secrecy, infidelity, betrayal, forbidden. If it was love, it was the love of Capital T Tragedies.

"I didn't want any of this to happen," she said.

"No. But it would always have been like this. No matter how I told them."

"I didn't want you to tell them. Why would you tell them anything? There's nothing to tell."

"Listen," he said, "I can't stay in town. I'm moving. I thought about moving into my mother's place in Colorado, but it needs too much work, and it's too far away anyhow. I found a place, a cabin in Kachina Village near Flagstaff. Far enough away but close enough to visit Dani. I'm moving in this Sunday, the twenty-second."

"First day of winter," she said. She cupped the heat vent, leaning close to it.

He gave a short laugh. "I guess so. Appropriate."

She faced him, leaning against the door, the handle digging into her spine. "So I won't see you anymore."

"I don't know. That's up to you. That's what I came to talk to you about."

She squeezed her knees.

"Everything's changed now," he said.

"Because we destroyed people's lives."

"Okay, yes. Yes. So the question is, was it for nothing? Is this nothing?"

She pressed her hands on the sides of her neck. "No," she said. But it wasn't something, either. Nothing, something, the space in between. She tipped her head against the window, the glass cold on her temple. "I'm completely turned around. I don't know what to think. I don't know what to do."

"You could come with me," he said.

The words floated in the close space, almost an incantation, as the air vents pushed warm air at their faces. She heard her mother's scoffing question: *You'll start a sweet little life together? Happily ever after?* She wanted to scoff, too. Going with him wasn't an option. Was it?

"Hear me out," he said. "You'll be eighteen in a couple months. You could finish school in Flagstaff, away from all this. A fresh start. You could go to college there. The university has a great forestry program, or whatever you decide you wanted to study. You'd be close enough to visit home. And we could see—" He pushed his foot against the gas pedal and revved the engine. "About us."

"We're not an 'us,' " she said.

"I love you," he said. "It's true, as much as everyone thinks I'm out of my mind. As much as, as Rachel said, I'm doubling down on it. Maybe so. But I know I want to be with you. I didn't know how to make it happen before, but now."

"We don't even know each other," she said.

He gripped the steering wheel and rested his forehead on it. "Do you love me, or don't you?"

Her heart thudded as if she had run fast up a hill. She felt a pulse of heat in her traitorous body.

He said, "Shouldn't we at least give it a shot? Shouldn't we find out?"

He reached out and took her hand, pressed it between both of his. The engine rumbled under her, and more warm air gusted from the vents. A drowsy, dreamy heat. She pictured it: A cabin in the woods. A man who loved her. College, her mother close by. A happy picture. Did they deserve to be happy after what they'd done? Her father must have believed it. He'd burned his bridges, scorched his earth, and walked right into the sunset.

He lifted her hand to his face, put his mouth on her wrist. "It's real, Jess. What can I say to make you believe me?"

"Don't say anything," she said.

He pulled her close, and she breathed in his woody scent. His beard brushed her cheek, and she trembled, the gearshift digging into her thigh. That thread of heat wound through her, taut and golden. Her body told her it was true. Believe, it told her. What if, for once in her life, this was right? *Un*expected. *Un*conventional. *Ir*regular.

"Beautiful Jess," he said. His lips were on her ear, his voice a low whisper, as if afraid to startle her from a trance. "My beautiful girl."

She pulled away at those words, curling her hands in her lap. Her father's phrase. His grumbly voice. She looked at her shoes, pressed her toe against the worn-thin canvas. Shoes she'd worn out with her walking. Feet to walk on, to run on. Her own two feet.

She grabbed the door handle. "I can't," she said. "I have to go, Adam."

"Wait," he said.

She knew what she had to say. "I don't love you. Okay? I don't. I don't want this. I don't want to be with you."

He slumped in his seat. "Just like that. It's that easy for you."

"Yes," she said.

And it was. The door swung open, and she stepped outside onto the pebbled pavement. She walked away. She walked through the darkness. She walked home.

Her mother was sitting on the sofa in her robe when Jess let herself in. They stared at each other for a moment.

"Were you with him?" her mother asked.

"Yes. Just talking. He wanted to talk."

"About what?"

Jess paused, trying to find the right words. She had yet to say the words to herself: *It's over. I won't be seeing him again.*

"Do not lie to me, Jess," her mother said. "Do not."

"I won't. He wanted to say good-bye," she said. "He's leaving town. He asked me to go with him, and I said no."

"That son of a bitch. For Christ's sake. Come here."

Jess plunked down on the sofa and leaned on her mother's shoulder.

"I'm proud of you," her mom said. "That was the right thing."

"Okay," Jess said, wishing she felt right. Normal. "I want it to be over now."

"I know you do. Hey, no more sneaking out," her mom said. "Don't make me wake up terrified."

"I'm not doing anything. Just taking walks. When I can't sleep."

"You can't go roaming around any time you want. Okay? It's not safe. You have to be careful. Even here. At the very least, leave a note." She sighed and pulled Jess closer. "What am I going to do with you, huh?"

Jess nestled into her mom's shoulder, wishing she could fall asleep and wake up with the world restored: a teenage girl with a father, with a best friend down the street.

The rain started Friday afternoon. The news predicted a two-day storm, a real gully-washer, with snow falling that night north in Flagstaff. So Jess and her mother went to the store, pulling up the hoods on their jackets and scurrying inside, where the bread and milk were already sparse on the shelves. As Jess pushed a cart down the aisle, its front wheel wobbling, she saw someone ducking around the aisle. Dani. Jess let go of the cart and ran after her, her mother calling out behind her.

She hit the corner and almost ran into a display of cereal boxes, knocking two loose from the stack. She tossed them on the stack and then walked fast past the packaged meats and deli, scanning the aisles for Dani. But she couldn't see her. When she reached the front of the store and peered out, she spotted a dark-haired girl dashing through the rain to a car parked behind a cluster of shopping carts. Jess couldn't tell if it was her. She'd started to run out into the rain when her mom grabbed her elbow.

All Saturday it rained, and Jess and her mom stayed indoors, playing pinochle and drinking hot cocoa, the windows foggy with the steam of their breath. Throughout the night, the rain drummed the roof, sneaking into Jess's dreams and startling her awake every hour or so with a sense of unease, a question at the back of her throat: *Who's there?*

Early Sunday, bleary from her restless night, she brewed a pot of coffee and decided to make buttermilk pancakes for her mother, frying them in butter in the skillet and heating the syrup bottle in a warm pan like her mother did. When her mom woke, she said, "Okay, who died?" and then laughed, ruffling Jess's hair. Jess ate three and a half, slathered with butter and syrup. Queasy, she loaded the dishwasher. Starting over. Back on the road to normality.

The rest of the afternoon, her mother napped on the living room sofa with the TV blaring news and reruns of cop shows. Jess stayed in her room. Cold and damp, she put on one of her dad's wool sweaters she'd buried deep in the closet, and it hung down to her thighs. She pulled his cards from the desk drawer and spread them across the bed before bundling them up again. She took a shower, the extra-hot water scalding her skin and scalp red. By late afternoon, she sat at the desk and watched the rain pummel the driveway, bend the branches of the jacaranda. The flat, gray sky muddled her sense of time, and she began to feel as if she were waiting for someone, listening for the sound of arrival. The hair on her neck rose. Not a welcome arrival. A sense of threat. Someone or something coming to get her.

Jess hunched in the desk chair, feeling the weight of herself, her breath feathery in her throat. She wrote:

> The first day of winter
> You wait in the dark
> for what lies in wait
>
> Wait, wait, don't tell me:
> You feel the full weight of your decisions
> Waiting for a weight off your mind
> Well, don't wait up
>
> Wait, I'm not finished.
> Wait, is this what I ordered?
> Waiter, there's a fly in my soup.
> Just wait till your father gets home.
>
> Wait a minute: how heavy is
> the weight of the world?
> How much weight can you bear?
> I'll wait for your reply

Then she scratched it out with ink, line by line, until it was illegible.

She jumped up and ran into the living room. Her mom was still asleep on the sofa, her arm dangling off the side, the cordless phone and a plate with crackers and cheese at her fingertips. Jess picked up both, putting the phone in the charger, the plate in the sink. She took deep breaths and paced in the kitchen. The oven clock ticked to 4:35, and the sense of foreboding swelled. She gripped the oven handle. She needed to go out, take a walk.

In the bedroom, she pulled her puffy coat from the closet, and tore a piece of paper from her notebook.

She wrote,

Mom,

I'm going out for a walk (it's about 4:45). I need to clear my head. I'll be back in a couple hours. Don't worry.

Love, J-bird

After taping the note on the coffee table under the remote, she shrugged on her coat, stuck her notebook inside against her chest, and zipped up. The bottom of the sweater hung like a skirt over her jeans. She leaned over her mother, picked up her dangling hand, and rested it across her chest. She unfolded a quilt and covered her. Her mother sighed, her eyelids fluttering, and Jess tiptoed backward. From the front closet, she dug out an umbrella—her father's, she realized, a black one with a heavy plastic handle—and she slipped outside.

She ran down Roadrunner Lane, her canvas shoes soaked within minutes. The rain, strong as a summer deluge, stung with winter ice. Running helped warm her, but her hand holding the umbrella ached, and she cursed herself for not grabbing gloves. With each splashing step, though, the glaze of dread began to slough off and fall away from her shoulders.

When she reached the first dip in the road, she paused. Water rushed across it, but the stream wasn't too wide, maybe three or four feet. She stepped a few feet back to get momentum, ran forward, and jumped, her heel clearing the water with inches to spare. She laughed, glad for once of her height and long legs and muscle memory, at the long-ingrained instinct to leap.

At the bottom of the hill, she turned on Quail Run and passed the orchard, glimpsing a blur of twinkle lights through the rain. She slowed to a walk, panting hard, after she veered down College Drive near the Syc's gates. The rain had drenched the legs of her jeans and the bottom of the sweater, but she was warm inside her coat. The campus looked abandoned, with students and faculty cleared out for the holidays. She didn't turn onto Piñon Drive as she so often had, but headed instead to Main Street and the District. There, she spied the bright windows of the Patty Melt, and she jogged toward it. A blast of warm, greasy air greeted her when she pulled the door open, and she sighed in relief.

Inside, Jess dried off in the bathroom as best she could with the hand dryer and brown paper towels, and then she ordered a Coke and a large side of fries at the counter from Rose Prentiss, who said hello and made a crack about the vacant restaurant, everyone afraid they'd melt in the rain. Snuggled in a booth by the window, Jess picked at the basket of fries at her elbow, dipping them in a glob of ketchup. She kept her eyes on the street, watchful, a twinge of unease lingering, but there was little traffic. Water pooled in the lot, sloshed against a concrete parking barrier. Even the gas station across the street was slow. A streetlight snapped on, fanned a glow across the sheets of rain. She pressed down all the buttons on her soda lid, liking the click and dent of plastic under her thumb. With her fingernail, she carved half-moon impressions into the Styrofoam. She checked the clock over the counter. Five o'clock on the first day of winter. Shortest day of the year. She was suddenly ravenous, and she stuffed several fries in her mouth, barely chewing and gulping them down, the salt and grease coating her teeth. The tension in her eased, and for the first time in weeks, she felt a little lighter, a little like she might be okay. She licked the tips of her fingers before wiping them on a napkin.

Rose came over to her table. "Hey, Jess? My manager said we're closing up early. You're the only customer we've had in hours."

"Oh. Okay," she said. She shoved the last fries in her mouth and pulled on her coat, plucking at the damp collar. She snapped the rubber band at her wrist. She didn't want to go home yet, but she wasn't sure where else to go.

"Do you need a ride?" Rose said. "Angie's coming to pick me up. I'm sure she wouldn't mind taking you home."

Jess smiled. "Thanks. That's okay. I'm already wet anyway. I think I'll walk a bit more."

"You sure?"

Jess nodded and licked the salt from her lips. She gathered her umbrella, swollen with water, from beneath the table. "I'll be fine."

For the first time, Jess crossed through the gates of the Syc. She wandered down the barren pathways and tried a few doors, but they were locked up for the weekend and upcoming holiday. She found a bench under a covered patio and curled up, holding her knees close for warmth. She thought about botany. The scientific study of plants. She tried to picture herself walking these sidewalks, leaning on lab tables, looking under microscopes. She thought of a dead horned toad, looking at a fragment of its eye with Dani at her shoulder. Could she stay in this town? Dani would move away, go to a good school somewhere in another state. She wouldn't have to worry about running into her. Maybe once she was behind these gates, she could be someone else.

Rain sluiced down the side of the building, gushed across the concrete. Another half hour, maybe, and she'd head home. Her mom would start to worry if she stayed out too long. Under her coat, she shifted her notebook, which dug into her ribs, and then tried to dry her face with her scratchy sweater. Too cold to sit still, she stood and began to pace. She jogged back and forth as the rain clattered on the roof like hooves. As she did, she caught sight of the sign on the door: Department of Theater. Dani's mom's building. She traced the sign's lettering. She breathed on the adjacent window and drew a crooked heart, and her optimism faded. Her throat ached as she thought of her best friend, as the shame and guilt swelled.

Shivering in her damp clothes, she opened the umbrella again and walked the two blocks down to Dani's. Adam's old car and Rachel's both sat in the driveway, but the lights were still off. Through the window next to the front door, though, she could see a faint glow coming from the other side of the house.

Jess let herself through the unlocked side gate to the backyard, staying in the shadows along the fence. From there, the light shone bright through the window. Dani sat at the dining table, reading a book. As Jess watched, Rachel came into the room. She paused and put a hand on Dani's shoulder, dropped a kiss on her head, and then moved out of sight. After a moment, the attic light snapped on.

Dani looked down at the book but didn't turn the page. From that angle and distance, she could have been her father, so closely did her face and posture resemble his.

Her best friend, reading a book. As if nothing had happened. As if no time had passed.

Teeth chattering, breath steaming, Jess walked toward the house, mesmerized by its yellow glow, a strange kind of fire in the rain. She climbed the stairs to the deck and crossed to the sliding glass door. She closed the umbrella, wrapped its band tight, and set it on the table. When she reached the door, she pressed both palms to the glass, and when the glass was cold, she gasped, so sure she'd been it would bring warmth.

HOLD STILL, THIS IS GOING TO STING

TO BE FAIR, THE DOG was dead. Dani had gone over to check the Captain's food and water, like she said she would, and found him lying on the kitchen floor. It wasn't as if she stuck him in the freezer *alive*. It was summer. What else was she supposed to do?

"You could've called the vet," her mother yelled through the receiver. "You could've called one of us." Static scratched on the line.

Dani said, "It was the weekend. I was working. I'm calling you now, aren't I?"

"Three days later."

"I didn't want to bother you during your—retreat thing." Her mother and her husband Hugh were at some mountain sanctuary outside Prescott, "realigning" themselves, as Hugh called it.

"It's not a bother to tell us our dog has died. It's not a bothersome detail." Her mother sniffled. "Did you cry? I know you didn't cry."

Dani said, "No." She hated crying. *Hated* it, that trembling feeling rising up, the burn, the lack of control. "But I wasn't glad. I didn't gloat. The dog was old." An understatement. The Captain was blind and tottered about in a striped baby onesie that covered his furless, mole-like skin. Her mother had gotten him soon after Dani failed out of Stanford seventeen years ago. Captain Asshole, the little mayor of bark town, destroyer of shoes and carpets. The Captain would snarl and lunge at her legs, corner her in the hallway, and once or twice she gave him a little kick, even though he had no teeth left and could only gum at her ankles. When she'd scooped him with the dustpan into the plastic trash bag, he'd weighed next to nothing. She'd cleared out a frozen pizza and a few bags of vegetables, and he fit right on the shelf.

Dani said, "I'll take the body down to the vet today. Okay? I'll go over and get him. It's my off day." She'd just worked four twelve-hour shifts back to back. She yawned and opened the morning's paper.

"Never mind. I'll do it. I'll be home tomorrow. Hugh's staying longer with Dr. Steve." She sighed. "Oh, Dani," she said, but what Dani heard was this: *I thought you were getting your act together. I don't know what I did to deserve this.*

Dani stared down at the newspaper. "Oh my god. Mom—"

But her mother had hung up. Dani kept talking to the dial tone. "They found Jess Winters. Or they think it might be her." The phone line started bleating. She clicked it off.

Dani smoothed the newspaper page. She got the scissors and cut out the article. She pressed her finger on the photo—that same old photo of Jess with curly brown hair and eyes lined with kohl. Dani could feel the metal heat of a Bic lighter on her thumb, the hot eyeliner thickening along the tops of her lids, Jess's breath on her face: *Don't blink*. Dani let the scrap of paper flutter to the coffee table.

Before she went to get the dog out of the freezer, Dani walked to the college to water the plants in her mother's office, which she had promised but forgotten to do, and then to the District to get a coffee at Alligator Juniper. She had moved from an apartment near the medical clinic into a studio guest house next to the college. She rented the place from Esther Genoways, her high school Humanities teacher, who had quit teaching a couple years ago to open Yum Bakery. "It's just Esther now, honey," she said, but Dani still thought of her as Ms. G. The guest house was tiny but clean and private, tucked under a large shady sycamore with a stone path and picket gate. For years Mr. Manning, her high school history teacher, had lived in it, but a few months ago he'd married his partner and moved to San Francisco. Dani didn't know if she'd call it home, but it was the first place she could see herself staying for more than six months or a year. She might even buy a frame for her mattress and box spring. The weather had cooled from last week's heat wave, and blooming milkweed, phlox, and globe mallow flung bright color along the street. Dry stalks of grass in the cracks of the pavement crunched under her shoes. A phrase began to loop in her mind, something she'd overheard years ago when she'd walked past some girls skipping rope in a driveway: *One, two, Jess is coming for you, three, four, she's at your door.* She said it now under her breath, a cadence, as she stepped over the cracks.

Most of the Syc students were gone for the summer, so the brick paths were open, the buildings cool and quiet. The theater building had a familiar smell of paint and sawdust and air-duct dust. Her mother's office: Prof. Rachel Fischer (formerly Fischer-Newell). Photo stills from New York stage shows she'd written or acted in and *Playbill* covers lined the walls. On the desk was a small framed picture of Dani at about age ten, standing on the front porch, her arms stiff at her sides. Back when Dani still had potential. The shadow of the photographer showed on the steps—had it been her mother? Or her father? As Dani poured water on a drooping philodendron, she argued with the imagined voice of her mother in her head. She *was* getting her act together. Yes, she had barely squeaked out a college degree after ten years in and out of school, and no, she never made it to med school, but she was a good phlebotomist, at the medical clinic for two years now. Her slim, tapered fingers—a surgeon's hands, her mother used to say—handled needles like a dream. Though her coworkers were standoffish—she'd hear them talk about her, calling her Miss Stick-Up-Her-Ass and Ice Queen—she got high marks on her employee evaluations. *Good rapport with patients. Natural acuity for venipuncture.* It was true: she could manage the difficult sticks, the ones whose veins kept sinking and sliding, the dehydrated elderly folks, the fainters and thrashers. She could even handle Jess's mother, Maud, coming in. Look to the side of her face. Push down the swell of emotion. It *wasn't* heartless to be good at her job, to keep a professional distance. To tell them matter-of-factly, "Hold still. Now this is going to sting," unlike the others who cooed and patted shoulders and called patients "baby." With the Captain, she'd acted with clinical instinct: Dead dog on kitchen floor. Hot. Preserve the body.

She was about to walk inside the coffee shop when she spied Paul Overton through the window. She backpedaled and pressed herself against the wall of the building, holding her breath. She knew from her mom that his wife had recently died of breast cancer, but she'd found out he was home with his little boy from Luz Navarro, who'd told Dani yesterday when she delivered the mail. Luz wasn't clear whether he had moved home for good. As Luz handed Dani her mail, she said, "Isn't it so sad?" and, "Hijole, time flies, huh?" Dani had nodded, but she thought now that time wasn't so much flying as disintegrating. That was another life ago, and she had spent so long trying *not* to think of it that when she did, it was as if her mental screen was smeared with thumbprints. Moments fractured into shards of color and smell and sound she strung together like a sad, crooked garland.

She moved behind the building and waited, peeking around the corner until Paul came out, coffee and keys in hand. There he was: still tall and lean with his round moon face, but all his black woolly hair was gone, shaved right off, making his ears look even larger—in the sunlight, the tips seemed to glow red. Even after all this time, she could feel the tension in her body, as if she had absorbed it into her cells. She'd dated other men over the years, had even joined an online site to meet people outside of town, but nothing stuck for more than a few months. No one worth letting in. She gathered the bottom of her T-shirt and wrung it like a washcloth. Paul Overton, her first love, the honest boy who had pulled the pin on her family's live grenade.

Dazed and jittery, Dani walked to her mother's house, her childhood home. *Five, six, she's gonna slit your wrists, seven, eight, lock the gate.* At her mother's house, she picked up the newspaper from the driveway, climbed the porch steps, and peered in the side window. Like going back in time, except most of the furniture from her first seventeen years was gone, sold or given away or stuffed in the storage unit, all but the refinished dining table and reupholstered blue recliners. Hugh had contributed a large leather sofa, glass-fronted bookcases, and some colorful rugs. Dani braced herself as she cracked the door, forgetting that the Captain wouldn't come lunging at her.

She dropped the newspaper and her keys on the kitchen counter and went to the freezer, took a deep breath, and opened the door to a hiss of mist. The compact plastic bag sat on the shelf, right where she'd left it. She reached in and touched the black plastic, but a wave of panic rose in her, and she yanked her arm back. She slammed the door shut.

Shaking, she sank into the recliner on the right—her father's.

She still thought of it as his, even though he'd been gone for eighteen years now. Since then, in the handful of times she'd seen him, usually when he dropped by unannounced at the holidays, Dani still couldn't look at him in the face—which was *her* face, as everyone used to point out (*Adam! She looks just like you!*): dark hair, blue-gray eyes, pointy chin, although she'd gotten her mother's straight nose instead of his hawklike one. A face she'd once loved beyond reason. Her funny, handsome Daddy who made her lunches and painted landscapes up in the attic and fixed up her car on weekends. Who gave her books and music as gifts and redmarked her Humanities papers but also made her take breaks and taught her to play card games—poker, pinochle, hearts—and easy sleight-of-hand magic tricks. The one who gave her a map and a pack of thumbtacks and said, "Mark it up, Dani. See the world. You can go anywhere you want. I want you to see as much as you can." In those days before he left town, she couldn't look him in the eyes. "Look at me, please, Dani," he'd said, pleading. "Please let me explain," but she couldn't. She plugged her ears and kept her eyes focused to the right of his cheek, on his trimmed sideburn, at the yellow pencil behind his ear. She asked him not to visit her or to ever talk to her about it, and she never visited him. What was done was done. Now she ignored his calls but read his letters, which he sent every couple of weeks or so. In them he recounted his sad life at his cabin in Kachina Village. In each he tucked a check inside, which she cashed once a month and used for rent. Perhaps he saw this as some kind of penance; she didn't ask. She didn't write back. She didn't say thank you.

She stood and went to the window that overlooked the backyard. The tall cottonwoods and shaggy cat claws and junipers no longer fit her memory. Obscuring the chain-link fence was a row of ocotillo Hugh had planted to keep the Captain from digging out. She looked at a spot near the left corner, where dry grass had attached itself in clumps to the lower diamonds of the chain link.

She walked down the hall to her old bedroom, which Hugh and her mother had turned into a room for the Captain: a dog bed, food and water, stuffed animals and squeak toys, a small TV they'd left on for him and which she'd shut off the day she found the Captain in the kitchen. She turned it on now. On the screen a blond teenage girl fought a vampire with a misshapen forehead. The girl stuck a stake through it, and it exploded into dust. Ashes to ashes, dust to dust. The young girl didn't seem to break a sweat. Dani clicked it off. In the room, her little wood desk was gone, and so was the travel map with its sunny push-pins. Gone was the microscope where she would prick her finger and look at her blood, confounded by the serpentine clumps of cells, thinking then she'd work with blood as a doctor or scientist. Gone were the rickety vintage twin beds, an arm's length apart, where she and Jess had once rolled around and kicked their bare feet and whispered secrets, where she had snuck Paul Overton in one spring afternoon when her parents were out and lost her virginity. Where she'd wake up in the middle of the night and see the empty bed across from her and wonder, Where's Jess? before falling asleep, sure Jess was in the bathroom or getting a drink of water. Where she'd later vomited off the side into a trash can, an image of her father and Jess in her head, her mother screaming in the next room. Where she'd lain awake in the dark after all those police interviews in the weeks after Jess disappeared.

She crossed the hall into the bathroom. The cream tile, that same tile, glowed under the fluorescents. Modern taupe hand towels now, instead of pink, hung on the sink rack. She fiddled with the light switch, flipped it on and off. Dark, light, dark, light. Tiny, tiny, tiny sparks behind her eyes.

Dani had met Jess late in the spring of junior year, but Dani had seen her and knew who she was, of course. Jess at first had hung around Angie Juarez, riding around in Angie's old red car, and the boys said, Oh, she's a big lezbo, too, angry such a pretty girl hadn't given them the time of day, and the girls said, She's such a stuck-up *bitch*. But then Angie went back to being the quietest person in school, grease on her necklines and under her fingernails, and still Jess wanted nothing to do with any of them. Graffiti popped up on lockers: "Jess Winters *spreads*," which wasn't true in the malicious, salacious sense they intended, but the rumor—*Jess Winters fucks her best friend's daddy*—didn't come out until later, anyway.

Dani hadn't cared about gossip. She'd barely noticed. Even when Jess started eating lunch in Ms. G's classroom with her, she hadn't paid much attention. At first it was because she was too busy being Dani Newell: studying, lost in a world of math and biology and pretests and scholarship applications, immune by then to the eye-rolls and snorts of her classmates. She shut them out; when she walked down the hall, clasping her books, she imagined herself behind protective glass, like the pope, except unlike the pope, she was mentally giving them all the finger. Professor's Kid and Most Likely to Succeed—goddamn *right*. But then she started tutoring Paul Overton, who she knew wrote for the school paper and had broken all kinds of records in track and cross-country—not that she'd ever been to a track meet. He understood trig almost as well as she did, but his father had died, and he'd fallen behind. Within weeks, she was so in love with Paul and so busy having sex with him—in her twin bed after he snuck in through the window, or in her car's back seat, or in his mother's pecan orchards on a blanket right on the dirt—she hardly noticed anyone else. All she saw those days were Paul's blue eyes and his black woolly hair; it was as if someone had replaced the lenses of her eyes. She clutched at those big ears of his like she might fall off a cliff if she let go. She didn't know her body, let alone her heart, could feel like that—unearthly, like a flare in the corona of the sun.

Then Paul's mom hired Jess Winters at the orchards. When Dani drove over one afternoon for Paul's tutoring session, her underwear stuffed in her purse, she found Jess behind the counter, head thrown back in laughter, her long hair brushing her arms. Paul laughed with her, leaning in, as if they were old friends. For a moment, Dani stood puzzled, unsure whether to be annoyed, but then Paul saw her. He turned away from Jess and in one swift movement pulled Dani into a hug, lifting her off the ground, her ballet flats slipping off her heels, her glasses knocked crooked. A breeze snuck up Dani's skirt and grazed her naked buttocks, the soft damp spot between her thighs, and she'd shivered with the sensation. She, Dani Newell, in the arms of a beautiful boy. Her whole body hummed, softened.

When Paul set her on the ground, she'd smoothed her skirt down, her cheeks buzzing. Flustered by her emotions, she turned to Jess. She'd babbled something about that idiot cheerleader, and Jess tossed off something tart and smart, making Dani smile. *This* girl was no idiot.

Paul took her hand, leading her toward his house behind the office, toward the desk in his bedroom, toward his bed.

"See you at lunch, then," Dani had said with a wave. Jess had waved back, her eyes shining like a planet, and Dani squeezed Paul's hand harder. If she could be a girlfriend, maybe she could be that, too. A friend.

And she had been. A friend. A best friend. With Jess, Dani got to try on yet another version of herself, one no one expected of her in that town, a girl who went camping in Mexico, her hair stiff with ocean salt, who wore kohl eyeliner and listened to music with atonal chords. With first Paul and then Jess, Dani felt *almost* wild, riding shotgun in a pretend life, skirting the edge of danger. She had not expected it of herself, so long had she known the safe, mapped-out direction of her life. She watched that shiny, exquisite version bounce and roll toward her, and she reached out to grab it.

A ball that turned out to be a hand grenade.

In the days and months after Paul blurted her father's secret at dinner, Dani didn't cry, or wail, or throw fits, or lash out like her mother had. She simply locked all the hot, lovely parts of herself away. She put up the screen of glass again, although this time it thickened into an opaque block of ice. Everything on the other side—her father on his knees, weeping so hard his eyes swelled shut, begging her to forgive him; her mother throwing all his clothes into the street; him driving away in her old car because she'd refused anything he'd touched; the row of solid Fs on her transcript after her first year at college, from 4.0 to 0.0 in a year, when instead of studying or going to class she spent her days huddled in a carrel in the library or riding the bus into San Francisco and wandering the streets she'd once read about; coming home to her old bedroom in this old town; the whispers and glances as she stocked shelves or mopped floors—was recognizable but distant, arctic, tinged blue.

Dani flipped the bathroom light off and hurried down the hall, pouring herself a whiskey from Hugh's stash in the cupboard over the stove. She didn't add ice, unwilling to reach around the Captain in the freezer. She couldn't even bear to touch the handle. She looked to the side of it, thinking of how she'd looked to the side of Maud's face as her blood flowed into the vial.

She sat in the window seat and rested her forehead on the warm glass, peering at the yard in the late afternoon, the shadows long and leggy. She looked to the corner of the yard again. *Nine, ten, she's coming again, one, two, Jess is coming for you.*

Dani drained her whiskey. She went to the freezer, and holding her breath, she pulled the Captain into her arms. Even frozen, he was still as light as a wrapped Christmas toy.

She stepped into the yard, hazy with the day's warmth and fading sun, and walked across the dry grass to the far left corner of the lot. She set the frozen dog on the ground and rubbed at her inner arms, the tender place where she prodded and flicked others before jabbing them with a needle. She kneeled and pressed at the plastic bag until she could see the dog's shape. The air was as warm as a bath, but she began to shiver.

That last night, Dani had looked up from reading her book at the dining table to see Jess standing on the deck, her hands pressed against the sliding glass door. Jess's brown curls, soaked from the rain, were pulled straight and stringy, and her mascara and eyeliner streaked under her eyes and down her cheeks. Dani should have been startled, but she wasn't. She looked up as if she expected to see her there, and there she was. The first thing Dani felt was happy to see her, and she started to smile. Then she remembered.

She rose and walked to the door, staring at her through the glass. Jess dropped her hands. The roof overhang shielded her from the rain, but her shoulders jumped, her lips trembling. Dani pulled the door open to a frigid gust.

"Look who it is," Dani said. "My best friend." She laughed. "Let me guess. You were in the neighborhood."

Jess pushed her hands inside her coat. "I wanted to make sure you were okay."

Dani laughed. "Never better. Perfect. A million bucks."

Jess reached out and grabbed Dani's wrist. "I'm so sorry. Please don't hate me. I didn't mean for any of this to happen."

Dani yanked her wrist away. "But it did happen. You did it."

Jess clawed at the air, got hold of the fabric of Dani's shirt, and pulled.

"Please," she said. "You have to believe me."

From behind the blue ice, Dani noted Jess's chattering teeth, and her first impulse was to pull her inside out of the cold. Instead she tugged her shirt from Jess's grip. Her knees shook until she remembered to lock them.

She said, "Stop trying to make me feel sorry for you. God, go home. You look terrible. You need to get out of the rain and get warm."

Jess swayed before grabbing the doorframe. "He asked me to go with him. But I said no. I couldn't."

"Go where?"

"With him." She looked at her feet. "To his new place."

Dani stared at her. "You mean, like live with him?"

Jess nodded.

Dani laughed. "Move in with my father. And be, what? My stepmother?"

"No. I didn't go. I told him no." Agitated, Jess unzipped her coat, catching her notebook as it slipped down.

Dani laughed harder. "How good of you. How *moral* of you. What a good friend you are."

"It wasn't like that," Jess said.

"I don't care what it was like." Dani stopped laughing and instead started to cry. Hot, fat, salty sobs that burst forth from her tight chest. Which infuriated her. She stepped across the threshold and pushed Jess with both hands, hitting her full force in the ribs. Jess stumbled into one of the wooden chairs but caught herself. Her notebook landed at Dani's feet.

The rain stung Dani's hands and arms and neck as she bent and picked up the book. She swatted it against her palm. "Oh, your precious notebooks. Your precious, precious writing. Did you write about him? Did you write him love poems?"

"No," Jess said.

Dani opened the book and flipped through it, rain spattering the pages, smearing the ink. Her eyes grew blurry again, her throat clenched and raw.

"Did you write about me? Or my mom?"

"No," Jess said.

"You better not have. You better not ever, ever write about me. I don't want your words." She walked to the deck rail, ripped out pages, and threw them into the yard. She tore out more and wadded them up, chucking them into the darkness. She flung the cover after them like a Frisbee.

She stood there panting and choking out sobs, her clothes and hair soaked, as she stared at the crumpled paper scattered across the grass. The wall of ice was gone, melted, leaving her with this terrible crying, this unbridled, bare-knuckled rage.

Jess said, "I know you don't believe me. I know you can't forgive me."

Dani turned and looked at her. "How do you know what I can or can't do? You don't know what I'll do." She clenched and unclenched her fists. "You don't know what I'm capable of."

In that moment, *she* didn't know what she was capable of. She looked down and saw Jess's umbrella lying on the table. She picked it up, tested its weight. Compact. Leaden with rain. Blunt.

"Dani," Jess said.

Dani stepped toward her, wielding the umbrella in both hands like a short bat.

Jess stumbled past her to the deck stairs. On the bottom step, she tripped and fell, landing face-first on the ground. Dani heard the air go out of her, even through the drumbeat of rain.

Dani followed her down the stairs.

Jess scrambled to her feet and started to run again. She seemed to tilt to the right. She slipped and fell again, this time landing on her hands and knees.

Dani hit the ground and chased after her, almost slipping herself on the muddy, slick grass. She reached Jess before she could get up.

On her knees, Jess looked up at Dani. Her mascara streamed black down her cheeks. She sat on her heels and lifted her chin, her eyes wide open. Seeing her posture, Dani thought of the Greeks, of supplication. She thought of her father, on his knees, too. Begging. *Please, Dani.* She waited for Jess to say the same.

Instead, Jess said, "Go ahead." She said, "If you're going to do it, do it."

"Don't tell me what to do." Dani lifted the umbrella over her head with both hands. She stared down at Jess's face, blurry now. "How could you? Why would you do this to me?"

"I didn't," Jess said.

"He loves you!" Dani said, and she raised her arms high.

"Dani!" her mother called. "Where are you?"

Dani and Jess stared at each other.

"Here, Mom," she said. She dropped her arms. She dropped the umbrella at her feet. She stepped away, her eyes on Jess.

Jess rose to her feet. The knees of her jeans were torn, her clothes smeared with mud. This time, she walked fast, taking long steps along the grass. She slipped once but caught herself, throwing her arms out for balance.

Dani ran up the deck stairs, where her mother stood in the doorway.

"You're soaked," she said. "What on earth are you doing?"

"I saw deer," Dani said. "Five of them. They ran off."

Her mom reached out and wiped water from Dani's cheek. "Come on. Strip down, and I'll get you a towel and your robe."

Later, after her mother had gone to bed, Dani went to get her clothes and towel from the dryer. The garage door was ajar. Dani opened it and flipped on the single light. A string with a rubber ball hung from the roof and dangled over the spot where her father had once parked the Squareback to work on it. Oil drippings stained the concrete. She stared at the brown-black stains until she began to see shapes in them: a ship with a mast, a seismograph reading, cytoplasm, a face in silhouette. She blinked up at the bulb, unsure of how much time had passed. On her father's workbench, she spotted a flashlight and a box of trash bags.

Bag in hand, she quietly slid open the glass door. The rain had become mist. She scouted the yard, her bare feet squishing in the soaked grass. She scooped up the sodden paper, wadded it, and threw it in the bag. She found the umbrella and put it in, too, its metal tip stretching the black plastic. The notebook cover was all the way against the fence, under the dripping branch of a juniper. She added it to the rest, spun the neck of the bag closed, and once inside stuffed the bag under the spare twin bed.

Dani never told anyone Jess had come that night. Never the police in all those interviews. Never her mother. Never Paul. What she told was the essential truth: the last time Dani had seen Jess Winters, she was alive. No, she hadn't harmed her. Never. She swore it. She didn't know anything else. She didn't know where she went or if she was with anyone. She buried the image of Jess—kneeling in the rain with her face upturned—deep inside the ice.

Over the days, and then weeks, and then months, and then years, Dani had imagined scenarios for what had happened that night: No, Jess was fine. Jess ran, warming herself as she splashed through the waterlogged streets. The rain plastered her clothes to her skin, and she lowered herself to a large puddle and washed her scraped knees and palms. Then she hitched a ride to Phoenix, drenching the car seat with rainwater. She stole a car, she rode a bus, she hopped a train—never mind there was no bus station, no train depot within fifty miles. Dani never had believed her father or anyone else was involved. Jess left on her own two feet, and she found her way out of this place—what she had always wanted. Or, at least, once had wanted. Dani retreated behind her ice wall, and she shut the rest of it out.

For the second time in her life, Dani went to the garage for a shovel. She ran her fingers around the curve of the metal spade, brushed at the flecks of dried dirt. Was this Hugh's, or her father's? Was it the same one? She began to dig. She dug next to the place she had dug almost twenty years ago, next to the secret she had buried to protect herself.

She panted, struggling with the spade in the hard, dry earth, and then she began to tremble so hard she had to sit down on the grass. Her teeth chattered, and she pressed her face to her knees and held on to her calves. She pressed her eyes, stifling the burn. No, she told herself, as she had told herself when she looked away from Maud. She squeezed her eyes shut tight, and then she could see her teenage self, calm, her mind at a clinical distance, focused on what she needed to do: dig, dump ruined notebook and umbrella from bag and into hole, shovel dirt, tamp down. The ground soft because of the rain, mud sticking to the spade. She saw the yellow pencil at her father's ear. She saw those serpentine clumps of cells through a microscope. She heard her own voice as it sounded now when she swabbed the soft, tender flesh of an inner elbow and raised the needle: *Hold still. This is going to sting.* She always looked away from their fearful, pleading faces, kept her eyes on the task under her hands.

Dani tried to stand up, but she couldn't get her legs under her. She tried to dig from a sitting position, with the shovel between her knees, but she couldn't put enough pressure on the spade. So she laid the shovel on the grass and used her hands.

The surface was so dry she formed her slim fingers into claws and scratched. Dirt crammed under her short nails, and one bent backward, but she didn't stop. By the time the sun set, she had marked the outline of a hole large enough to hold the Captain's small body but had scraped only two inches down. The dirt grew cool, crumbly, moister but not damp. Her clenched fingers ached as the sky turned to gray and then to black. Her eyes adjusted enough she could see her hands, but little else, the yard a charcoal sketch of itself. She flexed her hands and stretched her shoulders, and she kept on, scratching and scratching, wondering when she would feel it: the metal rod of a blunt instrument, flakes of decomposed paper. The earth gave way, inch by inch. She had no idea how long it would take to make a hole deep enough.

OUTSIDE THE WINDOW
August 15, 2009

Dear Dani,

Every time I start a letter to you, I never know how to begin, and so often I never do. Too often I have not said what I should say. I have left pages blank for too long.

I saw the news yesterday. It was in the paper here, and on the radio, too.

I am sorry, Dani, for what this news makes us examine again. As if we ever stopped. I am the first to say, I do not want to revisit that time again. But that is my fault, not yours. It was not hers, either. I am the one at fault. I know that. I have had eighteen years to turn it inside out.

We never have talked about what happened. I have respected your wishes that I stay away. I assume you read my letters, even though you do not write back. I know you cash the checks, which is fine. I hope the money helps in some way.

What you do not know, because I do not always send them, is I write letters to you every morning. It is how I start my day before I head in to work. I tell you what is outside my window that morning and throughout the day. Yesterday, I told you about a half moon hanging over the western sky. I told you the morning's temperature (today, 63). A few days ago, I told you about the deer grazing five feet from the window, so close I could see the ripple of their necks as they swallowed acorns they nipped from the grass. I have told you over and over about the winter pines and bare oaks in silhouette at dawn, about the stillness of the air, how it seems as though time stops on some mornings. Hardly newsworthy details. But something about sharing it with you makes it seem real. I often feel as though I am watching the world from a distance.

It hit me today that I have lived here, looking out this window I once found so alien, longer than I lived with you. Seventeen years with you, eighteen years here. I was forty-four when I left, I'm sixty-two now. Headed out of my second act and into my third, as your mother might say. Living in a cabin. Selling houses part-time in Flagstaff, painting houses in the warm months, painting mediocre paintings in a studio with southern light. In a life I never could have imagined then.

But here we are.

Still I do not know how to begin to tell you everything. So I will begin with the most recent news from my window:

It is barely light out; I have become an early riser though I still do not sleep well. The sky through the pines is blue this morning, with a fat white scar of a cloud. The cloud looks like a zipper, like a spine. Otherwise, the sky is as clean as a plate. I have the window open, and the air smells of pine needles. The wind has picked up, and the tops of the pines sway. What else? It is trash day. The neighbor is pulling in his bin. He wears a red wool cap even in summer. His name is Errol Jorgenson, and he's a retired army sergeant. A robin lands on the boulder to the left of the window, a worm hanging from its beak. Its breast is the color of rust.

Do you remember your old Squareback? The hood and tails and doors were thick with rust when I found it. I sanded it, primed it, and found the original green and repainted it. It may sound strange, but it is among the most satisfying tasks I have ever accomplished. I sold that car a few years ago to a young man hitchhiking on his way to Albuquerque. I never drove it anymore, left it parked on the side of the cabin. I drive a regular pickup now. With the roads here in

winter, it is good to have four-wheel drive. The drive into Flagstaff
is about a half hour each way, but I have come to like it, the time it
takes to transition from work to home. Everyone here on the road
in the Village knows each other, but we keep to ourselves. What
else? The kitchen could use a new coat of paint. Ironic, with all the
painting I do. This spring I had a new roof put on. We do not need
air-conditioning here, but we have a wood-burning stove.

We—just me.

Oh, Dani, how to begin? How to end?

I look at her photograph in the paper, and it is a wonder to me
that I have days now when I do not wake up seeing her face, that I go
full days without even thinking of her. There was a time I believed I
would not stop seeing her everywhere. That I would not stop waking
with her face behind my eyes. That I would not stop hoping she
would show up on my doorstep and come inside. I am sorry if that is
painful to read. But it is the truth, and the truth is something I think
you and I need a bit more of between us.

The night I left, you asked me: Why? Why her? Why did I do it? I
did not have an answer then. I don't know, I told you, over and over.
This question of course has haunted me. Why? Why her? A teenage
girl, my daughter's friend? Why would I walk knowingly into such a
minefield? Why would I do such a thing?

The first time I opened the door and saw her on the doorstep, I
thought not of her but of me. Of my awkward teenage self. Growing
up, I got teased a lot for my nose. Beaker and the like. I was skinny
and clumsy, had a habit of hanging on to my elbows as though I could
keep myself from flying apart. At first, I saw Jess only in the light
of memory. I looked at her as if on my former self: empathetically,
fondly, wishing for her to hang in there.

I still cannot pinpoint the moment it shifted—how it became what
it did.

I did love your mother. People ask, but were you in love? Or out? In or out. As if it is so clear-cut. I always loved Rachel, though it was honestly a more gentle love that had turned into friendship and familiarity. You know our story. College sweethearts, met when she took an art class on a whim. She always says she was a terrible artist, but she was not. She had a wonderful eye. Still does, I imagine. She and I grew up together in a sense, roaming around New York, she far away from her Midwest childhood and me removed finally from my lonely adolescence. The theater, art shows, clubs, waiting tables and living off soup and crackers and Chinese leftovers. We were not planning to have you when we did. Though we were old enough, we wanted to get ourselves established, get ready. Still, it was the happiest day of my life, Dani, when I got to hold you for the first time. We knew we could not stay in that loft on Wooster Street in SoHo, living off scraps; those were heady times in the art world, but we knew we had to change. Rachel got her position in Sycamore and we bought that sweet little house on Piñon and there we were. She had a good stable job, and I had, what? I did not know. I had you. I got my Realtor's license, and that became a way to contribute. I set up my "art studio," where I could pursue my pedestrian paintings that nonetheless fulfilled a restlessness in me. I was not unhappy.

Why not just say, I was happy? Well, I was not unhappy but I was not happy, either. A shifting, in-between place. Adulthood is full of such uneasy spaces, as I am sure you know. Happiness comes in waves, not as a permanent state. If I had to describe that time, I would say I was holding steady. I was helping raise you, a joy every day. I was helping Rachel, who was so busy and exhausted in her teaching and work that some weekends after a show she would sleep a full day without waking. I felt some days as though I was the kickstand of our marriage. My job was to prop Rachel up, to keep her—and you—from falling over. Which meant I could not teeter; I had to stand straight. Perhaps that is not a fair description. I'm not sure I felt this at the time, only in looking back. I'm not sure I was able or ready to admit we had a problem. A real problem.

Part of that problem, I know now, was my perception of how Rachel had begun to see me. That is, in my view, she no longer did. There was a time when she lit up when I entered a room, when we were two artists together, not one successful and one struggling— one failed, in fact. Before I was a man who could not finish a painting because he saw that it could not—should not—be finished because it would never be good enough. She would never admit it, but I knew: she had given up on me. I could see it in her face, a face I knew by heart: how it pinched up when I told her I'd started a new piece, the flare of her nostrils and cut of her eyes when I said I was going upstairs to work. I had lost her faith, if not her love. This was no one's fault but my own, but it was devastating if I allowed myself to think of it. Further, in my failure, she thrived. That symbiosis was not easy to know. I am not blaming your mother. Please understand that. My actions are to blame. Yet I think she and I both know now there were things we should have voiced. I should have voiced them.

I want to be clear, though: problems or not, I believed in that life. I saw it before me like a well-made table. Stable, sturdy, welcoming, a place of refuge and peace. I had no intention of leaving it. Until Jess, the most I envisioned for us was more travel, seeing more of the world.

That is part of what happened. But there is more.

When everything exploded at Thanksgiving, Rachel asked me, Is this about your mother? I denied it. Of course not. Why would it be about her? You know some of that story, most of it probably, though we have never spoken about it. My mother left my father, older brother, and me when I was fourteen—when I was that beaky boy who held his elbows. She was a painter, and she became famous in the years after she left. She did not stay in touch. No letters, no postcards, no phone calls. I believe now that is the only way she could live with herself for abandoning us—for choosing herself and her work over her children. My brother was seventeen, on his way out, already nearing adulthood, so perhaps she did not see it as abandonment, or us as children. I do not know. I know that he and I both struggled, though he turned away from her in anger, shut her out, while I tried desperately to get her back. Letters, postcards, unreturned calls. After a couple years I stopped trying to contact her, but I always followed her career. Her work hangs in the Museum of Modern Art, in the Art Institute of Chicago, many places. I knew she had left New York. I knew she lived in Colorado, not ten hours from us in Sycamore, on a small ranch outside Durango. The image I have of her, the one that persists, is a photograph taken when she was in her forties, about ten years after she left us. She sits on a tree stump outside her cabin, looking away from the camera, her dark hair swept by the wind. Frances Barnes. My mother, a beautiful stranger. She was not mine. I cut out the magazine page and kept it folded in a dresser drawer.

I never saw her again. I always believed someday I would. I did not.

When she died, at only sixty-four, she was alone. Alone in a small house on a large swath of land. They did not find her for three days. By that point, she had little money, but she had a number of paintings, which I kept with me for years. My brother and I have since sold them and divided the estate—the money I send you is from those sales, from an account I set up for you.

The irony is not lost on me. Here I am, alone, cabin in the woods, estranged from my child and former wife. History repeats itself.

So if you were to ask me the question now—Was it about my mother?—my answer is less emphatic. Because of course it was. How could it not be? She is the reason I wanted to paint. She is the reason I will never be good enough. She is, in a sense, the lost love of my life.

While I understand this truth now, it is also too easy to chalk my behavior up to the idea that I was traumatized, I was deranged by her absence, I was grieving, I was seeking my mother in a new love. That is only part of it.

Still there is more.

Trying to explain love is to lapse into cliché, is it not? It is like the language of sympathy, burdened with overuse and abstraction and inexactitude. (I am so very sorry for your loss. I wish you comfort in this terrible time of sorrow.) To speak of souls is laughably naive, sentimental. I have struggled—am still struggling—to find the right words, any words, to describe what I felt for her, my inappropriate, ill-advised, immoral love. But I will try again.

We humans speak of falling in love. Falling. Losing control. Taken over by gravity. Reeling toward the ground, toward scrapes and bruises and shattered bones, unless something—or someone— breaks the fall. Water. Soft mattress. Waiting arms.

Yet the sensation of falling is also the closest we have to flying. Something we can do only in dreams.

With Jess, I fell, as if from a great height. God, did I fall. I saw the ground coming, and I could not stop myself.

Why? Why her?

Because she was the sky.

Jesus, what does that even mean? All I can get at are strained metaphors. Here is what I think I mean: I looked up, and there she was—blazing blue, sun and shadow, air and cloud and lightning, a goddamn palette of nature, innocent and fragile but also strong, impervious. I could not stop staring at her shifting light.

Yet if I am honest, the power of the feeling intensified not because of how I saw her but because of how she saw me. She looked at me with such ragged longing, only in part sexual. There was a nakedness in her gaze, and I mean that both in the sense of straightforwardness and vulnerability. But more than that, in her eyes I saw reflected a version of me that I hardly knew myself. She did not know of my failure as an artist, or that my mother had left me, or that I would never be extraordinary. Under her gaze, I could forget those parts of me.

More truth, Dani? I wanted the physical, too. No, I did not touch her, but yes, I wanted to. I was willing to wait, but that waiting was not chivalrous or patient. I was mad with it, desperate, driven to distraction by the depth of that desire. This went beyond sex and pleasure, which I had had plenty of in my life. This was not a cliché, a middle-aged man frustrated in his bedroom. I felt more akin to a teenage boy, unable to control myself. The sight of her—smart, quirky, funny, radiantly beautiful—unleashed a wildness in me I still do not understand. Ferocious. Left me shaking.

I cannot speak for her, of why she was attracted to me. The obvious question: Was she trying to replace her father? It would be hard to say no. Even at the time, I recognized that likelihood. I knew she was confused and vulnerable; I knew the loss she sought to heal, even if she did not know it. I should have known better. I did know better. And I did it anyway.

Why, why, why, why, why? The question that haunts me. Hunts me, really. Chases me into the night, howling.

Today's answer: Because I loved her, because of my mother, because of my marriage, because of my fallibility, because of lust, because of my life at midlife. All of them are true, all at once.

Never was any of it because of you.

Please know, I am not speaking of love in how I love you, which is its own precious thing. She was not my daughter, though you were the same age; I did not see her as I see you. Never. I have no

predilections, no abstract desires. This was singular. I did not intend
to seek her out, nor did she seek me. I knew it was unacceptable
on so many terms—I was married, she was seventeen, she was your
friend—but there it was. I have loved that way once, and it was her.
I believed it like I believe in gravity.

Until then, I was not the sort of man who stepped out of line. The
best I can explain it is that Jess opened a part of me I did not know
was there. Let us say it was a circle. My life thus far was a line, and
here was a circle. One straight, one curved, both potentially endless.
Both perfectly lovely, both integral to the geometry of the world.
The absolute truth is, I did not want to choose. I wanted both lives.
The line and the circle.

I had not figured out yet what I wanted to do. I was trying to get
my head around what I felt. The whole thing was terrifying, deeply
distressing. Unbelievable, really. I do not blame Paul for what he did.
He had every right to protect you and your mother, and it would
have been unfair for him to hold that secret once he had it. It was
not his to hold. He was a good-hearted kid, and I bear him no ill
will, though I desperately wish it could have happened differently.
Of course, I know now there would be no way to make it okay. I
knew it then, too. None of it would have been easy, even had it been
real. That is, even if she had come here with me.

You should know: she was telling the truth when she said nothing
happened. Nothing physical. She also did not pursue me; I pursued
her, not the other way around. Yes, she was attracted to me, but she
turned me away. When I left town, I asked her to come with me, and
she said no. She did not want me. I am not sure if she ever loved me.
I only know it was real for me.

Perhaps this should go without saying, but I feel the need to tell
you: I hope it is not her in the wash. I want her to live. That night I
was stuck in Flagstaff in the snow, the night she disappeared, I sat

in my hotel, despondent, looking out the window. A young couple was out on the street, skating on the iced-over streets in their tennis shoes. All these years later, the image stays with me. Gliding down the deserted street, laughing, flinging their arms out for balance. If she can't be here, I want her to be out there, beautiful, dreamy, skating the streets of the world.

Dani, here is the truth: I have great remorse for the pain I have caused you and your mother, but I still do not doubt I loved Jess. That open circularity: I still feel it. Should I have ignored it? Probably. Many people do. I did not. I have been called everything from delusional, destructive, disgusting, despicable, and criminal to foolish, selfish, myopic, naive, and pathetic. Believe me, they have said it all, and perhaps you agree with them. Yes, I probably am all those things, too. Would it have worked out had she come here with me? Oh, good heavens. I do not know. Most likely not. Still—still, god help me—I wanted it to, even when it meant losing you.

But I didn't know what it meant to live with that. To really live with what I had done. To lose you. I knew at the time I caused pain and upheaval and ruin; I knew I destroyed our family. Yet somehow I thought your absence would be temporary. Somehow I deluded myself you would come back. I never thought you would not be part of my life permanently. I never imagined this version of us. I never believed I would repeat my mother's mistakes.

Yet I am not that man anymore. I am so far removed from him, I feel sometimes as if all this happened to someone else. I no longer know that man with the glowing hope in his heart, yet I am him. I no longer know that young painter with dreams of wildness that I could never capture, and yet I am him, too. I no longer know that middle-aged Realtor who spent his weekends holding open houses and fixing up a car for his daughter. I no longer know the boy who woke up one day without a mother and then lost her again at midlife.

Of course I am him, and I remain responsible for my actions. I am trying to understand something about time here. I do not know the shape of myself.

I cannot get this right. I can never get it right.

When you were little, before you would remember, our next-door neighbors' son drowned in a plastic play pool in their backyard. He was two and had wandered out of sight for only a minute. As if that were not terrible enough, there was a babysitter there that night. A young man, sixteen years old, a family friend. Whenever I think about that night, it is always the babysitter's screams I remember. Ghastly, high-pitched. Otherworldly. A banshee wail.

That is the sound I think of when I think of how I hurt you.

We are no longer the same people, you and me. I am still your father, yes, but I am not that man. You are still my daughter, yes, but you are no longer that teenage girl who could not look me in the face. Perhaps you still cannot look at me, but it is as a woman now, one deep into her life and career, her own loves and mistakes and regrets. A woman I wish I knew. You are so far away, Dani. I know who you were—every image of your childhood hangs in my mind like this morning's moon, a crooked eggshell of a thing, so luminous I cannot stop staring. But I want to know who you are now.

I would like to be a different man. I would like to be a different father, one you would visit. I would like to find a new shape.

I have never asked because I thought I knew the answer, but I know now how little I do know. And so I ask: Dani, will you come see me? Will you come see your old father?

I would like to show you my view.

Love, Dad

A RIDE HOME
December 22, 1991

JESS PUSHED THROUGH THE SIDE gate of Dani's house, and when she hit the driveway, she began to run. On Piñon Drive she ran straight down the center line, splashing through ankle- and shin-deep puddles. Her knee and palms throbbed from her falls, but she didn't slow down. She had no idea what time it was, how long she had been out wandering. She had been so cold, but now she was growing hot inside her coat. The rain had mostly stopped, though fat drops splattered down from tree branches. When she reached College Drive, with the gates of the Syc across the street, she paused, trying to decide which way to go. Left would take her home, up the hill, almost a mile away. Two blocks to the right was the District, where she could see the lights from the gas station. She jingled the change in her front pocket. She'd call her mother from the pay phone there. She'd say, Come get me, Mom. And her mother would—she'd come get her, let her slide inside the warm car. She might yell, say Jess was stupid to go out in the rain, but to Jess even that was fine. She could get a hot cup of coffee and wait for her mom to pull in.

At the intersection of Main, she spied a lone car in the distance. As the car drew closer, its headlights foggy, the earlier apprehension returned, a strange hand clamping down on her shoulder: *Got you.* She darted into the street. Her pant legs dragged in the pooled water as she raced to the gas station. She reached the door at the same time that she realized the store lights were dimmed. A sign in the window read "Closed due to storms." Jess cupped her hands to the window and peered in. No one there. She smacked her palm on the glass.

The pay phone was on the corner of the building, and she shuffled to it, feeling in her pocket for change. As she did, she heard the squeal of brakes. In the street a car swerved. As if in slow motion, its tail slid sideways, and it went over the curb and up on the sidewalk before it shot across both lanes. The car stopped with a jerk, its front end facing Jess, its headlights illuminating the station.

Jess let out the breath she was holding. The car reversed and then pulled into the lot of the Woodchute, across the street. She turned and dropped change into the pay phone. After she punched the buttons, she listened to the phone ring, tracing hatch marks on the metal box.

No answer. Her mother was either still asleep, or in the shower, or had the TV up too loud. She hung up before the machine picked up, before she would hear her own voice, too: *You've reached Jess—and Maud—Winters. You know what to do and when to do it, so do it.* Her laugh at the end—her father's laugh. The returned coins clanged in the dish, and she fished them out through the metal flap.

She stared at the buttons, thinking of her father's cards in her desk drawer. *Call if you need anything.* What could she say? *Come get me. I need a ride home.* His home was not hers anymore. He lived five hundred miles away, with a new family, a little girl who was probably walking now. His beautiful girl. Soon he would walk her to school in tennis shoes he'd bought just for her. Soon she would learn to cross-country ski and keep her eyes on his back. Soon she would swim in the ocean and look for him on the shore.

She dropped in the coins and more from her pocket and then punched in the numbers she'd memorized.

Her father answered on the second ring. Even after all this time, she knew his voice instantly.

"Hello?" he said. "Hello?"

She breathed into the receiver, the words stuck in her throat. *It's me. It's Jess.*

"Hello," he said. "Is anyone there?"

I am. It's me. I am, you are, she is.

An automated voice interrupted, asking her to deposit more money.

She hung up the receiver, cutting both voices off.

She slumped against the wall. She was so tired, so sleepy. She wanted to climb into bed. She touched the torn denim at her knee, pressed against the scrape on her skin. She was hot, too hot. A mile home. She'd have to walk.

Across the street at the Woodchute, the door of one of the rooms opened, letting out a slash of light. To Jess's surprise, Angie Juarez and Rose Prentiss came out. Jess looked at the car that had pulled into the lot—Angie's Impala. She hadn't recognized it through the mist. Rose said something and laughed as they shut the door and walked toward the car.

Angie. Her old friend. Her first friend. Angie would give her a ride home. Jess bolted through the gas station lot and across the street as Angie and Rose climbed into the passenger side.

"Wait!" she called out. "Wait for me."

THE HUNGER YEAR

AT FOUR IN THE MORNING, Roberto Navarro climbed out of his bed but paused as the springs creaked. The young woman tangled in his sheets kept snoring softly, hugging her pillow. The stove light cast a glow around the small studio apartment. His footsteps muffled on the carpet, he went to the closet and pulled out a milk crate of old school folders and carried it into the bathroom. He sat on the side of the tub under the buzzing bulb and the whirring exhaust fan. Though he smelled of a stranger's sweat and stale cigarette smoke and spilled beer, he didn't turn on the shower. He riffled through the folders, stuffed with loose-leaf paper, finding the ones scrawled with HUMANITIES on the covers. "Beautiful," Esther had said a few hours ago at the bar. He scanned pages for the line she'd mentioned, from an assignment she'd given.

There: "The ship sailed across the sky."

He read on: "In that sky were stars and comets and other bright shards that reminded the pilot of shattered stained glass. He gazed through the ship's rear window as if to see the marble of his planet, but it was gone from sight. He sat and watched the silent universe spark and glow as the ship glided through it. Somehow, he smelled the bitter tang of the tomato plants in his mother's garden, he saw the sway of a pine tree's matchstick branches, he heard the organ pipes of Sundays."

He ran his finger over the markings in the page's margin: "Kick ass, Beto!" Jess Winters had written. "Took my breath away."

Jess had been his partner during the class exchange. He traced her handwriting now, chill bumps rising on his arms. He remembered she had written a poem about the earth and sky changing places. He'd not written anything in her margins but told her instead, "It's perfect." Her note was too kind—after that paragraph, the story devolved into ridiculous details about the spaceship itself and a human-robot war that had destroyed the Earth. He smiled. God, he'd been obsessed with space then. He would sit with Tomás in the carport as he worked on his truck and reel off facts about constellations, about NASA's launch that year of the Hubble telescope—about the images he'd seen on the news of exploding stars and the inner core of Comet Levy and the rippled window-curtain structure of the Orion nebula. With a laugh, Tomás would say, "Mission control to Beto. Hand me that wrench, hombrecito." Little man, Tomás had called him, teasing, pinching his round cheeks back when they were still round. At home and in the world, he was Beto instead of Roberto. Always diminutive.

Roberto rubbed his neck, smelling the young woman on his hands. He splashed cool water on his face, and his stomach rumbled awake. There was a time when it had always rumbled—the year he turned sixteen and grew three inches, the same year Jess Winters arrived in town, a month after two men in uniform showed up on his family's doorstep. Back then, he felt as if his stomach were eating itself. After his paper route, he would run past his sister Luz scrambling eggs and chug whole milk straight from the jug. Luz would say, "Jesus, Beto, slow down. We gotta make it till Friday with that." When she wasn't looking, he would sneak extra bologna or turkey from the fridge, wrap it in a paper towel, and put it in his pockets; as he walked to school, he pulled out the meat and wolfed it, barely chewing, trying to stop the ache.

Quarter to five now. The young woman hadn't budged. He remembered how she'd called out his name—his full name, Roberto. He trailed his fingers across her shoulder before he pulled on jeans, boots, and his work shirt. He left her a pot of coffee, a blueberry muffin, and a hand-drawn smiley face on a Post-it note. In recent years, since he finally grew into his body and became a man who turned heads, he'd made up for lost time. He met someone new every couple weeks. He took home college students or just slipped with them out to the alley of the Pickaxe, up against the concrete wall. He was thirty-four now, an age when he ought to be doing more than screwing his way around town, but he couldn't seem to stop himself.

Outside, a mottled yellow moon skulked behind the Black Hills. The sky had begun to lighten but was still dark enough he could see bats at the end of their night hunts, their strange staccato flutter at the corners of his vision. Whippoorwills trilled and then hushed as he passed their roosts. He looked up in a way he hadn't in a long time, checking the summer stars. Vega. Ursa Minor. August—time for the Perseids. He scanned the sky, but saw no meteors.

He walked to the shop via the route he always took: down Main through the District. In a town this size, Roberto didn't have to drive much outside of his job—thank God. As everyone in town knew, he was a great mechanic but a terrible driver. Six fender-benders and scrapes since the first in driver's ed, when Mr. Valenzuela yelled, "Brake! Brake!" but Beto hit the gas instead, plowing straight into a neighbor's prized roses. So he walked or biked everywhere, head down, ignoring hollers and the occasional thrown cups from passing cars. The cops left him alone because they knew him—because Gil Alvarez was a family friend—though he still knew enough to look straight ahead and take his hands out of his pockets if he saw a patrol car.

As usual, Main was quiet at this hour, the only lights on at the Woodchute and at Ms. G's bakery. As usual, he paused across the street from the bakery and watched her through the illumined window. Ms. G—Esther—kneaded dough, her curly hair pulled up in a bun under a green bandana, her loose pants swishing. Because it was dark outside, she couldn't see him standing there, a bit of predawn magic. His stomach growled harder. He wished he could get a cinnamon roll hot and fresh from the oven. He wished she would open her door to him the way she once had at school: *Come in, come in. What's going on?* He remembered her past words: *You can't see my heart. My heart is an inferno*, and he wished he could confess to her: mine isn't. Nothing but stone, ash, even when he fucked so hard he sweated through the sheets. Though she couldn't see him, he waved to her, tucking his shirt collar tight against the sudden chill.

At the shop, Roberto climbed behind the wheel of the old blue Cherokee Jeep, Iris's orchard workhorse. He clutched at the wheel, wringing it like a wet towel. He'd never been able to make sense of it. He understood cars and engines the way good cooks knew spices or mathematicians knew numbers or pianists knew keys. He listened to an engine and knew it was a busted gasket, a loose nut, the carburetor, a cracked block. But all that changed when he slid behind the wheel. He knew his problem was related to Tomás's death, but it wasn't as if he pictured Tomás in the crushed Humvee (although he did so at other times, often before bed, imagining twisted metal, a crushed roof, blood pooling on a dusty road). In the driver's seat, all his intuition and knowledge disappeared. It was as if he'd never seen a car before—heck, it was as if he'd never *sat* before, as if he'd never seen his own hands and feet.

With the radio tuned to the local station and his hand poised over the keys in the ignition, he began his mantra: *You are one with the car. You and the car are one.* For whatever reason, and embarrassing as it was, it worked; he hadn't had an accident since he'd adopted it. The news came on. A wildfire on the Rim. Traffic jam on I-17. Updates about the Jess Winters case. He stopped his mantra and turned up the volume. The forensics team would arrive today and begin its investigation. Detective Gil Alvarez cautioned against speculation. He urged patience and privacy for the family.

Roberto looked over at the shop's open bays. Angie stood in the first bay, her white hair sticking out from under her ball cap. He hadn't had a chance to talk to her yesterday after the news broke. He'd been so distracted and tired this morning he'd forgotten to say hello. He got out of the jeep and shut the door. Angie looked up. They met each other's eyes. After almost twenty years, he knew when she'd been crying.

Beto had first met Jess at Allen's Thrift, where he liked to go on the weekends even though he had no money. He liked to wander the aisles and try on clothes, and the older women who worked there would give him butterscotches from the dish at the register. Jess was there with Angie Juarez, sorting through racks in the men's section. He remembered it was cold because he was wearing Tomás's wool church suit. Since his growth spurt, his own jackets and pants had gotten too short, but the suit was still a little big. The sleeves hung past his wrists, his fingers poking out from the wool, and he'd safety-pinned the waistband of the pants. The jacket still smelled of Tomás, hints of peppermint and chicory coffee and sweat.

He'd seen Jess in Humanities and in the halls, of course. The

Phoenix Girl, people called her. He knew Angie, too; they'd gone to school together since they were babies, though they'd rarely spoken. Well, she hardly spoke at all then. Jess and Angie held up clothes to each other as he watched.

Jess caught him staring, but instead of making a face or looking away, as girls at school did, she waved at him.

"Hey, Slim," she said. "What do you think of this shirt?" She held up a black stretchy thing with a narrow neck. She shone like a new penny. He wanted to hold her in his pocket.

"It's nice," he said. "Looks like something on *Star Trek*." He heard Tomás's voice in his ear: *No, no, no* Star Trek *talk, hombrecito. No space shit. Be cool.* He blushed.

"Cool belt," Jess said, pointing at the one he held. "You going to get it?"

"Maybe," he said. He gripped the leather, heat in his cheeks. It was only a dollar, but he had fifteen cents in his pocket. He made next to nothing on his paper route, and money was tight at home, with Papi's bum back and Abuela in the nursing home and Mami asleep half the day since Tomás's funeral, the folded flag on her dresser. Luz was working two jobs, waiting tables and cashiering at the HealthCo. "I'm nineteen and look at me," she'd said the other day, pointing at her stained shirt and holding up her chapped hands. "I think you look great," he said, and Luz had hugged him. "I know you do, Beto."

Now Jess said to Angie, "Hey, we should jam if we're going to make the movie." She looked between Angie and Beto and cocked her head. "You want to come with us? Lunch at the Patty Melt and then to the Palace to watch the same movie for the fiftieth time in a row. Heaven forbid we should get a new release. Still, what else are we going to do around here? Watch paint dry?"

Beto clutched his belt. He didn't think of sitting next to Jess, her long curly hair tickling him as they bumped elbows on the shared arm, or that the movie was a sci-fi one he loved. Instead he pictured a cheeseburger with bacon, ketchup dripping onto his fingers. A chocolate milkshake, sucking it through a straw until he got brain freeze. Plump hot dogs rotating on silver wires, popcorn smothered in butter, and fat red licorice ropes and candy boxes displayed like fine jewels. His stomach growled so hard he caught his breath.

"I don't have any money," he said, before he could think of another excuse.

Jess's brow wrinkled, and she said, "Oh." Then she smiled and said, "Well, hell, I can spot you. Come on." She took the belt out of his hands, dropped it in her bag, grinned, and sauntered out the front door.

Beto and Angie stood together, watching her go. He looked at Angie, and she looked at him. They both started laughing. He'd never heard Angie Juarez laugh that way. A great big laugh that reverberated like a canyon echo. Her eyes lit up like someone had flipped a switch, the silver streak in her hair almost glowing.

Soon after, something happened between Angie and Jess. To this day, Roberto didn't know exactly what had caused the fallout, though he could guess. (Love. Wasn't it always love?) It was right around the time the lake disappeared, he remembered, because he'd ridden his bike to look at it and found Angie's Impala parked there. After the bike ride, he was hot in Tomás's coat, but he kept it on. It was starting to smell a little, like a wet towel left in the washer. He saw Angie sitting on the dock by herself, swinging her legs.

He rode over to her, his tires bumping over the rocks and tufts of bear grass. Two days after the lake story ran in the paper, the mud was dried up and cracked, scaly even. It looked like pictures Ms. Genoways had shown in class of the drought in Ethiopia during the famine. He thought of those pictures, those babies with their big heads and swollen bellies, when he was feeling hungry. At least he had food. What did he have to complain about?

Angie waved at him but didn't say anything. She folded her legs under her on the dock.

He parked his bike and set the kickstand. He pointed at the empty lake. "Crazy, huh?"

She nodded.

"Where's Jess?"

She shrugged.

Beto sat on the dock next to her. He wished he knew what to say. Tomás would know. Whenever Beto would blab on about nebulas or supernovas or tell him about another girl turning him down for a date or ignoring his smiles, Tomás would crack his gum and shake his head. "Stop trying so hard," he'd say. "Girls can smell desperation. Just let it happen. Be yourself."

Finally, Beto said, "Are you okay?"

She nodded but then said, "My car won't start." She brushed at her bangs. "Battery, I think. Not sure. Might be the alternator."

Before Tomás signed up at the army recruitment office, he was often out in the carport tinkering on his truck. When Beto wasn't reeling off news about the Hubble, he was watching, taking in the names and shapes of engine parts. He'd hand Tomás tools or hold a flashlight, liking the clang of metal on metal, the pungent oil and gas fumes.

"Want me to look?" he asked Angie.

"You can," she said.

He walked with her and his bike to the Impala. She popped the hood and tried to crank the engine.

He leaned over the engine, listening. He tugged at the spark plug wires and wiggled the distributor cap. "I think your cap's loose. Do you have a Phillips head?"

She opened the trunk and pulled out her toolbox. She handed him the screwdriver and leaned next to him as he tightened down the cap.

"There," he said. "Try again."

She did, and the engine turned over. She smiled, her face as bright as it was that day in the thrift store. He tossed the screwdriver in the air and caught it with a grin. Angie laughed, but then her face crumpled. She started to cry.

He opened the passenger door and slid in next to her. "What's wrong? What happened?"

Angie Juarez never talked, so in a way it made sense that when she did, it all came gushing out. Had to come out sometime. She leaned her head on the steering wheel and told him her secret, about liking girls. She'd been damming it up so long, it was a wonder she hadn't cracked at the center like the lake.

"It's okay. You can like whoever you want. I won't tell anyone," he said, before she could ask. "Who am I going to tell?"

She smiled and hiccuped a couple of times. "Thanks. Thanks for listening."

He nodded. He lifted the collar of the suit coat and sniffed. He thought he could smell peppermint. "I miss my brother," he said. It was the first time he'd said it aloud.

"I'm so sorry, Beto," she said. "I really am."

"Yeah. Thanks." He was still holding the screwdriver. He set it on the dash.

"Want to come to the shop with me? Come. Meet my papa. You know, he's planning to hire a mechanic. I think he wants full-time, but I don't know. Maybe you could work after school?"

"I have a job," he said.

"Weekends, then," she said. "Come on. Put your bike in the trunk."

He did, tying the trunk down with a bungee cord. He slid in next to her.

"Let's ride awhile," she said. "Do you want to drive? You fixed her."

"No," he said. "You. I don't have my license yet, anyway."

"When are you sixteen?"

"I am. I just don't have my license." He hung his head. "I'm not a very good driver."

"Well, that's okay. Maybe you just need to practice."

"Maybe," he said.

The car roared to life. He heard Tomás in his ear: *Be yourself.* Over on the passenger side, Beto did feel like himself. He felt fine. Better than fine. His new friend Angie drove, and she talked. A lot. It was as if she'd flung open a cellar door and they'd stumbled out into the open. All the shadows went away and left him with sun. He even forgot his gnawing stomach. He hung his arm out the window, dove his hand through the wind, thinking he was touching the dust particles of the universe. In that moment he felt, as Ms. Genoways always said, like a million bucks.

Beto started working at the auto shop after school and on weekends, doing oil and tire changes and shadowing Mr. Juarez. Angie would invite him for dinner. Mr. Juarez made simple meals of enchiladas or hamburguesas and sides from boxes and cans—rice and beans, macaroni and cheese, au gratin potatoes, butter noodles. Beto ate and ate and ate, and Mr. Juarez laughed. Growing boy, he said, patting him on the back, a good strong slap, but Beto saw Mr. Juarez had teared up, which he knew had to do with Tomás.

After dinner, in the last strains of the day's light, with the bats winging and dodging overhead, Angie and Mr. Juarez would take him out in the Impala to practice driving. He hadn't been behind the wheel since Tomás had taught him to drive a stick; then, they had lurched around the neighborhood, the truck smoking by the time Beto pulled into the driveway, Tomás doubled over laughing on the passenger side. Mr. Juarez was patient, even when Beto almost sideswiped a parked motor home and backed up onto his neighbor's lawn. "Esta bien," Mr. Juarez said, patting Beto's arm. "Relax. Take your time." But Beto couldn't relax. His joints felt rusted, and he hunched like an old man at the wheel, clenching his jaw until it ached.

When Beto got them home safely to Angie's house, he came in for dessert and ate a half a pan of brownies and a whole sleeve of mint cookies before walking the four blocks home. He checked the winter sky for Orion and the Big Dipper—he arced to Arcturus, sped on to Spica—and then searched for the Pleiades and Aldebaran and Sirius, the brightest and nearest in the whole galaxy. He wished he could tell someone these facts. When he got home, he pulled the meat loaf Luz had made from the fridge, unwrapped it, and ate it cold while standing on the back steps, looking up at the winking sky. Where was the Hubble now? What was it capturing and sending home? Sitting out in the winter dark, looking up, the line came to him: *The ship sailed across the sky.* That was the night he wrote the story, hunched over the kitchen table with a pan of meat loaf at his elbow. For a few hours, he left behind that hunger year, flying away into his imagination, into an imagined future.

Funny how quickly friendships and relationships shifted and re-aligned then, as if their teenage lives were playing cards shuf-fled and redealt every few months. Jess started hanging out with Dani Newell and Paul Overton, a holy trinity of cool smartness, about the same time Rose Prentiss rocketed into Angie and Beto's sphere, all corkscrew hair and doll-blue eyes and attitude. When Rose wasn't working at the Patty Melt, she was in detention. To be fair, every time she got in trouble she was defending Stevie. Rose was tiny, but she threw her body into revenge against shit talkers; recently, she'd rammed a CPR dummy into a boy's chest in health class. With Rose in their orbit, Angie laughed her canyon laugh, her eyes a galaxy.

On weekends, the three of them started going to Rose's par-ents' motel, the Woodchute. Rose had a key to the Woodchute's office, and once she knew Stevie had gone to her room and put up the after-hours sign, she would sneak in and get a room key. Unlike other teenagers who went to parties at Peck's or the Drag, who locked faces near the fire, rubbed up against each other, or ducked away into the scrub, the three of them sat around and sipped on crème de menthe Rose had stolen from her par-ents' liquor cabinet and watched cable TV. But Angie and Rose watched each other, too. Beto understood those looks without anyone saying a word. Hungry. They were hungry, too.

Beto wrote more, filling up his loose-leaf with silly stories about talking spaceships and doppelgänger planets and human-robot love. Once he went to see Ms. G after the last bell, to show her some of these wonders. He'd knocked and then turned the unlocked knob, stepping inside before realizing she wasn't there.

Her desk was strewn with student papers, stained coffee mugs, and pencils sharpened down to nubs. He hurried forward and set his stapled pages on top of a stack of papers, tiptoeing away as if he'd just done something wrong. He heard keys jingle outside the door, and he panicked, as if he *was* doing something wrong. Near the door, he ducked behind a coat rack bursting with abandoned jackets, umbrellas, and book bags.

Ms. G walked right past him, trailing smells of vanilla and coffee and French fries, and sat down at her desk with a sigh. He stood frozen behind the rack, stifling a sudden urge to cough. Holding his breath, he peered through the coats. She held his pages in her lap, her reading glasses perched on her nose. She smiled and let out a short laugh. His stomach growled so loud that she glanced up, frowning at the vents.

He didn't know how long he stood there watching her read. She scribbled something on a page before she grabbed her purse and a stack of papers, strode past him to the door, and turned out the lights behind her.

Beto stood in the dizzying dark of her room, breathing in the mustiness of strangers' unwashed coats. He stepped from behind the rack, his head abuzz, his limbs tingling. She'd left his story on the desk, and he snatched it up, scanning the page. Next to the line "The solar wind howled and beat against the ship's window, a monster trying to break inside," she'd written, "Beautiful. Just beautiful." He pressed the paper against his rumbling belly.

The December night Beto first drove by himself was the second night of the storms. He was almost seventeen now but still hadn't gotten his license. That night, the streets and lots pooled with water, the ditches rushing, but none of that stopped Angie and Rose, who had gotten off shift early from the Patty Melt. Angie pulled the Impala into the flooded motel parking lot, and Rose opened the passenger door and ran through the rain to the office. Before Angie even turned around to him in the back seat, he knew he wasn't invited to come in with them.

"Take the car," Angie said. She held out the keys. "I don't mind."

"I don't have a license," he said. "I'm failing driver's ed. Again."

"So what? No one's out. You'll be fine. You're careful. Go get some fries or something."

"Okay," he said, although he couldn't because he didn't have any money, and he was too embarrassed to ask for any, even from his best friend. He took the keys. "What time should I come back?"

She said, "I don't know. An hour? Take your time."

He checked his watch. It was five thirty. He said, "So about six thirty?"

"Yeah," she said, but she wasn't looking at him. She was watching Room 7, where Rose stood in the lighted window. She flung open the car door and left it ajar as she splashed through puddles to the room.

Beto climbed into the driver's seat and shut the door. The rain thudded on the metal roof. His breath fogged the windows, and he rubbed at the windscreen with the sleeve of Tomás's coat. The sleeves were shorter now, the bones of his wrists sticking out like knotted rope. He ran through the steps in his mind. Gear in park, foot on brake, check mirrors. Turn ignition, headlights on, wipers on. Put in drive, let off brake, press accelerator.

He lurched forward, alternating gas and brakes. At the turn onto Main, he stopped, looked both ways three times, though no one was on the road, and pushed the gas pedal. And there he was, driving down Main, by himself, in the rain, the tires spraying water onto the sidewalk. It felt okay. He felt okay. He heard Tomás in his ear: *Don't try so hard. Be yourself.* His shoulders relaxed an inch. He thought of Ms. G, and he whispered, "My heart is an inferno." And it was, supernova hot, ready to burn right through his chest, and no one knew but him. He smiled.

He stayed on Main. Most of the businesses were dark, closed early because of the storm. The rain battered the hood, and the windshield wipers thumped in a steady rhythm. He drove maybe twenty miles an hour, looping between the exit to the highway and the motel. Back and forth, north and south, up and down, for about forty minutes.

He was getting the hang of it when he thought he saw something sleek and low—a cat?—dart out in front of him. He swerved right, and the Impala went up on the sidewalk before he overcorrected and shot out in the street, bouncing, the chassis scraping the pavement. He slammed on the brakes in the middle of Main, and the tires skidded. His heart hammered his chest, and he gripped the wheel, looking at the beam of the headlights on the gas station. That was when he saw a figure in the rain. Jess Winters, as he told the police multiple times later.

She stood under the awning, next to the pay phone. She was wearing a red coat with a long sweater beneath it over jeans. Her hair and clothes were wet.

That was what he told Detective Alvarez. No, he didn't speak to her. No, he didn't know where she was going.

"How'd you know it was her?" Detective Alvarez had asked. "It was dark, not to mention pouring rain. How'd you recognize her?"

"Her jacket at first," he said. "Her hair. The way she stood. I don't know, I just did."

"You're sure it was her?"

"Pretty sure," he said. "Ninety-eight percent sure."

"What were you doing out in Angie Juarez's car?" Detective Alvarez asked.

"She let me borrow it," he said. "I work for her father."

"It was a bad night. What were you doing out?"

He didn't want to get Angie in trouble or tell her secret, so he had to lie about that part. That was the one thing he'd lied about.

"Practicing driving."

"In the storm? The streets were flooded."

"I was hungry," he said. "I went to get fries."

"You don't have your license, Beto. The stores were closed."

"I know." He pulled Tomás's coat tighter around him. "Am I in trouble?"

The detective sighed. "Don't go out driving when there's flash-flood warnings from here to kingdom come. It's not safe, and it's especially not safe for you if you get pulled over. Entiendes? Use your head. What if something happened? Dios. Where was Angie?"

He'd started to say, *At home*, but then he realized they'd find out. "At the motel with Rose."

"Why the motel?"

"We go there sometimes. We don't do anything. Just hang out. We can watch cable."

Detective Alvarez had looked at him over his reading glasses. He took off the glasses and hung them on the front of his shirt, raked his fingers through his hair. "Go home, Beto," he said. "Don't let me catch you driving without a license again."

"Yes, sir," he said.

But that was later. That night, after he saw Jess, he drove past the station and pulled into the motel lot to pick up his friends. He waited in the car, pulling Tomás's coat tight. Stevie's car now was parked in front of her room, the light on in the window. In a few minutes, Angie and Rose stumbled out of Room 7. They climbed in the back seat, still holding each other.

"You drive, Beto," Angie said.

He was shaken up from his spinout, chilled and damp, and hungry as always. As he looked at their glowing faces, he was angry about something he didn't understand yet.

He threw the car in reverse and gunned it too hard. They shot backward until he slammed on the brakes. The car jerked, throwing them forward.

"Beto!" Angie said. "Stop."

"I am," he said. "I did."

"What was that?" Rose asked. "What was that noise?"

The windows were even foggier now with three of them breathing, craning their heads.

"Did we hit something?" Angie said.

"I don't know," he said. "I can't see."

Rose said, "Shit. Well, go. I don't want Stevie to see it was us. Go, go."

He put it in drive and hit the gas. They barreled forward, and the front left tire almost clipped a porch post.

"Beto, watch out," Angie said. "Jesus. Papa is going to kill me."

Rose started laughing. "You're the worst driver, Beto," she said. "The worst in the world." She laughed harder, and Angie did too, her big echoing laugh.

"Sorry," he said. His hands were sweating, and he could smell the stinking wool of Tomás's jacket, and he hit the accelerator too hard again. They skidded out into the street, splashing in a giant puddle. The jolt sent both girls sliding across the seat, and because they were tipsy, and in love, they started laughing harder.

Beto wasn't laughing. He was shaking, and sweating, and he could barely see past the headlights. He just wanted to get home. He was starving.

Roberto bolted upright in the shop's office. He blinked at the windows and then at his watch. Eight o'clock now, well past his dinner time. His stomach churned. He hadn't eaten anything but a convenience-store turkey sub that Angie picked up for him at noon. His hands were shaking—he could blame too much coffee, but he knew it was more than that. Angie had gone home at six, but he'd said he'd close up. He hadn't wanted to go home to his empty apartment, to see the tangled sheets imprinted with the body of another stranger. He had sunk down into Mr. Juarez's recliner, replaying the memories that had erupted throughout the day. He heaved himself out of the chair now, and his legs wobbled before he caught his balance.

Roberto walked home in the near dark. The day had reversed itself: dawn turned to deep dusk. He reversed his route, too, down Main and past Esther's closed shop. The other stores were bright and busy now, the street alive with cars and headlights. The scent of char-grilled carne asada wafted from Casa Verde. He'd stop there in a minute, wolf down tacos and take home another batch, and the owner would say, as she always did, "Hijole, mi'jo, where do you put it?" But he stopped first across from Esther's, staring at the unlit window. The bats were out again to feed, their wings beating fast after a day at rest. He tilted his head and watched them dart and swerve after invisible prey.

He saw himself—that boy, Beto, the boy who dreamed of flying through space. A boy whose brother died, whose friend disappeared, whose body grew too quickly. Somehow he'd shut off his heart and mind and let his body take over, consume him.

A kind of self-protection, yes, but where had it led him? Scarfing food, holding down three jobs, walking and biking instead of driving, having rip-roaring sex in dark parking lots. And here he was: still hungry, a gnawing pain he could not shake.

Tomás, again, always: *Don't try so hard, hombrecito. Be yourself.* Little man, all grown up. But into whom? He wished he knew. Maybe it was time to figure it out.

Standing across from the bakery, Roberto stared upward. It was not yet night, but the planets and stars swam in the murky aquarium sky. Something bright streaked high in the east, and he squinted. A meteor? No, a satellite. Or a ship sailing across the sky. He rose to his tiptoes, rocking on the balls of his feet. A car honked, and someone catcalled, "Whoooo, Beto!" He waved automatically. He looked to Esther's window, and the line came to him: *He was pure moonbeam, traveling by the light of himself.* He put his head down and began to walk at a fast clip. He passed the restaurant and instead headed straight home. He needed to write it down before he could forget.

SAY YOU SEE THE WORLD

THEY FOUND YOU. AT LEAST that's the word on the street. About a half mile north of the motel, in the wash where I gather stones for the lake. All this time, you've been that close. All this time, I could have been the one to find you.

They'll be knocking on my door soon enough, I'm sure. Going over it all again. I can't tell them any more than I did then. I was the last to see you. I still don't know where you went. If that's you in the wash, I have no idea how you got there.

All I know is that was the fall of falls. That's how it has become entwined in memory for me. Fall the season. Falling down. Falling for the pharmacist.

I had graduated high school, and I should have been at Arizona State on an art scholarship, but instead I was stuck helping my parents with the motel until my mom got on her feet after her double mastectomy. I had moved out of the room I shared with Rose in the house I grew up in and into the Woodchute's Room 11, with its king-size bed, kitchenette, pink-and-turquoise southwestern art and dusty gold curtains. What could I say: at least I had my own space now. I shoved my clothes in the closet, my toiletries in the bath, my drawings and half-used paints and drawing pads under the bed, along with a shoebox where I stashed my savings.

The first fall happened sometime in October, I think. I remember tufts of yellow and red on the Black Hills. I was at the motel, carrying a load of bedding from a room to the laundry bin, when

I got distracted by the sky, by the riotous clouds casting shadows on Mingus Mountain. Distraction. That's how I thought of it. Still think of it. My space-outs, Rose calls them. The best I can describe it is that it's like seeing a flash from something, the face of a watch, maybe, or a car hood, a hubcap at the bottom of a river. Behind my eyes, colors and shapes take flight, and I can't seem to help it: I stop and stare. That, on top of my face, and you can imagine the assumptions: I'm crazy, or mildly retarded, or possibly autistic, or, well, *not quite right*. People say these things in front of me. I'm sure they said them in front of you, as well as others: Space Cadet. Prentiss Dementis. Hickey Face. Tard. Deformo. They stare at my cheek but won't meet my eyes, or whisper to each other when they see me coming, their eyes fever-bright with malice or pity. My own parents never really noticed when I was in a room—not after Rose, their "surprise," the un-blemished daughter, came along. It's like I'm either too visible or invisible, which is a strange place to inhabit.

Anyway, that day at the motel, I stepped on a dangling sheet and, boom, down I went to the pavement, scraping the hell out of my knee and elbow. The first fall.

That also was the first day I spoke to you.

At the HealthCo, I was standing in line at the pharmacy, my basket full of antiseptic and bandages, when I turned to see you watching me, touching your cheek in the spot where my mark was. I knew who you were. I'd seen you at school earlier in the spring, of course, but I also knew you as the girl who walked at night. I knew before anyone about you and the man and the dark house. But I never told. I'm good at secrets, even if no one asks me to keep them.

I said to you, "It's not contagious." Out of habit, it came out with more sting than humor, and you dropped your hand as if you'd burned yourself, as if your own perfect skin would ever harm you.

"Sorry," you said, your voice softer than I'd expected.

I looked at my feet, sorry I'd made that red flush creep into your face. The fact was, I felt a kinship with you even though we'd never met. You haunted the streets at night; I did, too, although I drove instead of walking or sat on the motel's roof, where no one could see me but I could see all. You had found an older man; I knew I needed someone older, too, at least that's what my mom had told me the night of my senior prom as I stayed home and ate my TV dinner. As I stuffed in a bite of metallic apple cobbler, my mom had said, "Older men don't get hung up on looks."

I looked up to speak to you again, but you were walking away with Dani Newell. Smartest girl at school. Everyone knew she'd probably go to some Ivy League college. Dani wasn't one of the ones who teased me, but she wasn't exactly warm, either. Thought she was better than everyone. Turned out she wasn't. She stayed here too.

I ran my finger along my birthmark. Like a map of the world, you said once, later. What I saw in it depended on my mood. Lichen. Inkblot. Palm print. Oak leaf. Phlegm. Some days, when I was feeling especially silly and dreamy, I saw it as France: Paris on my jaw, Marseille on my throat, the outcrop of Brittany jutting toward the Celtic Sea of my right eye. Mostly, though, I tried not to see it at all.

"Next," the pharmacist said.

That's when I first got a load of Tom Donahue, Pharmacist. He came out from behind the partition at the Formica counter, stringy black hair brushing the collar of his white smock. His Adam's apple ran up and down his skinny neck like a mouse in a maze. Ten years older than me, maybe. He had acne pocks on his

cheeks, and a scar ran from his right temple to the corner of his
mouth. He would know the Question, too, then: *What happened
to your face?* I swore I would never ask him.

I looked down at my torn red sweatpants, at my T-shirt with
the coffee dribble. I ran a hand over my unwashed brown hair,
my cheek, and I thought about all the ways people knew me, or
thought they did. I thought, He knows none of that. I pulled my
hair forward over my cheek. Right there among the aisles of Q-
tips and hemorrhoid treatment, I thought, I could be anyone.

Tom smiled and rang up my items. "Will this be all for you?"

I handed him my debit card. I stifled a wheezy cough and
nearly choked on my gum. "Are you new here?"

He nodded. "Moved to town a couple months ago." He held
up the card and read my name. "Stevie Prentiss," he said.

I said, "I go by Prentiss. I'm an artist."

Now where did that come from? I did not go by Prentiss. But
I *could*. An artist? I hadn't drawn anything since I'd graduated,
but what the heck. It sounded better than the manager of a run-
down motel. Maybe I *could* be an artist. I suddenly had the sense
things were going to change.

"Prentiss." Tom Donahue rubbed his jaw, and he smiled a
little. His scar reminded me of a seahorse, a jutting V near his
temple, a curled tail near his mouth. "That's nice. Sounds French
or something."

I stopped myself from touching my face, my own imagined
country. I swallowed my gum, and the mint trailed down my
throat. "Have you been to France?"

"Once. Before," he said.

"Before what?"

"Oh, who knows. Another life, I guess." He gave a short laugh
and then cleared his throat. "How about you?"

I nodded. At least I planned to go, someday.

He said, "Well, *bonjour*, Prentiss."

I smiled at the sound of my new name in his mouth.

The whole time I was talking, Tom looked me straight in the eye, which was more than I could say for most people, who either stared or looked past me like a memory. Not Tom. He didn't just look. He saw me.

Until I met Tom Donahue, Pharmacist, my days revolved around the motel. Mornings, I set up a continental breakfast, and then my mom came in for an hour so I could run errands and fetch supplies. Afternoons, I answered phones, took reservations, balanced the books, cleaned the rooms, and did laundry when employees called in sick. I usually had one day off, Mondays, when a student from the Syc covered the office.

Evenings, I visited my folks, helped cook, loaded the dishwasher. My parents loved me, I'm sure—Stevie is, after all, a combination of their names, Steve and Marie—and I loved them, but I often felt like background noise. Mostly they talked as if I weren't in the room. Dad talked about his jerk bosses at the cement plant, where he'd picked up shifts to help with my mom's medical bills, and how it was a relief to have gas prices down after the Gulf War. Goddamn Saddam, he said. My mom talked about what was on sale at Bashas', but she was tired, and she absently rested her hands where her breasts used to be. Rose was often out, either working her shifts at the Patty Melt or with her friends Angie Juarez and Beto Navarro. I knew Rose was sneaking into the motel with Angie and Beto. When I confronted her, Rose had begged me not to tell. "Please, Stevie, for me," Rose said, as she always did when she wanted her way, which was always. So I didn't tell. I might have been a lot of things, but a narc wasn't one of them. I could keep a secret, and as much as a pain in the ass as Rose could be, she was my little sister. Since she was born, I've wanted to protect her. When my parents brought her home, a squeaking swaddled peanut, I hugged her too tight, eager and clumsy, thinking I was making her safe, and they took her away from me. Once, thinking she was cold, I covered her head to toe with blankets, nearly suffocating her, for which my father smacked me on the backside, yelling, "Don't you touch her, you hear me? Don't touch her." So I didn't much after that. At night in our shared room, I told her stories, about us flying into space and going roller-skating on the moon. She'd laugh and say, "Stevie, you can't roller-skate on the *moon*," and I'd say, "Sure you can. You'll see." Funny she spent most of her time in high school defending *me*. Five feet tall with her pipe-cleaner blond hair and fuck-you fists, bright as a welder's spark. Baby Rose, I still call her.

Anyway, those days and nights were hardly the life I'd dreamed. In those dreams, I got on a Greyhound bus, twenty pounds lighter after a summer of drinking banana yogurt shakes, and I left behind my parents and young sister in a house behind the high school. I left this little Arizona town with its slow, shady river and headed to the sprawling streets of Phoenix and Tempe. In my dreams, I sketched drawings and wrote essays and ate lunch on urban patios. I lived in a fifteen-story dorm with a roommate named Laurel or Traci with an I, or Renée with an accent on the first *e*, a city girl who taught me to wear eyeliner and how to use cover-up on my mark and let me borrow her best jeans. I drank beer from kegs and lost my virginity with a boy named Dylan, or Alex, or Ryan, a smart boy, an older boy, an art major probably, who knew nothing about me but who knew enough of the world not to care about my face, who traced it and said I was beautiful not *despite* it but because I *was*. On summer vacation, I backpacked through Europe and smoked Gauloises and drank black coffee, all the things I had read in books from one library and seen on my parents' one television and in movies at one theater. My dreams then were as real to me as the river running through town, as sure as the square charcoal between my fingers. When my mother was losing her breasts and my father was sleeping at the hospital in Flagstaff, those dreams started to slip away like air from a leaky tire.

All of which is to say, I was conscious *in the moment* the life I was living was not the one I had dreamed, and it brewed restlessness in me. I have wondered so often if this was true for you, that sense of living in contradiction to what you desired. What was it that drove you out at nights? That drove you into the rain that last night?

In the summer, I often climbed a ladder up to the motel's roof, a blanket under my arm. No one ever saw me. Did you ever notice that no one ever looks up? You didn't, either. The night I first saw you, you ran across the street and ducked into the alcove of the vacant office building. We both watched the high-schoolers gathered at the gas station. They leaned up against car hoods, snuck sips of wine coolers. We both watched the college students drift out of the Syc's gates and cruise to the Pickaxe and the Patty Melt and Casa Verde, all the Laurels, Tracis, Reneés, Dylans, Peters, Ryans. We both saw Jerome's tiny blanket of lights, the Milky Way as bright as tourmaline, the illuminated smoke billowing from the cement plant.

Other nights, with the same restlessness that drove me to the roof, I drove around town. I drove up and down Main through the District, past the single-story shops closed for the night. I drove out to the fairgrounds and climbed up the mountainous slag heap, the shiny pieces sharp under my hands and feet, thinking of Mordor. I drove up College Drive and through the iron gates onto the Syc's campus, a whole other world even though it was only across the street, where even in summer young men and women walked with their arms full of books across the neatly clipped quad. I drove into the neighborhoods, parked in dark graveled cul-de-sacs. That's where I caught sight of you one night in late summer. You were jogging toward a house with a For Sale sign. I ducked down in my seat and watched as you walked to the front door and let yourself in. As if it was your house. As if it was yours for the taking.

It was like watching in a dream. I wanted to get out and follow you, but I couldn't move. All I could do was sit and wait. A police car pulled up, its headlights on but its blue warning lights off. I thought I was in trouble, and I slunk farther down, waiting for the officer to knock on my window. But when I peeked up, he was standing at the door, talking to someone. A man. Older, but I didn't know him. The door closed, and the officer drove off. Soon enough, you came out, and this time you ran, leaping off the front step and stumbling on the path. You ran to the dark street. The man stepped on the porch. He watched you go. He never looked in my direction, but I could see even from a distance how he was watching you, holding on to the porch post. Like if he let go, he might fall down.

I drove to the motel that night, alight with something I didn't understand. That secret of yours. I wanted it to be mine. I climbed onto the motel roof, and freak that I am, I touched myself, my hands on my two good breasts and inside my pants, thinking of you and the man at the house, of Tom Donahue and his seahorse scar, until my eyes rolled back and the sky washed over me. Then I crawled into bed, thinking about my drawings and paint tubes under the bed, and all the places I hadn't been, shivering in the loneliness that swelled large and gaping in the dark.

I fell again when I was unloading groceries from the trunk and stepped in a small pothole. My ankle turned, my bags went flying, and I landed hard on my wrist. Sprained it, or at least it swelled up. Tom Donahue touched my hand that day. He picked out a splint and an ACE bandage and showed me how to wrap it. Dani Newell was working that day, too. She asked after my mother. I didn't know yet about her father, that he was the man on the porch at the dark house. No one did. Except you.

A week later I fell again, tripped over the curb in front of the office, and I hollered so loud the guests in Room 10 came running out in their robes. At the HealthCo, Tom knelt and prodded my scraped, swollen knee.

As he pulled Bactine, Neosporin, and gauze from a shelf, I imagined him pulling me into the break room.

He would lean close—as close as you and the man on the porch must have been—and say, The truth is, I haven't been overseas. I got fired from my last job in Phoenix, and my great-aunt lives up here. I got this scar in a fight. So you see, I'm not perfect.

It doesn't matter, I'd say.

I'd say, Where should we go?

And he would say, Anywhere. Anywhere you want.

Other times I hadn't fallen, but I pretended I had a sore throat or food poisoning, snatching up Sucrets and Pepto. I said I needed things for my parents: Bengay, vitamin B, glucosamine, cortisone for a rash. I told him about my mom, and he told me he was sorry, and he looked sorry, shaking his head and rubbing his jaw. Each time Tom threw in extras, or wouldn't charge for everything, or rang in coupons I didn't have. Each time he looked me in the eye, and each time I could feel my glowing heart, and I felt, well, almost pretty.

I felt like you must have felt walking into that house.

But then I overheard my parents talking about a letter that showed up in our mailbox: Adam Newell, Dani's father, in love with an underage girl. They didn't know it was you, but I could put two and two together.

After that, I didn't see you again until that last night, but I did see him once. He stayed at the motel. He checked in late; it was evening, but he was wearing sunglasses. He had a shadow of beard on his face. His car was piled with crap. He nodded his thanks, took the key, and let himself into his room. The whole time, I wanted to say something. I wanted to tell him I understood. I wanted to say, *Sometimes that's how love goes.* As if I knew. But of course I didn't say anything. I heard his car pull out late and then return around midnight. When I got up at six to set up the office, he was gone.

The night you disappeared was the weekend before Christmas. The motel usually was busy with tourists from Phoenix on their way to see the lights at Tlaquepaque, but because of the storms, everyone had canceled. On that Sunday, after I checked out the last couple and closed the office and left the after-hours sign in the window, I went to my parents' house, driving carefully through the waterlogged streets, keeping to the center lines to avoid the deepest parts. Inside, I reheated some tuna casserole.

"Where's Rose?" I asked.

"Staying the night at Angie's," my mom said. "School's out tomorrow."

"Right," I said. Meaning Rose probably would be at the motel with Angie and Beto, damn her.

My dad clicked the TV volume up. "Snowing in Flagstaff. Expecting eight inches or more."

My mom said, "I heard the river's up almost up to the bridge."

I stood at the counter and watched the backs of their heads in the TV's glow.

I said, "I changed my name." They didn't respond. The TV showed a graphic with rain sheeting out of gray clouds. I raised my voice. "I said, I changed my name."

My mom swiveled her recliner to look at me.

I gripped the edge of the counter. "It's Prentiss now. I go by Prentiss."

She glanced at my dad, who also swung his recliner until their feet were almost touching. He ran a hand over his face.

"Isn't that a bit strange?" she said. "To go by your last name?"

"No. It's not strange at all."

"What's wrong with the name we gave you?" he asked.

"Nothing." I touched my cheek. "I wanted a change. Also, I've met someone," I said. "His name is Tom Donahue. He's a pharmacist."

"Tom Donahue," she said. "At the HealthCo?"

"Yes."

"You're dating?"

"Not yet."

They exchanged another look. "I see."

"Stop doing that." I threw the casserole spoon into the sink. "I'm standing right here. I can see you."

"Little girl," my dad said as he let down the recliner's leg rest, "hush now."

"No, you hush. You hush." I slapped the counter. "I stayed here. I stayed here for you."

My mom said, "We appreciate your help, Stevie. But we want you to have your own life."

"My own life." I laughed. "I still could go. I could."

My dad said, "Go where?"

"To art school, for one thing. I won a motherfucking *scholar-ship*."

"You watch your language, girl." He looked at my mom. "What in the world has gotten into her?"

She shrugged. "Beats me. Tired, probably."

"I'm right here!" I said. "Can you even see me?" I pulled my hair back, exposing my cheek. "How about now?" I traced it, moving my finger furiously across the rough skin. "Your gift to me. Marked from birth."

My mom frowned. "Stevie, honey. Calm down. Why don't you stay here tonight?"

I turned off the oven and grabbed my purse. "It's *Prentiss*. It's probably French." I slammed the door.

I drove up and down Main, stopping at the two traffic lights, water lapping the sidewalks. Because of the storm, the parking lots were barren. No cars parked in haphazard rows, no young men and women leaning on the fenders, strolling and laughing, their whole lives wound silken around their shoulders.

I drove to the river and parked on the bridge. The rain fell more gently now, but the swollen river churned, cresting a foot from the bottom of the bridge. I left the headlights on and looked out at furious water, at branches stuck on the banks. The rain fell and fell and fell. I rubbed my sore knee, my bruised palms. I thought about the times I had spent drawing down by the river, my toes buried in the dirt. I studied my hands resting on the steering wheel. They were dry and cracked from cleaning solution, the nails short and ragged. In the deepening lines, I saw my father's titanium-white dust and pity, my mother's disappearing body. In my freckles, I saw my sister, sweet Baby Rose, who I once hugged too hard, who I smothered with my love. In my knuckles were my big-city college dreams, sun-yellow and fading fast. Embedded in my palms were the names, the whispers, the black corners of my life. My love line forked at my wrist, trailing off into the veins, and it was red all right, primary red, deep-rooted, primal.

I drove to the motel and parked in front of my room. No cars were in the lot, but a light was on in Room 7. Baby Rose. Dang her. I grabbed the extra key and walked to the room under the tin awning. The rain was a sleety mist now. I knocked on the door, calling out Rose's name. I could hear the TV blaring. She didn't answer. I tried the door, but it was locked.

At the window, there was a crack in the curtains. I stepped close to the glass and peered in. They were on the bed, on top of the sheets, the covers kicked down and rumpled on the carpet. Rose and Angie Juarez. Not Beto, as I'd suspected, but Angie, the quiet one with the streak in her hair. Naked and exposed, the blankets tossed away. I stood still at the window, holding my breath, but they didn't look my way. They didn't look at anything but each other. I turned away.

Across the street, I saw someone at the gas station pay phone, caught in a beam of headlights. The person turned, and I recognized you then. The new girl, the girl I'd talked to at the pharmacy, the girl I'd seen out walking at night, the girl at the dark house. I hurried to my room and waited for Angie and Rose to come out.

That was the last time I saw you, across the street. About six thirty or so, I thought, yes. No, I didn't see which way you went. No, I didn't see anyone pick you up. That was what I told the police.

It wasn't the last time, but I never told them the rest of it. I never told.

But you already know.

I went in my room, but I heard the sound of a car engine in the lot. I heard the slam of Room 7's door. I stepped out of my room and stood under the tin awning. Rose and Angie stumbled to the Impala, which shone under the streetlight like a pomegranate seed. Someone sat in the driver's seat, and I knew even with the shadows it was Beto Navarro. I pulled in a breath to call out to Baby Rose, to say, Hey! Come here, you. To tell her, Goddamn it, be careful. To squeeze her shoulder and smile, say, Angie's a nice girl. To tell her I would keep her secret.

I saw you then. You ran across the street, stopping on the curb under the streetlight. Your hair, red coat, sweater, and jeans were soaked from the rain, your breath a trail of smoke. You stood in the rain and waved. You called out, "Wait. Wait for me."

But they didn't see or hear you. Rose and Angie disappeared into the car, and the engine roared to life.

You jogged toward the Impala as the headlights and taillights flared to life, as the reverse lights popped on.

They didn't see you.

The car sped backward. The tires screeched.

You fell.

You landed on your back, splashing into a large puddle. I didn't see so much as feel your head jerk as it hit the pavement. The Impala wrenched forward, nearly clipping a pole, and then pulled away into the street, my baby sister inside, oblivious to what she'd done. The Impala's taillights bumped off the curb into the road, faded into the night.

I ran to you, kneeled at your side. The pooled water was deep, and your face was almost underwater. I pulled you up by the front of your coat and got a hand under your neck.

"Are you okay?" I shook your shoulder. "Jess. Hey. Are you okay?"

You opened your eyes. You looked at me. "What time is it?"

"Are you okay? Jess?"

You blinked a few times as the rain misted down. You struggled to pull yourself up to sitting.

"I'm okay," you said. You touched your head and winced. But your hand came away clean. No blood.

"Should I call an ambulance?"

"No," you said. "I think I'm okay."

"They didn't see you," I said.

You laughed a little. "Yeah, I got that." You laughed again. "This has been a hell of a day."

"Can you stand? Let me help you." I reached under your arms and lifted. Your puffy coat squished. You smelled of wet wool, sweat, a tinge of laundry soap or lotion.

"I need to get home," you said. "What time is it?"

"I don't know," I said. "I think it's six thirty or so."

You got your feet under you. You stood up, leaning on my shoulder. You stepped on each leg and held your arms out, testing your weight and balance.

"See? I'm okay," you said. "I should get home. What time is it?"

"I don't have a watch," I said. "I'll check inside."

You followed me toward my room. You limped a little, but you were upright. Standing. Walking. Talking. You stopped at the bumper of my car. "I need to get home," you said, your voice agitated now. You flapped your hands as if shaking them dry.

"I can drive you, if you want. I can give you a ride."

I opened the unlocked passenger side for you, and you sat down, your knees out, your feet on the pavement. "I'm all wet," you said.

"Don't worry about it. It's okay."

"I lost my umbrella. It was my dad's."

"Stay here," I said. "I'll get my keys."

You looked up at my face. You touched your cheek. "Like a map of the world," you said. "The world in your face. That's how I think of it. I hope that's okay. I hope that's not rude."

I stared at you as the colors began to swirl kaleidoscopic in the rain.

You smiled and looked down at your hands. Your wet hair swung as you shook your head. "Never mind," you said. "Sorry."

I wanted to say, Thanks. I wanted to say I wanted to be you.

Instead, I said, "My keys are inside. I'll be right back."

Inside my room, I grabbed my purse and keys and thought of how wet you were. I pulled some towels from the bath and then the comforter off the bed, folding it over my shoulder. I'd cover you up, warm you, but not to suffocating. I stopped and looked in the mirror. I traced the mark, its frayed edges, its dips and whorls. A map of the world.

When I returned, you weren't in the car. I stopped and stared at the closed door and empty seat. I stared and stared, for the first time uncertain of my own sanity, wondering if I'd imagined the whole thing. I dropped the bedding and towels on the concrete and walked to the passenger side. There, on the seat: your red coat. I opened the door and picked it up. You were real. I hadn't imagined you. I ran to Main Street, looking up and down the road, squinting in the mist. I couldn't see you. I called your name. I went to College Drive and peered up the street, looking for a figure in the dark. I couldn't see you anywhere. I squeezed your coat into a ball, hugging it to my chest.

Of course, I know *now*, I should have gotten in the car. I should have looked for you. I should have called the police. I should have called your mother. I should have realized, She's not thinking straight. I should have done more. Partially I thought I was protecting Rose, worried she'd get in trouble. But the awful truth is, in the moment, I was offended. You didn't want a ride from me after all, the weirdo with the world on her face? Fine. Walk then. See if I cared. I took your sodden coat inside. Hung it on the shower curtain rod to dry. You could come and get it then. I wouldn't bring it to you.

Two days later, the paper ran the article. You were missing. You hadn't come home that night.

The police came, said you'd been spotted in the area that night. Asked if I'd seen you.

By then it was too late to tell. Your red coat, washed and fluff-dried in the laundry room, was bundled under my bed, next to the drawings and half-used paint. By then, I'd found a pencil in its pocket and taken it, put it in the cup on my desk. By then, I couldn't tell about Rose, Angie, and Beto and the car, about Rose and Angie's secret in the motel, about watching you fall but then get up. It would seem as though I were hiding something. What if they didn't believe me? *I* barely believed me: A car hit you. You fell hard and smacked your head, but you got up. You stood, talked, and walked. You sat in my car. And then you walked away. I threw a blanket over all of it, smothered its memory until it stopped kicking.

I told them instead I saw you across the street at the gas station when I came home from my folks' house. About six thirty.

Did I speak to you? they asked.

No, I told them, as I saw Baby Rose swaddled in a blanket, as I heard your voice in my ear: *What time is it? I have to go home.*

After my interview with the police, I went to Room 11. My room. My life. I flipped on the light and sat hunched against the pillows on the bed, looking at the dingy walls and the paintings of cactuses and coyotes. And then I saw something else. Colors. Shapes.

I took down the ugly paintings and dug out my art supplies from under the bed. With your pencil, I set to work on the white wall. When the sun rose, I tore down the gold curtains and opened the door, the air fresh and painful, like the river in spring. The rain had stopped three days earlier. The water had stopped rushing, slowed to a trickle, soaked into the porous earth, and the sun reappeared as suddenly as if it had tunneled through a brick wall. Back to normal. I didn't open the front office, left the phone number in the window, but no one called. I painted until my shoulders and arms ached.

It was late afternoon by the time I sat on the bed and looked at what I had done. The colors sharp and lush, reds and violets and golds. A woman, alone, standing on the rim of a low canyon, a suitcase by her feet. The woman, tall and round at the hip, standing sideways to the viewer, her face turned away. The canyon, a gouged bowl, slashed with shadow, a gash in its core. The woman, looking past the canyon at the sky, which was a deep burning orange tinged with black and brown. No. She was looking *past* the sky, into the long distance.

When I wandered into the HealthCo some time later, Tom was at the counter.

"My goodness. Are you all right?" he asked. "Are you hurt? What can I do?"

In the security mirror, I saw myself. My hair was knotted in place with a paintbrush, my full face exposed. Veins and patches of red stood out on my skin, and wild paint colors streaked my arms, legs, even my feet in their flip-flops. The neckline of my T-shirt scooped low, my nipples clear against the thin fabric.

"I've been working. Drawing, painting."

"You look cold," Tom said.

I shrugged and looked him in the eye. "I'm not cold here."

"Oh," he said, looking down. He looked up and smiled a little. I saw it in his eyes then, the pity. I don't know how I'd missed it in the first place, as clear and shining as it was. I could see everything now.

I said, "I'm not what people say. I'm not crazy."

He shook his head. "No."

Tell him, I thought. Tell him about the car. About the coat. Ask for his advice.

Instead, I lifted my chin and pointed at my cheek. "What does this look like to you? What do you see in it?"

Say the world, I thought. Say you see the world.

"Stevie," he said, "are you okay?"

"I'm asking you what you see," I said. "Do you see me at all?"

"I see you fine," he said. "I think you look fine. But I think you better go home now. You need to take care of yourself."

I said, "I'm going." I hiked up my bra strap. For no reason—or maybe because I was thinking of that woman on the wall with the suitcase at her feet—I said, "In fact, I'm leaving town today. This'll be the last time you see me."

For a second, I hoped he would say, No, wait, or, I'll come with you, but he didn't. Of course he didn't.

My nose started to run, and I wiped it on my wrist. I was angry at myself and terrified of what I knew, of that coat under my bed, and of you, still missing. I pointed at his seahorse scar. "God. What happened to your face?"

He looked down at the counter. "Go on now, Stevie," he said.

"That's not my name," I said.

He said, "Go on."

As I walked out the exit, I saw the first MISSING poster. There you were, fluttering in the breeze, invisible tape across your perfect cheek.

I sat shivering in my car in the HealthCo parking lot for I don't know how long. When the sun hit the horizon, I sat straight up and stared at the colors, which hovered and bled and shifted. I thought of the colors on my wall, that low canyon. I recognized it then, the gouge in the earth. I had seen it. It was real.

I drove to the old lake and stepped out to its emptiness. There was the gash at the bottom, the same one on the wall of my room. I looked at all the exposed cracked dirt in the bowl of the lake, and I wanted to protect it somehow, keep it safe, make it beautiful. The rocks and patterns took shape behind my eyes. I climbed down into the basin and started at the center. At the heart, and moving outward. That day I placed three stones. One for each day I didn't tell. One for each day I didn't chase after you. One for each day the red coat beat under my bed, poetic in its telltale fervency. One for each day I wish I'd known what to say to make it okay, to make you stay, to drive you home to safety. And I've placed one every day since. Marking the days: 6,669 as of last week, from the day we got the news. Circling, circling, feeling my heart expand even as I continue to live small.

It's a terrible truth that I found my art when we lost you. I made the lake, with its 6,669 stones. I painted every room in the motel with its own themed mural: Fall, Winter, Spring, Summer, Earth, Fire, Water, Air, Sunrise, Sunset. I painted the doors in bright citrus hues, restored vintage metal porch furniture, updated curtains and bedding to make each room its own. I turned my car into a mosaic, with bottle caps and wine corks and shards of colored glass. In "The Best of Indie Motels" in the latest *Arizona Highways*, there's me, standing atop the motel in the rooftop garden, with a streak of purple dye in my hair, my whole face exposed to the world.

That painting in my room has faded in the last few years, its colors grown softer, less luminous, but it is still there. Still that woman stands on the precipice, looking into the distance. Is she you? Or me? I have never been sure what I intended. What does she see out there in the burning sky? What is she waiting for?

Today, I grab a felt-tip pen and sign my name in the lower right corner of the wall, near the woman's foot. Prentiss. I haven't called myself that in years. Not since the day I made this painting. Only Father Tom still calls me that. The pharmacist turned priest, the man who I believed saw me for the first time, who sees me now at the grocery store and waves, kindly, because he was always kind.

But it was you who saw me first.

Today, I see something else in the painting. This time, the woman does not look past the sky at the distance but sees herself *inside* the distance. A place where old dreams and desires rise.

I watch the woman on the wall. I see myself letting go of the wheelbarrow that strains my back, whose handles leave deep marks and splinters in my palms. I see myself letting go of the rocks I carry so carefully in the curves of my arms. I stop marking the days. I stop trying to cover the injured earth. Stop trying to save it, transform it, make it beautiful again. I see myself turn away from the edge. I see myself turn toward a new horizon.

Go on, Father Tom said to me that day.

Maybe I can. Maybe I can go now.

THANK YOU FOR CALLING

MAUD WAITED. FOR THE FIRST time in years, she took vacation, letting a sub cover her route. For the first time in years, Maud hadn't wanted to keep moving. She wanted to keep still. For two weeks now, she had stayed on the sofa. She sat, reclined, lay down flat. She rose to use the bathroom and to get snacks from one of the many containers people had dropped off, but mostly she stayed still. She slept, on and off, kicking her blanket on and off. She watched television. She watched the walls. She watched her hands and feet. She watched the driveway, waiting for Gil Alvarez to arrive with the news. She watched the clouds, the mailbox, the oil stain under her sedan. She watched the window itself, where the husk of an insect hung from a spiderweb in the corner. The same window where she'd watched and waited on the last night.

That night, she'd woken with a start, groggy, the room gray and dim, the sky nearly dark. 5:10 p.m., the stove clock read. The hard rain had turned to a drizzle. She found Jess's note and sat on the couch with a sigh. Frustration tinged with relief. At least she'd left a note this time. Her headstrong, independent girl. Tomorrow, they'd go get a Christmas tree. Pull out the decorations buried somewhere in the storage shed. She still needed to buy presents. She'd been too upset and distracted to shop. Maud flipped the porch light on, and then she took a shower to shake off the bleariness and chill in her bones. She even took time to diffuse her hair with the blow-dryer.

At six thirty, she put out fixings for their dinner. Grilled cheese and tomato soup: warm food for a rainy night. She dumped the soup in a pan and put it on the stove to simmer. She slapped thick slices of cheddar between the bread, buttered one side—extra butter for Jess's sandwich. She checked the window. The rain was a mist now, seeming to float rather than fall. She held her elbows. Almost two hours. She should be home now. Her stomach began to flutter with worry, even as she told herself, Come on, Maudly. She's fine. She's a smart kid. Out for a walk. Maybe she's with a friend.

Except Jess didn't have any friends. Not now.

At seven, she began to make calls. She called the Patty Melt, but it had already closed. She called Hector Juarez. No, Jess wasn't with Angie. Angie and her friend Rose were there, watching a movie. Wait, Rose had seen her earlier. At the Patty Melt. She'd come in for fries. Around five. Maud called Esther. No, Esther hadn't heard from her—she'd call if she did, and she'd call and check back. Maud called Iris. No, Jess hadn't been to the orchard. She'd keep an eye out and call if she saw her.

Around seven thirty, Maud turned off the burner under the soup, covered the buttered bread and cheese with foil. She grabbed her keys. The flutters in her stomach had turned to clenching, even as she assured herself she was being overprotective, paranoid, worried for nothing. Any second Jess would walk in the door. She left her own note: "J-bird: went out to look for you. Worried, dang it. Stay put."

She drove the short way to town, down Roadrunner to Quail Run instead of her normal route, the longer back way that would dump her out on the other side of the District near the post office, avoiding campus traffic. Coming up on a low dip in the road, she stepped on the brakes as her headlights showed a slash of water in the road. She turned on her high beams. The stream was low and running slow, more mud than water. Must have been rushing through at some point but then slowed once the rain let up. That was the way of flash floods: come in a flash, gone in a flash. She let off the brake and drove across it at good speed, the tires splashing but firm on the pavement.

In town, she drove slowly through the puddled streets, wrapping her arms around the steering wheel and peering through the windshield. No one out walking. She drove onto the high school campus, onto the Syc campus, turned around in the Woodchute's parking lot, deserted but for one car. She stopped at the Pickaxe, even though Jess wouldn't have been allowed in. Neither the bartender or any of the three people nursing drinks had seen her. She stopped in the one fast-food restaurant open near the highway. No one there had seen her, either. She drove through the neighborhoods. She stopped in front of the Newells'. No porch light. No Christmas lights. Dark house. No sense in knocking on that door.

Back home, she flew inside and called out Jess's name. No answer.

No blinking button on the answering machine, but she pushed play anyway. No messages.

She waited until midnight, Jess's official curfew, to call the police. Seven hours after she went out, five hours after she said she'd be home.

At midnight, she opened the front door and stood on the threshold, calling her daughter's name.

No answer.

No answer ever again.

As she waited, sometimes she answered the telephone, which had been ringing like gangbusters. She told the callers, No, thank you, I'm fine. I appreciate that. No, I don't need anything. Thank you for calling. She told the newspaper, No comment. When Gil called with updates about what stage the forensic anthropologists had reached, she listened and said, I see, and, Okay, good to know. She told him, I appreciate it, Gil. Thanks for calling. Sometimes she held the phone up to her bad ear so all she could hear was the vibration of voices against her cheek. She thought about the calls she'd made that long-ago night, the calls she'd received from Esther and Iris and Hector, checking in. She thought about how phone calls themselves had changed: caller ID, voice mail, ringtones, cell phones that fit into front pockets. She thought about the bulky answering machine and its tin-can message. *You know what to do, so do it*. Maud did know. She waited.

About the waiting, people said, This must be so hard, but after eighteen years, a few more days were a drop in the bucket. She'd been through it before. Whenever bodies were found in Arizona, or across the United States, Jess's file came up in the Missing Persons database. Most of the first tests ruled her out—the timing, the sex, the age. One time, Maud did have to look at the objects of a young female victim to see if she could identify them. A necklace with a gold half-heart. Jess would never have worn such a thing. No, the hard part had already happened: the years of not knowing even though, deep down, she knew. The years of hoping, of imagining otherwise, despite every intuition to the contrary. Hope: humans' greatest strength and their greatest flaw. Hope had saved her, but it also kept her in limbo, kept her from moving forward. Kept her right here, waiting.

This time, Maud wasn't *really* waiting. She already knew. She knew the moment she kneeled in the dry wash with Gil and saw the bone protruding from the earth, and again when she returned and walked through the wash. Some part of her had always known. The part of her that knew the sun would rise and set each day, perhaps, or the part that understood the earth was spinning on its axis even though she couldn't *see* it spinning, couldn't *feel* it move at such stunning speed.

Jess wouldn't have run. Maud had always known that. Of course she would be nearby.

Gil had said they couldn't guarantee they'd be able to identify the body. He noted how much time had passed, the harsh sun and hard rains, mineral and acid levels, the tendency of animals to dig and scatter bones. He'd raked his fingers through his hair and said, "We don't know if we'll find answers, Maud." He'd reached out and touched her shoulder in his calm way.

Maud had her answer, whatever the tests revealed. It was what she had known all along.

Jess wouldn't have run.

The phone rang again. Again, she said, Yes, no, I appreciate it, thank you, thank you so much for calling. She ate a blueberry muffin from the box Esther had dropped off. She watched the monsoon clouds gather on the horizon. Afternoon already. The clouds looked weaker now, here in late August. The monsoon would fizzle soon, and the sky would dry out like a cotton sheet on a line. Come September, it'd be blue for weeks.

She heard the mail truck before she saw it; even with her ears, she knew the low stop-and-go hum. She went outside and waved at Luz Navarro behind the wheel. Luz stopped and called out, "Hey, mamí, how are you? How you holding up?"

"Fine, Luz, thanks for asking. I'm all right."

"We're all thinking about you. My mom's got you in her prayer circle, for what it's worth," she said. "Father Tom, too."

"Thanks. I appreciate it."

"Let us know if you need anything."

"Thanks. I will." *Thank you for calling.*

In the mailbox, mixed with bills and mailers, she found "Thinking of You" cards from co-workers and folks on her route. Soon, her box would be flooded with "In Sympathy" cards, her doorstep busy with flower deliveries. She knew this, too. She already knew.

The phone rang again. Maud picked up, but no one responded.

"Hello? Anyone there?" she said.

She was about to hang up when someone spoke.

"Is this Maud?" A man's voice.

"Who's asking?"

After a pause, the man said, "Adam Newell." He paused again. "Please don't hang up."

She didn't say anything at first, but then she sighed. "I guess I've been waiting for this. I guess I knew you'd call again eventually."

"I've tried. Many times."

"I know. What do you want?"

"I promise I won't call again. I promise I'll let you be after this. But I've been wondering something, and I need to ask you. I need to know the answer. Okay?"

"Ask," Maud said.

He sighed. "She ran away because of me, right? Because of what I did?"

Maud held the phone away from her ear. She looked at the holes in the receiver and then out the window. She stared at a dark cluster of clouds. The sky had been darker that long-ago afternoon. She'd been sitting on this same sofa.

"Maud? Hello?"

"I'm here."

When he finally spoke, his voice had grown soft, barely audible. "It's my fault. I know it's my fault. I just wanted to tell you."

She nodded in the stillness of her living room.

"Maud?"

"Here."

His voice sounded shaky, thin. "I know it's not enough to say I'm sorry. I know that, too."

Maud said, "She didn't run away."

"I don't understand. She ran off."

"No. She went out, but she was coming back. She left a note, remember?" Maud didn't need to look at the slip of paper she'd taped in the notebook. She recited it from memory. " 'I'm going out for a walk. I need to clear my head. I'll be back in a couple hours. Don't worry. Love, J-bird.' "

"I know." He paused and then let out a hard breath. "But I assumed she changed her mind."

"That's like you. To assume."

"I'm saying I'm the reason she changed her mind. I'm trying to say something here."

Maud said, "No. She didn't change her mind. She wasn't running away. She went out for a walk. That was the plan. Back in a couple hours. She was coming home. To me, not to you."

He didn't answer. The silence strung across the line.

Finally, he said, "I wish you'd talked to me about it. I wish you'd told me more."

"I'm sorry, do you think I owe you something? Do you think I owe you explanations?"

He raised his voice. "I wish you talked to me," he said. "Jesus Christ. All this time, I believed she'd run away."

"Fuck you, Adam. She *was* running. Emotionally, anyway. She couldn't sit still because of what you did." She dropped her head onto the sofa cushion.

He breathed on the line.

Maud grabbed one of the muffins from the box and squeezed it until it squished out between her fingers. She thumped the cushion, smearing crumbs and grease on the fabric.

"I was asleep," she said. "When she left. I had no idea she'd go outside. Why in the world would she? I woke up, and I wasn't even worried at first. Exasperated, maybe. You know what I thought? I thought, Tomorrow, we'll go get a Christmas tree. We'll get a tree and we'll decorate it. We'll get out all the decorations! All of them!" She realized she was yelling, and she stopped.

"It's not—"

"Don't say it," she said. "Don't you say another word."

His voice cracked. "But it's not your fault, Maud."

"Of course it's not." But of course it *was*. Deep in her heart, she'd always known the truth, even when she couldn't look at it in the face. She was the mother. She'd failed to protect her. She'd failed to do the bare minimum: be awake. She wanted to yell, No, it's *your* fault, because it was, ultimately, but she couldn't get the words out.

"Maud, I loved her," he said.

"No, *I* loved her," she said. "I did."

"Can't it be both?" he said. "Can we both have loved her?"

Loved. Past tense.

"I have to go," she said.

"Maud, wait. Please. I know I have no right to ask this. I know I don't."

She tightened her grip on the phone. "Say it," she said.

"Will you let me know? Will you call me and let me know when you do? Not because you owe me anything. That's not what I'm saying."

Maud wiped her greasy fingers on her pants. He still had hope. This man who had loved her daughter, who had wanted to hold her in his arms.

"Okay," she said.

"Thank you," he said.

"Thank you for calling," she said automatically and hung up.

The phone rang again, and Maud didn't answer. She turned the ringer off and pulled the blanket over her. She clicked through the TV channels, drooling onto the pillow. Her arm grew numb beneath her, and she shook it out. She picked up most of the ruined muffin from the carpet and threw it in the kitchen trash. She ate another one, letting the crumbs drop straight onto the tile. Lifting the tinfoil off a dish, she fished out a bite of noodles with her fingers.

The doorbell rang. She turned and blinked. Okay. Okay. This was it. She brushed crumbs from her shirt, smeared the noodle sauce on her pants. The wait was over.

She opened the door, and there stood Esther, Iris, and Rachel. They all held bags and boxes and bottles.

"The gang's all here," Esther said. "A gang of what, I don't know, but we've got booze."

Maud smiled in spite of herself. She started to say, Oh, I'm fine, no need. Really. I'm not feeling up to company, thank you for calling, but by the time she found the words, the three of them had pushed their way inside. In the kitchen, they unloaded sacks, uncorked bottles, turned the oven to 350. They washed the dishes and wiped down countertops and bagged up the trash. Iris got out the broom, swept up crumbs, and then ping-ponged through the house. Rachel, who had subbed for a sick student at play rehearsal and was still in costume as Big Mama, pearls at her throat and her face thick with pancake makeup and eyeliner, handed Maud a glass of Chablis. Esther unwrapped a deli tray piled high with shaved meats and fresh wheat rolls. "Real food. Not all this bakery crap," she said. She smiled. "Who's plying you with all this shite, anyway?"

Eat, they said. Drink, they said.

Tell us, they said, if you need to. Or don't. We're all yours tonight, Maud. And tomorrow. And the next day. You're not getting rid of us that easy.

Maud nodded. She didn't have to thank them, these women she had known as long now as she had known her own daughter. She looked at the deepening wrinkles on their cheeks and necks and hands, the soft stomachs, the fragile skin under the eyes. She had watched them age. They'd watched her age, too, watched her fuzzy curls turn salt and pepper and now almost fully gray. They'd watched her every step of these last years, even when she hadn't known they were watching. They were waiting, too.

"Thanks," she said, anyway, even though she didn't have to.

No problem, they said. We're here for the haul, you hear?

You're not alone, they said.

Of course she was, but she knew what they meant. They meant well. Good eggs, every last one of them.

A couple hours later, after Maud had forgotten she was waiting, when she had forgotten to keep watch, a door thumped shut in the driveway. They all swiveled to see who was coming up the walk. Except Maud. Maud turned away suddenly, her back to the window.

Without looking, she knew it was Gil Alvarez. She knew his silver hair was glinting in the fading sunlight. She knew the slump of his shoulders, the deep-set weariness in his face from seeing what he'd seen all those years. She knew how he would comb his hair with his fingers. She knew he'd look her in the eye and say, Maud, can I speak to you?

She knew it, just as she'd known the truth when she returned to the wash and walked through it, slipping on the hot stones, until she reached her own street, Roadrunner Lane. The place where the road dipped, where that fateful night she'd paused upon seeing a slash of water and mud and thought of flash floods. She'd known her whole life how desert washes turned to wild rushing rivers that could knock trucks sideways. She knew the rules: Do Not Cross When Flooded. Turn Around, Don't Drown. She knew about drivers who didn't listen, who stalled out in six inches of water and climbed onto their roofs as the cars washed downstream. She knew about hikers swept miles from their tents, crushed under mud and stone.

She knew all of it.

The sun was on its way west again. It would set, and tomorrow it would rise. The world spun on its axis. It spun, and spun, and spun, and here she stood.

Her friends murmured. They touched her back, her arm. They said, Shit.

Maud felt the warmth of their skin. When her knees buckled and she started to go down, they took her weight and pulled her up. They held her steady. We've got you, they said.

Still she couldn't turn around. She stood facing the wall, and she thought, No. Wait. Not yet. I'm not ready yet.

MASS AND GRAVITY
December 22, 1991

JESS WALKED UPHILL TOWARD HOME—HER familiar route up College Drive, past the Syc on the right, past Piñon Drive and sleepy neighborhood houses on the left, onto Quail Run, past the orchard. Her teeth had stopped chattering, and her head had begun to throb, a knot the size of a tangerine. Her father's sweater was so wet it hung almost to her knees. She was so hot. As she hit Roadrunner Lane—the road to home, she was almost home—she peeled off the sweater and tied it around her waist, remembering now she had taken off her coat and left it on Stevie Prentiss's car seat when she'd decided she needed to walk home. Why had she done that? Stevie had gone inside her room to grab her keys, and Jess had thought, I need to go home *now*. She'd shrugged off her coat, climbed out of the car, and started to run. She made it halfway up College Drive before her throbbing head stopped her.

What time was it? The events of the evening had become muddled. She remembered Dani holding an umbrella over her head. Jess's umbrella. Her father's umbrella. She remembered bright taillights, lying in a puddle, the yellow sign of the Woodchute above her. She kicked at the pavement. Her toes were numb, but the rest of her was feverish, sweating. All she wanted was to lie down, to pull the covers up, to sink into oblivion. All she wanted was for her mom to sit next to her and put a cool hand on her burning forehead.

When she reached the dip in the road, the one she'd jumped

over on the way into town, she could hear the water before she could see it. A staticky gush, like a bath faucet on full blast. The sky dark now, she squinted, trying to gauge how far across it was. Six feet? About as wide as a car. No telling how deep.

Shit. She paced across the road, alongside the water, trying to find the narrowest part. If she had to turn around and take the long route to her house, that would be at least another half hour. She began to cry a little. Why hadn't her mother come to find her? What time was it?

It's time, she heard a voice say, a voice inside.

She tasted salt in her throat. Okay. She could do this. She composed her breath and pushed at her eyes. She stretched to her tallest self, brushing her wet hair out of her face. Okay.

She assessed the distance again. If she got a running start, she could make it.

She walked back several yards, turned, and took a deep breath. An easy jump across. A leap she'd done a million times—over puddles and streams, over crevices, off steps. Out of necessity but out of joy, too. To leap, to defy gravity for one tiny moment.

"Don't blink," she said.

She ran toward the rushing water. When she hit the edge, she sprang off her left foot and leaped, kicking her right foot out, throwing her body forward.

She didn't count on the mud, the silty slick layer lurking beneath the surface. When her left foot hit and she pushed upward, she slipped. Her foot went out from under her, and she landed hard on her side, splashing into the center of the stream. As she hit the water, she cried out, "No!" because she knew. She'd seen it on the news—how cars, let alone bodies, could be swept away by a current. She scrambled for purchase, lunging for the pavement above her, but the water was too strong. *Swept* was the wrong word. It *shoved, pushed, thrust, heaved* her off the road and into the narrow chasm of the wash.

She thrashed and blindly snatched at rocks and dirt, trying to stop herself as she spun and tumbled in the violent current. *Get on your back*, the voice inside said. Her father's advice about riptides. And then it was his voice, the one she'd always known, the one she'd heard again on the payphone: *Don't fight it. Let it take you. Ride it out. Keep your eye on the shore.*

But there was no shore, only darkness and sharp rocks, a roar of rushing water, choking mouthfuls, the grit of sand in her eyes and teeth.

Her mother's voice now, the voice she knew by heart: *Buck up, J-bird. You have so much to live for.*

I'm trying, she thought as she thrust her mouth toward what she thought was air. But the sky had disappeared, and the earth, too, the elemental world upended. The water did not heed her will. It did not care about her lungs and their need to breathe. It did not know of her desires or dreams or fears. But it also did not act upon her; this was not about punishment, or judgment, or morality. It simply followed the laws of nature. The larger the mass, the stronger the force of gravity. Her young, slim body in all its desperate exertions could not compete. She breathed in water instead of air—eighteen years later, forensic scientists would find that water in her bones as diatoms and know she drowned, would know it was her bones from DNA tests. They would know her body was pushed into a crevice in the side of the wash, trapped and buried by tons of mud, unseen until the dirt began to erode with wind and more water. They would find a piece of her tennis shoe and a silver earring buried with her in the dirt.

In the end, she did not think in language. Words, her beloved words, could not save her. Not *love*, nor *home*, nor *friendship*, nor *beauty*, nor *truth*, though these surely would have been among the last on her tongue if she could have brought them forth. She did not think in images, either. Her young life did not, as they say, flash before her. No glimpses of Mom with a bowl of popcorn on her knees, her laugh as loud as a freight train. No Dad raising his glass to toast her on her sixteenth birthday: *Here's to my beautiful girl. Go get 'em*. No Dani giggling in a tent on a beach. No Adam, begging her to love him.

Instead, what Jess saw was light: millions of sparks behind her eyes. Before she lost all consciousness, she understood these sparks as galactic light, dust from the universe. Ancient light that had traveled for millions of years and only found its way to her now. The light of dreams. The light of both the past and future. Nameless light, unknowable light, but for a moment, hers.

SUNDOWN AT THE ORCHARD

ON THE DAY OF THE memorial service for Jess Winters, the morning dawned bright and clear, the air warm but drier now on the cusp of fall. Out at the orchard, Iris and Paul finished setting up chairs and tables on the redwood deck. Esther, along with Rachel, Hugh, and, surprisingly, Dani, had dropped off trays of food and set up the kitchen and living room. Maud hadn't wanted anything big. Simple, she'd said. Thank you. Thank you, she kept saying, her hands fluttering until she grabbed onto her elbows and held tight. Iris turned and scanned the view from the deck. They'd get to watch the sunset, maybe even glimpse the nearly full moon. At least they didn't have to worry about the weather. They could give Maud a nice night. Pay their respects. Say good-bye to Jess. Finally.

Paul looked at his watch. "We have to get to T-ball, Mom," he said. "Are you coming with us?"

"Can't this time. I need to keep an eye on the irrigation," she said. This time of year, with less rain, watering was crucial to make sure the kernels filled out the shells. Soon enough, it'd be harvest again. Soon enough, she'd be going twelve hours a day for three months straight. All those shells. She'd be a shaking shell of herself by the time it was finished. But this would be the last time.

Paul leaned to pick up his coffee cup, and he let out a small grunt. His left wrist was healed, but his shoulder would be in a sling for a few more weeks. Iris started to ask him if he was all right but stopped herself. He was all right. He was putting his house in Phoenix on the market. He'd given notice at the news-paper and enrolled Sean in preschool and T-ball here. He was coming home. For now, he said. Who knew for how long. The *Sycamore Sun* had an opening for an editor. Half my current salary, he said with a laugh.

"Will you take over the orchard?" she'd asked.

"I don't know, Mom," he said. "I don't know yet. For now I'll help out. I'll help as much as I can."

She'd nodded. It didn't matter. If he didn't want it, she'd sell it, then, though she hadn't told him yet about her plans.

Now Paul said to Sean, "Go get your glove, buddy."

His son ran to the house at full speed, his short legs chugging. Paul laughed. "It's like he's set on one speed: Go!"

"He's growing," she said. "Already I can tell he's taller."

"Yeah. I guess they do that."

She patted his unslinged arm. "He'll be tall like you. Like Beau."

They leaned on the railing together, staring into the trees.

She said, "It was good to see Dani."

"Yeah," he said. "I thought it'd be, I don't know." He shrugged. "Different. But it was good to see her. She looks good. She looks the same."

But she wasn't the same, Iris thought. None of them were after all this time. After everything. Ruled an accidental drowning. No foul play. But it was still foul. Iris couldn't get the detail of Jess's earring out of her mind. That little piece of silver sunk into the earth as her flesh rotted away.

He said, "I need to go down to Phoenix next weekend. To deal with the house. Can you watch him?"

"Of course," she said, and her heart lifted. "Of course."

"I'm not ready," he said. "I don't want to pack up yet. I don't know what I'm doing."

She thought about those weeks and months right after Beau died. She'd shaved her head as if going into battle, and in some ways she had been. She fought through the days, taking care of Paul, of the orchard, of everything, because if she stopped to look around, she might blow into bits.

"Do it anyway," she said.

"Thanks." He reached over with his good arm and put his hand over hers. "I couldn't do it without you."

"Don't worry about it. I'm happy to help with Sean."

"I don't know how you did it then." He shook his head.

She smiled. "I had you."

He smiled and rubbed her head. He walked toward the house, pressing at his shoulder. The rest of him was healthy. Tall, with those long, muscular legs, like Beau's. His head shone in the morning sun, his big ears jutting out. She touched her own head, tugged at the short tufts. Maybe she wouldn't cut it today. Leave the clippers in the drawer. Maybe she'd let it go for a while, see what happened.

She straightened a chair, reattached a wire to a nail, and reached down to yank out a tuft of rattlesnake weed that had snuck up through the planks. She turned and looked at the orchard, at the cool shaded rows. She'd looked at this her entire adult life. Come next fall, it wouldn't be hers anymore. She'd have to find a new view.

She hadn't told Paul, or Esther, or anyone. Except Beau. She told him, out on the deck, late at night in one of her talks. *Buster, it's happening.* She told him this winter would be her final Sundown nights. Told him she was going to buy a little cottage near the Syc, with a guest room for Sean. After so much land, so much space, the thought of smallness appealed to her. Told him she was going to college. Her. Ha. Told him she had no idea what she was going to study. She'd take whatever struck her. She'd be undecided for a while.

Oh, of course she was going to miss it. Like hell. Like she missed him. But she was doing it anyway, because goddamn, buster. This life. She didn't know how much of it she had left.

The trees were ripe, she told him. They were almost there.

***

On the way to the ball fields, Paul glanced in the rearview at Sean buckled in the back, a small leather baseball glove on his right hand. The glove was too stiff. They needed to break it in. Paul wondered where his old glove had ended up; he'd have to remember to ask his mother. Probably somewhere in a closet, and he thought of his own closet down south full of Caryn's clothes, and he thought he smelled vanilla. His son's knees and elbows had healed, the skin pink but scab-free. Sean stared out the window, growing glassy-eyed as he often did in the car. The drive was short, but Sean would zonk out within minutes, so Paul asked him questions to keep him awake. Asked about his new preschool, about baseball, about the lizard he'd seen that morning. In the rearview, Paul caught a glimpse of his own collar. It was smudged with black. He rubbed at the mark.

She'd looked exactly the same. That had been his first thought. Like time had stood still. Sleeker, more modern than he expected. Her dark hair was shorter now, curved in a bob around her pointy chin, contacts instead of glasses. She'd lined her eyes with kohl with an elaborate swoop at the corner. When she smiled, he could see the crow's feet, the vertical creases in her cheek. Otherwise, the same.

"Dani, you look great," he'd told her. "Exactly the same."

"You too," she said, smiling. They chatted about how long it had been, about the weather. She pointed at Sean and said, "Oh, wow. He looks *just* like you."

"Yeah," he said. "Check out those ears. Poor guy."

Her smile faded. Without warning, she'd started to cry. She took three steps, closed the space between them, and hugged him. Closed the gap, the literal one, and the festering one. She wrapped both arms around his ribs, squeezing. His shoulder protested, but he didn't move. He stood still, silent, and everyone else fell silent, too, watching them. She stood on her tiptoes, pulling at his good shoulder, and he bent down.

"I'm sorry about your wife, Paul," she said into his ear. "I really am."

"Thank you," he said. He lifted his good arm and put it around her. "I'm sorry, too. Me, too."

They stood there on the edge of the orchard, on the edge of their past lives. He held her, and he could feel her shake, and he shook too. Since Caryn died, he hadn't hugged even his mother this way, only Sean. Dani Newell, his first love whose heart he'd broken, leaving her retching her Thanksgiving dinner on the carpet. And here they stood, in the orchard again, bound by time and memory and all the things they'd once said, and the things they hadn't known to say. I love you, they'd once said. God, I love you so much, they'd said, over and over, and they had meant it, their bodies joined under the naked sky. They hadn't known any better then. They hadn't known anything yet.

At the ball fields, Paul unbuckled Sean's belt with his good hand. He bent down and checked his reflection in the side mirror. His eyes were puffy, a bit red, but he looked okay. He could use a shave, but oh well. He greeted the other parents, some of whom he knew from high school—there was Warren Smith, Smitty, his track mate, now plump around the middle and holding his chubby son's hand. He said to Paul, Good to see you, good to see you. He whacked Paul on the back with a meaty paw.

Paul met Sean's T-ball coach, Coach D, who'd been sending e-mail introductions and reminders. He hadn't realized D stood for Drennan, and she was the woman he'd seen walking on the trails. The woman who'd found the bones. The new professor at the Syc. Coach Laura Drennan.

Laura gathered her young charges while Paul and the other parents lingered behind the fence. She squatted at eye level and spoke in a loud, cheerful voice. "We're going to learn so much about baseball and sportsmanship, but your number-one job is to have fun, okay? Do you think we can do that? Let me hear you."

The girls and boys cheered, hopping up and down. The kids took turns swinging wildly at a Wiffle ball on a post, and Coach D helped them choke up on the bat, showed them how to stand at the plate. Eye on the ball, she said. She clapped at every single swing. When Sean got up to bat, he turned and looked for Paul. Paul waved, his eyes filling. His first milestone without Caryn. Sean connected, and the plastic ball dribbled toward the mound. Paul yelled, "Go, buddy, go!" But Sean took off for third instead of first, hopping on the bag with both feet. Everyone cheered anyway, and Coach D guided him over to first.

After the game, while the kids sucked on orange slices and juice boxes, Coach D handed out schedules and snack rotation lists to the parents. Paul thought she looked different, though he couldn't pinpoint why. Calmer, maybe. More open. Out on the trails, she'd struck him as one step away from falling down.

Someone asked how she was settling in at the Syc.

"Great!" she said, still in her coach voice. "Keeping busy." She clapped. "Okay! See you next Wednesday night for practice!"

While the parents gathered up their kids, Paul lingered as Sean stood with another boy at the pitcher's mound, throwing rocks toward home plate. He introduced himself to Coach Laura, sticking out his good hand to shake hers. She had a strong grip.

He said, "We've crossed paths before, I think. Out on the river trail."

Laura tilted her head. "Right. You're the runner." She seemed to blush when she said it. Perhaps because she didn't want to talk about the bones. She let go of his hand and pointed at his arm in the sling. "You're having a bad day."

"Lost a fight with a ladder," he said.

"Ladders. Sneaky sons of bitches."

He laughed. He nodded at the field. "Hey, thanks for doing all this. I'm sure you're busy."

She shrugged. "Busy's good. I like busy."

"I haven't seen you out lately. Walking."

"No," she said, looking down. She tapped the tips of her tennis shoes together.

He said, "Are you coming tonight? To the orchard?"

"The memorial? Oh, I don't think so. I didn't know her," she said. "I'd feel out of place."

"I always feel out of place," he said, "and I'm from here."

She smiled. "I actually would like to pay my respects to Maud. She's a great lady. The first one here to welcome me." She pulled on her ponytail. "It's been very strange. A lot of people know who I am, but I barely know anyone."

"I can introduce you. If I don't know them, my mom will."

"Thanks. Maybe. It'd be nice to know people. It's been a long summer." She pulled a baseball from her shorts pocket and gripped it in her right hand. She threw the ball, hard. It went all the way to the right-field fence.

He whistled. "Good arm, Coach D."

She grinned and pointed at the field. "Looks like we're the last ones standing."

Sean sat on the pitcher's mound, alone, burying orange slices in the dirt at his feet. "I should get going," Paul said.

"Me, too." She nodded. "It was nice to meet you. See you later. Or next practice."

"You bet," he said.

He watched Laura Drennan walk toward the neighborhood behind the fields, her ponytail swinging between her shoulder blades. He called to Sean, who jumped up and ran at him, his knees and hands brown with dirt. Forgetting his shoulder, he swung the boy up in his arms. He cringed, biting at the pain, but he didn't set him down. He shifted Sean's weight, smelling oranges. He tightened his grip.

"You did great," Paul said. "You played like a million bucks."

***

Laura Drennan walked home. She walked through the metal gate, trailing her fingers on the latch. She walked, and her stomach growled, and she thought of the leftover burrito in her fridge. She thought of the quizzes she needed to grade, the prep she needed to finish. She walked across the bridge and down the gravel path that led to the streets of her neighborhood; she walked the same path to and from the college on her teaching days, too. She walked, and she said the street names in her head before she reached them. She knew them now without looking. She knew her students' names, too, here with classes a month in.

She knew her new colleagues' names, the names of campus buildings, the names of the mountains, the names of trees. She knew the name of her mail carrier and the name of her mail carrier's daughter, the girl whose bones she'd found in the wash. She knew the name of the woman who served her pastries at the bakery. She knew the names of her T-ball kids. She knew the names of the T-ball parents. She knew that father back on the field was the runner with the sexy legs on the river trail. She knew the woman at the auto shop and her chatty wife—look, there they went now in their cool vintage car, their teenage girl at the wheel. Laura waved, and they waved back.

Before Laura reached the street, she turned and looked behind her. The grass of the fields rippled in the gentle wind. Paul Overton, his arm in a sling, carried his son across the gravel parking lot. She turned and kept walking. She smiled. It was almost fall, she was coaching Little League, and the sun was shining on her face. When her feet hit the pavement, she gave a little skip. Skipping. What a childish thing to do. What was next, hopscotch? Hush up, you, she told herself. Just be among the goddamn living. She skipped, the soles of her tennis shoes scuffing the pavement, until her breath came hard and fast, heavy in her ears. She skipped all the way home.

***

From the passenger side of the Impala, Rose said, "Ten and two, Hazel. Stop slouching."

Hazel shifted her hands on the wheel. "I'm not slouching. These seats are slippery."

Angie sat in the middle of the back seat, offering advice and directions. Hazel was a good driver, attentive, cautious, defensive. Better than Rose, that was for sure, who'd always been a lead foot and a talker at the same time. A damn sight better than Beto, god love him. Hazel's personality probably came from her father, though Angie had never met him, so she couldn't say for sure. She didn't know much about those two years after Rose had called off their secret relationship, their clandestine trips to the motel, to the alleys of Jerome, to the desert pullouts outside of town, atop the slag heap behind the fairgrounds with the sharp ore cutting into their skin. She only knew Rose finally came home—with Hazel.

Rose turned around to Angie in the back seat.

"I said to her, I said, Stevie, where is this coming from? Why do you suddenly want to go to Paris?"

"Watch this corner, Hazel," Angie said. "People speed here."

Hazel said, "Got it." She slowed down, looking both ways.

Rose slapped the dash. "She bought a one-way ticket. Got right on the Internet and ordered it up. Says she'll be home in a few months. I swear to God. I swear to *God*. Mom's about to have kittens."

Hazel said, "I think Aunt Stevie is smarter than everyone gives her credit for."

"I agree," Angie said.

"I'm not saying she isn't smart. That motel is the tightest ship in town. But there's smart, and then there's prepared. There's smart, and there's—whatever it is she does. My sister wandering the streets of Paris, having one of her space-outs. How's that going to go?"

"Fine," Angie said. "It will go fine."

"What if it's not? I mean, what if we never hear from her again?"

"That's not going to happen."

"It happens," Rose said. She was suddenly near tears. "You know it does. We all know that. Look at Jess."

Hazel braked at the stop sign on Arrowhead. "Which way? Right or left?"

"Left," Angie said. "Then take a right on Main."

"Where are we going?" Hazel said.

"Not Paris!" Rose folded her arms.

Angie laughed. "It's a surprise," she said. "I was going to show you after the service tonight, but let's go now."

"A surprise?" Hazel and Rose said together.

"Jinx, you owe me a Coke," Hazel said, grinning at her mother. She reached over and punched Rose gently on the arm.

Rose reacted in mock pain and then tucked a piece of Hazel's hair behind her ear. "Watch the road," she said.

"I am."

Nearing the Woodchute on Main, Angie said, "Turn left here."

"Here? The motel?"

"Yep."

Hazel turned the car in smoothly, slowly. She pulled into a parking spot in front of the office.

Rose stared at the front office, where a college student was filling in. "I can't believe she did it," she said. "I can't believe she's not in there. She's always in there."

"Things change, hon," Angie said. "It's only for a few months. She's coming home."

Rose turned around again. Her blue eyes, those sweet, coy, flirtatious baby blues she'd first seen over the Patty Melt counter when they were both teenagers, when things like eye color and hair curls and beauty obscured everything. For nineteen years now, she'd seen those eyes flare in anger, crinkle shut with laughter, well up in fear and sorrow like they were now.

"What if she doesn't?"

They were, Angie thought, like the blue of a winter sky at dusk. Someday, she would see them close forever. Like she'd seen her father's. Or Rose would see Angie's that way. But not yet. Not just yet.

"I love you, Rosie. Did you know that?"

Rose nodded and wiped her eyes. "I love you back."

Hazel sighed. "Oh my god. Get a room, you two."

"We are," Angie said. She climbed out of the car and headed toward Room 7. She unlocked the door and looked in at the decorations, at the banner, the plane tickets and hotel reservations she'd spread out on the beds. She turned around, and she met Rose Prentiss's eyes again. They both grinned. Their room. That crazy, sexy girl. Somehow they'd made it. Past the looks, past the sex, past the immaturity and denial and secret shame. They'd made it this far.

Hazel let out a whoop. "Disneyland! Are you kidding? Cool! Oh, wow." She threw her arms around Angie, and Angie remembered that day in the mud, her father lifting her, pulling her to safety. How much he could carry. Love, that glassy orb of a word, took shape over Hazel's shoulder, and Angie coughed.

"You don't turn sixteen every day," Angie said. She held up the car keys. "I think it's time the Impala had a young driver again."

Hazel screamed. She hugged Angie and hugged Rose and hopped around the room and out into the parking lot.

Rose sat on the corner of the bed. She looked at Angie now with solemn eyes.

"I've been feeling stuck. Wanting to get away."

Angie nodded. "I know."

"How? I didn't even know. Not really."

"Rose. Come on. I know you."

Rose threw out her arms. "I want to go places. I want more. It doesn't mean I don't love you or our life."

"I *know*," Angie said. She sat on the bed next to her. "I used to want that too. Then we got busy, with Hazel, the shop, the motel, family. All of it. Somehow it got lost."

"Yeah," Rose said. "Lost."

So much lost. Angie thought of heart-shaped rocks, of bones beneath the earth. But so much found, too.

"Run away with me," Angie said. She pulled out the tickets she'd been hiding under her shirt and inside her waistband. "Paris in December. You and me. Your mom will keep an eye on Hazel. We'll meet up with Stevie." She flapped the tickets against her palm.

Rose stared at Angie, at the tickets. She took the tickets and held them in her lap. "Oh, you're too much, Angela Juarez. Too damn much."

Hazel yelled from the parking lot, "You guys, come on! Let's go for a ride in my new car!"

"Roller-skating on the moon," Rose said. She stared out the open door.

"What?" Angie pulled at one of her curls.

She smiled. "Nothing. Something Stevie used to say." She laid her head on Angie's shoulder. "But I know what she means now."

***

Down the hill in Phoenix, Stevie Prentiss sat buckled in her window seat on the plane. She patted her money belt inside her new jeans, where she had carefully placed several hundred-dollar bills. She had her hotel reservation and a new cell phone with overseas access. She had her neck pillow and eye mask and a coupon for one free drink. One suitcase was in the bin over her head, another was in the belly below, a puffy red coat nesting in the bottom-most layer. The rest, she'd buy when she got there. Paris. She reached up and adjusted the air vent, smelling the jet fuel as men with orange jackets and sticks bustled under the wing.

She turned to the woman sitting in the aisle seat. "I've never been on a plane before," she said.

The woman smiled and nodded. "Oh, sugar, no need to be nervous. People fly every day."

"I'm not nervous," Stevie said. She hardly knew what she was feeling. Antsy. Elated. She fiddled with the knob on the tray table. She touched her cheek.

Back home in Sycamore, they were saying good-bye to the girl tonight, paying their respects to the mother. Stevie had already said her good-byes. She'd sat on the bed facing the mural on her wall, and she told the girl, one last time: It *was* an accident. They didn't know. I'm sorry I couldn't save you. She told her, I'm taking your coat to Paris. I'm going to wear it as I walk along the Seine. She addressed the woman in the mural, the woman she now understood to be the mother: the mother standing on the canyon rim, looking into the distance, waiting for her girl to come home. To *her*, Stevie had said, I'm sorry I didn't follow her. I'm sorry I didn't call for help. I'm sorry you had to wait so long.

The plane pulled away from the terminal and bumped along the concrete to the runway.

She closed her eyes as the plane accelerated, the force pushing her into the seat. She opened them the exact moment the wheels lifted and the plane left the earth.

She looked out the square little window and watched the houses and cars and trees and swimming pools and jagged mountains grow smaller, shimmering in the heat and dust of the desert.

The plane climbed and bounced on air pockets, and her stomach dropped. She peered out and saw a cloud above them, and soon they were inside it, a gray mist that obscured her view.

She had never seen anything like it. Never. And she'd been looking her whole life. She laughed.

The woman on the aisle leaned over. She pointed out the window. "It's real pretty, isn't it?"

"It is," Stevie said.

She pressed her fingers on the glass, and the colors stayed still. She could see clearly all the shining world below.

***

Saturdays, Esther closed the bakery at three for the rest of the weekend, and usually she beat it out of there, knowing she'd have to be back before dawn on Monday. Today, she lingered, thinking she'd make a fresh loaf of banana bread to bring to the service at Iris's this evening. She'd already overloaded Iris's kitchen and dining room with platters of pastries and carafes of coffee and tea, and Hugh had made pinwheels and lasagna bites. No one would be going hungry, and she needed to remember to bring plastic to-go containers. But banana bread was Maud's favorite, and tonight—well, she might need banana bread. By god, Esther could make banana bread.

She poured the eggs and overripe mashed bananas into the creamed butter and sugar and turned on the mixer, old Spinster. She watched Spinster's paddles whirl. Spinster was a good old gal. Esther laughed. *Gal.* What a word.

Someone tapped on the window, startling her. Esther sighed. Not for the first time she regretted installing a window that left the kitchen exposed to the sidewalk. She loved the light, but not so much the rubbernecking mouth breathers. She needed to put up a sign: "Beware, Menopausal Baking Season. Please Do Not Tap Glass." She plastered a smile on her face and looked up.

Beto Navarro stood at the window, straddling his bike. Roberto. Roberto now. He smiled and waved, and she waved back. She gestured to the door and mouthed, Come in, come in, and walked around to the front.

"Hi," he said. "Esther."

"Hey yourself. Roberto." She tilted her head to look up at his sharp, lean face. She again felt that snaking heat from the night in the bar. "How long have you been this tall?"

"A while now," he said, laughing.

"I guess I was sitting down at the Pickaxe. And a bit drunk to boot."

He smiled. He pointed down Main. "I was at the shop, but we closed a little early today. You're usually not here when I ride home."

"No. I stayed later today," she said, thinking, Does he look for me? She opened the door wider. "Do you want to come in? Are you hungry? I have some day-olds I was going to freeze."

"I'm always hungry," he said.

"You've come to the right place."

He smiled, and Esther noticed a tender blue vein at his temple. She had the strange thought she would like to rest her thumb on that spot. Jesus, what was wrong with her? He had been her *student*.

They sat at a table in the break room, and she unwrapped the morning's tray of leftover bear claws, apple fritters, and blueberry scones. He took one of each. She watched, a bit astonished, as he ate them one by one.

"These are delicious," he said.

"I'm glad."

He swallowed and wiped his mouth with a paper towel. "I've been wanting to ask you, why'd you decide to stop teaching?"

She waved her hand. "Oh, it was time. I'd been there twenty-three years. Literally half my life, and I was tired. I wasn't doing the job I needed to be doing anymore. I looked around and realized I better figure something else out."

"You were a great teacher," he said. "Best one in the school. And you were so young to leave."

"Thanks," she said. "That's nice to hear. About the teaching, not the youth. Although that's nice, too."

"It's the truth." He popped in the last bite of a scone. He looked at her, chewing, and then down at his hands. "I've often thought about you. Over the years."

"Is that right." Her pulse jumped, and she pressed two fingers against her throat. "That's also nice to hear."

"Okay." He let out a shaky breath and checked his watch. "I guess I should get going. The memorial's in two hours, and I should shower."

"Right. I need to finish my banana bread."

Neither of them moved.

He scratched his neck and then looked at her again. She looked, too, the heat wriggling around her belly.

"You're thirteen years younger than me," she said. "Is that right?"

"That's right," he said.

She rested her elbows on the table. He did the same, wadding up the paper towel between them. He clutched it, tearing at the edge. She watched the rise and fall of his Adam's apple as he swallowed.

He said, "I walk by in the mornings, or ride my bike when I

deliver the paper. Early. I see you in here. The lights are on, so you can't see me, but I see you."

"You should have stopped."

"You were working. I was working." He shrugged. "Then you came into the Pickaxe, and I thought, Maybe it's a sign."

Esther smiled. She used to believe in signs.

"You were my student," she said.

"A long time ago."

"People will talk." She gave a wry laugh. "Although, who cares, right? Since when do I care what people say?"

A rhetorical question, but she answered to herself: always. She heard Grandmother's voice in her ear. *You don't watch it, you're going to end up washed up, a fat spinster with no one but that queer friend of yours for company. You're going to die alone.*

She leaned away from him, her smile fading. "It's nice to see you, Roberto."

He nodded and looked toward the door, a flush on his cheek. He stood up, his lanky frame seeming to teeter. "I better get going."

She blinked down at her lap.

Instead of walking out the door, he walked around the table and crouched next to her. She heard his knee joints crack. He reached out and touched her cheek, surprising her enough she sucked in her breath.

"Your heart is an inferno," he said.

She pressed her cheek into his palm and let out a small sigh. How nice. How nice it was to be touched. "Is that from a poem?"

"No," he said. He laughed. "That's you. You said that once."

"I did? You're kidding. You remember that?"

"Sure. I was an impressionable kid." He ran his hand down her neck, stroked her collarbone.

"Beto—"

"Roberto," he said. "I'm not a kid anymore, Esther."

"No." And he wasn't, was he? The look in his eyes was not of a wide-eyed boy with a crush but of a serious young man with desires about which she knew nothing. Really, she knew nothing of him, nor he of her. He might as well be a stranger, as far as they had moved from those past lives.

He shifted to kneel and leaned close to her neck. "You smell like butter. And bananas."

"*This* is bananas," she said.

He kissed her neck.

"Christ." She turned her face to his.

Well, this was a first. Making out with a former student in her bakery. He got to his feet and pulled her up from the chair, pulled her against his lean young body. She lost her balance and flung out her arm, knocking a metal tray to the floor.

"Wait," she said, almost panting. "We can't."

"Why not?"

Indeed. Why not? If it was a mistake, so what? So *what*, as Iris had said about Sam. The one thing she did know these days, pushing hard into middle age, was how much she didn't know.

Roberto bent down, wrapped his arms around her waist, and *lifted* her, straight off the ground. She cried out, "Don't!" but then he set her on the counter.

"There," he said. "Face to face."

She blinked. And what a face he had. That forehead. She reached out and put a thumb on that vein at his temple and then dropped her hands to his shoulders. Never in a million years could she have imagined this. She leaned in, and her heart gave a funny little cough. There you are, old gal, she thought. She laughed. What a word. What a life.

***

Dani put on her dress for the memorial, a simple black cotton one whose drooping hem she'd had to rig with double-sided tape. She scrunched up the toes of her flimsy black pantyhose and pulled them up her legs, hoping she wouldn't snag the fabric on a fingernail. She slid on low black pumps whose scuff marks she'd filled in that morning with felt-tip pen.

When she looked in the mirror, she startled herself. Her hair, chopped off to her chin. Her eyes, lined like she'd seen in a fashion magazine while waiting for her hair appointment. That morning, she'd pulled out a stick of eyeliner, found a box of matches, and lit the end of the liner, smearing it hot across her lids. The sulfur from the match made her nostrils flare.

Don't blink, Dani.

Jess had laughed. "Stop blinking. You're making me smear it." Dani had squeezed her eyes open and shut, feeling the liner and mascara wet on her cheekbones and brow bone. Jess laughed harder, her breath warm and minty. "Nice job, raccoon face," she'd said, holding up the mirror, and Dani had laughed too, seeing the fat dark rings around her eyes and giddy with that new strange thing. Having a best friend. Being girly. "Now you," Dani had said, picking up the eyeliner and the Bic. "Okay, now you don't blink," she'd said to Jess, and Jess said, "I won't." She'd held her eyes open.

But she'd missed everything anyway.

Dani blinked now, smoothing down her dress, turning sideways. She'd already messed up her makeup once today, crying on Paul's shoulder out of the blue like a maniac. It had come up out of her like a wave. Like a flash flood. She got out the eyeliner and matches again and set to work repairing the mess. When she was finished, she pushed at the corner of her eyes and straightened her shoulders.

Time to go.

Dani climbed the steps to her mother's front door. She stood on the porch of her childhood home in her worn funeral dress and peered in the sidelight window. She could see Hugh in the kitchen, lifting a steaming pot from the stove and carrying it to the sink. Her mother stood at the dining room window, looking out at the yard.

Her mother turned, smiling, probably at something Hugh said. For a moment, Dani almost didn't recognize her. From that angle, she saw what she didn't see in passing every day: time. The softening of the skin along the jawline, the puffiness of her cheeks, the slope at the top of her back, the silver at her temples. Her mother was growing old, and Dani had missed it.

Dani was about to knock, but her mother glanced at the front and saw Dani standing in the window. In that split second, Dani saw her mother's whole face, her whole posture, change. In her mother's face, Dani saw herself peering through a microscope for the first time, when the tiny unseen world suddenly snapped into sharp glorious focus. Oh! Look! Look at that! her mother's face seemed to say. Dani realized now her mother had never stopped looking at her that way; Dani had missed that, too.

Her mother opened the door and smiled. "Dani," she said. "You're early."

"I'm here," she said.

"I'm glad," she said. "Hugh!" she called. "Dani's here."

Hugh only had fifteen years on Dani, but he'd always seemed older than his age, puttering around the kitchen with hokey aprons that said things like "Kiss the Cook" or "Danger: Man in Kitchen." About as exciting as sliced cheese, really, but innocuous. Plus, he made her mother smile like she was now, big and toothy.

"Well, there she is," Hugh said. "Don't you look nice."

He put his arm around her mother's shoulders, and Rachel leaned into him. That part had never gotten less strange, seeing her mother with another man, even after all this time. Those early images of her parents, embedded in her from infancy, had been difficult to shake. Mother, father, child. The family unit. Oddly she thought of images from the atomic bombing in Hiroshima. The explosion was so hot that the shadows of objects burned into the concrete. That was how it felt sometimes, that old bond, that old life. Burned straight into her, casting a permanent shadow.

Her mother smiled again at Dani in the doorway. "You really do look wonderful, sweetheart. Your hair. I do love it. It suits you."

Her mother's voice seemed to take on an exaggerated pitch when she spoke with Dani—to hide what Dani had believed was disapproval lurking below. But Dani understood now it was only awkwardness, her mother's attempt to bridge the distance Dani had put between them when she'd walled herself off. Her mother, who'd taught her to use a microscope. Who'd first showed her the unseen world around her.

Dani did what she'd done earlier at the orchard. She flung herself at another human being and burst into tears.

"Okay." Her mother held her. "Okay."

"Oh, goodness," Hugh said. He patted her shoulder. "Tea. I'll make tea."

"I can't stop," Dani said. "I can't stop crying."

"It's okay," her mother said. "I know."

Dani relaxed in her mother's arms.

"I failed," Dani said. "I'm a failure. Me, smartest girl in school. Everyone must be having a good laugh."

"No one's laughing. And you're not a failure."

Dani lifted her head. "I'm a mess."

Her mother laughed a little. "Your face is."

"I know." She started crying again. "See? I can't stop."

"So don't," her mother said. "Don't stop. It's okay."

"I can't go to the orchard like this. Will you tell Maud I'm sorry?" She hiccupped. "Tell her I'm sorry. Tell her—oh, I don't know what to tell her."

"I'll tell her," her mother said.

"She was my best friend," Dani said, burying her face into her mother's shoulder and smearing her with black. "My first real friend."

"Yes, she was." Her mother rubbed her back. "It might help to say good-bye."

But Dani had already said good-bye.

As she'd lined her lids in the mirror *again* before she left her little guest house, she'd thought, How to begin?

With what was in front of her.

She'd said to the mirror, I live behind Ms. G's house. Remember when we wondered if she and Mr. Manning were a couple? Um, no.

She said, I still live in Sycamore. I take people's blood for a living. Go figure.

She said, I hated you for what you did. I hated you. I wanted you to be here so I could hate you some more. Blame you some more. You and my dad. But that's not working out so hot for me. I always pictured someday being able to yell at you, to have it out again. To make you sorry. I always believed, really believed, you were out there. And some day, you would come home.

Then she'd had to redo her makeup *again*.

She'd said, Don't blink, Jess. Blink and you miss it.

She said, I've missed too much now.

She said, I don't know if I still look like him. I don't know what he looks like anymore.

On the front porch, Dani let go of her mother. She said good-bye, went down the porch steps, and walked toward her guest house, on that old street in that old town she knew by heart.

She didn't need any more good-byes.

How to begin?

***

He usually liked to paint this time of day. The bedroom he had turned into his studio faced west, but the oaks and pines filtered the sun. The soft, low light of late afternoon. But today he took a walk instead. Today, he wanted to be outside. She had liked to be outside, and since he could not be there to say a formal farewell, he would say one here.

He had almost gone down to Sycamore today. Maud had called him with the news, as promised, and he had not asked, but she had told him: "There's a memorial. Out at Iris's place." She hadn't invited him. He'd found the time and date in the paper, and he had written it on the calendar pinned up next to his desk. He'd thought he could go and stand in the back, stay hidden, but he knew he would not be welcome. And he had promised he would not bother Maud again. He could keep that promise. He would not interfere with a place that was no longer his.

This was his place now.

He walked through the forest behind the cabin, his shoes crunching on the pine needles. He had no destination, really, just to be outdoors. He reached the Griffith Spring Trail, and he thought the spring was as good a place as any for what he had in mind. He wanted to sit for a few minutes on a boulder and watch the sun sink behind the trees. It did not really matter where he sat, or that it happened at a certain time, or even that it happened today. He was not sure, actually, what it would change. But he found himself wanting the ritual. To mourn properly, with solemnity. To lay her, if not himself, to rest.

When he reached the spring, he sat down on a slanted boulder near the water, feeling the ache in his hips, in his left knee, knowing he would struggle to rise from this low position. The spring, full and lush this time of year after the summer storms, trailed downhill to fill Oak Creek and Pumphouse Wash to the south. Soon it would slow to a trickle, come to a standstill.

He had not prepared a speech. He had not thought about what he would say. So he sat, staring at the water. Really staring through the water, at the mossy rocks and silt below. How clear it was. How calm.

He took off his shoes, rolled up his pant legs, and stuck his bare feet in with a small gasp. He pushed himself off the rock and walked out into the spring, holding his arms out for balance and stepping carefully on the slippery rocks. When he reached the center, he stopped and looked around. He reached up and brushed back his hair. A yellow pencil fell out from behind his ear. He had forgotten it was there, *again*. He reached down and plucked the pencil from the water, slid it behind his ear. The water dripped on his neck.

You would have loved this place, he said to her. You might not have wanted to come here, but you should have lived to see it.

He waited, listening to the wind in the tops of the pines, listening to his own breath.

That was all. That was all he had.

Nothing had changed that he could tell. The sadness was part of him now, so long had he lived with it.

He stepped out of the spring, rolled down his pant legs, slipped his shoes on, and headed to the cabin. Home. He still had plenty of light left. Perhaps he would go to the studio after all. Make dinner, a steak and salad, have a glass of wine, then get out the paints. Perhaps that was the way to end the day.

When he reached the cabin, the sun was low, near to setting, casting shadows across the house. He did not see her at first. She was sitting in one of the two rockers on the porch. Even when he did see her, even when she rose from the rocker and stood at the railing facing him, he did not immediately understand. Who was this woman with the dark short hair on his property? Was she lost, looking for a neighbor?

She lifted her hand to him, and still he did not know. Still.

And when he did recognize her, when he did finally see it was his daughter standing before him, he clenched his fists, digging his nails hard into his palms. To make sure. To make sure he was standing there. That she was.

She came around to the steps of the porch, in full view. A streak of light made its way through the trees and lit her. She looked straight at him. Right in the face. The child he once knew. The woman he did not. Both of those at once.

He did not know what to say. He opened his mouth and closed it. His throat tightened. She stepped closer, and he felt a shiver of alarm. What if she had come to berate him, to say the words he knew she had wanted to say but could not? Fine. If she must, she must. He braced his shoulders and swallowed hard. She stood a few feet in front of him now, her gaze steady behind the dark makeup around her eyes.

She said, "Hi, Dad."

He laughed, almost a croak, startled by the simplicity. "Hi, Dani."

She smiled a little, and he did, too.

He cleared his froggy throat. "You came."

"I did."

"I thought you'd be at the memorial."

"I did, too." She tilted her head. "You've gone gray."

He touched his hair. "A while ago, yes." He touched the pencil, pulled it from behind his ear. "You look well," he said. She was grown, his daughter. So grown. *Perfect* is what he meant. So he said it. "Perfect."

She smoothed the sides of her hair, tucked it behind her ears. "I don't know what to say. I hadn't exactly planned this. I got in the car, put your address in my GPS, and here I am."

He nodded. "Well, are you hungry? We could go to town. Or I have some steaks and salad. Wine."

"Okay. Let's eat here. Sure. Dinner. We'll start with dinner." She looked down, biting her lip. He could tell she was fighting not to cry. He wanted to lean over and pat her shoulder, comfort her, but he dared not touch her for fear she would bolt.

He climbed the porch instead and opened the unlocked door. "Come on in," he said.

She followed him inside. He showed her his bedroom and studio, the small kitchen, the tiny bathroom, the cubby where he had his desk, where he wrote to her each morning.

"It's not much," he said.

She sat down at his desk and looked out the window, her back to him. "It's just how you described it. Exactly."

"Is it? I'm glad."

Outside the window, the light had turned hazy, soft with a tinge of pink.

"The sun's setting," she said.

Down the hill, the memorial would be starting. "Yes," he said.

"I'm not ready to talk about it," she said. "I'm still very angry. I still don't know how to forgive either of you. I don't know how to tell you things. I have things to tell you."

"Okay," he said. "I'm still glad you're here."

She folded her hands on his desk. She shook her head, her short hair swinging. "Where do we even start?"

He got a chair from the kitchen and pulled it up to the desk. He sat next to her. He set down the pencil he forgot he was holding.

"Here," he said, pointing out the window, at the best light of the day. "Tell me what you see."

***

The cars kept streaming in after the service began, even though it had started a little late. They scrambled to set out extra chairs to fit people in, but there weren't enough for everyone. People leaned along the far rail of the deck. They squeezed in the doorway of the living room. They spilled out onto the lawn. And still the cars came, their headlights cutting across the dimming sky. They parked far down the driveway and on Quail Run, their tires tilted in the drainage ditch. In the waning sunlight, they walked toward the orchard, toward the twinkle lights that beckoned from the deck, toward the trees that sighed in the breeze.

Father Tom said, "We come here today to remember Jess Winters. We come to say good-bye to one of our own. We come to comfort her family in this time of sorrow. Let us pray."

Maud bowed her head but didn't close her eyes. She wasn't Catholic, or even religious, but Father Tom had assured her there wouldn't be a mass. Just a gathering, he'd said. A few words.

She watched the cars and the people with their eyes closed. All those old familiar faces. Literally old now, some of them. There were her parents, sitting next to her, her mother more shrunken, her father hollow in the cheek. On her other side was her ex-husband Stuart—alone, his wife and now-college-age daughter in California—his jowly chin shaved clean though she'd never seen him without a beard before. There were Esther and Beto Navarro and Luz Navarro, there were Angie Juarez and Rose Prentiss and their girl Hazel, there were Iris and Paul and little Sean, Rachel and Hugh. There was Laura Drennan, the young professor. There was Gil Alvarez, who caught her eye and nodded with a small smile. There was the woman on Bottlebrush with the metal sculpture in her yard, the butcher at Bashas', the woman who ran the snack shack at the ball field. People she hadn't seen in years, people she'd forgotten, people she knew by heart.

Maud looked at her hands folded in her lap. This was for them, too. Jess Winters was her daughter, but she was theirs, too. She was bigger than herself by then, more than a girl who Maud had once cradled in her arms. Jess Winters was their story, as much a part of Sycamore as the land itself, as the land that had swallowed her whole. Jess Winters was their worst fear come true (look what can happen, in an instant). Jess Winters was their ghost. Jess Winters was their metaphor: loss, secrets, guilt, failure, embedded in one shining, curly-haired girl.

But she was Maud's daughter, and hers alone to bury.

And she would. But not here.

After the service, Maud stood at the railing next to Stuart and shook people's hands. Good night. Thank you for coming. I appreciate it. Retiring, yes, I can hardly believe it myself. I'm not sure yet what I'm going to do. You're right, a vacation would be nice. Thank you. It was good to see you, too. Good night. She was on autopilot now. The hard part was almost done. The hardest part was next. Of course, it would never really be over. Not exactly, in the way that sometimes she dreamed she could hear out of her left ear, that she still had all her senses. When she woke, she had to start all over again. You cannot hear, old girl.

You cannot see her anymore.

But the service was over, and she was home, with four stacks of Tupperware trays and a freezer packed with casserole dishes, and a mailbox and desk full of sympathy cards. Her mailbox overflowed these days. So many letters and cards and padded envelopes, her box stuffed because some days she forgot to check. She had no reason to check anymore.

The doorbell rang, and she thought about not answering, but then she saw the police cruiser out front. Gil Alvarez.

She opened the door. "Gil. Is everything okay? Come in."

"No, that's all right. I don't want to bother you."

"Did you need something?"

"Nope, no. Don't want to keep you. Just wanted to stop by and check on you." He gave a wry smile. "Old habits, I suppose."

"Thanks." She shook her head. "Thank you for all you did. For trying to find her. I'm not sure I've ever really thanked you."

He sighed. "I'm sorry, Maud. You know I am." He raked his hair with his fingers, the way he always did.

She flapped her hand at the living room. "Do you want to come in? Really."

"Not tonight. But maybe another time."

"Sure. That'd be nice."

"If you need anything." He held his hand out.

She shook his hand. As she did, he reached out with his other hand and covered hers. A warm, reassuring pressure. He let go, nodded, and then walked down her driveway. She stood in the doorway, staring at the street after he'd driven off.

She picked up the phone and called Esther. "Can you come over?" Her voice came out low and shaky.

"Oh, Maud. I'm on my way."

Maud hung up and sat down hard on the sofa. She retired to the sofa, she thought with a laugh. Retirement. She had two months left at the post office, and it was true, she really didn't know what she was going to do now. She needed a plan. *This*— eating too much, staring out the window—could not be her plan. She owned this house outright and had a good pension. Her parents wanted her to move home. Come home, they said, hugging her. Stay with us awhile till you get on your feet. But that was not home. This was home now, whether she'd planned it or not.

And she hadn't planned it. She'd been flying high on anger at Stuart and grief and a sudden gaping freedom that seemed to have cut out a vital organ—her brain, maybe, because she sure hadn't been thinking straight. She'd accepted the transfer to the Sycamore post office, packed up her house, packed up her only daughter, and *fled*. To the safe haven of a small town in northern Arizona. A safe place, she'd thought, for now. She'd thought, This is temporary. I'll figure it out. This is just for now.

The endless now.

Here she was, facing her future, whether she wanted to or not.

The next day, Maud headed to Mexico with Jess's ashes in a little red balsa-wood box on the passenger seat. She'd told Stuart, I'm doing this my way, and he had not argued. It had been a long time since they'd argued, anyway. Nothing to argue about anymore. In Calexico, she stopped for gas. She watched the sun glare off the hoods of the cars in line for the border. Exhaust fumes wavered off the asphalt. The gas station was too far from the ocean for her to smell it, but she thought she did, a tangy, humid brine.

Two hours later, Maud pulled the truck into a tiny beach inlet off the rutted track to their secluded spot near San Felipe, Mexico. She hadn't seen another car on the road in over an hour. Nothing for miles but ocean on one side, desert on the other. Sparse *cardón* cactus and ocotillo dotted the bone earth, too spindly to offer shade. Sweat soaked her tank top and the waistband of her cotton shorts. She could feel it pooling under her breasts, soaking the bathing suit she wore underneath. She wiped her damp forehead, patted her curls, put her hand on the red box. The vise grip in her chest loosened as she stared at the expanse of the blue-gray Sea of Cortez. She murmured, "We're here, J-bird."

At the water's edge, Maud stripped off her shorts and tank top and kicked off her flip-flops, down to the one-piece she'd dug out of a drawer as she packed, the elastic shot at the straps and legs. She cradled the little red box. She couldn't see anything but land, sky, and sea. The water, warm in the shallow part around her ankles, grew colder as she waded deeper. She stumbled into the waves with a gasp as the water hit her overheated skin and stiff muscles. She turned onto her back, the box propped on her chest, and started kicking toward the horizon.

She stopped and floated, closing her eyes against the trumpet-bright glare. The salt water held her up, took her weight. After days of little sleep, and after the long, dusty drive, she breathed deeply.

I wish I could write you a poem, J-bird. To really tell you how I feel. How hard this is. How hard it is to let go.

All right, Starshine. All right, my blue-winged girl. It's time for you to go now.

Maud sat up, treading water, holding the box above the surface. Then she set the box on the water and gave it a little push. The balsa wood floated away, a sad and listing ship. Eventually, it took on water, the gritty ashes inside growing heavier, and it went down. It sank out of view, the quick flutter of a fish, the strange flash of a firefly.

Maud climbed to the beach in a worn swimsuit that gapped around the thighs. She returned to the hotel. She stripped off her suit, showered, and then went outside onto the balcony, wrapped in her towel. Here she was, in her safe place. She thought of her nice counselor, trying to get her through it. What do you see for yourself, Maud?

She saw herself standing on a hotel balcony in Mexico. Not the balcony she'd stood on during her honeymoon, when she was young and slender and wide-eyed, reaching for the sky. No, she saw herself now, an hour or so after she had let the little red box sink.

She dropped the towel and stood naked, facing the water. There she stood, sagging at the breasts and belly, gray up top and down below and wrinkled and with a fat varicose vein blooming on the back of her thigh. She lifted her arms, the skin beneath drooping—flying squirrel wings, Rachel called them, flappity-flap. She saw a glint, a flicker of light in the distance. And what do you know. There was the whole wide world. It was still there, waiting.

ACKNOWLEDGMENTS

I AM INDEBTED TO THE Alabama State Council on the Arts, the University of North Carolina at Charlotte, and the University of Montevallo for financial support during the writing of this book. Enormous thanks also to Poets & Writers and Maureen Egen for the Writers Exchange Award and the Jentel Artist Residency, where I completed the first draft.

Different versions of two chapters first appeared as stories in literary journals: "The New Girl" in *The Fourth River* and "Say You See the World" (as "In My Former Life") in *Cutbank*. I remain grateful for those first publications and for lit journals everywhere.

To my agent, Henry Dunow: Thank you for your belief, encouragement, patience, sharp eye, advice, and good humor. To everyone at Harper who shepherded this manuscript, especially my editor, Emily Griffin, a brilliant reader with a wicked eye and a gigantic heart: Thank you for your love of books and for putting mine into the world.

Thanks to the members of the Faculty Workgroup at the University of Montevallo, who plowed through the first messy pages and helped me find my way. Timothy Winkler and Elizabeth Wetmore, whom I trust with my life as well as my words, read from top to bottom repeatedly and saved me from myself. All flaws are mine, not theirs.

My writing path has been forged through invaluable mentorships and friendships. At Vanderbilt, I thank my lucky stars for

Lorraine López, Tony Earley, Nancy Reisman, Peter Guralnick, Kate Daniels, Mark Jarman, Rick Hilles, Mark Schoenfield, Dana Nelson, Teresa Goddu, and Margaret Quigley; big love to my MFA classmates for their talent, humor, and kindness, especially Meredith K. Gray and Alex Moody. I owe so much to the remarkable teachings of Ron Carlson, Maxine Clair, Pam Houston, Jill McCorkle, Richard Bausch, Bret Lott, and Ann Cummins. Boundless thanks to the wondrous Tayari Jones, Joy Castro, Kevin Wilson, Toni Jensen, Matthew Pitt, Mike Croley, and Mare Biddle. Side Hugs Forever to Marjorie Sa'adah, Justin Quarry, Nickole Brown, Jessica Jacobs, Nina McConigley, Derek Palacio, Jennine Cápo Crucet, Alejandro Nodarse, Stephanie Pruitt, Lee Conell, BG Cross, David Roby, Amy Arthur, and Robie Jackson. I send bouquets of thanks to my superb students, colleagues, and friends from UNC-Charlotte and the University of Montevallo, with extra love to Stephanie Batkie, Matt Irvin, Betsy Inglesby, Jen Rickel, Glenda Conway, and Steve Forrester.

To the old-school crews: Nikki, Missy, Gigi, Brando, Beth, Jorge, Tiffy Sue, Rick, Case, Dr. JJ, and all the kiddos in between: Look at all these years, friends. Miss and love you always.

To all my families, born and made: the Chancellors, Winklers, Cowans, Dozemans, and Skaggses. I always feel you with me. To my mom, Cathy: You're my shining beacon. My late father, Alan, is always in my heart.

Again, and always, to Timothy Winkler: You make this whole wide world go 'round.

P.S.

Insights,
Interviews
& More . . .

Meet Bryn Chancellor

Bryn Chancellor's story collection *When Are You Coming Home?* (University of Nebraska Press) won the Prairie Schooner Book Prize, and her short fiction has appeared in *Gulf Coast*, *Blackbird*, *Colorado Review*, *Crazyhorse*, *Phoebe*, and elsewhere. Other honors include the 2014 Poets & Writers Maureen Egen Writers Exchange Award in fiction, literary fellowships from the Alabama State Council on the Arts, the Arizona Commission on the Arts, and the North Carolina Arts Council. She teaches at the University of North Carolina at Charlotte. *Sycamore* is her first novel. ❧

Questions for Further Discussion

1. What does the title of the book evoke for you? How does the town itself operate as a character in the book?
2. Chancellor includes thirteen different points of view in *Sycamore*. How does she use language to create different points of view for each of these characters, even when a given character's chapter isn't told in the first person?
3. The reader is given a window into Jess's mind through the close third-person point of view in her chapters, but also more directly through the poetry she writes. What do her poems say about the kind of person she is?
4. The teenage characters in the book—Jess, Angie, Dani, Beto, and Paul—are not in the popular crowd at their high school, but they seem to form deep connections with their friends. When Jess and Dani play dress-up, Dani asks Jess, "Who do you want to be?" Is that a question that all teens are asking one another?
5. What do Maud's decision to keep Jess's room the same and Stevie's creation of the spiral jetty have in common? In what ways are they paying tribute to Jess's life? ▶

6. Some of Chancellor's characters live with people who are no longer alive or otherwise no longer with them. Iris Overton, for example, speaks to her dead husband at night. Is it rational to believe in ghosts or to speak to the dead?

7. When Laura discovers the bones, she has a feeling that they belong to "a girl who, not so long ago, stood somewhere, her gaze long and steady, as if she had all the time in the world." What does time represent to Laura? What about to Maud? And Stevie, who counts time in daily units?

8. Discuss the author's choice to craft one of the book's climactic scenes— the Thanksgiving dinner—as a play. What did this allow her to do? How is it different from the rest of the prose?

9. What might have happened if Paul hadn't overheard the conversation in the orchard? How might these events have unspooled otherwise? Was Adam's obsession with Jess always destined to come to a crisis point?

10. What do you make of Adam's letter to Dani? Does anything he says in it excuse his behavior or justify it?

11. Throughout the book, water comes in as a motif—the disappearing lake, the night of heavy rain when Jess disappears, and so on. How does Chancellor use water in a desert landscape to provide support for her themes?

12. Who holds the ultimate blame for Jess's disappearance? What or who might have kept her from going missing?

13. Did the characters who were close to Jess achieve closure by the novel's end? Is closure ever truly a possibility after a tragedy?

14. What do you think comes next for these characters? What do you hope for them? ∿

A Conversation with Bryn Chancellor,
Author of *Sycamore*

Is the town of Sycamore based on a real place? Why did you decide to set the novel in a fictional town?

While Sycamore is imaginary, it's based on places in the region where I grew up: the small town of Sedona, Arizona, and the neighboring towns of Cottonwood and Clarkdale, where I attended junior high and high school. A fictionalized version allowed me the distance to rearrange and create features and timelines I needed.

I've lived in the American South now for about twelve years, and I haven't yet been able to set any stories here. I've tried. Personally, I'm quite mesmerized by the landscape—leafy trees! rain!— but I can't get inside it the way that I can with the territory that I moved around in for thirty-plus years. The landscape is a major feature of Sycamore, as it's a major feature of the real place. The desert is *weird*, in the best of ways. When we went to visit recently, my husband commented it was like walking around Mars. A place of contradictions, both tough and fragile. A ferocious beauty.

As with much of my writing, I wanted to explore the lives of working people who are sometimes overlooked, both in literature and in life. My settings often are unexplored corners of small-town

Arizona and unseen avenues of urban Phoenix—a West with which many people are unfamiliar, and one I hope to bring into focus as more than myth or stereotype, to show the complexities of the land and its people.

I'm often told, and I accept, that I write about ordinary people, though I do find myself questioning what we mean by *ordinary* and why that strikes us as notable. One of my favorite responses from a reader so far is that the book illuminated the poetry of the ordinary and prompted him to start writing poems in the mornings. That makes me unbearably happy. For me, the world would be far better off if we all started our mornings writing poems.

Which of the characters' points of view came easiest to you? Which was the hardest?

Writing from Adam's perspective was hands down the hardest. I resisted wrestling with his motivations, the harm he caused, his immaturity and selfishness. Of course, I had to. I had to know why he acted badly, how he had lived with it. I only could do it when I hit on the idea of him writing to Dani. He became complex and sympathetic to me then, this aging father writing a letter to the adult daughter he's lost because of his actions, grappling still with his mother's abandonment, his career failures. That letter feels like the first time he's been honest, both to her and to himself. ▶

**A conversation with Bryn Chancellor,
author of *Sycamore* (continued)**

This may be surprising, but I wrote Jess's chapters last. I think part of me resisted writing in the voice of a teenager, not to mention the logic of how to write from the perspective of someone missing. I worried about clichés and inauthenticity—I don't see this book at all as a "missing girl" story, and perhaps I was overly self-conscious about that trope. Initially I conveyed Jess only through her notebooks, messy entries and poems, but that narrow first-person felt flat, and I knew I needed to bring her more fully into the picture. So I pulled way back, perspective-wise, to an omniscient point of view, so I could see her first before seeing through her. For whatever reason, that opened up her story and character for me, as well as the two-timeline structure of the book.

I don't know if any characters were easy for me—I tend to pull out my hair more often than not—but I did have fun writing Rose and Iris, those short, voice-driven monologues. I'm also quite partial to Esther, who carries a lot of the book's humor and who, in some ways, I see as my funnier, more outspoken alter ego. But I love all of my characters, even when they're not at their best—maybe even more then.

Did you sketch out the entire plot before you started writing? If not, did you have a sense of what was going to happen in the end?

When I started, I had no clue what had happened to Jess. I had to solve my own mystery. I didn't know her, or any of these characters, much at all. I knew I didn't want to solve her disappearance with tricks or surprises or even a crime—or at least the possibility that it wasn't a crime. I thought about never answering the question of what happened. In the end, I gave readers the truth, but the characters will never know exactly what happened.

Part of the joy of writing for me is figuring it all out, that thrilling sense of surprise and discovery as you get to know your characters and place and what happens next and next and next. Even with a book with so many components, I didn't really outline, just tried to feel my way through, unlock the answers as I learned more about the characters and the place. During early drafts, I pinned all the characters' names to a bulletin board and kept notes on a large whiteboard as I plugged away.

Ultimately, I had to stop worrying about what it was going to be—stories? a novel in stories? an unfinishable disaster?—and just get down the story in my head. I wrote the first (messy) draft quickly, which is unusual for me. The heavy lifting came in revision, about seven drafts total. Revision is where I figure out what I'm really trying to do. ▸

A conversation with Bryn Chancellor,
author of *Sycamore (continued)*

Who are your biggest literary influences?

As is the case for many writers, I was a
reader long before I tried to make my
own stories. My mom likes to tell how I
surprised her by reading a note aloud
when I was around three or four years
old. Startled, she said, "I didn't know you
could read," and I shrugged my
shoulders and said, "Yeah." In some
ways, that's how reading still feels to me:
like something I have always known how
to do. Yet it also stands out as one of the
saving graces of my life, the act to which
I have turned again and again to find
solace, to escape, to expand and enrich
my mind. What a wonder a book is:
through the art of language, we are
transported to worlds that we would
otherwise never know. Reading is
simultaneously the most ordinary and
the most wildly magic habit of my life.

It's hard for me to narrow down
specific writers because there are so
many I admire and I'm constantly
reading and discovering more. More
broadly, I tend to favor fiction, both
novels and short stories, but I am also a
fan of poetry, narrative nonfiction,
graphic narratives, and film. A good
story often has many qualities, but I am
most drawn to those that have deeply
complex, original characters in whom I
am absolutely invested. I want to *feel*
something at the end, to recognize a
change, to glimpse some aspect of the

human condition. If I'm weeping at 3 a.m. when I finally close the cover, success! I like dark humor, mesmerizing language, and experimental voices. I'm also a sucker for a story with secrets. We're always holding our breaths a little as we wait to find out how or if the truth will be revealed, or we see how a secret weighs on a character and shapes their actions; I especially love when the reader is privy to the truth and we see connections the characters don't. *Jane Eyre* and *Frankenstein*, two old favorites, come to mind, but I also was mesmerized by J. Courtney Sullivan's recent *Saints for All Occasions*, a beautiful family drama in which an old secret ripples across a lifetime.

What's your favorite piece of advice that you give to your creative writing students?

I like to say, "Come on, break my heart." Meaning: when it starts to get hard, keep going. Dig deep. Don't hold back. Make every part count.

The more I teach, the more I find myself stripping down to basics, starting with observation. We practice how to notice. To really pay attention, to look and look again. I want them to wonder about others, to marvel at what they don't know. Sometimes I think when we activate our writing eyes, it's like when Neo finally sees the Matrix: stories and details *everywhere*.

I also remind students that as ▶

A conversation with Bryn Chancellor,
author of *Sycamore* (continued)

writers, the one true thing we can control is the writing. The work on the page. All you can do is write your best version on your terms. I tell them to hold on to that process, as messy and hard as it is, because that's what will sustain them. ⟋

Bryn Chancellor's Five Favorite Books about Small Towns

Many wonderful contemporary novels and story collections are set in small towns and rural areas, but I've narrowed my choices here to books with expansive perspectives in which the town and place are amplified, in the spirit of Sherwood Anderson's *Winesburg, Ohio,* or Carson McCullers's *The Heart Is a Lonely Hunter.*

1. *Olive Kitteridge* **by Elizabeth Strout**
Somewhere between a linked story collection and a novel, this book brings to life not only the indelible main character Olive Kitteridge but also dozens of others in and around Olive's town of Crosby, Maine. It's impossible to imagine these stories taking place anywhere but this captivating and at times insular and frustrating town. I could read this book every year and find something new in it, and I never fail to get choked up in the last pages as I leave this place and people behind. Strout's most recent, *Anything Is Possible*, works in a similar vein for Amgash, Illinois, the hometown of her character Lucy Barton.

2. *Plainsong* **by Kent Haruf**

A quiet, humane, and achingly beautiful book. Through its interwoven multiple ▶

perspectives and unadorned prose, we are immersed in the world of Holt, a rural town in Colorado that forms the core of Haruf's several books. The cast of characters—a high school girl, two teachers, young boys without their mother, and a couple of cantankerous bachelor brother farmers—are rendered so truthfully and with such great heart that I still feel their presence years after I last read this book.

3. *LaRose* by Louise Erdrich

Erdrich's first book, *Love Medicine*, a story cycle, was my first exposure to her work and is itself an excellent example of small-town literature, but *LaRose* is a book in which Erdrich is writing at the height of her powers. Omniscient and multigenerational in its scope, with a multitude of fascinating characters including the Iron and Ravich families and the Irons' young son, LaRose, this sweeping story of family bonds, tragedy, grief, revenge, and forgiveness also is inextricably bound to a tight-knit town in the North Dakota Ojibwe reservation.

4. *Empire Falls* by Richard Russo

Funny, touching, and heartbreaking, *Empire Falls* is among the finest in Russo's several novels that lovingly explore blue-collar towns in the Northeast. *Empire Falls* interweaves a cast of characters, at the center of which is Miles Roby, the middle-aged owner of a struggling diner, his daughter, ex-wife, and ne'er-do-well father, among many others. I also love the sneakiness of the title, which suggests an outsize Romanesque tragedy—and reminds us that big things happen in small worlds.

5. *The Bluest Eye* by Toni Morrison

A Nobel Laureate and one of America's most revered writers, Morrison obviously is known for her unflinching exploration of Black American life, history, and racial oppression, along with her rich, mesmerizing style, but she is also one of the finest writers of small towns. I could just have easily picked *Beloved, Sula, Song of Solomon, Love, Home,* or others. *The Bluest Eye* evokes the struggling coal town of Lorain, Ohio—Morrison's hometown— in powerful ways and makes us see yet again how place and experiences are intertwined.

Bonus

A few more must-read books evoking small towns and rural places: Claire Vaye Watkins's *Battleborn,* Jesmyn Ward's *Salvage the Bones,* Marilynne Robinson's *Gilead,* Sherman Alexie's *The Absolutely True Diary of a Part-Time Indian,* Jill McCorkle's *July 7,* Dorothy Allison's *Bastard Out of Carolina,* and Tim O'Brien's *In the Lake of the Woods.*